Brotherly Love

Also by William D. Blankenship

THE HELIX FILE
THE PROGRAMMED MAN
THE LEAVENWORTH IRREGULARS
TIGER TEN
YUKON GOLD

Brotherly Love

A Novel by
William D. Blankenship

ARBOR HOUSE
New York

This book is dedicated to my agent, Bill Berger, who believed in it from the start, to my brother, Don Max Blankenship, and to the memory of Harold Rupert, a valued friend

Sunday

CHAPTER I

THE TALL man with the deep tan spent a pleasant afternoon watching the Ryders through his binoculars from a hilltop overlooking Compo Beach. They made a handsome family, Ben and Donna and the kids. A regular Norman Rockwell portrait.

Young Jeff reminded him very much of Ben and himself when they were kids. Jeff was rangy with wide shoulders and powerful legs, advanced for a boy of eleven. And at fifteen Sharon Ryder was already a young lady.

Ben has a great deal to lose, he thought. And that simple fact gave him a deep sense of pleasure.

Now and then he would make an entry in his notebook, his hand moving automatically to imitate the distinctive flourishes of Ben's handwriting. It had taken almost a year to perfect that handwriting, but the result was worth the effort. He felt confident that he could stroll right into Ben's bank and draw out his savings, if he chose to. But he wouldn't. Money wasn't an issue here.

Let's see . . . Ben is wearing the gray swimming trunks from Klein's . . . the blue knit shirt from Bloomingdale's . . . brown thongs . . . yellow tinted sunglasses.

He had those same articles of clothing in the closet of his own apartment. In fact, he had duplicated Ben Ryder's entire wardrobe as closely as possible, down to the Seiko quartz watch on Ben's left wrist.

Frequently he would study Ben carefully through the binoculars, comparing his own features with Ben's by peering intently into a small pocket mirror he carried for just that purpose. He noticed that Ben had gotten a haircut on Saturday afternoon and made a note to have his own hair cut to exactly the same length the following morning.

There is no difference between us, he decided. We look more alike now than ever. More than the year we played football at Pasadena High. More than the summer we spent logging together in Oregon. And more than the year Ben could have saved me from being sent away, and *didn't.*

The familiar rage began building inside him, turning his head into a crucible of pain. The bastard. After all I did for him, and he wouldn't lift a finger to help me. But he fought the anger. Closed his eyes and willed himself to be calm . . . to control the hatred . . . to channel it into his plan. Unfocused anger is stupid, he reminded himself. Besides, Ben will pay for his disloyalty soon enough.

Gradually the pressure inside his skull diffused and he relaxed again, lifting his face to catch the sweet warmth of the afternoon sun.

BEN RYDER LAY on an oversized beach towel staring up into the June sky, his eyes comfortable but troubled behind the tinted lenses. He was trying to tell himself that his fears were groundless, that his life was on the same straight course he had steered for the past several years. There were no waves big enough to swamp the Ryder family ship. Everything was beautiful. This would be another perfect summer.

Ben dug his toes into the sand and levered himself up on one elbow to take a long, thirsty pull from the cold beer in his hand.

Yes, his life on this corner of the planet known as Westport, Connecticut, was very pleasant indeed. After seventeen years of marriage, he and Donna were still capable of discovering new joys in each other. Together they had produced a pair of children in whom they took a quiet pride. He had started his own industrial design business five years ago, and prospered. There was a comfortable bank account—enough to live on for perhaps a year if the economy went soft again—plus some quality stocks and the equity in the house. Everything had seemed perfect.

Then, without warning, a threat to his carefully structured world had appeared.

Correction: such a threat *may* have appeared.

He still couldn't decide whether his fears were real or imagined, and it was the doubt that tortured him. The uncertainty. If the threat was real, he would find a way to handle it. But these hints of trouble . . . these shadows. How do you handle a shadow?

He finished his beer and tucked the bottle into the brown bag behind the cooler, aware that Donna's instincts for thrift would be bruised if he tossed away an empty that could be turned in for a nickel deposit.

"What's on your mind?" Donna asked. "Something to do with sex, I hope." She was stretched out on a towel next to him, her long slim legs and rich blonde hair taking on additional sheen from the sun.

"Please note that I have saved one empty beer bottle, and credit the nickel deposit to my account."

"It's about time you remembered to do that. But you're dodging my question. What's on your mind? Why have you been so preoccupied lately?"

He sat up and tucked his legs under him in what he often heard referred to as "the lotus position," which was what everyone had called "Indian style" when he was a boy, and took a few seconds to admire his wife.

Donna's hair was the shade of wheat but the texture of silk. And though it was long and luxuriant, she spent little time caring for it; a daily shampoo and fast pass with a dryer and comb was about as much time as Donna believed her hair was worth. Her eyes were a primary blue. As a student, Donna had been the Kansas State Womens Gymnastics Champion and her slim, tautly muscled body reflected the fact that she still enjoyed frequent workouts on a set of parallel bars at the Family Y. She had a pug nose that she hated, but which Ben thought her best feature, and a mouth made for smiling. Best of all, at thirty-six she still retained islands of freckles under her eyes. To Ben each freckle was as valuable as a one-carat diamond.

"I repeat . . . what's wrong? Have you suddenly realized what a hag I've become?"

Ben laughed.

"Then tell me. I've watched you brood over something for more than a week now." She had a sudden thought that made her clutch at his arm. "You had your annual physical last week. Did they . . . did Dr. Hart find something wrong?"

"No—nothing like that." He scooped up a handful of sand and poured it into a conical cone between them. "I've had a peculiar feeling lately that . . . well . . . that Harry is around." He chuckled to show how ridiculous he felt about that.

"Your brother Harry?"

"No other Harry could make me feel so jumpy."

"But why would you think he's here? He's still in that hospital in California."

"No, he's not. When I started feeling this way, I put in a long distance call to Camarillo. Harry was released from there eighteen months ago."

"Released? But he *murdered* someone. They gave him a life sentence."

"Like everything else, a life sentence doesn't last as long as it used to. The administrative physician told me that over the last few years Harry had responded to treatment, that his quote compulsive anti-social behavior unquote had disappeared. His personality has become, you should forgive the expression, socially realigned. Harry was eligible for parole after fifteen years, but they kept him for an additional two years for observation. Finally he was released. Not just paroled, by the way, but given a straight discharge. That means they have no way of telling me where Harry is right now."

"Socially realigned," Donna said in disgust. "I hate those bull-shit psychological phrases."

Ben couldn't help grinning. "You always lapse into profanity when you're really upset. Did you know that?"

She managed to return the smile. "That's a fucking lie."

There were shouts of anger from the general area where Sharon and Jeff were swimming, and they looked up to see what was wrong.

"Hey!" Ben called. "Sharon . . . stop teasing Jeff."

"I'm not teasing him. He's being a *cretin* again."

"I am not. They won't let me swim with them—"

"He won't leave us alone," Sharon complained.

"You'll have to get along with each other—or come out of the water," Donna ordered.

There were grumbles, but both children quieted down and went splashing off in opposite directions.

"Who's that boy with Sharon?" Ben asked. "Have I seen him before?"

"You've seen him a dozen times. That's Oop."

"Oop?"

"I believe his full name is John Chambers MacRae. Oop to his friends. You know . . . after that comic-strip character, Alley Oop. The caveman with the huge arms and chest."

"Ah, yes. I see the resemblance. Good Lord. He isn't Sharon's new boyfriend, is he?"

"I'm afraid so."

Ben groaned. "Where does she find them? Oop, for Christ's sake. Well, I hope she dumps him as fast as the others."

"I wouldn't count on that. I was told in strict confidence that they've exchanged pillows."

"What does that mean?"

"Sharon has given Oop her pillow to sleep on, and vice versa."

Ben made a theatrical gagging sound.

"Stop it. Don't you remember the time you gave me one of your snotty old handkerchiefs? You wanted me to sleep with that. I did, too, after I washed it."

"That was different. I was a sophisticated college man twenty-one years of age. Oop is a kid of about sixteen with no forehead."

"He's a very good student. His name was in the newspaper last week for taking high honors."

"He probably stole them."

"Poor Oop," Donna said. "We're slandering him to avoid talking about Harry."

"My brother Harry," Ben sighed. "My *twin* brother."

"That makes it worse, doesn't it."

"Yes, it does. Being twins, you know, especially identical twins, you're always together. Same classes in school . . . same friends . . . same everything . . . so much that you become counter-

13

parts of each other. Exchangeable parts, I should say."

"Except that you and Harry had such different personalities."

"Harry was always the wild one . . . the risk-taker. He dominated me, I've told you that. But he always looked out for me, too, in his way. Even when we played football in high school, Harry would run the blocks and I'd sail through for the touchdowns. 'All part of the service,' he used to say. For a long time I wondered why Harry wanted to play on the line when he was by far the best broken-field runner of the two of us. Finally I realized he preferred to knock people down, it was that simple. I mean he just *loved* to flatten people."

Silence. Then Ben continued: "Thinking back, I guess Harry was probably out of his mind from the start. I couldn't see that when we were kids, of course. Maybe mom did. She used to remark that Harry was *moonstruck,* her way of saying he was different. He didn't get along well with most people, for instance. As a boy Harry was always in a fight with someone; any little thing would send him into a rage. Later, in high school and at U.S.C., he had a reputation with girls as a bad date. He could lose his temper and get a little rough if a girl didn't, as he said, come across.

"Then, in our junior year, he was arrested for raping and killing that girl. I couldn't believe it. *Wouldn't* believe it. But when I visited him at the L.A. county jail he admitted to me that he'd killed her. Bragged about it, in fact, because he wanted my help. He had a crazy idea that if I confessed to the murder, his lawyer could get the jury confused as to which of us had done it, because we're twins.

"I couldn't, of course. I couldn't confess to a murder, not even to save Harry. He went into one of his rages, tried to get at me right there in the visiting room, and the guards took him away. At the trial, after the judge pronounced sentence, Harry turned to me and said, 'I'll kill you for this, Ben.' Those were the last words he ever spoke to me."

Donna let Ben retell the story, even though she had heard it in even greater detail many years before, and in bits and pieces since then, because she realized he needed to talk.

Ben cleared his throat. "You know all this, but there's one thing I've never told you. That day in the visiting room at the L.A. county jail, Harry said, 'She wasn't the first one, either. I've killed before,

Ben, and gotten away clean. That's why I know I can beat this one, with your help.' It's haunted me all these years, wondering how many other bodies of young girls Harry left behind."

"My God." She gripped his arm tightly. "I used to wish I'd known Harry, so I could understand you better. Now I'm glad I never met him."

They lay back on their beach towels, fingers entwined.

"He's been out of Camarillo for a year and a half?"

"That's right."

"Well, maybe he's really changed, if he hasn't come around here in all that time. What makes you think he's in Westport?"

"Nothing specific. Just a feeling, and some hints."

"Hints? Tell me."

"Oh, I ran into Joe Powell last Wednesday in Playhouse Square. He asked, in a joking kind of way, why I'd snubbed him the day before. Joe claimed he passed me coming out of the Red Barn on Route Thirty-three and that I looked right through him. He swore it was me, but I haven't been in the Red Barn in a couple of years.

"Also, last week I was driving up Main Street and saw a reflection of myself in one of the store windows. Except there was no reflection of my car. At least there didn't seem to be. It came to me a few blocks later that maybe I'd seen Harry's face.

"But what bothers me most is a feeling I have of being watched. Sometimes the hair will rise on the back of my neck and I'll twist around to see who's staring at me, but there's never anyone there. I don't know, maybe I'm imagining all this because I know Harry is out."

"You said you had the sensation before you knew Harry had been released."

"Yes, I did."

"All right then . . . what shall we do about it?"

"I've been thinking about calling Lieutenant Conde down at the state police barracks and ask him to trace Harry. We've known each other for a few years now. I think he'd follow through for me."

"Do it," Donna said promptly. "Neither of us will have a good night's sleep until we know where your brother is."

Jeff appeared above them, soaking wet and dripping water onto their beach towel. "Can I have forty cents for a snow cone?"

15

"You've had two snow cones already," Donna reminded him.

"They're only water, with a little flavor. Water's good for me. You tell me to drink water all the time. You say water's good for me, but you won't let me have a snow cone. I don't get it."

All said in a rush of words designed to confuse the issue. Donna did not fall for the ploy. "No, you may not have another snow cone right now. As you pointed out, snow cones cost forty cents. Water is free. If you want a drink of water, there's the fountain. Help yourself."

"Gee. Forty cents isn't much."

"It is when you're overdrawn on your allowance, which you are. And you owe me two car washes besides. No more snow cones or other treats until you're paid up, buster."

Jeff turned to his father. "Am I big enough to get an American Express card, dad?"

"No, thank God."

"Gee, the world isn't made for little people, is it."

"The world *is* made for little people," Ben said, "but you won't appreciate that until you're a big person, with a big person's responsibilities."

Jeff turned back to the waters of Long Island Sound, throwing himself headlong into the surf with a splash that swamped some of the smaller children playing in the shallows.

"You know something else that bothers me?" Ben said. "Sometimes Jeff reminds me too much of Harry. Jeff is demanding . . . aggressive . . . rough on people around him—"

"You've just described half of the eleven-year-old boys in the world," Donna replied.

Ben shrugged and let it go. But it's true, he thought. Jeff has an inner toughness much like Harry's, something I've always lacked. Harry was hard, and I was soft. *Am* soft? If Harry has come back, can I handle him? Or will he still be able to run roughshod over me, after all these years?

In one of those moments of insight experienced by people who are truly close, Donna said, "Don't worry about yourself, Ben. You're a gentle, loving man. I wouldn't have it any other way, and neither would the kids."

"Thanks for the vote of confidence. But the fact is, I never in

16

my life won a fight with Harry. Not once." The confession made him restless. "I'm going in for a swim."

As he climbed to his feet, Sharon and Oop emerged from the water laughing and pushing at each other. He noticed with fresh pride how mature Sharon had become. Her figure, so boyish a few short months ago, had blossomed into a delightful variation of her mother's sensuous body, and her face had evolved from the flat angles and planes of a tomboy into the warm curves of young womanhood.

At that moment a nasty memory presented itself. Ben saw with startling clarity the raw black and white police photos of the young girl Harry had raped and murdered back in Los Angeles. She had been seventeen, only two years older than Sharon was now. He could recall with detailed accuracy the way her body had been found; she lay with arms and legs akimbo under a big pepper tree in an isolated section of MacArthur Park, hair spread around her head like a thin pillow, neck corded with dark bruises, tongue disgorged in a swollen mass from the side of her mouth, a plaid skirt pulled up roughly around her waist to reveal naked legs and buttocks.

Ben ran down the beach and plunged into the sound. But the refreshing waters could not purge the cold fear that was beginning to eat at his stomach.

AT FOUR P.M. Harry Ryder decided to move from his position overlooking Compo Beach. He knew from prior Sunday afternoons that his brother would pack up the family shortly before five P.M. and head home. He walked quickly to his car, which he had parked on a cul-de-sac off Blue Water Lane, and drove to the Greens Farms area of Westport where his brother lived.

Ben Ryder's home, built several years ago when prices were reasonable and interest rates low, was situated on an isolated piece of property that perfectly suited Harry's needs. The house, too, had advantages for him. It was a contemporary structure of wood and glass built on the highest portion of four acres of heavily wooded property. He had been able to set up an observation post, of sorts, in a stand of hickory trees about one hundred yards opposite the wide front windows.

17

He parked on Clapboard Hill Road and, after making sure there was no traffic coming in either direction, hiked up a hill, the summit of which overlooked Ben's property. He picked his way down the opposite slope using the route he had traveled many times over the past weeks. A three-minute walk brought him out of the woods at the rear of Ben's house, where he took out a key from his pocket and entered the house through the garage door.

The Ryder family cat, an old tabby named Whiskers, purred lightly from his bed when Harry entered the garage. Whiskers had been mildly surprised the first time the stranger who looked like his master had appeared, but soon became accustomed to the man's comings and goings. The fact that the man always came into the house when the Ryders were away had no significance for Whiskers, whose life was totally centered on the two red bowls that held his food and water.

Harry thought it stupid of Ben to have a cat for a pet when he lived in such an isolated house. A dog would at least make some noise when a stranger came around. But Ben's complacency was to his advantage, so he could hardly complain.

He glanced at his watch and gave himself only ten minutes inside the house; the Ryders could conceivably leave Compo Beach early. His only mission today was to assure himself that the batteries for the listening devices planted in the house were still operable, and to check Ben's closet for any new articles of clothing.

Harry tested the device hidden in the base of a living-room lamp first, then the others in the kitchen, dining room and master bedroom. All were in working order and tuned to the same frequency. That sometimes became a problem when people were talking in more than one room, but he couldn't risk the noise of more than one receiver at his listening post.

As always, Harry ended a tour of his brother's house in the bedroom. He stared at Ben and Donna's bed, envying the years they had spent together there. *He's had sixteen years with her, and I spent more years than that jerking off alone in a locked room in Camarillo.*

That wasn't fair, Ben. Not fair at all.

He found that Ben had bought two new pale blue business shirts. They had Robert Peck labels and he made a note to visit the nearest Peck store in Norwalk to pick up two of the same shirts for himself.

His watch said four twenty-six, so Harry quickly let himself out of the house and retreated through the woods. He circled through the trees and brush to his observation post in the stand of hickories and settled down to wait for the family.

The humid weather had dramatically increased the population of mosquitos and other flying insects. To make the long wait bearable Harry had brought along spray cans of Off and Garden Bug Killer. He sprayed the woods around him with the bug killer, then closed his eyes and dosed his face and back of his neck and arms with Off.

The Off worked reasonably well, but he still found it necessary to spray the area around him every ten or fifteen minutes to keep the mosquitos at bay.

At about five-fifteen the Ryder family station wagon came up the long curving driveway to the house. Jeff and Sharon jumped out and raced for the garage door. Jeff won. He reached into a nearby planter, took out a key and unlocked the garage door, throwing it open with careless energy.

Harry had taken note of the spare key during his first week of watching the house. A few days later he had made a wax impression, from which a locksmith had made him a duplicate key. Since then he had been able to come and go in his brother's house whenever he chose.

Ben and Donna followed the kids into the garage carrying beach towels, folding chairs and the cooler.

Harry waited until they were inside, then turned on his portable transceiver. He kept the volume very low. Even so, he could clearly hear the family's activities in the four major rooms of the house. Donna was in the kitchen transferring the extra sodas from the cooler to the refrigerator. Sharon was on the phone in the same room talking to a girlfriend, while her brother was in the living room begging his father for a .22 rifle for his next birthday. He could hear his brother replying, "No way, sport. Not until you're at least thirteen. And not even then, if you haven't learned better discipline."

"Aw, dad. Tony has one."

"I think his parents were wrong to buy Tony a gun. He's not ready. Tony and his twenty-two should be locked away in a window-

19

less room for the next three years."

"Aw . . ."

Harry grinned. Just like Ben to veto the gun. Anything even slightly dangerous would turn his legs to water. How did I ever get such a gutless wonder for a brother?

For the next hour he listened to the mundane sounds of a family gathered for a casual dinner of hamburgers, potato chips, beans and lemonade.

Shortly before seven P.M. he focused his binoculars on the TV corner of Ben's living room. As expected, Ben was sprawled in the easy chair waiting for *Sixty Minutes* to begin.

You are so predictable, Harry smiled. So pathetically predictable. That'll be the death of you, brother dear.

Later, when the kids were scattered in other parts of the house and the TV had been turned off, Harry heard the first conversation that genuinely interested him since he had settled down in the woods.

Donna was saying ". . . ought to call Lieutenant Conde right now."

"On Sunday night?"

"Policemen work funny hours. He might be there."

"All right."

Harry heard the phone being dialed and studied Ben and Donna through his binoculars. The sun was behind the hill and they had turned on a light, so he could see their faces perfectly. This was no casual conversation. Their expressions were too serious.

"Lieutenant Conde, please," Ben said.

A few moments of silence.

"Jim? Hello, this is Ben Ryder. I'm glad I caught you, though I'm sorry you're stuck down there on a Sunday night. Yes, I know we've had a lot of burglaries in town lately. Where'd they hit this time? Hey, that's a shame.

"No, I'm calling about a personal problem that may end up involving the police. Jim . . . I don't quite know how to begin. This is painful and sort of embarrassing for me. You see, I have a twin brother. An identical twin. His name is Harry and until last year he was serving a life sentence for rape and murder out in California. What? Yes. Harold Raymond Ryder." He paused while Lieutenant Conde presumably wrote down the name. "He's been locked up in a state hospital in Camarillo, California. Yes, he was confined there for seventeen years. Finally got out on what they call an administrative discharge. I think that means a panel of doctors have declared him safe and sane. The problem is, Jim, he may be in this area, and he could try to hurt me or someone else in my family. Well, the last time I talked to him, which I'll admit was a long time ago, he threatened to kill me. So the reason I'm calling . . ."

There was a long silence while Ben listed to Conde. When he spoke again, his voice was full of relief.

"Jim, that's great. Exactly what I was going to ask. Thanks. Sure, I'll be in my office most of the day tomorrow. Okay. Talk to you then."

Ben put down the phone.

Harry quickly scanned their faces and was delighted to see that the lines of tension on Ben's face had eased. Good. Let him feel nice and safe. That will make it so much harder to face the truth later on.

"Conde will put a tracer on Harry. He says the police out there keep pretty good track of anyone who's been convicted of a serious sex crime, even if they've left the state. He may have word on Harry's whereabouts tomorrow afternoon or evening."

"Good. I hope he tells us Harry is working in a shoe store in Los Angeles, or something."

"So do I."

They embraced, which pleased Harry. Touching, he thought. And useless. It won't be that easy to keep the boogeyman away.

He had seen and heard everything he wanted for tonight. Ben sensed he was in Westport, and that was good. He had wanted Ben to know . . . and yet not know. To feel harrassed and uneasy without knowing exactly why.

Now I'll tighten the screws. Give him something to *really* worry about.

He turned off the transceiver, gathered up his mosquito repellant and quietly made his way through the trees and brush toward his car.

Two hours later Harry was driving down the Merritt Parkway toward Greenwich in a relaxed and cheerful mood. He had just enjoyed a steak and scampi dinner at the Pepper Mill, enhanced by several martinis and a bottle of Cabernet Sauvignon, followed by Cherries Jubilee.

Aware that he had consumed too much liquor, he was taking pains to drive carefully when a young hitchhiker appeared in his headlights. A girl of twenty or so. Long dark hair and nice tits. Impulsively, he pulled off onto the grass and waved to her through the rear window.

She ran up and jumped into the front seat.

"Thanks, mister. I'm headed for New Jersey."

"I can take you as far as Greenwich," Harry said, pulling out onto the parkway.

"That'll help."

They drove along in silence while Harry assessed his passenger. A college girl, he decided. Just out of school and heading home. Strong face. Italian, perhaps. He liked the mole on her left cheek; it made an elegant beauty mark. And her tits were not just nice, they were *terrific.*

She was carrying a rucksack which she had dumped in the back seat. Harry wondered idly what it contained. No bras, that's for sure. But lots of panties. I wonder what color panties she wears. His cock hardened at the thought. He cleared his throat. "I hardly ever stop for hitchhikers. It's not safe, they say. But you looked harmless enough. Going home for vacation?"

"Yep. I was up in Cape Cod looking for a summer job. It would've been neat to stay on the Cape all summer, but the good jobs are already taken."

"What kind of work are you looking for?"

"Oh, waitress, I guess. Or lifeguard. I have my Red Cross lifesaving certificate."

"Good for you. Don't worry, you'll find something in New Jersey."

"Yeah, but Jersey is the pits. It's the only state so dumb that people abbreviate the name—*Jersey.* You don't hear people calling New York just *York* or New Hampshire just *Hampshire.* But everyone says *Jersey* like it's so grungy you could get sick saying the whole name."

Harry laughed. "I never thought about it, but you're right."

"Where are you from, mister?"

"L.A. I moved out here a few months ago."

"I'd love to live in California. Why'd you come here?"

"I have some business to settle. Then I'll be heading west again."

"What kind of work do you do?"

"Actually, I'm retired. This is personal business."

"You don't seem old enough to retire, nice-looking fella like you."

Harry felt his cock swell larger. He thought he'd give the girl a bit of a laugh. "I look even younger without this." He peeled the mustache off his lip.

"Wow! A false mustache!"

"And I don't need these either." Harry removed his glasses and showed them to her. "You see—plain glass."

"That's wild! Why do you wear a false mustache and fake glasses? Are you an actor or something?"

"I have a twin brother. We're identical twins. Ben's his name. We're both thirty-eight but sometimes I want to look older or maybe a little different than Ben. So I put on these glasses and the mustache. Other times, when I do want to look like him, I take them off."

"It must be weird to have an identical twin. I can understand why you'd want to change your appearance now and then. I mean, like, in order to be your own person."

"Exactly."

"Thirty-eight. You don't look it."

"Well, I had this operation. Monkey glands. Made me feel ten years younger."

"Monkey glands! Isn't that dangerous?"

"Not at all. The toughest part is catching the monkey."

She giggled. "Now you're putting me on. Were you kidding about being a twin too?"

"No," Harry said softly. "I do have a twin brother. That's an absolute fact. But we're alike in looks only. In other ways we're very different."

"That's interesting. In what ways?"

"Well, for instance, old Ben is what's called a monogomist. He'd never cheat on Donna, his wife. But me—everyone knows I'll

23

fuck anything that's warm and wet." He laughed, looking directly at her.

The girl joined his laughter, uneasily. And she turned her head to look out the opposite window. End of conversation.

Which made Harry sore. Just a touch sore. I didn't mean anything, he brooded. A little joke to pass the time. The bitch flashes her fanny to hook a ride, then turns up her nose at a harmless remark. Not very polite.

His head began to throb.

"Say, why don't we stop for a drink?"

"No, thank you. I'd like to be home before midnight."

"What's the hurry? You're only going to *Jersey.*" He parodied the word exactly as she had done, but now his humor seemed to escape her. To Harry her silence was a calculated insult. "Wake up, kid. That's your own gag."

"Maybe I'd better get out here. Would you pull over, please?"

"I said I'd take you as far as Greenwich."

"I'd rather get out here. Stop the car. Please."

"Sure, whatever you want."

They were approaching one of the New Canaan exits. Harry turned off the Merritt and around the curve. "I'll have to stop up there. Too much traffic behind me."

"That'll be fine. Thanks for the lift."

As he came off the ramp, a side road presented itself to the right. He braked to a stop under some trees and, without thinking about it, flicked off his lights and killed the motor.

"Thanks again. Goodbye."

Before she could open the door, Harry's left hand closed around her wrist and he slid his right arm over her shoulders. "What's the hurry? Look how private it is."

"Let *go.*" She spoke in a tight voice, struggling to reach the door handle.

"I love that mole on your cheek. It's sexy. Are you Italian? Greek?"

She continued to struggle, then accepted that Harry was just too strong. Her mouth opened to scream.

"No." Harry released her arm and clamped a hand over her mouth. "Let's keep this just between us. No one else needs to know.

24

Especially your folks. I'll slip you some money afterwards, enough to give you a couple weeks of pure vacation up on the Cape. What do you say?"

Her elbow crashed into his cheek, snapping back his head.

"Hey! What the hell's wrong with you?"

She was biting at his fingers too, so Harry slid his hand down around her throat and squeezed hard enough to cut off any sound. The way she wriggled around, with her big ass and tits humping up and down, made him even hornier. He discovered that his pants were unzipped, although he couldn't remember opening them. He wondered for a moment whether she had done that. Wouldn't be the first time a girl had teased him that way.

"Easy now, no one's going to hurt you."

He wished he knew her name. It was more exciting to whisper a girl's name while you banged her. Her jeans ripped as he yanked them down over her knees and she made a gagging sound when he rolled over on top of her. For safety's sake, he kept a firm hold on her throat.

There. Lots more room without that damn steering wheel. Her legs jerked convulsively as he entered her. He peered into her eyes, trying to determine whether she was at last finding pleasure in his boldness, but they had gone glassy and fixed.

Harry rammed himself home several times, lost in the heat of the moment. That beauty mark, how he loved it. She was magnificent. She was giving him . . .

Everything.

LATER HE COLLAPSED at her side, breathing hard and sweating like a long-distance runner. The only sound was of a mosquito buzzing at his ear. He brushed it away and rested his head on the back of the seat, eyes closed.

Another car turned off the parkway and its lights swept the trees nearby.

He straightened up and zipped his pants.

The girl lay crumpled next to him, not drawing a breath. Taking her pulse would be a waste of time. He knew the posture of death too well.

He was angry with himself. This was a mistake, a breach of the plan. You promised to lay off for a bit, Harry. Save it all for brother Ben.

Fortunately his instincts hadn't failed him completely. He had picked a fairly dark and quiet spot. But there were houses terribly close.

He switched on the lights and turned over the engine. Keeping the car to a moderate speed, he continued up the road into New Canaan. He saw lights from houses to his right, but only darkness to the left. Woods? No, a park. That would be perfect.

Harry turned into the park entrance and drove a hundred yards or so, until the main road was well behind him. It would be foolish to drive very far into the park without knowing the road system.

He chose a bridge that ran over a little creek, parked and went quickly to the other side of the car, opened the door, dragged out the girl's body.

With a grunt he pushed her down the embankment. She made a violent crashing noise as she rolled through the brush, paralyzing Harry with fear until she came to rest near the bottom.

He tossed the rucksack after her and was walking around the car when a funny thought struck him. Why not incorporate this into the plan? That way the poor kid's death would at least count for something.

There were only seconds available to improvise, but he hit on an idea immediately. He was wearing a cotton sports shirt with a buttoned-down flap on the pocket, a shirt identical to one owned by Ben. He tore off the button, wiped it clean with his handkerchief and flipped it down the embankment toward the girl's body.

The police dearly loved their clues. Now they would have one.

He climbed into the car and drove away, whistling.

Monday

CHAPTER 2

BEN SPENT most of Monday morning working on a project for a new account, an automotive company that had hired him to design the interior of a new line of busses. Since he liked nothing better than working on a complex set of design and economic problems, he was mildly annoyed when someone entered his office just as he was setting in place a key strut of the scale model he was building.

"Mr. Ryder?" A young man stood in the doorway holding a large cardboard carton. "Delivery."

"Okay, put it anywhere." Clients and vendors often sent samples of materials to his office, so he accepted the delivery receipt and signed it automatically. It took a minute for the label on the box to register in his mind. When it did, he left his board and opened the box. "What the hell is *this?*"

He picked up the phone and called The Wet Spot, a liquor store where he often shopped for wine.

"Hello, Bob. Ben Ryder here. Say, there's been some sort of mistake. Your boy just delivered a full case of champagne to my office."

"Yes, Mr. Ryder. Anything wrong? A bottle damaged?"

"No. The problem is, I didn't order any champagne."

"You mean you want something else?"

"I mean that I didn't order any wine at all today. Not a single bottle, much less a case of champagne."

"But Mr. Ryder, you did. You came by a couple of hours ago. Ordered a case of champagne, paid cash and asked me to deliver it to your office."

"Look, I've been here in my office all morning. I could use a free case of champagne, but the person who paid for it will be calling you any minute to find out where the hell it is."

Bob West laughed self-consciously. "Mr. Ryder, you came in this morning at about ten o'clock. Said you were having a party and wanted a case of Chateau Rothschild. I tried to steer you onto something just as good, not so expensive. You said no, you wanted the best. This is going to be a special party. You peeled off five one-hundred-dollar bills from a big roll of hundreds—pardon me, I couldn't help noticing—and paid me cash. You're a good customer, Mr. Ryder. So don't think you have to be embarrassed about returning some bottles of wine. I understand. I can send the kid back for them later today."

While West was talking, the truth hit Ben. *Harry.* Harry had bought the champagne. "No, that's all right. I'll keep it, Bob. I was a little confused."

He put down the phone and stared at the case of champagne.

Harry loved champagne. When they were college students and could hardly afford beer, Harry would sometimes order champagne for a tableful of his friends. And it would be like Harry to carry a big roll of bills. Ben remembered how Harry would change two tens into singles, then wrap another ten around the twenty singles to make his small bankroll look bigger.

In a way it was a relief to know he hadn't been jumping at shadows. Harry was here. No question. The champagne was his calling card.

The phone rang and Ben answered it cautiously. "Ryder Industrial Design."

"Good morning, Ryder Industrial Design. How are you?"

Ben relaxed slightly. "Hi, Donna."

"You're in a very extravagant mood today. I've never been so surprised in my life."

30

"Extravagant mood?"

"Yes! The skis just arrived. Ben, they're beautiful! You really went all the way this time, Benjamin. Skis. Boots. *And* ski suits. The works for both of us. What came over you?"

"Wait a minute. Are you saying someone has delivered ski equipment to our house?"

"Yes, of course."

"What makes you think it came from me?"

"From your note, you modest thing. 'I'll see you on the slopes of love.' " She chuckled. "Kind of a tortured metaphor, but I like it. What really surprised me was that you got my size right on everything. You've never managed that before."

"Do you have the note? Does the handwriting look like mine?"

The tension in his voice finally reached Donna. "Yes, I have it right here. It's your handwriting." Pause. "Isn't it?"

"No. *Harry* sent that stuff. And The Wet Spot just delivered a case of champagne to my office. I called Bob West over there and he swore I'd been into his place earlier today. Donna, I've been *here* all morning."

"But this *is* your handwriting. I've seen your scribble a million times."

"Hon, that's not my writing and I haven't bought any ski equipment for either of us."

"It's uncanny," she said. "Especially since we talked so recently about taking up skiing this winter. Ben—how would *he* know that?"

"I can't tell you. But obviously I was right about being watched. Harry is in Westport and he's playing some kind of sick game with us."

"He must . . . he must still look very much like you. I mean, all those years of being locked up haven't aged him too badly if he fooled Bob West."

"Apparently not. Where did the skis come from?"

"Allen's Outdoor Shop, over near the Clam Box Restaurant."

"Yes, I know the place." He felt a sudden desire to get out of his office. To do something. To *act.* "Donna, I'm going to Allen's. Maybe they can tell me something about Harry, anything that might provide a lead for the police."

"Lieutenant Conde hasn't called?"

"Not yet. If I don't hear from him by four o'clock, I'll go to the police station."

"Yes, you'd better."

"Until then . . ." He searched for a casual way to introduce his greatest fear, but found none. "Until then, keep the doors and windows locked and the kids in the house."

"Sharon has a piano lesson this afternoon." Donna's voice had begun to tremble.

"Cancel it. Keep them home until I get there. Tell them I'll explain everything tonight. . . . I'd hoped they'd never have to know about Harry."

"Their Uncle Harry." Donna shook her head. "My God."

ALLEN'S OUTDOOR SHOP was located on Post Road just past the turnoff for Sherwood Island. Ben drove there and found the windows covered with signs: GIANT WINTER SPORTSWEAR SALE! BUY EARLY AND SAVE!

He went into the shop, which was crowded with shoppers buying beachwear, plus a few people trying on the winter sale items.

"Mr. Ryder, I didn't expect to see you again so soon. Did you forget something?"

He turned to find a rather pretty girl smiling at him.

"Did your wife like the outfit? If not, she can exchange it."

"You know me." Ben made it a statement instead of a question.

"Certainly."

He smiled, trying to preface what was bound to be a difficult conversation with pleasantness, then plunged ahead. "This will sound a little crazy—when do you think I was in here?"

"Why . . . right after we opened this morning. Nine thirty or so."

Ben glanced at the name tag on her blouse. "Miss Mills, I have a twin brother. *He* was in here this morning, not me."

"A twin? That's amazing." She studied Ben's face. "I'd swear . . ."

"We're identical twins. Would you tell me what name he gave you?"

She went to the cash register and picked up a sales book. "Here, the skis and clothes were purchased by Benjamin Ryder, Clapboard Hill Road, Westport."

"No, *I'm* Ben Ryder. That was my brother. The . . . uh . . . gift he sent us was quite a surprise. We didn't know Harry was back in Connecticut."

"But, he said the woman's outfit was for *his* wife, Mrs. Benjamin Ryder. He knew the sizes and everything."

"That was part of Harry's surprise, I guess."

"Oh . . ."

"It's confusing, I know. My big question is, does Harry still look *exactly* like me? I haven't seen him in several years."

She squinted at Ben. "Very much so. Even now, I can't believe that wasn't you this morning. You were talking about . . . I mean *he* was talking about how much his wife liked yellow and that sort of thing. And you *sound* alike too."

"Did he have any scars? Or special mannerisms I don't have?"

"Not that I noticed."

"Did you happen to see what kind of car he was driving?"

"I'm afraid not."

A customer came up to the counter with a bathing suit. Miss Mills rang up the sale, put the bathing suit in a bag and thanked her.

"My brother didn't mention where he's living? A town? The name of a hotel?"

Miss Mills shook her head. "As I said, he gave the Clapboard Hill address and said he wanted everything delivered right away because his wife would probably be going out around noon for lunch with a friend."

Ben felt the tightness in his stomach again. Donna often went out for lunch with Babs Colton on Mondays. How could Harry know *that?*

Suddenly Miss Mills produced a triumphant smile. "Wait, this must be some kind of joke. If you and your brother haven't seen each other for so long, how is it that he was wearing the same clothes you have on right now?" Another customer came up. "Excuse me, I'll be right back."

Ben was shaken by the depth of his brother's knowledge. Harry knows that Donna and I have decided to take up skiing. He knows

33

her sizes and favorite color. Where I shop for liquor. How I dress. He's obviously put months into researching us. And what else does he know? The places where Oop and Sharon hang out? The location of the secret tree house Jeff and Tony built up on the hill?

And why? Ben didn't want to face the whole answer . . . Harry had something in mind, a plan. Harry was always making big plans.

Miss Mills returned. "Am I right? Is this some kind of joke, Mr. Ryder?"

"Yes, in a way. Thank you, Miss Mills. Thanks a lot."

HE COULDN'T DEVOTE the rest of his day to the problem of Harry, much as he wanted to. The Truro Company, a California manufacturer of gardening equipment, had sent an executive all the way from Los Angeles to talk with him about the design of a new hedge trimmer. The man would be arriving at his office about one o'clock.

A few days ago the idea of designing a more efficient machine for the tiresome chore of trimming hedges had looked like an interesting project. Now he could summon up only minimal interest in the meeting with Truro's man, who turned out to be a marketing type full of jargon about "demographic dynamics" and "the profit picture for electric trimmers."

Usually he took it slow and easy with his clients, gave them first-class treatment. But today he had trouble just sitting still while Bob Drummond, Truro's new products-marketing manager (who insisted on being called "Bobby"), rattled on with his vague descriptions of the product.

When he could no longer bear the man's chatter, Ben said, "Didn't you bring any blueprints? Any mechanical drawings of the working parts?"

Drummond looked surprised. "No. I thought we'd yak some about it first."

"This is useless. Before I can design the body of a product I need to know precisely how the guts of the machine will work. Isn't there a technical man I can talk with?"

"Why, sure . . . We got a full team working on this. But I thought I'd save a little loot for old mother Truro by coming out here alone. The old man . . . our chairman . . . really liked your design for the new Mackey power saw. That's why we asked you—"

Ben cut him short. "I'll have to talk to your technical people. It would be best if I came out to your plant in Los Angeles. Can you set up a date for that?"

"Yes, I guess so."

"Do it." Ben stood up, signaling an end to the meeting.

"But don't you want to hear about our sales campaign? Listen, we've got a series of TV ads planned—"

"Some other time." At the hurt expression on Drummond's face, Ben softened his voice. "It's been a pleasure talking with you . . . Bobby. And I look forward to meeting your team in L.A. You've got a fine product. I'll try to do it justice with my design."

Drummond brightened. "You're damned right we got a fine product! Okay, Benny, I'll set up that meeting and call you next week. Meanwhile, get that old thinking cap on!"

Ben ushered Drummond out of his office and immediately went to his phone. He called the Connecticut State Police and asked for Lieutenant Conde. A desk sergeant informed him that Conde couldn't take any calls at the moment.

"Tell him that Ben Ryder is coming over. I want to see him as soon as possible. It's urgent."

Ben switched on the telephone answering system and left his office. He drove to Troop G, the Connecticut State Police barracks that served the Fairfield County area, ticking off in his mind the points he would make.

Conde was still busy when he arrived, so Ben tried to relax for a few minutes by thumbing through a few of the old magazines in the waiting room. They made him wonder if somewhere there existed a single person in charge of ordering all the magazines for all the waiting rooms in the world. Part of that person's job would be to send women's magazines to offices where men waited, and men's magazines to waiting rooms for women. That person would also make sure that all magazines delivered to waiting rooms were at least two years old and so tattered they fell apart in your hands.

Presently Jim Conde came striding down the hall.

"Come in, Ben. Sorry to keep you waiting. We finally nailed the second-story man who's been hitting all those houses west of the Merritt. I've been interrogating him for the last two hours. He's a kid. Only sixteen and already a seasoned pro. Would you believe it?"

He followed Conde into his office and took a chair.

Conde went around the desk and plopped himself down, sweeping a pile of manila folders out of the way. "Damn paperwork. That's half the job these days." He was a burly man of Ben's age, but with hair so thin and gray that he appeared much older. He had youthful eyes, though, and a good-natured face that no amount of police work could sour. "The sergeant you spoke with told me you sounded spooked."

"I'm worried, Jim. I found out this morning that my brother Harry is definitely in Westport."

"What? You've seen him?"

"Well, no. But other people have."

"Did he phone you?"

"No. But—"

"I know." Conde smiled and leaned forward. "You're sure he's around anyway."

Ben had an uneasy feeling that somehow he had lost Conde's support before he started. For the first time in their casual acquaintance he noticed the trace of flinty suspicion lurking behind the friendly eyes. "Yes, that's right. Harry found a unique way to let me know he's in Westport."

He told Conde in detail about the two deliveries made that morning to his office and home by The Wet Spot and Allen's. The main points he wanted to make were that Harry had somehow acquired a great deal of information about his family, and that he believed his brother might still be a very dangerous man. He listed all the things Harry appeared to know about the family and explained how certain actions, like peeling off five one-hundred-dollar bills and ordering expensive champagne, were part of *Harry's* personality. He talked for a long time, trying, without success, to generate a sense of urgency in Conde.

Finally he said, "You don't seem impressed, Jim. Or convinced."

Conde took out a pack of cigarettes. "Mind if I smoke?"

"Go ahead."

He lit up, put a pad of yellow lined paper in front of him and picked up a pencil. "Ben, you and I have been bumping into each other around town for half a dozen years. We've worked together on a couple of civic committees. Our sons were on the same Little League team one year, and we spent some frustrating Saturday mornings wondering why the hell they couldn't remember to tag up on an outfield fly. Occasionally we run into each other at Stop and Shop. You always seem to have a list of what's on sale, which tells me you're better organized than I am. And I've heard you're a damned good industrial designer. But that's all I really know abut you. Ben, my point is, I just don't know you well enough to move on this without some evidence of criminal intent by someone. So let's nail down a few facts, okay?"

"Shoot."

"What time of day were those orders placed at The Wet Spot and Allen's?"

"I don't know exactly. About nine thirty at Allen's. Midmorning at The Wet Spot."

"Where were you then?"

"In my office."

"Who was with you?"

"No one."

"Don't you have a secretary? A partner?"

"No, my business is kind of a one-man show. I have a telephone answering system, an outside accountant to handle my books, and my typing and other office work is done by a secretarial service in the building."

Conde wrote those facts on his pad of paper. "In other words, you can't prove that the person who bought the champagne and ski equipment was your brother."

"Who else could it be?"

"Well, it's possible that you might have gone to The Wet Spot and Allen's and bought that stuff yourself, then claimed your twin brother was there."

"Why the hell would I do that?"

"I wouldn't know. And I'm not saying you did. But since you have no witnesses to where you were this morning, the man who made those purchases could have been you."

Face it, Ben told himself, Conde didn't believe him . . . had already written off Harry Ryder as a threat. He felt a growling anger

37

take hold of him. "What the hell is this, Jim? I have a brother who's a homicidal maniac. You know that's true if you've checked his record. And I can bring you birth certificates, old snapshots, whatever else you want as proof that Harry and I are identical twins. Identical in every way. I just brought you evidence that he's here in Westport trying to impersonate me, but you seem to believe *I'm* impersonating *him*. Why? Why won't you believe me?"

Conde picked up one of the manila folders he had set aside earlier. "Ben, your brother Harry is dead."

"What?"

"Your brother died about six months ago in California. I got the word this morning."

Ben sat stunned and disbelieving. Harry dead? That couldn't be. "You're *wrong*. . . . Harry is here in Connecticut—"

"Not possible." Conde opened the manila folder, which contained a computer printout and a sheet of the yellow lined paper covered with handwritten notes. "After you called me last night I ran a search on your brother through the California Law Enforcement Survey Center. That's a computerized system for tracking individuals convicted of major felonies in the state of California. The query came back: *Deceased.* But I didn't stop there. The printout told me that Harold Raymond Ryder had died in an auto accident last November in Ventura. This morning I called the Ventura County Sheriff's Office and talked to a clerk who gave me the name of the California Highway Patrol officer who was on the scene of your brother's death. I spoke with the investigating officer, who confirmed that your brother and his wife—"

"Wife?"

"Yes." Conde looked through the file. "Your brother married an Ellen Rafferty shortly after his release from Camarillo. Anyway, they were driving north on Highway One on the evening of November 9 when your brother lost control of his car. They went off the road and down a cliff onto some rocks about a hundred feet below. There was an explosion. The car burned. Your brother and his wife were probably killed outright."

"Their bodies were burned?"

"Extensively."

Ben jumped on that. "Then it wasn't Harry who died in that car.

38

How could they identify him if he was so badly burned?"

"From personal effects, such as his wedding ring. Also, the wife's father positively identified both bodies. He's completely legitimate, Ben. Sean Rafferty is a well-known and highly respected businessman out there, I was told, and apparently he was no fan of your brother. Rafferty identified your brother's remains but cursed his soul with just about every profanity that officer had ever heard. So Rafferty would have no reason to lie. Ben, your brother is dead."

Ben shook his head. "You don't understand. Harry and I are *identical* twins. We come from the same damned cell. There's a union between us that few others in this world have. If Harry had died in that crash, I would have felt it. Here—in my gut." He saw Conde's open skepticism. "I know that's hard for you to accept. Okay. But I wasn't the one who went to The Wet Spot and Allen's, and there's only one person who could impersonate me so convincingly—Harry."

Conde shrugged.

"You really believe I set up my own impersonation?"

"I think you've been under a lot of tension since you learned your brother was released. And I don't blame you. The system kicked out the record of that murder and it sounded pretty grisly, even on a computer printout. I'd be shitting yellow bricks if a lunatic like your brother had threatened me, and that's no lie. So maybe, not knowing he was dead, you invented some proof that he's in Westport, to guarantee police protection . . ." Conde's voice dropped into an even more compassionate register. "Was that what happened? If so, let's just forget it. Like they say in basketball, no harm, no foul."

"No harm?" Ben was annoyed to hear his voice shaking. "No, not yet. Well, I guess what they say is true, after all."

"What's true?"

"There's never a cop around when you need one. Thanks for nothing, officer."

LIEUTENANT JIM CONDE had, more than most people, a fear of being wrong—of making The Big Mistake. In his first year as a policeman, up in Hartford, he had arrested a burglary suspect and given court evidence with such skill and authority that the accused was convicted after a very short jury deliberation.

The man had been in prison for almost a year when a major fencing ring was broken by the Connecticut State Police. One of those caught in the roundup confessed to a number of burglaries in Hartford, including the break-in for which the man Conde had testified against was then doing time. He even led the state police to some of the unrecovered loot from that burglary.

The convicted man was pardoned, and young Jim Conde considered getting out of police work. He was honestly upset by the consequences of his testimony. An innocent man had lost a year . . . a whole year . . . out of his life. And then an older cop had taken Conde aside and told him, "Boyo, you can only do your best and hope to God you're right. That goes for surgeons and presidents and schoolteachers too. You'll make mistakes . . . they can't be avoided. Just be sure your mistakes don't come from slipshod work. Those are the ones that haunt you forever."

With those words once again in his mind, Conde was wondering if he had listened closely enough to Ben Ryder. There was something wrong about Ryder's reaction to the news of his brother's death. Ryder should have been relieved, but he wasn't.

"I'll be out for an hour," he told the duty sergeant.

Conde drove out to The Wet Spot and went in to find the proprietor, Bob West, restocking his vodka shelves.

"Hello, Bob."

"Oh hi, Jimmy. What's up? Another bad-check artist in town? I hope not. By God, it's tough enough with so many regular customers bouncing paper. Times are not good, Jimmy. In fact, the economy is in the toilet, you want my opinion. I can always gauge the economy by how many of my regulars are overdrawn at their banks."

"I'll bet you can." Conde smiled. "The government should put a few of their hotshot economists behind cash registers. They might learn something."

"Amen to that."

Conde took a package of salted peanuts off a rack and tossed a quarter on the counter. "I understand you had a difference of opinion this morning with a fella named Ben Ryder."

West abandoned his shelving. "Now how would you know that?

What's happened, Jimmy? Does Ryder say I overcharged him or something?"

"No, nothing like that. Ryder has a twin brother who's something of a pain in the ass. Has a lot of traffic warrants outstanding, that sort of thing. Ryder says his brother is in town and was in here this morning."

"A twin brother? I never knew Ryder had one."

"The twin doesn't live in Westport."

"Oh. Well, he may have a twin, but it was Ben Ryder who came into my shop this morning. I'm certain of that."

"How?"

"He says to me, 'Mornin', Bob, how's Lucy?' Now how would some brother I never met know my wife's name?"

"Unlikely."

"Plus which, Ryder admitted he'd been in here later on, when I talked to him on the phone."

"He did? Are you sure?"

"Yes. At first he gave me that funny stuff about not having come in, not ordering the champagne, then he apologized and said he was confused. That's the very word he used—'confused.' But the main thing is, Jimmy, when I've done business with a man for five years, I *know* him. Some brother, twin or not, couldn't possibly fool me."

"Okay. Thanks, Bob."

As Conde was leaving, West said, "I think he spent too much money on champagne and his wife gave him hell, that's what I think. Mrs. Ryder is careful with a dollar, you know. He didn't want to ask for his money back straight out, so he claimed he didn't place the order. People are strange, aren't they, Jimmy?"

"And getting stranger every day."

Conde next drove out to Allen's and talked to Miss Mills, the clerk Ryder had mentioned. She also believed Ben Ryder had come into her shop twice that day. And, like Bob West, she claimed that Ryder had backed away from the idea of a twin brother at the tail end of their conversation. Her most telling argument was that Ryder had worn exactly the same clothes both times he appeared in the store.

"How could someone you haven't seen for years own exactly the same suit? *And* shirt and tie?"

41

Conde said he had no answer to that question.

As Conde considered Ben Ryder's actions, his suspicions grew. Not of the brother, Harry. Harry was obviously dead. But of Ben Ryder.

For some reason Ben Ryder had desperately wanted the police to believe his brother was in the Westport area. It was almost as if there was something . . . a crime? . . . that Ben wanted to blame on his brother Harry. Apparently it had ruined Ryder's plan to learn that his brother was dead. He hadn't counted on that. Conde itched to know what Ben Ryder had wanted to pin on his brother.

Well, it would come out one day. Those things usually did.

CHAPTER 3

BEN TURNED onto Clapboard Hill Road as the last gusts from a briefly violent thundershower pelted Westport. By the time he reached his driveway the storm had moved west away from the Connecticut shore.

As always, he felt a rush of pride as he approached the home he and Donna had worked so hard for. The house was built of prime California redwood with decking around three sides and big front windows overlooking a picture-book setting of forested hillside. There were five bedrooms, one a guest room and the other extra room planned as a nursery for a third child who, sadly, had never arrived. Donna had personally chosen each of the big flagstones that made up the face of a huge living-room fireplace as well as the oak plank flooring for the room, salvaged from a junkyard in Stamford that specialized in dismantling old houses and reselling the materials.

Now, for the first time since their move to Westport, Ben felt some regret at building on such an isolated piece of property. But they had wanted enough privacy to be able to yell at the kids or throw a noisy party without drawing complaints from the neighbors, and that's what they had. From the front door you could see only a piece of the steep roof of the Campbells' saltbox colonial, and during winter the roof lines of four other houses along the ridge were clearly visible. But during summer months the foliage created an impenetrable screen that guaranteed their privacy.

At odd moments Ben told himself that in many ways he had become a character from a *New Yorker* cartoon: the Connecticut exurbanite who frets over inchworms while the rest of the world goes to hell. Still, most people fell into one stereotype or another, and he guessed his was as good as any. At least he was pleased with his life; so many of his friends seemed unhappy with theirs.

The tires made a pleasant crunching sound as he parked on the wet gravel driveway. While he was gathering up his coat and briefcase from the back seat, Donna came out and met him in the middle of the parking circle. They kissed and she took his coat.

"I'm glad you're home. I was starting to worry."

"Nothing to worry about. I have Lieutenant Conde's solemn word on that."

"Uh oh. What did he say?"

"He thinks I'm a liar or a nut case. Maybe both."

She patted his shoulder. "You'll want a drink."

Just inside the front door were two pairs of skis, ski boots and two brightly colored ski suits that had been stuffed back into their plastic garment bags. Donna, without a word, waved in their direction and shrugged.

Ben went into the living room and dropped into a chair. He reached automatically for the newspaper on the end table and glanced at the headlines and photos in the first few pages. There was little relief or distraction in the news: inflation was up in the double digits again . . . prospects for peace in the Middle East had fallen to yet another low . . . a girl had been found brutally murdered in New Canaan . . . real-estate taxes in Westport would be going up by several mills on the new list . . . a deer had wandered into a shopping center in Fairfield, jumped through a plate-glass window and bled to death.

Donna came back to the living room and handed him a glass. "Try this. Myers's rum, lime and coke. Not Tab, mind you. *Real* Coke."

He raised an eyebrow. "You let a carbohydrate in the house? You're more upset about this than I realized." He took a deep

44

draught, enjoying the distinctive taste of Myers's and the luxury of drinking it with Coke for once instead of Tab.

Donna sat on the arm of his chair while he finished the drink and recounted his conversations with the clerk at Allen's and Jim Conde. She surprised him by finding a few positive aspects to his day. "Well, we've learned a lot. One: Harry is definitely here. Two: He has plenty of money. Three: He's been watching us. Four: This is just the beginning of—something. Unless . . ."

"Unless what?"

She bit the corner of her lip. "Unless Lieutenant Conde is right. Could you possibly have been worried enough about Harry to sort of make up the business at Allen's and The Wet Spot? I mean, I suppose you *could* have gone into those places yourself—"

"Jesus! You, too? No wonder Conde won't believe me if my own wife—"

"I'm sorry. It's the card that came with the skis . . . I'd swear you wrote that note."

"Did you save it?"

"Sure." She went into the kitchen and returned carrying a plain white card.

Ben examined it carefully. "You're right, this looks exactly like my handwriting. But I did not write this note. Wait . . ." He put the card carefully on the end table. "Fingerprints. We could prove Harry wrote this if he left fingerprints on the card."

"Damn! I've been picking it up all afternoon. And now your fingerprints are on it too."

"Yes, but if there's just *one* print of Harry's, Conde would have to eat his goddamn computer printout. You know, I'm getting very tired of computer mentality. Some people believe that any information produced by a computer must be true, forgetting it all depends on who programs it. I'm afraid Jim Conde is one of them."

Donna plucked the lime out of Ben's glass and nibbled at it. "There must be a way to prove Harry isn't dead."

"I hope so. But while I was being belligerent to Conde, I looked at the report from California and saw the word 'Cremated' under a heading 'Disposition of Remains.' So whoever took Harry's place in that car has been reduced to ashes." Ben suddenly came out of his chair. "I've got it again, that feeling of being watched." Restlessness drew him to the front windows. "Where are the kids?"

"Sharon's on the phone."

"Naturally."

"And Jeff is in his room. But not because of all this. I found three cigarettes hidden in his bureau under the T-shirts. I swatted him good and told him you'd be mad as hell, so back me up."

"A few cigarettes hardly seem important right now."

"I *told* him you'd be angry. Jeff must believe that we stand together on these things or he'll play us off against each other. Kids are good at that."

"Okay, I'll be properly outraged."

"It would help if you meant it."

"Sorry. You're right, I can't let the problem of Harry affect the way I deal with the kids."

"Ben, we've had things too easy for too long, haven't we?" The irritation had gone out of her voice, replaced by a scratchy echo of fear. "It's hard for me to accept the idea that we might be in real danger. I spent all afternoon finding ways to pretend that nothing has changed—scolding Jeff and trying to balance the checkbook—while I should have been circling the wagons, or something."

"Oh, things aren't that desperate. We do have a credibility problem with the police, but one solid piece of evidence that Harry is alive will change that."

Donna gestured toward the telephone alcove in the hallway. "Sharon has a date with Oop tonight. Shall we let her go?"

"We can't keep her or Jeff locked up like prisoners. Not for long, anyway. I'll have a talk with the kids tonight, and with Oop."

"Sharon will hate that. She thinks we should communicate with her boyfriends through diplomatic couriers."

"I know." He looked through the front windows again. "Harry could be out there in the woods right now, watching us. I'm going to take a look around outside before dinner."

"Ben, is that necessary? The woods are drenched from rain and the mosquitos will be out in force. Your brother wouldn't sit out in some wet crawly place any more than you would."

"You're probably right, but I'll change my clothes and poke around anyway."

46

AT HIS LISTENING post, Harry nodded approvingly. Good thinking, Ben. Too bad you telegraphed your plans.

Although there was plenty of time to gather up his equipment and disappear while Ben was changing, Harry elected to sit tight. He'd always wondered just how safe he was. This would make a good test of his security, and would add some spice to the day as well.

Of course, there was always the possibility that Ben might actually stumble on him, which would be a shame. He would have to kill Ben, ending the game terribly early.

He turned off the transceiver, gave the six feet of space around himself another dose of bug fogger and drew farther back into the brush with his damp olive-drab poncho pulled tightly around his shoulders. Five minutes later he heard the front door open and the sound of Ben's footsteps on the gravel drive. Harry listened intently for sounds of brush being trampled down, but Ben was moving quietly through familiar terrain.

Good, Harry thought. Let him surprise me. That would make the contest halfway interesting.

Presently he heard Ben's footsteps somewhere off to the right. After a long interval a red shirt became faintly visible through the brush and Harry almost burst into laughter. A *red* shirt. Only a fool would wear a shirt like that while he was prowling the woods for an intruder.

Harry smiled as he took out a knife from his pocket that had been lovingly manufactured by a craftsman in Oregon who turned out only one perfect spring knife per week. A safety latch slid back at the flick of his thumb. He pressed the lever beneath the latch and a six-inch blade slid from the handle and locked into place. There was no harsh clicking sound, only a whisper as the lock closed behind the shaft. The blade itself had been hand-forged and honed to razor sharpness. It would slash through Ben's flesh as easily and silently as a laser beam.

Ben came to a halt no more than ten yards away. Through the foliage Harry caught a glimpse of a scar on his brother's neck, a crescent wound so old and weathered as to be hardly visible. It would not even be noticeable to someone who didn't know it was there.

The image startled and troubled Harry. He had almost forgotten the scar, which was the one physical difference between himself and his brother.

It brought back disturbing memories . . .

THEY WERE THIRTEEN years old and living on Marengo Avenue in Pasadena in a big house that had been broken up into tiny, cheap apartments. The old man was dead by then and mom was working for the *Star-News* selling classified ads over the phone.

Two days before Christmas he and Ben had pedaled their bikes down to the park across from Caltech to watch the floats being decorated for the Rose Parade on New Year's day. There were flowers stacked all over the place, tons of them. Roses. Gardenias. Carnations. Orchids. Every flower imaginable. The flowers had given him one of his great inspirations.

"Ben, let's swipe some of those roses. The guard's an old fart, we'll get around him easy."

"I don't know, Harry. If they catch us . . ."

"Nobody's gonna catch us, or miss a few roses. Come on, Ben. Don't be an asshole. Think what a great Christmas present for mom those roses would be."

"Oh, all right."

They ditched their bikes in the trees and walked up to the roped-off area where at least fifty high school and college kids swarmed over the skeleton of a float they were slowly turning into a gigantic flowered stagecoach. The guard was pacing the area inside the rope, but his main job was keeping onlookers away from the float rather than guarding the flowers.

When the guard turned his back, Harry whispered, "Now!" and they ducked under the rope.

They each grabbed an armful of flowers, all the roses they could carry.

"Hey, you kids! Stop!" The guard waved a billyclub and charged after them.

"Move!" Harry commanded.

They dived back under the rope and ran for their bikes while the guard shouted at them to halt. Some of the kids working on the float yelled encouragement, but they didn't need anyone's urging to run. The guard was surprisingly agile for an old man. He almost grabbed them before they reached the woods and lost him for the few precious seconds it took to recover their bikes. Then they were free and pedaling madly, leaving a trail of scattered red roses all the way to California Street.

It took considerable skill to operate the bikes with enormous bunches of flowers in their arms. Harry guessed that they had at least fifteen dozen roses between them, enough for a nice present for mom with plenty left over to sell. Lots of people would want to buy a dozen roses at a good price during the holidays. It would be a happy Christmas for the Ryders after all.

But at the corner of Los Robles Avenue and California Street Ben misjudged a turn and his front tire scraped the curb. Harry saw him wobble and fight to control his balance. The front wheel went sideways, hitting the curb a second time, and Ben catapulted over the handlebars, showering the street with flowers as he landed face down in a terrace of ivy.

Harry's first instinct was to laugh at his brother's comic landing. The laughter faded when Ben struggled up from the ivy with a stricken expression on his face and a shiny object attached to his neck. It took a moment for Harry to realize that the object was a long shard of glass from a broken bottle that had been lying in the ivy, and that the glass was imbedded in Ben's throat.

"Harry . . . help me."

Harry dropped his bike and the roses and rushed to Ben's side. He yanked the spike of glass from his brother's throat and immediately realized his mistake. The blood came pumping out faster than ever. With trembling hands he tore off the tail of his own shirt and wrapped it around Ben's throat, stanching the flow of blood to a slower rate.

"I'm dizzy, Harry."

"Get up here and hang on!" The handlebars of Harry's bike were equipped with an L-bar for carrying the newspapers he delivered after school. He helped Ben up onto the L-bar, steadied the bike and pushed off. Ben held on with one hand and kept the bandage tight to his throat with the other while Harry pedaled away at top speed.

"I can't make it! I'm gonna fall off!"

"Shut up and hold tight!"

California Street became a steep downhill grade at Marengo Avenue. The pedaling was easier, it was almost a glide if he could keep his balance with Ben sagging on the handlebars. Harry's arms were aching from the strain of keeping Ben upright, but he gritted his teeth and kept on pumping the pedals.

Five minutes later he turned into the hospital's emergency entrance, abandoned his bike and dragged Ben inside. A nurse came to his aid and immediately took Ben away to have the wound sewed up and properly bandaged.

Later, a doctor congratulated Harry on his quick thinking. "That was nice work, son. You probably saved your brother's life."

Harry was still so frightened that he could only say exactly what was in his mind. "I had to save Ben. I love him."

LOOKING AT THAT wound from ten yards and twenty-five years away, Harry felt an abrupt and overwhelming sense of loss. It was true. He had loved Ben more than anything else in his life.

The years again receded and he saw bright, swift images of Ben and himself. Color frames of the two of them beginning when they were about fourteen. Bike rides to the top of Lake Avenue in the Mount Wilson foothills. Lazy days of cookouts and surfboarding at Zuma Beach. Double dates at the Hollywood Palladium. Cramming for exams. Their first walk through the U.S.C. campus, and the shared feeling that they were finally becoming *men*. Beer busts. Waiting on tables at that coffee shop on Jefferson Boulevard for pocket money.

They had considered themselves twin princes of the campus. Nothing would ever separate them; they had sworn an oath to that during a night of heavy drinking after finals week. It was only the girls, and the things Harry liked to do with girls, that finally came between them.

He remembered how it felt the first time he killed one, how he had returned to the dorm that night scared silly and expecting to be arrested any minute. He had almost gone straight to Ben and told him about the girl. About the way she had cockteased him until he just had to show her what he could do, what a stud he was. Instead, he had showered off the smell of her and gone to bed. And the next day, to his relief, turned out to be just a regular day—breakfast and classes and working in the coffee shop from one to six. The girl wasn't even in the newspapers until two days later when someone found her stuffed in that drainage pipe up in El Tujunga. Even then she was only worth a half-column story on page five of the *Times*.

In the year that followed, he killed four other girls—all of them cockteasers who made the mistake of thinking they could slip Harry Ryder a little tongue and walk away. They found out that he didn't settle so cheap. He'd get it all, or they'd be sorry.

Even when he was arrested for killing the last one, the girl in MacArthur Park, Harry wasn't worried. Ben would get him out of the jam because he had sworn to stand by him always.

Which was why he had been so stunned by Ben's refusal to fake a confession to the killing. Sure, it was sort of a wild idea. But there was a ton of evidence against him, from fingerprints on the girl's purse to scratches on his face and his skin under her fingernails. A confession from a twin brother might at least have confused the jury, hung them up, kept them from reaching a verdict. And even if it hadn't worked, at least Ben would have *tried* to help.

But to *refuse* and never even come to see him during the trial . . .

Once again his anger over that act of betrayal caused a white-hot pain to blossom inside Harry's head. He found his breath coming in gasps and his hands shaking like a drunk's. Impulsively, he stepped from his hiding place with the knife poised.

One slash . . . one split second of action would free him from the smothering weight of the past.

Ben didn't love me enough. It's that simple.

The lethal edge glittered, but found no target. Ben was gone.

He heard the front door of the house open and close and felt cheated. He wanted to go into the house and finish it, kill them all. But he fought that temptation because there was too much fun to be had at Ben's expense. His brother had become so proud of his place in the community and his expensive house and beautiful family. Ruining all that for Ben promised to be great sport. For that reason only, he would let his brother live a while longer.

Harry knew he should settle back and switch on the transceiver.

They would be talking about him seriously tonight. Making plans against him. But he felt drained and exhausted, and for some reason he wanted to cry. That really bothered him. He collected his gear and once more found his way through the trees to Clapboard Hill Road.

Funny, what a few memories could do.

IN THE RYDER household the dinner table was always the best place to raise an important subject. Tonight Ben waited until dinner was almost over before bringing up the issue of Harry.

"Kids, your mom and I have something to discuss with you."

"Oop is taking me to a rock concert tonight," Sharon said. "He'll be here any minute."

"This is important." Ben brought out a shoebox he had scrounged for in the attic just before dinner and put it on the table in front of him. "There's something about me that you kids have never been told. It's sort of wild, but true." He paused. "I have a brother. A *twin* brother, no less. His name is Harry and he looks exactly like me."

Sharon and Jeff exchanged skeptical glances. The idea of their father having an identical twin was hard to swallow. They knew very well that he was a person of few secrets.

Ben removed the top of the shoebox and began passing around some of the faded old snapshots from inside. "Here, this is Harry and me when we were about . . . oh . . . twelve. We're on the beach at Santa Monica. And these . . . well . . . you can see for yourself. Birthday parties. Our first bikes. Summer vacations. It's all there." He sat back and let the photos do the work of convincing them.

Jeff pounced on the pictures as if they were free baseballs. "Wow, dad, it's true! There's *two* of you . . . why didn'tcha ever tell us?"

Sharon was equally amazed, and interested, but her reaction was quiet, pensive. "Why do the pictures stop when you're both eighteen or nineteen? Did your brother die or something? Is that why you never mentioned him?"

"No, Harry is still alive. I didn't want you to know about him because, well, Harry is a sick and very bitter man. Mentally sick. In fact, he's spent almost half his life in prison, for murder."

52

"Murder!" Jeff's eyes seemed to double in size. "Wow!"

Taking note of the measured strain in her father's voice and the somber cast of his eyes, Sharon said only, "Dad . . . I'm sorry . . ."

Her insight surprised him. "Thanks, hon."

"Who'd your brother kill, dad? Some gangster? A spy?"

"No, Jeff . . . and this isn't pleasant but I'm afraid you kids need to know now . . . he raped and then killed a young girl. Someone not so much older than your sister." As best he could, and in a way he hoped would be understood, Ben patiently explained what he knew of Harry's mental illness and his crimes, the one he had been convicted of and the others he had admitted to Ben. He also told them why Harry blamed him for his conviction and how he had learned that Harry was now in the Westport area.

The children listened quietly and with close attention, even though Ben took a great deal of time.

When Ben had finished, Donna added, "Your father has told you all this to make you understand that Harry might do something to hurt one of you because of his hatred for your father."

"It's hard to believe anyone could hate dad," Sharon said.

For some reason the remark nettled Ben. "Your old man is too doddering, not up to having enemies, you figure?" He felt foolish the moment the words were out of his mouth.

"No, dad . . . I just meant it's sort of hard to believe that a brother you haven't seen in all these years would still want to hurt you, or Jeff or me. Especially when Jeff is nothing but a little toad." She mussed Jeff's hair and drew the usual snarl from him. "I mean, it's too much like a *Kojak* rerun. Killer stalks glamorous teen debutante and ugly-duckling brother in revenge for past grievance. Come *on,* dad."

"Listen to me, Sharon—this is a serious business. Don't give me any of your smart-ass remarks or you'll find yourself grounded until this problem is resolved. Do you understand?"

Sharon's eyes smoldered, but she averted them from her father's uncompromising glare. "Yes, *sir,* I understand."

"Harry might try to pick up one of you kids somewhere, in the neighborhood or at the beach, for instance. Believe me, his appear-

53

ance would fool you. Even our parents couldn't tell us apart. And once he got you into a car, anything could happen."

"Hey!" said Jeff, "I know a secret handshake. Look, dad, hold your big finger like this when you shake my hand. Then I'll know it's you."

"You're on the right track." Ben smiled at him. "But shaking hands whenever we meet might be awkward. Instead, why don't I have a private signal I can use whenever we run into each other around town, or when I pick you up in the car. Something that's just between us."

"A secret signal!" Jeff exclaimed. "Great!"

Sharon rolled her eyes, but remained diplomatically silent.

"Tell you what—whenever we meet outside the house I'll do this . . . tug at my right ear." He gave the lobe of his right ear a pull.

"Gawd," Sharon said.

"I know, it looks dumb. But it's a simple way for you to know whether you're talking to me . . . or to Harry. So pay attention, Sharon. Look for that signal. You too, Jeff."

"Neat idea," Jeff agreed, "and I can rub my nose like this, see, as a . . . whadayacallit? . . . *countersign.* I saw that in a movie."

"That won't be necessary. We know there's only one of you."

"Thank the Lord," Donna murmured.

The doorbell rang and Sharon jumped up. "I'll get it. That's Oop."

"I want to talk with him before you leave," Ben said.

"Dad."

"Either I talk to him or you stay home. I'll give you time to explain the problem yourself, in your own way."

She went off grumbling and Jeff asked, "Can I be excused too?"

They stared at him in amazement.

"What are you up to?" Donna demanded.

"Nothin'! Why?"

"You *never* ask to be excused from the table."

"I've got some new stamps to put in my album, that's all. Panama-Pacifics."

"All right, go ahead."

Jeff rushed from the dining room and went up to the second floor two steps at a time.

54

Donna tapped her fingers on the tabletop and looked over at her husband. "Yep, he's up to something."

"That he is," Ben agreed. "I only wish Jeff's escapades were all we had to worry about. Is there any more hot coffee?"

JEFF WENT STRAIGHT to his room. But instead of working on his stamp album he took a metal box from his secret hiding place behind a loose board at the back of the closet. The box contained the money he had been saving for Christmas presents, plus a Swiss army pocket-knife he had shoplifted from the sports department at Sears and a collection of nude photos of women that he had won in a game of pitch-penny.

There was twenty-eight dollars and forty cents in the box. Not enough, probably. But the dirty pictures might make the difference.

He returned the box to its hiding place and went to the phone in the upstairs hall. He dialed quickly and a moment later said into the phone, "Hello, this is Jeff Ryder. May I speak to Tony? Thank you." After a pause, "Tony? Jeff. Can you talk?"

"Sure. What's up?"

"Remember how you said I could rent your twenty-two rifle for a couple of weeks? I've got the money after all."

"Fifty dollars?"

"No. Twenty-eight dollars. And forty cents."

"I want fifty dollars."

"I don't *have* fifty."

"Then forget it."

"No, wait. How about *one* week for twenty-five dollars."

"You said you had twenty-eight."

"I'll give you twenty-eight if you throw in six bullets."

"No bullets. Get your own."

Jeff paused. "Twenty-eight dollars and you can have the dirty pictures I won pitching pennies at the Y. But I want the bullets. Otherwise, no deal."

"What dirty pictures?"

"Pictures of naked women, in color. They're neat, Tony."

"I've seen pictures of naked women. My dad buys *Hustler* and *Penthouse.*"

"You haven't seen pictures like these. In one of them, a girl is doing it with a *sheep.*"

"I don't believe you."

"It's true! And in another there's three women all doing different things to each other."

"What kind of things?"

"It's hard to explain. They're in bed together kissing each other between the legs and stuff like that."

"What for?"

"Who knows?"

There was silence as Tony considered the proposition. "Okay, it's a deal. But if all of a sudden my dad wants to see the gun, you'll have to give it back right away."

"I know. I don't want trouble about the gun any more than you do."

"Come over in the morning. I'll wrap it in a beach towel and you can sneak it out the back door. You can have the bullets, too, but only six of them."

"Swell! Thanks, Tony."

"Bring the money . . . and the pictures."

"I will. See you tomorrow."

Jeff put down the phone and drew a deep, satisfied breath. Mr. Harry Ryder will get a big surprise if he tries to hurt *my* dad, he thought.

BEN AND DONNA finished the last of the warm coffee and tried to chat about things other than Harry. After about ten minutes Ben stretched and rose from the table. "I'll talk to Oop now." A disturbing question occurred to him. "Oop *can* talk, can't he?"

Donna produced one of her mysterious smiles. "I'll let you find out for yourself."

He went into the living room to find Oop and Sharon huddled at the end of the couch. Oop was leaning forward to catch the whispered gist of Sharon's conversation, which was obviously about Harry. She was showing Oop some of the old photos.

"Good evening."

The boy came to his feet with the speed of a West Point plebe.

56

"Sharon's told you about our problem?"

"Yes, sir."

The *sir* was an agreeable surprise. "Sit down, please." Ben took the chair nearest the couch. "Okay, the story is this. My brother was released recently from a mental hospital. He's killed people, and he may still be dangerous. Furthermore, he has a grudge against me and might take out his anger on my family. The fact that we're identical twins creates special problems. For instance, neither of you could tell him apart from me, even up close. I don't want to ground Sharon, so I'm asking that the two of you go places with other people, the bigger the group the better. Also, until my brother is found I want Sharon home no later than midnight whenever you go out."

Oop was a young man of massive proportions. Large head that seemed to rest on wide shoulders without the aid of a neck. Square dimpled jaw. Small blue eyes. Thick pads of muscle on his chest and shoulders. Narrow waist. And the placid, trance-like stare of a bull waiting to be released into an arena. Unsure whether his words had sunk into the boy's brain, Ben asked with some irritation, "Do you understand anything I'm telling you?"

"Yes, I do," Oop replied in a serious voice. "I'm aware that sexually disturbed paranoids can be very dangerous. You can be sure I'll do everything in my power to protect Sharon. She's a very special girl, if I may say so."

The boy's response so startled Ben that he missed the wicked smile that quickly crossed his daughter's face.

"Where the hell did you get the name Oop?" Ben asked.

"It's a burden," the boy admitted.

"I like the name," Sharon said. "There are a million boys called John. Oop MacRae. That has style."

Oop gave Sharon a look that was both proprietary and submissive. Realizing that, he quickly returned to a businesslike manner with her father. "We're going to a rock concert in Bridgeport tonight. We have friends who are going too. I'll see if we can ride with them. I'm sure they won't mind leaving in time to get Sharon home by midnight. You might want to turn on your outside lights for us, sir, for safety's sake. And I noticed as I drove up that someone left a ladder lying alongside the house. It should be locked up in the garage. No point in locking the ground-floor doors and windows if someone can use your own ladder to climb in a second-floor window."

Ben recalled that he had left the ladder outside on the previous weekend after cleaning the rain gutters. Oop's demeanor and powers of observation suggested so much intelligent competence that Ben felt dull and deflated by comparison. He couldn't recall meeting anyone else whose appearance was in such total opposition to his personality. "Thanks, I'll put it away tonight."

"It may also ease your mind to know that I have a brown belt in judo."

"A brown belt," Ben repeated. "Yes, I'm glad to know that. However, you're a sixteen-year-old boy with decent instincts. My brother is a psychotic killer."

"I'll remember that. Mr. Ryder, may I ask a personal question?"

"Be right back," Sharon interrupted. "I'm just going to get my purse." She left the room with a smug grin, basking in the favorable impression Oop had made on her father.

"Go ahead," Ben said to Oop.

"Well, from what I know about identical twins, you and your brother come from a single cell that separated into two parts early in its development. And I've read that twins who come from a common egg cell often develop opposite characteristics. For instance, one will be right-handed and the other left-handed. One will part his hair on the right side, the other on the left. Was that true with you and your brother?"

"No, we're both right-handed and part our hair on the same side. We even have identical moles on our right shoulders. When we were kids our family doctor said he'd never heard of a pair of twins so alike. How is it that you've been studying twins?"

"I haven't exactly studied twins, but I have done a lot of reading about human cell structure. I'm planning a career in medicine."

"Sounds like you've already chosen a specialty."

"Yes, sir. Research. My goal is to find a cure for cancer, if no one else does before I graduate from medical school."

"That's a high ambition."

"I had a younger brother, Timmy, who died of leukemia a couple of years ago."

"I'm sorry, I didn't know."

"He gave me my nickname." He smiled with a ghost of sadness. "I let people call me Oop because it's sort of a legacy from Timmy. Otherwise I'd mash a few noses."

"I'll bet you would."

Sharon returned looking radiant and happy. She slipped her arm through Oop's. "I'm ready."

"May we go now, sir?"

"Sure. Have a good time. And, Oop, please keep this matter to yourself."

"I understand, sir. I won't spread it around."

"We'll be back early." Sharon reached up and planted a kiss on her father's cheek. "Really, don't worry about us. We'll run with the pack tonight, and for as long as you say."

"Thanks, kid. It seems you're growing up after all."

He switched on the outside lights even though it wasn't quite dark yet and watched through the front window as they went to the car and drove away. After they left, he walked around to the side of the house, found the ladder and locked it in the garage. He inspected the outside of the house on all sides looking for other weak points that might make it easy for Harry to force an entry. There were no broken latches on windows or sliding glass doors with faulty burglar bars. That made him feel better.

It was dark when Ben went back inside the house. Donna was in the living room, a mischievous gleam in her eyes.

"Did you make a complete or only a partial fool of yourself?"

"Complete." He winced and added, "I even asked Oop if he understood what I was saying."

"I tried to tell you that he's a smart kid. Sharon will be safe with him, as safe as anyone can be."

"I didn't know they came like Oop anymore. I thought they were all hair and muscle with eight-track tape systems for souls. Oop gives me hope for the future." He sat down on the couch next to Donna and put his arm around her. "Although somehow the future doesn't seem as promising as it did yesterday, before we knew for sure about Harry . . ."

"I have an idea." Donna snuggled closer to him. "Let's make a pact not to mention Harry for the rest of the night. Tomorrow we'll tackle the problem. But tonight we'll put Jeff to bed early, make another dent in the Myers's rum while he's falling asleep, then climb into the sack ourselves. We both have a lot of tension to work off, I'd say."

"Mmm, especially in the important muscles, where I always tense up the most."

"Where? Here?" She began to gently knead his thigh.

"Higher. You never did have a sense of geography—"

Her hand slipped upward until it was stroking one of the important muscles he had mentioned.

Ben leaned back. "Jeff!" he called. "Bedtime!"

Tuesday

CHAPTER 4

LIEUTENANT JIM Conde arrived at the Westport barracks of the Connecticut State Police, Troop G, promptly at eight thirty on Tuesday morning. As he entered his office, Conde tossed his hat across the room with a skimming motion that brought it to rest neatly on top of a filing case. It was a daily ritual that gave him a small sense of satisfaction. More important, he was happy to shed himself of that damned hat for a few hours.

Conde always thought of his regulation headwear as "that damned hat." He despised the hat because it looked exactly like the one worn by the Northwest Mounted Police and Smokey the Bear. The design had obviously been chosen to evoke an image of the tough lawmen of yesteryear. In Conde's opinion, the hat only managed to turn Connecticut State policemen into ridiculous Nelson Eddy lookalikes. Over the years he had written dozens of letters complaining about the hat to his superiors. Somehow they hadn't shared his acute discomfort. He had tried not to think about the damn hat, but often out in the streets he felt that people were laughing at him on account of it.

There was a rap on his office door and Conde barked, "Come in!"

Sergeant Eddy Trelska entered, holding an official form as if it were holy script. "Lieutenant, we've got a positive ID on the girl."

"Good. Let's see it."

Trelska passed over a Form CG-72 and watched the lieutenant's face with shrewd anticipation.

"My God! She's Tony Scar's daughter? Are they absolutely certain?"

"Yes, sir. Remember that rucksack we pulled out of the creek? The lab techs dried it out in an oven. One of the things they found inside was a student identity card from Holy Cross with the girl's name and photo on it. Then, to double check, they compared prints taken from the body with ones on file from when the girl worked on a Christmas job with the post office last year. The match was positive. It's her, all right, Catherine Anne Scarnato. Do you think this might be a mob killing?"

Conde scoffed at the suggestion. "No! The one thing they don't do is kill each other's daughters. You say she worked in the post office last Christmas? That's funny. Tony Scar has all the heavy money in New Jersey, and most of the loose change." He considered the implications of this information. "Has Scarnato been notified?"

"The coroner reached him at home about half an hour ago, as soon as the prints were confirmed. Freburg says Scarnato took the news hard, very hard. Oh, Freburg also said to tell you he gave Tony Scar your name, since you've got the file. Scarnato's on his way here right now."

Beautiful, Conde thought. Marvelous. Tony Scar's daughter has been raped and murdered and I've got the file.

"Thanks, Eddy. That's all for now, but stand by. You'll have to take Scarnato to the morgue after I talk to him."

"Right, lieutenant."

After Trelska had gone, Conde took out the dead girl's file and wrote across the top with a black felt-tipped pen: CATHERINE ANNE SCARNATO. He flipped through the photos from the crime scene, shaking his head and wondering, as he always did in these cases, what made the killer tick.

He saw from the form Trelska had brought in that Catherine Anne Scarnato had been nineteen years old, weighed one hundred and twelve pounds, had dark brown hair and brown eyes and a strawberry birthmark on her right shoulder. She had died from

64

asphixiation as the result of a crushed trachea. Swelling, bruises and sperm samples from the vaginal area indicated she had been raped prior to or concurrently with her death.

That would be some picture to paint for Tony Scar.

What I need is advice, Conde decided. Advice and information on how well-connected Tony Scar is in Connecticut.

Among his fellow officers Conde was admired for his dogged determination to nail down every fact and piece of evidence that could be found on each case he worked, large or small. He was also considered politically astute and benefitted from the fact that he wore the uniform of the state police very well. But a large part of Conde's success was attributed to his "rabbi," the man higher in the chain of command who had spoken up for him at promotion boards and nursed his career in other ways, especially by providing advice and counsel.

Conde's "rabbi" was Commander Bob Spence, presently chairman of the state Organized Crime Investigative Task Force. Spence was in exactly the right position to provide information on Tony Scar. He called Spence's number at the Task Force offices in Meriden, a suburb of Hartford, and was put through quickly.

"Hi, Jimmy," Spence began. "I just heard about your bad luck. Are you sure the girl was Tony Scar's daughter?"

"Her prints check out, along with a Holy Cross student ID found near her body."

"Scarnato has been told?"

"Yes, he's on his way here."

Spence gave a low whistle. "You'll have the media on your ass before noon. I hope you have some kind of statement for them."

"I will by the time they get here. The reason I'm calling, Bob, is to find out what Tony Scar has in Connecticut. I mean, besides his piece of the jai alai in Milford. I know about that."

"Nothing else," Spence told him. "At one time he ran the loan sharks for Jack Castanza, but that was a sideline. Gambling has always been Tony's racket. Especially the numbers. He's been plugged into that golden pipeline for years. Lately he's been trying to wangle himself a casino license in Atlantic City through a front group. He'll get it, too. No, Tony doesn't have anything in our territory except the jai alai. Of course, he has lots of friends on this side of the Hudson."

"Are any of those friends connected with the State House? Does the mob own anyone important in Hartford?"

Spence's voice tightened. "You shouldn't ask questions like that, Jimmy. Not over the phone."

"If your phone isn't safe, we're all cooked."

"All right." Spence spoke carefully. "They've got two state senators, and Tony has friends in the Stamford and Bridgeport city halls. One of them may call and threaten to fuck with your promotions if you don't find the girl's killer fast enough. My advice is, ignore them. This isn't Jersey. The mob doesn't run Connecticut . . . not yet."

Conde enjoyed the sweet sensation of relief.

"Watch yourself, though. Tony Scar has more lawyers than the Justice Department. Don't give him an opening to say you mishandled the case."

"I won't. And I appreciate your advice, Bob, as always. Good talking to you."

"Ah . . . before you hang up, one other thing. I've been told you've written another letter about hats to the commissioner."

Conde squirmed in his chair. "Well, yes, I did. You know how I feel about those damned things. They're ugly. And *stupid.*"

"You've come a long way in the last ten years, Jimmy. Built a good reputation for yourself. I'd hoped to have you with me in Hartford soon. That won't happen unless you drop this . . . crusade —or whatever the hell it is—to change the uniform. Honest to Christ, you're making a damn fool of yourself on the subject."

"I don't want to change the uniform, Bob. Just the *hat.*"

"Jim, you've written your last letter about hats. Understood?"

Conde's ears were burning. "Understood."

"Good luck with the Scarnato case."

OVER THE NEXT hour Conde prepared for his meeting with Scarnato by arranging for a speedy release of his daughter's body and by juggling the Troop G duty roster to provide more investigators for the case. He also requested additional manpower from Hartford and

Southbury, and received the promise of three more men. The criminal-science lab was sending a second team to the crime scene in New Canaan to go over the ground once more. Scarnato wouldn't be able to say that the Connecticut State Police wasn't doing everything in its power to find his daughter's killer.

Conde was writing out a statement for the press when Eddy Trelska came back. "Scarnato is here, lieutenant."

"All right, send him in." He tidied the stacks of paper on his desk and stood up. Even a pig like Scarnato deserved a civil greeting at a time like this.

Tony Scar's face was familiar to Conde. He had seen it on organized crime dossiers circulated by the FBI and, occasionally, on television or in the newspapers. It was a strong face, heavy and cruel, dominated by arrogant eyes and a flat nose that had been broken more than once. When Scarnato entered his office he was shocked to see the toll this tragedy had already taken on the man. Tough Tony Scar's eyes were red and puffy and totally lacking in arrogance. His complexion had gone pasty, his square jaw slack, his powerful frame was bent. In no way did he resemble the Tony Scar who stonewalled grand juries and terrorized the competition.

"Mr. Scarnato, my condolences. I'm Lieutenant Jim Conde, the officer in charge of this case. Please sit down."

Without a word Scarnato took a chair and stared at the floor.

"I'm Peter Wells, Mr. Scarnato's attorney," said a man who came in behind him. "Before we go any farther, Mr. Scarnato wants to be certain the victim is really his daughter. Can we do that without actually viewing the body? From photographs, perhaps?" Wells had a rich, cultured voice that Conde decided could only be a product of the Ivy League. He was tall and extremely well dressed, but his smooth face held a jittery concern that looked foreign to it.

"Yes, of course." Conde opened the file and chose the least offensive photo of Catherine Anne Scarnato's body. She was shown from the waist up, lying on a morgue slab.

Wells, rather than Scarnato, accepted the photo. He took a pair of glasses from an inside coat pocket and slipped them on to examine the photo. "I'm sorry, Tony. It's Catherine."

Scarnato snatched the picture from Wells's hand. "No! . . . Not my baby . . ." The gravelly voice disintegrated on the last word. Tony

Scar gave the photo a single swift glance, then threw a thick hand over his face and began to sob. His head dropped down between his knees as he gave way to his grief, sobbing and cursing in thick, primitive Italian while Wells and Conde waited and avoided each other's eyes.

It was difficult for Conde to match this pitiful figure with the Tony Scar who had been responsible for so much crime and death over the past quarter of a century, the Tony Scar whose trademark was a meathook in a corpse's throat.

ANTHONY SCARNATO HADN'T set out, as so many others had, to become a racketeer, or a killer. In the beginning all he wanted from life was a steady job and enough extra money to have a little fun. In the late 1950's he was a young truck driver who delivered meat from the dock terminals to wholesale butchers in northern New Jersey. Tony was strong, everyone knew that. He had to be, to lift two-hundred-pound slabs of beef with only a meathook. He lived alone in a rooming house in Paterson and tried to save his money, but that wasn't easy on a small salary.

Tony sometimes got into debt and borrowed a few dollars from the loansharks, but he always repaid those loans right on time. He played the numbers too, and once hit the bank for a big payoff—five hundred dollars.

But the inevitable finally happened. Tony found himself owing both the loanshark and his numbers man, an impossible parlay. He scraped up enough money to pay the loanshark, but the numbers bank would have to wait. He made that clear to the runner.

The man who ran the bank, Joe Franzece, didn't see it that way. He sent a thug to teach the Scarnato kid this simple lesson—if you owe both a loanshark and a numbers man, you pay your numbers man first.

The morning after the thug was supposed to have beaten that lesson into him, Tony showed up for work without so much as a black eye or split lip. In fact, he seemed especially cheerful. That puzzled Franzece. But what bothered him more was the fact that his hired muscle had disappeared. Franzece was still pondering this turn of events three days later when his thug finally turned up . . . a barge captain spotted him floating in the Hudson River a half mile off the Forty-second Street pier, a meathook imbedded in his throat.

Clearly, Franzece decided, he had misjudged Tony Scarnato. The man was something more than a truck driver. He had talents that should not be wasted. Franzece approached Tony Scarnato on a more friendly basis and found that the young man had been expecting him. They both had the same idea, that Tony should go to work for Franzece as a collector and runner at considerably more money than he was making as a truck driver.

For a year or so the arrangement worked well. Franzece was delighted with his new employee's ability to shake money out of people. Scarnato was not only tough, he was smart. He instinctively understood which customers needed only a gentle reminder to pay up, like a brick thrown through a living-room window, and which required more direct persuasion. With Tony's muscle behind him, Joe Franzece expanded, taking over the territories of two other numbers bankers, who like his former muscleman were found in watery graves with meathooks in their necks or hearts.

The future looked rosy to Joe Franzece. Then, late one evening after the central bank had been locked up and his employees sent home, Franzece looked up from his desk to find Tony smiling at him. It wasn't unusual for Tony to be in the bank late at night since he served as a bodyguard when there were large amounts of cash to be handled. So Franzece thought nothing of the strange smile until he noticed the object in Scarnato's hand—a meathook.

Franzece lunged for the pistol in his desk drawer. His hand came within inches of reaching it before Scarnato's powerful arm whipped across the desk. The tip of the hook caught Franzece squarely at the base of his skull, severing his spinal cord and exiting his throat under the chin, slicing the jugular as well.

Franzece died wearing the expression of a startled monkey.

Days before the body of Joe Franzece was found in the Jersey meadowlands, almost on the spot where Giants stadium now stands, both the police and the mob already had recognized Anthony Scarnato . . . Tony Scar . . . as the new boss of the numbers in northern New Jersey.

Tony celebrated his ascension by marrying a shy church-going girl from Newark, a girl who would ignore his business affairs while, he hoped, bearing many children.

From there Tony moved with authority to consolidate his position. He bought up dry-cleaning shops, vending-machine companies and small family restaurants throughout his territory. He welded them into three chain operations: Teddy Bear Coffee Shops, Mr. Speedo Dry Cleaners, and The East/West Vending Company. Those operations were fairly profitable in themselves, but their primary purpose was always to serve as conduits for the cash flow from his gambling operations.

Over the next two decades Tony took over most of the organized gambling in northern New Jersey, and was granted pieces of other rackets as well by the ruling council of the mob. In that time he used his meathook personally only twice, although scores of others died on his command.

In only one area was Tony frustrated. His wife, still shy and quiet, bore him only one child—a daughter, Catherine Anne. But his disappointment faded as the girl grew, for she was a delightful child with a great love for her father and a zest for life that Tony appreciated.

There had been only one dark year in his life, the year Catherine was sixteen and finally discovered the true nature of her father's business. She was shocked and angered by that truth. For two months she refused to talk to her father or even sit at the same table with him. Those months were a special hell for Tony. He thought he had lost his daughter for good.

But gradually they had reached a truce. Catherine agreed to continue living in the house and giving him the respect and love due a father, but she would no longer take his money. The presents and privileges he had begun to give her were rejected. No more expensive clothes. No car. No exotic vacation trips. No jewelry.

The only thing of substantial value that she took from Tony after that was her college tuition. Even then, she called it a "student loan" and insisted that Peter Wells draw up a formal loan agreement, which she signed. For room and board at Holy Cross she worked as a waitress in the student dining hall and as a lifeguard at the pool.

Tony disliked the arrangement, but was prepared to accept it so long as his daughter continued to let him love and cherish her. And now Catherine was gone, snuffed out before she could taste the pleasures of life . . .

At this moment Tony Scar would have traded his entire splendid empire to have his daughter Catherine standing safely in front of him.

When Scarnato's wounded-lion sounds tapered off, Wells pressed a handkerchief into his hand. Tony Scar wiped the tears from his cheeks. His back straightened and his head raised. Some color returned to his face and Conde felt a chill as he watched the pain in those deep brown eyes gradually evolve into a fiery hatred.

"What's your name again?" Scarnato asked.

"Lieutenant Jim Conde."

"Conde," he repeated, deliberately dropping the rank. "How soon can I have my daughter's body?"

"Tomorrow morning."

"Tomorrow? Bullshit. That's my *daughter*. I want her *now*." His fist slammed down on Conde's desk.

"Don't pound on my desk again," Conde said mildly, "or I'll see that she isn't released until next week."

"You can't do that—"

Wells put a restraining hand on his client's arm. "Actually, tomorrow sounds reasonable, Tony."

"*Reasonable?* I'll give you reasonable—"

"I'd like to ask you a few questions," Conde broke in. "You may have information that can help us find your daughter's killer. May I turn on a tape recorder?" He indicated the console to the left of his desk.

Scarnato looked at Wells. He said nothing, but his eyes conveyed a message.

"No recorder," Wells said.

"For Christ's sake, your daughter's been murdered, Scarnato. Help us."

"Was she . . . abused?"

Screw him, Conde thought. I tried to go easy. "Yes, she was raped and strangled."

For a moment Scarnato couldn't breathe, felt like he was being strangled. When he could speak, he said, "Where did it happen?"

71

"We don't know exactly. She was found in a public park in New Canaan very close to the Merritt Parkway. Her rucksack was nearby. We think she was hitchhiking, that whoever picked her up may have attacked her on the spur of the moment. Unfortunately, that's a fairly common scenario. Did Catherine hitchhike often?"

He hated hearing a cop call Catherine by her Christian name. "Yeah, sometimes. I didn't like it, but she was an independent kid."

With Scarnato finally speaking for himself, Conde switched on the tape recorder. When no one objected he continued with his questions. "Which direction would she have been heading?"

"Home . . . Jersey."

"Where had she been?"

"Up on the Cape looking for a summer job. Like I said, she was independent. Earned her own pocket money. She called a couple of nights ago, said all the summer jobs up there were taken, she'd be home in two or three days."

"Was she with anyone?"

"A girlfriend. They were both going home."

"What's the girl's name?"

Scarnato rubbed his eyes wearily. "Molly something. Henderson, that's it. She and Catherine were classmates. This Molly, she's from Portland, Maine. Why do you want to know about her?"

"Catherine may have met some guy on the Cape, a new boyfriend. Maybe they were driving down to New Jersey together and had an argument on the way." He let his voice trail off. "Her girlfriend might give us a lead to such a person."

Scarnato waved his hand violently. "Catherine wouldn't take up with anyone like that."

"Probably not, but we have to check."

It occurred to Scarnato that the police might never find his daughter's killer. "You don't know a damned thing about this creep, do you?"

"We have very little physical evidence," Conde admitted. "That's why your help is so important."

Scarnato pointed at the recorder. "Turn that off."

Conde did, sensing that Scarnato had stopped answering questions anyway.

The racketeer's face was stiff as he listened to the memory of

72

Catherine's voice. "Are you really *trying* to nail the guy who did this?"

"I have more manpower than usual for a case like this. We want to find him, and we will."

"That's good. I wouldn't like you to deliberately blow the case because Catherine happened to be Tony Scar's daughter. So you'd better find the creep, and you'd better do it fast."

Wells cleared his throat in warning, but Conde let the implied threat pass. Fathers of murdered girls were entitled to demand justice. Even Tony Scar. "Sergeant Trelska will take you to the morgue for a formal identification of the body. I'm sorry, but we can't release Catherine otherwise. It's a legal requirement. Mr. Wells can make the identification for you, if you prefer."

"No, I should be the one." Scarnato drew himself up, summoning his reserves of strength. "You got any more questions, send them to me through Peter."

Wells passed his business card across the desk.

Through his window Conde could see that two television crews had already set up their equipment outside the front door of Troop G headquarters and that half a dozen reporters and photographers were standing nearby comparing notes. "The press and TV people are already here. I'll go talk to them while Sergeant Trelska takes you out the back door."

Wells stood up. "Thank you, lieutenant. You've been very considerate. I'll be in touch with you about arrangements for the release of Catherine's body. And please call me if I can help in *any* way."

While they shook hands, Scarnato walked wordlessly from the room. Wells offered a smile as an apology for his client's behavior and followed him out the door.

This is going to be a rough one, Conde thought. With a sigh he picked up his written statement, straightened his tie and put on his hat. He didn't know which he hated more—Tony Scarnato, or that damned hat.

AT BREAKFAST DONNA and Ben planned their strategy for the day. Sometime during the morning Ben would take the card that had accompanied the skis to Jim Conde and ask him to check for his brother's fingerprints. Oop had offered to take Sharon and Jeff to the beach for the day, which would free Donna to help in the search for Harry without worrying about the children. For additional security Oop had invited along four other boys, all hefty members of the football team.

"Remember," Ben told the kids again, "if you see me somewhere, look for this . . ." He tugged at the lobe of his right ear.

"I gotta go to Tony's for a few minutes," Jeff said, gulping down the last of his milk. "Okay, dad?"

"Go ahead, but stay out of the woods. No shortcuts. Got it, sport?"

"You bet." Jeff put his empty glass and cereal bowl in the sink and ran out the door.

"Don't be long," Sharon called.

"I won't."

"That kid." Sharon tossed her head. "He's got as much sense of time as a gypsy. Mom, if Oop comes while I'm still in the shower, please tell him I'll be ready in a shake." She bounded up the stairs.

Donna returned to her list of things to do and people to see. "I feel like a general deploying troops. How long do you think this will last?"

"I don't know." Ben's eyes shifted around. "Let's just take it day by day."

She was beginning to worry about Ben's nerves. The strain on him was greater than he wanted to admit. He was trying to appear confident that he could deal with Harry, but beneath his businesslike attitude was an undercurrent of self-doubt.

"Ben, why don't we just pack up and leave Westport for a while? Take a vacation somewhere. Get *away* from this."

"I've thought about that. It's a tempting idea, but what good would it do? Harry would still be here when we got back."

"You're right. I just feel like such a prisoner."

"I'm doing the best I can!"

"I know that." She realized her complaints were only making things worse, so she began putting away things in an attempt to establish a calmer atmosphere.

"Besides," Ben continued in a milder tone, "I'm in the middle of a couple of big jobs. Financially we can't afford any long trips until

74

those projects are finished. They're our bread and butter for the rest of the year."

"I understand." Donna discovered she had been aimlessly putting away pans and silverware in the wrong cupboards. "As you said, we'll just take it day by day."

And try not to go out of our minds.

A FEW MINUTES past ten A.M. Harry came out of Grand Central Station and walked to a bar on Forty-eighth Street just off Lexington Avenue.

There was only one customer in the bar, an elderly gentleman who had just ordered a glass of port with a raw egg broken into it. His breakfast. The bartender was vacuuming the carpeting. He switched off the machine and came around to take Harry's order. "Yes, sir," he said, giving the countertop in front of Harry a pro forma swipe with his bar rag.

"I would like . . ." Harry paused and fixed his face in thought. "I would like two double shots of rye, in two separate glasses. Cheap rye. The worst brand you carry. You know, the stuff you give to customers who order Chivas Regal when they're too drunk to tell the difference."

For a moment the bartender suspected his customer of being an inspector for the Liquor Control Board. But no, he was too handsome and well-dressed. The inspectors always had tired eyes and wore suits from Alexander's. "Yes, sir. Two double ryes straight up." He reached below the bar and brought out an unlabeled bottle, from which he poured the two drinks.

Harry rubbed his hands together. "Splendid. Thank you so much."

"Five bucks."

Harry separated a ten-dollar bill from a large roll and pushed it across the bar. "Keep the change. This is a special occasion."

The bartender took it in stride. The ten disappeared with a flick of his fingers. The five-dollar tip, he figured, obliged him to exchange a few polite words. "What kind of occasion?"

"I'm telling my boss to go to hell today."

The elderly gentleman at the end of the bar raised his head from

75

his port and egg. "Think twice, son. Good jobs are hard to find, and harder to keep. I'm one that knows."

"Thank you, sir. But my resolve is firm. Cheers." Harry lifted one of the glasses and downed the cheap rye. He came up coughing. "God, that's miserable stuff."

"Your choice," the bartender reminded Harry.

Harry raised the second glass, but instead of drinking from it he put the tips of his fingers into the rye whiskey, washed them around and began patting his neck and face with the whiskey-soaked fingers as if he were applying after-shave lotion. He repeated the process over and over, working the liquor into his skin until the glass was empty.

The bartender and elderly gentleman watched the performance quietly but intently. When Harry was done, the bartender said with a straight face, "Care for another one, sir?"

"No, thanks. Two is my limit. Good morning to you, and have a nice day."

When Harry had left, the elderly gentleman took a sip of his port and raw egg and said, "Jesus, wasn't that disgusting?"

HARRY WALKED QUICKLY up Lexington Avenue, a briefcase identical to the one used by his brother Ben swinging nonchalantly in his hand. Occasionally a passerby would catch a whiff of Harry's whiskey-soaked face and turn to grin, or to cast a pitying stare.

At Fifty-sixth Street Harry turned west and walked another block before entering an office building and taking the elevator to the twentieth floor. Immediately facing the elevator banks on the twentieth floor was the plushly furnished reception area for Allied Motors. He approached the receptionist and announced, "Mr. Ben Ryder to see Walter Stanton."

The receptionist's nose wrinkled but she diplomatically ignored Harry's ripe aroma. "Yes, sir. I'll let him know you're here. Please have a seat."

Harry sat down in a red leather chair while Stanton's office was called. After a brief conversation the receptionist reported, "Mr. Stanton's secretary will be right down. She'll take you to his office."

"Thank you."

"She says you don't have an appointment."

"I'm sorry, I should have called ahead."

"Mr. Stanton is a *very* busy man."

"I'll keep that in mind in the future."

The receptionist nodded, as if an unruly servant had been put in his place.

A few minutes later a rather beautiful girl stepped from one of the elevators. "Good morning, Mr. Ryder."

For a second the name of Walter Stanton's secretary slipped Harry's mind. He had rehearsed it carefully, but the double rye had given him a slight buzz. Finally it came to him. "Good morning, Helen." He rose and retrieved his briefcase. "How's the boss today?"

Helen grimaced in spite of herself. "Busy, and feeling harrassed. I do wish you'd have called first. I'd have suggested that you come in another time."

All of which was music to Harry's ears. "Don't worry, I'll be in and out in ten minutes."

When they entered the enclosed space of the elevator, the smell of cheap whiskey on Harry's breath and person took her by surprise. "Mr. Ryder, are you *certain* you want to see the boss this morning?"

"Absolutely." Harry beamed.

They moved upward in silence with Stanton's secretary becoming more agitated by the moment. Before they reached the twenty-sixth floor she blurted out, "Look, Mr. Ryder, I must say this. It's obvious you're not yourself today . . . I don't think Mr. Stanton would appreciate seeing you right now."

"I insist," Harry said loudly, taking pains to slur the word.

She dropped the subject as if it frightened her. "It's a beautiful morning, isn't it? I walked all the way to work."

"I didn't notice." Harry yawned.

When they exited the elevator on the twenty-sixth floor he followed Helen along a wide corridor that rippled with activity. Most of the offices he saw contained drafting boards as well as desks, and the people in them bore the unmistakable stamp of technicians and engineers.

The door of Stanton's office, which was adorned with his name and the title "Vice President, Engineering," was closed. "He's been on a transatlantic call," Helen said, "but it can't last much longer. I'm sure he'll be free in a minute."

"Good." Harry collapsed into a chair. "I'm in a hurry."

Helen gave him a nervous smile and occupied herself with busywork. Two minutes later the door opened and Walter Stanton came out. "Send copies of these to Charley Lee at the Glasgow plant, Helen." He dropped a roll of blueprints on her desk. "And get Reeves and that twerp from finance . . . Hollis . . . in here for a budget meeting at two." He glanced at Harry and his irritation faded slightly. "Hello, Ben. Didn't expect you this morning. But come in, it'll be a pleasure to talk to someone who doesn't have a complaint."

Harry followed Stanton into a large sun-filled office, the walls of which were covered with copies of original designs of trucks, busses, bulldozers and other heavy equipment. They had been framed and hung with a reverence usually reserved for paintings by old masters. One corner of the office contained a floor-to-ceiling showcase that held scale models of many of the same vehicles portrayed on the walls.

Stanton threw himself into the chair behind his desk like a hockey player entering the penalty box. "How's my baby?"

"Your baby? Oh, the design for the new bus. Yes, that's why I'm here."

Stanton suddenly sniffed the air. "Jesus, is that you, Ben? You smell like a goddamn distillery."

Harry made a little motion of nervousness, as if Stanton had caught him out. "I did have a few drinks last night. Sorry if the bouquet has hung on."

"Last night?" Stanton cocked an eyebrow. "Come on, Ben, you're talking to an old railroad engineer. I know when a man's been knocking them back before breakfast." He shrugged. "None of my business, I suppose. You just surprise me, that's all."

"Can we talk about the design?" Harry put a reed-like quiver into his voice, as if Stanton had embarrassed the hell out of him.

"Of course. How's it coming? Will I see a scale model next week?"

"No, there's no chance of that. I'm bogged down, Walter."

"Bogged down?" The elaborate web of lines in the older man's face hardened. "We aren't paying you to bog down. What's the problem?"

"I'm afraid you'll have to make some engineering changes before I can go on."

"Engineering changes? That's impossible. We're too far along. Why, half the tooling for the parts has been done."

Harry leaned across Stanton's desk. "Look, you'll have to change the engineering anyway, and not just for me. This bus is a piece of junk, you must know that by now. You need another two feet in width, and the passenger section must be at least six inches higher for proper headroom."

"You were hired to design the interior of the bus," Stanton said coldly, "not to suggest engineering changes. And you're wrong. This bus will be roomier and more comfortable than the industry standard in every way."

"Don't give me that bullshit, Walter. I've studied the blueprints, remember?" Harry made a point of spraying the top of Stanton's desk with a fine mist of spittle.

Stanton was perfectly deceived by Harry's careful parody of a blustering drunk. Drawing well back from Harry, he said in a slow voice, "I may have made a mistake about you, Ben. You have all the right tickets, but no one told me that you don't stay sober during business hours."

"What you mean is, you don't like to work with someone who isn't a yes-man."

"I despise toadies. But that's beside the point. Will you finish the design work on time, and to our specs, or not?"

"Listen," Harry slurred, "I hate to have my name associated with a piece of shit. You can understand that, can't you, Walter? Right, Walter?"

Stanton looked at him, his face going beet-red.

"So why don't you get those gnomes of yours . . ." Harry gestured toward the corridor where the engineering staff worked ". . . to give me some new specs. Then I'll get back to work and you'll have your damned design in a couple of weeks."

"Don't bother." Stanton spoke calmly now. "We'll find someone else to do the work."

"Someone else?"

"That's right. There *are* other industrial designers, you know."

"You can't fuck with me that way. I have a contract with you people."

"Read it," Stanton said shortly. "According to our agreement we can terminate your services whenever we aren't satisfied with your efforts." He smiled tightly. "You may keep the initial payment we made to you, of course."

"B.F.D. My kids say that. You know what it means, Walter? Big . . . fucking . . . deal."

"Get out, Ben."

Harry lurched to his feet and fumbled for his briefcase. "Sure. Yeah, I'll get out. But don't blame me when this project blows up in your face."

"I'll send you a registered letter today confirming that our agreement has been terminated," Stanton said.

"The sooner the better." Harry stamped from Walter Stanton's office, barely suppressing the wild laughter bubbling inside him.

CHAPTER 5

BEN FOUND the level of activity at the state police barracks much higher than the previous day. There were mobile vans parked outside, cables running all over the lawn, reporters and technicians scurrying around and three times as many uniformed police on duty.

A muscular sergeant in a tight-fitting uniform was briefing some of the reporters, usings maps of New Canaan and a drawing of the Merritt tacked to a wall. They were talking about a girl who had been found murdered in a park. Ben vaguely recalled the headline from yesterday's paper and the photo of her body half submerged in a creek. For some reason the photo stuck in his mind.

He went down the corridor to Conde's office expecting to be stopped by someone. Jim Conde was tough enough to reach when he had nothing more than a teenaged housebreaker to worry about. Today, with a big murder case brewing, there would probably be a dozen people in his office. To his surprise he was allowed to reach the office, where he found Conde alone and hunched over his desk.

"Jim? Can I come in?"

Conde looked up in a preoccupied way. "Hi, Ben." He made a discouraged face. "Look, I'm very busy. People and problems coming out of the woodwork at me."

"I'll only take a minute." He slid inside before Conde could give him a definite order to leave. "I'm here for another favor. I'd like you to send this to whatever agency traces fingerprints for you."

Despite the dozen things he had on his mind, Conde felt a reluctant fascination for the object Ben Ryder held out to him. People were always thrusting bizarre things at policemen. At one time or another he had been handed a sugar cube laced with arsenic, a severed human leg, some black hairs supposedly from Hitler's mustache and a live hand grenade. But what Ben Ryder held out was disappointingly common—a clear cellophane envelope containing a small white card.

"What's this supposed to be?"

"The card that came with those skis. The handwriting looks like mine, but it isn't. Harry wrote this, I swear it. Maybe he left a fingerprint. Will you check that for me, Jim? The police in L.A. would have his fingerprints."

Conde groaned. "Are we still on that subject?" His arm stretched to encompass the outside world. "Don't you see all the activity around here? Can't you understand that I have a *live* killer to worry about?"

Ben held his temper. "I'm not crazy and I'm not lying. Harry is here. This card might prove it. I'll pay for the lab work myself, if you want."

"It's not a question of payment. Your brother's fingerprints . . . yours, too, probably . . . are on file with the FBI. I could find out whose prints are on that card overnight—but I won't. I want to stop this before it goes any farther. I'm just too damned busy to play charades with you." He paused for effect. "Your brother is dead."

Again Ben swallowed his irritation. Snapping back at Conde would be the worst thing he could do. "You know, Jim, in some cultures lunatics are humored, even revered. So humor me just once. See if your experts, your damn 'criminologists,' can find just one of Harry's fingerprints on this card. I'm betting they will."

The muscular sergeant who had been briefing the press appeared at the door. "The team from the science lab has arrived at the crime scene, lieutenant. They'll be starting another search of the area in a few minutes. And the coroner is sending over the prelims on the forensic. He says no sweat about releasing the body; he's found everything he's gonna find."

"Thanks, Eddy. I'm on my way to New Canaan, too. I'll take Johnson . . . Saderholm . . . and White with me. I want them canvasing houses near the New Canaan exits of the Merritt. I have a hunch the killer pulled off somewhere nearby while he did his work. Then he looked around for a place to dump the girl, and the park was handy."

"Makes sense," Trelska nodded. He gave Ben a curious appraisal. "Anything else for me?"

"If you're through with those media people, get on the computer and pull the names of all known sex offenders in Fairfield County. Put the rest of the men to work on that list. Oh . . . we've got three more investigators coming in from Southbury and Hartford. Tell everyone there'll be a progress meeting here in my office at seven P.M."

"Overtime." Trelska grinned. "That's fine, I need the money."

"You always need money. You'll get more overtime than you want before this case is closed."

Trelska left and Conde raised his shoulders in a gesture of appeal. "You understand what I'm saying, Ben? This case isn't about some phantom brother. This one is the real thing, a girl who's been raped and murdered. So be a good guy and let me get on with my job, okay?"

Ben stubbornly replied, "All I'm asking for is a fingerprint check. You said the FBI would do it for you."

"All *right.*" Conde threw up his hands. "I'll do it. But when the report comes back negative, I want your promise I'll never hear about your damned brother again."

"Deal." Ben felt triumphant for the first time in days. Harry's prints were on that card, he'd bet on it. He gave the envelope containing the card to Conde and tried to thank him, but Conde had already found the proper form for submitting fingerprint ID requests and was hastily filling it out.

Ben left the office quietly.

"HOW MANY BEDROOMS are there in your home?"

"Five," Donna replied.

"Number of doors leading outside?"

"Three, including the sliding glass door to the deck."

"Windows?"

"You mean the number of windows? I don't know." The question seemed so offbeat. "The usual number, whatever that is."

Donna had two projects for the day. The first was to arrange for a burglar alarm system to be installed in the house. The second was to call the better hotels in Fairfield County and Westchester to see if a Harry Ryder might be registered in one of them. It was a very long shot, but Ben was convinced his brother would be staying someplace he considered classy and expensive. That was Harry's style. But under his own name . . . ? Well, sometimes the obvious . . .

She was sitting in the offices of Crane Security Services, a private detective agency that bore absolutely no resemblance to the private-eye offices in the movies. It was furnished in a bright, modern style and the man in charge was the kind of successful young businessman you met at Westport cocktail parties. His name was Carter Phillips and he wore a class ring from Princeton.

"Does your garage door open electronically?" Phillips asked, referring to a checklist of questions in front of him.

"No."

"How many people live in the house?"

"Four."

"Names?"

Donna gave Phillips their names, wondering when these questions would end. Landing her first job after college had been easier than this.

Phillips smiled apologetically. "I'm sorry. I know this is tedious, but you said you wanted a cost estimate today."

"Yes, I do. Please go on."

For the next five minutes Phillips asked about the voltage of their electric wiring, types of window frames, attic access and similar questions that Donna found difficult to answer. In conclusion he studied the snapshots and original blueprints of the house she had brought along.

"It's impossible to give you a pinpoint estimate before we actually survey the house," Phillips said. "But my best estimate right now is five thousand dollars."

"Five thousand!"

"Yes, and that's a minimum figure. It could run closer to seven K. I'm sorry, seven thousand."

She would have laughed in his face except that he seemed so earnest. "That's a hell of a lot of money."

"Indeed it is. But the safety of your family and your property must be in doubt or you wouldn't be here."

Donna didn't know what to do. Five thousand dollars. Maybe seven. A few short years ago that had been a fortune. Even today you could buy a lot of groceries and make a lot of mortgage payments with that kind of money. Her thinking shifted abruptly. What good was five thousand dollars, or seven, if you couldn't feel safe in your own home?

"Survey our house as soon as possible and give us a final estimate. We'll go ahead, if we like your recommendations."

Phillips smiled and closed his file. "I'm sure you will. We've installed dozens of home security systems in Westport. None of those homes have been burglarized afterwards. I could arrange for you to visit one or two of them if you'd like. That's how satisfied our clients are; they let us use them as referrals."

Phillips abandoned his businesslike manner and said in a more personal tone, "Excuse me, Mrs. Ryder, but I have a feeling there's more to your visit than the usual fear of burglary. I see a lot of people across this desk and I know when someone is frightened. If you tell me your problem, perhaps I can help."

The police had been so skeptical that she hesitated telling anyone else about Harry. But Phillips seemed genuinely concerned, and it was his business to protect people in ways the police couldn't, or wouldn't.

"We're being harrassed by someone. Actually he's a member of the family, my husband's brother. Ben's twin brother. This brother . . . Harry . . . recently got out of a mental institution in California. He's a convicted killer and rapist and he has a grudge against my husband. He seems to know all about us. We're afraid he might try to get into the house or hurt one of us in some way."

"You've been to the police?"

"Yes. They were no help at all. You see, the police claim to have proof my brother-in-law is dead."

85

"But if you've seen him . . ."

"That's the problem. We haven't seen him. We know he's here only because others have seen him and thought he was Ben. They're identical twins."

Phillips frowned and toyed with his class ring. "Are you positive he's not dead? I mean, if you haven't seen or heard from him directly . . ."

Donna now understood exactly what Ben had been up against with Lieutenant Conde. "Yes, we're certain he's alive."

"You're right to be worried then. In our experience mentally unstable relatives are highly dangerous to their families. Now, there are a couple of ways we might help you. We provide uniformed guards for both industry and private individuals. We also have a staff of investigators working out of our main office in New York who might be able to locate this brother-in-law. And it sounds to me like you may have bugs in your house."

"Bugs?"

"Electronic listening devices."

"That's ridiculous. We'd know if someone had been poking around inside our house."

Phillips smiled at her naiveté. "That's what most people think. But we often find listening devices in private homes. If your brother-in-law knows a lot about you, it's possible he's listening to your conversations."

The idea was like a physical blow to Donna. Her home was a refuge. She didn't really believe Harry could have planted . . . bugs . . . in her home, but now she had to be sure. "How much would it cost to find out?"

"We could sweep your home for five hundred dollars."

The term *sweep* made it sound like light housecleaning. "All right."

"And what about your husband's office? Does your brother-in-law know what's going on there? If so, we should sweep the office, too."

"For another five hundred dollars," Donna said, not bothering to hide her sarcasm.

"Yes."

"Okay, do the office, too. How soon can you arrange for that?"

He pulled a looseleaf notebook across his desk and consulted its pages. "This is Tuesday. We can sweep both your house and your husband's office tomorrow, but we can't survey your home for the alarm system until Friday."

"Not before then?"

"I'm afraid not. But, as I said, we can provide one or more guards for your home in the meantime."

Donna was beginning to realize that she'd fallen into the hands of a very smart salesman. First he had scared the hell out of her, and now he was selling her everything in his shop. He probably didn't believe in Harry's existence any more than Lieutenant Conde did, but for a price he would send out legions of guards . . . investigators . . . and little men with electronic boxes to protect them against Harry's mischief. Phillips was a newer, smoother version of the salesman in suede shoes who once had almost sold her a complete aluminum siding job—on a house they were only renting.

"What's the daily rate for your investigators?"

"Three hundred dollars a day per man. I know that sounds steep," he added hastily, "but they're top professional investigators. Former FBI agents, most of them, and they don't watch the clock. If one of our men turns up a hot lead on your brother-in-law, he'll stay with it all night if he has to. And you won't be charged extra in a situation like that. I'd say three investigators working for two days should be able to turn up your brother-in-law, if he's around here and using his own name."

Another two thousand dollars. "And the uniformed guards? Are they all 'former FBI agents' too?"

This time Phillips acknowledged her sarcasm with a self-conscious grin. "No, of course not. They're older men, often retired police officers. Their prime function would be to sound an alarm if they saw someone prowling on your property."

Donna thought of all the elderly guards she had seen in banks and at the gates of industrial complexes, frail men of uncertain health. None of them would be a match for Harry. He might well hurt them, and she didn't particularly want that on her conscience. "I don't think so. But I do want your team of investigators to look for Harry. What kind of information do you need about him?"

Still another checklist was produced and Phillips began asking questions about Harry. Donna was able to answer most of them. When he asked for a photo of Harry, she gave him one of Ben from her wallet.

"You're sure they still look exactly alike?" Phillips inquired.

"I am."

Finally, with an appearance of great reluctance, Phillips addressed the question of money. "We'll need a deposit, Mrs. Ryder."

"How much?"

Phillips said with a regretful shrug, "Two thousand dollars would be sufficient."

Donna took out her checkbook and swiftly wrote a draft for that amount. "I want a daily report from your investigators."

"Certainly."

She was about to leave, in fact she had risen and walked toward the door, when she felt the need to ask one more question. "Do you think we're seeing ghosts? That if the police say Harry is dead, then it's true?"

For a split second Carter Phillips lost his Princeton smile, but he shifted gears quickly. "That's not for me to say. You're afraid of him and it's our job to help you erase that fear."

"Then work fast, Mr. Phillips."

A BLACK LIMOUSINE left the Henry Hudson Parkway and went up the ramp onto the George Washington Bridge toward New Jersey. Inside, Tony Scarnato sat with one hand gripping an armrest to hold himself upright.

"I think I'm gonna throw up, Peter."

Peter Wells looked anxiously down at the Hudson River. "We'll be off the bridge in a minute. Can you hold it till then, or shall I tell Vincent to pull over?"

Scarnato swallowed hard. "Never mind. It's going back down. I just have to find a way . . . some way . . . to take my mind off Catherine . . . off the way she looked in that damned *icebox.*"

It seemed to Wells that Tony Scarnato's face was becoming more pale by the second. "Hold on, Tony. You'll be home in thirty minutes. Try to think about something else."

Scarnato thought of his quiet wife, Teresa. This would destroy her. "No one's told Teresa yet?"

"Everyone thinks the news should come from you."

"Yeah, that's right." Another cramp struck his midsection. He gripped the armrest still tighter and willed himself to stay upright. "I'm calling a meeting for tonight at the house. Torre. Costello. Bloom. Frederico. Ponte. And Genovese. Seven o'clock. Call them as soon as we're home. Tell them to bring their wives, for Teresa."

"Will do."

"Peter, dump the stuff out of your briefcase fast."

"What?"

"Gimme your goddamn briefcase!"

Wells opened his two-hundred-dollar Gucci briefcase and let the papers inside spill to the floor of the limo. Scarnato snatched the briefcase from him and emptied the contents of his stomach into it in one long, gagging convulsion.

Peter Wells wondered what Signor Gucci would think of that.

By early afternoon Ben had put aside the threat of Harry as he found himself caught up in his work, specifically the interior bus design for Allied Motors.

Allied had given him the mechanical specs for the new bus and a bogey figure for the interior furnishings—eight thousand two hundred dollars per bus. The figure was supposed to provide for all seats, carpeting, foot- and headrests, lavatories and magazine racks.

Eight thousand two hundred was not a princely sum, but Ben had felt he could hold to it and still design an interior that would be roomier and more interesting than the average long-haul bus. That was before he came up with a sensational idea which . . . unfortunately . . . had shot the hell out of Walter Stanton's dollar bogey.

Ben's idea was to build into the back of every seat a video system so that each passenger could either play a video game or watch a closed-circuit TV show during his ride. No other long-haul bus, not even the busses used by Greyhound and Trailways, could offer anything comparable. The problem was that such a system would cost almost seven hundred dollars per bus. He had visited every manufacturer of in-flight video systems for airlines, and that was the bottom line.

By cutting back elsewhere he had fixed the overall interior cost to eight thousand six hundred and twenty dollars, but there was no more give in that figure. So he had a choice. He could give Walter Stanton an attractive, conventional design that could be built for eight thousand two hundred, or a genuine breakthrough design that would bump up his costs by more than four hundred dollars per bus.

There was a third option, of course. He could give Stanton *both* designs and let him make his own choice.

Ben pondered that option, then rejected it. Regarding most things in life he took the path of least resistance, the best compromise. But when it came to his work he never backed away from a tough decision. So to hell with the additional cost. That problem could be managed. By submitting a conventional alternative he would only be undercutting his own best design. Besides, this was just the kind of breakthrough a man like Stanton would appreciate. It could give Allied a leadership position in their market for two to four years. Greyhound and Trailways would stand in line to buy a bus that raised their passenger satisfaction to the levels this one would.

The decision to bet all his chips on a single roll of the dice gave Ben such a sense of excitement that he couldn't have worried about Harry if he'd wanted to. Instead he bent to his worktable, using an Exacto knife and strips of soft wood to carve out the contour of the seats as he visualized them in his mind's eye. This was the most exciting part of his work, that moment when the vague form in his imagination began to take on a tangible shape. If someone had asked him how he did it, he wouldn't have been able to tell them. He only knew that a strip of wood or a hunk of modeling clay transformed itself into startling new shapes in his hands. He never thought of his talent as a gift. He was too much of a professional for that.

The new shapes were developing nicely when a messenger came in with a registered letter. Ben broke off from his work to sign for the letter, saw it was from Allied and tossed it in the general direction of his desk. He missed. The envelope dropped to the floor.

An hour later Ben decided to take a break. As he was pouring himself a cup of coffee, he noticed the envelope near his feet and picked it up. Relaxed for a minute, with his feet on his desk and the coffee at his elbow, he opened the letter. It was from Walter Stanton. The letter read:

Dear Mr. Ryder:

This is to inform you that the agreement between the Allied Motors Corporation and Ryder Industrial Design regarding design work on an Allied Motors project designated *Ivanhoe* is hereby terminated.

According to the terms of that agreement, monies already paid to Ryder Industrial Design will be retained by your company, but no additional funds will be forthcoming. All engineering drawings, specifications, blueprints or notes regarding this project are the property of Allied Motors and must be returned immediately.

Yours very truly,

Walter Stanton

Ben read the letter twice before its meaning became perfectly clear to him. He'd been fired! But why?

With exaggerated calm he picked up his phone and dialed Walter Stanton's direct number. On the fourth ring he was answered by Helen Neary, Stanton's secretary.

"Good afternoon. Mr. Stanton's office."

"Helen, this is Ben Ryder."

"Oh . . . How can I help you?"

Ben puzzled briefly over her aloofness. Helen had always been cordial to him. Even supportive. "I'd like to speak to Walter."

"Mr. Stanton is busy."

"But he's in?"

"Yes," she conceded.

"Helen, I just received a crazy letter from Walter firing me from the project." He gave Helen an opportunity to reply, to tell him it was a mistake, but she said nothing. "I don't understand. What's wrong? Has the project been canceled?"

"Please, Mr. Ryder. You know as well as I do why Mr. Stanton sent that letter."

"No, I *don't.* That's why I want to talk with him."

"It wouldn't help." She injected a sigh of regret. "He's already called in someone else."

The image of another designer bringing those complicated specs to life gave Ben a violent jolt of jealousy. "Put Walter on the line or I'll plant myself in his outer office until he sees me. I don't care if it takes *weeks.* I won't settle for a damned letter, Helen. He must know that."

She made a small exasperated noise. "Just a moment, I'll see what I can do."

While he waited, Ben stared at the scale model on his work table. Its sleek, half-finished lines had taken on the tragic aura of a stillborn baby. He flexed and unflexed his free hand, fighting the impulse to reach out and smash the fragile structure into a pile of broken sticks.

Stanton was suddenly on the line. "Yes, Ben. What do you want?"

"I want to know the reason for this letter. Why am I being dumped?"

"You know very well why."

"Don't talk in riddles. When you saw my sketches two weeks ago, you were crazy about them. At least that's what you said. Why have you changed your mind?"

"Are you sober now?"

"Sober? Of course I'm sober."

Stanton became incredulous. "You really don't remember what happened this morning, do you? Now that you've sobered up."

"I don't understand—"

"Don't you remember visitng my office this morning? Coming in drunk and full of insolence? Calling the new bus 'a piece of shit'?"

Ben's stomach churned. Of course . . . so that was it. Harry had struck again.

"I'd like to come in and try to explain that."

"It's too late. I've already contacted another designer."

"Maybe it's too late for this job, but I'd like to work with you in the future. Walter, you don't understand what's going on here.

This will sound crazy, but that wasn't me this morning. I have a twin brother . . . an *identical* twin . . . named Harry. He's been playing tricks on me, impersonating me here in Westport. This morning he must have gone into the city and visited you. That was *Harry* acting drunk in order to cause trouble for me. I can prove—"

The receiver went dead. Milliseconds later a dial tone buzzed rudely in his ear. Stanton had hung up.

He replaced the receiver with care, obscurely proud of his self-control. Harry was testing him. Prodding. Trying to weaken him. Ben summoned up the image of a noisy, dusty bullfight, with the arrogant matador working hard on each pass to tire the bull and bring his head and horns lower and lower—until he thrust home his sword.

The image was gaudy, but too close to the truth.

Ben drummed his fingers across his desk. Allied Motors was gone, and that was a big piece of business to lose. Now what about his other accounts? Warner-Bengelheim, for instance. If Harry knew about his design work for Allied, did he also know of the series of packages he was designing for Warner-Bengelheim? The company was a German pharmaceutical manufacturer with U.S. headquarters in New York City. They had commissioned him to design an entirely new look for their line of vitamins, at a hefty fee.

I can survive losing Allied, Ben thought, but I'd be in big trouble if I lost Warner-Bengelheim, too. It would take months to drum up enough new business to offset the loss of those two accounts.

With considerable nervousness he dialed the number of Art Manning, Warner-Bengelheim's marketing director for packaged products. He answered his own phone with a curt . . . "Manning here."

"Hello, Art. This is Ben Ryder."

"Ben! You've got some nerve calling me after what you pulled. What the hell got into you?"

Ben's spirits dropped another notch. "What happened?" he asked gloomily.

"What *happened?* You don't remember? Christ, you must have been tanked to your damned eyeballs. You remember going into Harley's office, *don't* you?"

Harley was the vice president for mass marketing, the man

93

Art Manning reported to. "No, I don't remember that, but I can explain—"

"You walked in there smelling like a damn pub. Knocked over that little red gizmo on Harley's desk, the Calder thing he paid a fortune for, and practically passed out in a chair. But you came around fast and started popping off. Bad-mouthed our products. Made fun of a picture of Harley's wife. Said you didn't want to work for a gang of Nazis. And told Harley he's nothing but a prick with ears—which is true, but you didn't hear it from me. Hey, you did everything but crap on Harley's desk!"

Trying to explain over the phone would be as useless as it had been with Stanton. The only way to handle this would be to see Harley and Manning personally, go in with a set of pictures that would prove he really did have a twin brother and a copy of Harry's criminal record. That just *might* convince them.

"Art, I want to talk to you and Harley. Bear with me, please. Arrange a meeting for me with Harley. There's an explanation for all this, I promise you."

"Sorry, pal. Starting now, we don't even know your name around here." The familiar sound of a phone being hung up on him was repeated, followed quickly by the dial tone.

Ben put down the receiver and stared at the wall beyond his desk.

THE AREA WHERE Catherine Ann Scarnato's body had been found was still roped off and the criminal science lab team was making a search of the area for physical evidence. Conde arrived to find the lab's chief technician, Lew Wineman, personally directing the search. This pleased Conde. Wineman was not only a fine technician. He was also very attuned to the politics of the cases he handled.

"Hello, Lew."

"Jim . . . good to see you."

"You got here awfully fast."

Wineman, a pencil-thin man who looked sickly but who every year won or took runner-up in the Connecticut men's racquetball championship, unveiled his famous cynical grin. "I'm like the cat on the hot tin roof, Jim. When the capitol dome heats up, I do my dance."

"Are they nervous in Hartford? Bob Spence says Scarnato doesn't pull much weight up there."

Wineman hauled out a handkerchief and wiped away the cascades of sweat along his jawline. "Spence should know. But I'll tell you this—I got the *word* that I'd better find *some kind* of evidence for you, Jim."

"From whom?" Conde said quickly.

With deliberate ambiguity Wineman answered, "The honcho's office."

Conde took his circumspect reply to mean the office of the Commissioner of State Police. He quickly ticked through in his mind the names of several people in that office who might have made such a call. "That's good to know. Thanks."

"Anytime." Wineman turned back to the crime scene and pointed down into the gully. "The New Canaan police did a fair job of sealing the area. Unfortunately they drove their cars and an ambulance right up to the place where the killer must have dumped the girl."

"Stupid assholes." A trio of boys eleven or twelve years of age, curious for a closer look at the lab team, snuck under the rope and crept to the edge of the gully. "Move on," Conde yelled at them. "Get away from there."

"Yeah, we might have found a tire track, or a footprint. However, in sifting the dirt around the stream bed we did find one piece of evidence."

Conde's senses hummed. "What is it?"

Wineman showed him a small brown button that had been packaged in a special dust-free plastic pouch. "This was only thirty inches from where the girl's body was found. She may have torn it from the killer's shirt. Or, more likely, the killer lost the button when he shoved her down that incline. You can see the torn threads. The button isn't weathered at all, so it must have been lost there within the last day or two. It belongs to the man you're looking for, I guarantee that."

They walked together to the edge of the roped-off area. Below them three men in the special blue and white uniforms of the criminal science lab were systematically raking the earth and examining the branches of each bush within the perimeter.

"Watch out for that poison ivy," Wineman warned, placing a restraining hand on Conde's arm. "It's all over the place. Unusual, for a park."

Conde moved grumpily away from the reddish plant near his leg, thinking that this entire case was riddled with poison ivy. Then he brightened as he considered the possibility that the killer could have brushed up against that clump of red leaves. In that case he might have a rash on his hands or arms. Conde took out his notebook and made a note of the possibility.

A button and poison ivy. Not much to work on.

CHAPTER 6

HARRY'S FIRST act on arriving home was to mix himself a large Cubra Libre—Myers's rum with Coke and lime. He wasn't particularly fond of rum, but that was Ben's drink and Harry believed that for his plan to be successful he must drink Ben's favorite cocktails, eat Ben's favorite foods. Literally walk in Ben's shoes. It was a pity his brother had such plebian tastes. Harry doubted that his digestive tract would ever fully recover from the Big Macs, strawberry Fribbles and Nathan's hotdogs he had consumed in his quest to get inside Ben's personality.

These days "home" for Harry was a furnished condominium in Cos Cob, a small enclave of Greenwich tucked into the Connecticut shore about fifteen miles south of Westport. The apartment was small but expensive. Its furnishings were of solid oak, with the chairs and couch covered in genuine leather. Signed lithographs by well-known artists adorned the walls and a sideboard in the dining area had been handmade by Thomas Castbridge of Boston in 1795.

The place had several advantages beyond its comforts. Cos Cob was a pleasantly isolated little community, but still only fifteen minutes from Westport via the Merritt Parkway. The people who owned or rented condos in this complex were wealthy and traveled a great deal. Most didn't know their neighbors on sight. They came up from the city for weekends or used their apartments when visiting from London, Paris or wherever. They were handsome, rich, insulated people like himself. He would be very difficult to find here, if anyone started looking for him.

He carried his drink and the phone out to a private deck, playing out the cord behind him. The deck offered a splendid view of Long Island Sound, where at least a hundred sailboats raced before a fifteen-knot wind. At one time all those sails would have been a traditional white. Now many were striped with reds and blues. Colorful, yes. Even beautiful. But Harry preferred the pristine purity of a white sail.

It was just after five P.M., two o'clock in the afternoon in California. He dialed the 213 area code and a Pasadena number. As he did so, he mourned the passing of the telephone exchanges of old. When he was a boy the exchange for Pasadena was Sycamore. Sycamore 3-7380 had been their phone number for years. What bothered him most following his release was the displacement of names by numbers. The rise of the computer during his imprisonment had resulted in a digitized world that still seemed faintly alien.

"Patterson, Hill and Wyman, Pasadena office," said an eager female voice.

"Hello. Put me through to Oliver Crandall, please." He sipped his drink and enjoyed the brisk breeze.

"Crandall," a cheery voice announced.

"Hello, Ollie. Harry Bond."

"Harry! Where the hell are you?"

"Still in New York. I thought I'd best give you a call. Sorry I haven't checked in this week, I've been busy as hell."

"On that restaurant project?"

Ollie Crandall was a Pasadena stockbroker who believed Harry's last name was Bond and that he was a Los Angeles real-estate developer visiting the East Coast to put together a deal to build a chain of fast-food restaurants.

"The restaurant project, and other opportunities. How am I doing this week?"

"Your account is in good shape. Mohawk Data is up two points, I'm sure you're aware of that. You've made about seven thousand on it."

Ollie had recommended the Mohawk Data and was fishing for his compliment. Well, why not? Everyone needs a bit of stroking. "Nice work, Ollie." Harry waited a beat to let Ollie savor his moment. "Sell."

"Sell? No! It'll move up another point before the end of the month."

"Sell," Harry repeated.

"I know you crave action, but you can pick up another seven K just by sitting tight! Why kiss off that kind of money?"

"Got anything new and hot?"

"Well . . ." There was a rustle of paper as Ollie pawed through the "buy" recommendations on his desk.

"Never mind. Give me a minute and I'll find something myself."

"Harry, you aren't going to throw those damned darts again, are you? You know how I feel about that."

"Just having some fun," Harry laughed.

"I'll hang up!"

"No, you won't. Hold on."

Harry put down the phone and went into the living room. From behind the couch he took four large pieces of cardboard to which he had taped the New York Stock Exchange listings from the *Times.* He propped up the sections of cardboard against the cushions of the couch and took two red darts from the drawer of an end table.

Stepping back exactly ten paces, he put one hand over his eyes and tossed a dart. He heard it thud into the cardboard and smiled to himself. The second dart went wild. Harry winced as it smacked into something solid. "Please, not the end table." He took down his hand to find the dart dangling from a picture frame on the wall. He removed it carefully and rubbed his finger over the tiny hole made by the steel point. "No harm done."

His next throw was better. The dart struck one of the center boards. He went to the couch to see what luck had brought him. The darts had pierced the listings for Honeywell and the St. Regis Paper Company. Returning to the deck, he picked up the phone and said, "Ollie, take the cash from Mohawk Data and buy Honeywell and St. Regis."

Ollie groaned. "That doesn't make sense. You're just swapping one computer company for another and putting the rest into a cycli-

99

cal stock that's on the downside of its cycle. Think about this, Harry."

"The darts say buy Honeywell and St. Regis."

"It's insane. I should have put a stop to those darts the first time we met."

Harry remembered that first meeting with Ollie Crandall. A year ago he had walked into the Pasadena office of Patterson, Hill and Wyman and selected Ollie from among all the other salesman because he was the only one wearing a bow tie. Even such a small flag of individuality in the sea of stockbroker conformity deserved to be rewarded. He had marched over to Ollie's desk, evicted an odd-lot customer with a hard look and taken his chair. Ollie's initial hostility over his rudeness vanished when Harry dropped a cashier's check for one hundred thousand dollars on his desk. "My name is Harry Bond," he had said. "Buy me some stocks."

"Which stocks?" Ollie had asked in a flustered way.

Harry had shrugged. "I don't care, so long as I have some fun while I'm making money. It might be amusing to use the dart system for selecting stocks."

"The dart system? Is that some kind of syndicate pool? What the Boston brokers call 'rifling'?"

"No, I'm talking about actual darts, the ones you see in pubs. Let me show you."

Before Ollie could object, Harry had tacked the financial section of the L.A. *Times* to the nearest bare wall and was limbering up with a set of darts he had purchased that morning in a toy store.

"You can't do that in here!" Ollie had objected, tugging at his arm.

"Watch me."

A crowd gathered as Harry began tossing his darts at the financial section. The onlookers were quick to grasp the purpose of Harry's dart game and they responded to each toss with cheers and laughter. There was even a swell of applause when his fourth dart pierced the listing for Chrysler Motors. The commotion brought the branch manager out of his office. When he saw what was happening he threatened to call the police, but withdrew the threat when Ollie showed him the cashier's check.

Over Ollie's objections Harry had invested the money in the six stocks his darts had hit at random. Every week or two he sold everything and chose another group of stocks. He often used his dart system, but frequently he took Ollie's advice just to give the poor fellow a sense of worth. To Ollie's dismay, the stocks Harry had bought and sold through his dart system had outperformed those recommended by the highly paid security analysts employed by Patterson, Hill and Wyman. In the past year his one-hundred-thousand-dollar stake had grown to almost a quarter of a million dollars. The dart system worked! Even so, Ollie remained adamantly opposed to it.

"I'm telling you," he now warned Harry, "your 'dart system' will turn around and bite you in the ass as soon as the market goes bearish again. And when that happens, don't say I didn't warn you."

"I won't," Harry promised. "After all, it's my money. I can invest it any way I choose. Just take your commissions and smile."

Harry reflected that he'd made somewhat of a misstatement. The money wasn't legally his. The original hundred-thousand-dollar investment had been part of a much larger sum he had stolen from his wife's estate. It was an academic matter, of course, now that she was dead.

Reluctantly, Ollie accepted defeat. "Okay, I'll place a buy order for Honeywell and St. Regis, and sell off Mohawk Data. But can't you at least give me your New York phone number, or your address? I'd like to be able to reach you when the market's moving fast."

"I can't do that, Ollie. Sorry, but there are personal reasons. Just hang in there. I hope to be back in California in two or three weeks."

"New York," Ollie sneered. "I've never been there, but I hate the place. Do you know what time I have to get up in the morning? *Five A.M.* Why? Because the New York Stock Exchange opens at nine A.M.—six o'clock California time. Every broker on the West Coast hates New York."

Harry chuckled over Ollie's frustrations. "Look on the bright side. You go home at three in the afternoon."

"To a wife whose hobby is castration."

"Someday, Ollie, when I know you better, I'll show you how to deal with a wife like that."

"Just come home," Ollie pleaded, "but leave your damned darts in New York."

"I'll talk to you soon."

"While you're back there, will you do me a favor?"

"Sure. What is it?"

"Tell New York to go fuck itself!"

Ollie hung up before Harry could tell him New York had already done just that.

His thoughts had been nudged into memories of dear, dead Ellen. She had been such a mouse. Loving and meek. Eager to please. Like a declawed cat. It was a shame she had to die, but he couldn't have tiptoed into his new identity with Ellen around.

She had reminded him very much of his mother, another very plain woman also given to fits of self-doubt and bouts of melancholy. There were many differences, of course. Ellen had been unfailingly sweet, while ma could sometimes show a mean streak. Harry had always thought that was because the old man had died when she was still relatively young, leaving her alone and somehow unable to find another husband.

Yes, ma could show a temper when she wanted. He remembered one night when she really went off the deep end . . .

HARRY WAS FOURTEEN years old, and unlike most boys his age he liked to go to bed early and sleep the night through like a fallen tree. He always slept well and never understood people who said they "tossed and turned" all night. Sleep was like halftime in a game that's going your way, a rest between periods of exciting combat. That's why he was so surprised to find himself coming awake in the middle of the night. Something terrible was wrong with him, that's all he knew.

"Ben?"

No answer, though they slept in beds scarcely three feet apart. Then he remembered that Ben's hacking cough had turned worse near bedtime and ma had taken Ben into her room—into her bed, in fact, like she always did when he was sick. He felt a jealous stab, but it passed quickly under pressure of his fears.

Blood! He could feel the sticky wetness of blood below his waist.

102

"Ma! Ma! Help me!" He threw back his blankets and jumped from bed.

Ma could be heard stirring in the next room, gathering up her bathrobe and turning on a light. "Be quiet, Harry. You brother just went to sleep. His cough is just terrible—"

Ben . . . it was always *Ben* with her . . .

"I'm bleeding, ma!"

"What, a nosebleed?" She yawned as she came across the hall to the boys' room, drawing her robe around her and scratching sleepily. "Little nosebleed doesn't mean anything."

"It would if Ben's nose was bleeding."

The accusation snapped her awake. "I told you to keep your voice down, young man. Now let's see that nose."

"It's *not* my nose. I'm bleeding down here somewhere. On my legs. I woke up feeling funny and wet. It's all over the place, ma." He wiped the sleep from his eyes and looked down at himself. Ma had turned on the light. Strangely, there were no bloodstains on his pajamas or on the bed, yet he knew he was bleeding.

"What have you been doing in here?" she asked sharply.

"Nothing, ma. I told you, I woke up . . ."

"Have you been . . . playing with yourself?"

"Huh?"

"Just answer me. Have you been doing something with yourself? Doing something sinful, taking advantage of your brother not being here? You know Ben would never approve anything like that. You're the one who causes all the trouble around here." She made a sound like a rattlesnake about to strike.

"What's wrong?" Harry cried out. "What'd I do?"

"You *know* what you've been doing." She advanced on him with her hand raised.

"No, ma! I feel feverish, I swear I do—"

She struck him across the face with a hand that was not fully open, a slap that had the power of a punch. "You've been playing with yourself. *Masturbating.* There, you've made me say the word." Her face was livid. She grabbed his ear and dragged him over to the bed. "Can you deny it? Look, there's your evil seed all over my clean sheets. How could you *do* such a thing?"

Harry saw that the wet sheets were stained white, not red. He

103

felt shame without understanding why. He only knew he'd been dreaming. There were dark shapes in the dream, wild flashes of light. And then an explosion down below.

"Take off those pajamas and go straight to the washer with them. Your sheets, too. Then take a shower. And don't ever do that horrible, shameful thing again." Her lined profile was filled with revulsion. "Look, just *look* at yourself and try to tell me you weren't playing with that—that *thing* of yours. Oh!" She stomped from the room.

He looked down at himself and saw what she meant. His cock was standing out like the barrel of a gun. He knew he'd done something horribly wrong, made his mother angrier than he'd ever seen her. Confusion tore at him. Crying, he took the sheets from the bed and ran to the bathroom. Never again, he promised himself. I'll never make her ashamed again. But Ben . . .

SITTING ON HIS deck in Cos Cob, sipping the Cuba Libre, Harry wondered why it had always been Ben with ma, and with the others. We look exactly alike. We sound exactly alike. And yet the women always somehow went for Ben. Donna, for example. Now there's a beautiful woman. How had Ben snagged someone like her? It seemed to Harry that his brother's soft, amiable ways should have turned off the girls. Instead Ben always had more women than he could handle.

Suddenly restless, he swallowed the last ounce of his drink and went in to change his clothes. It would be fun listening to Ben and his charming family tonight. They would be starting to sweat now. His performances at Allied Motors and Warner-Bengelheim had been boffo, as they said on Broadway.

But the next impersonation would be much more difficult—a command performance for little Sharon. Could he convince Sharon that he was her father? He'd see.

THE SCARNATO HOME in Short Hills, New Jersey, didn't look much different from the neighboring houses. It was slightly larger and with an acre more of property, but a close examination would have revealed the significant differences—an electrified fence hidden by a perimeter of bushes and a small guest house used between shifts by the guards who patrolled the grounds.

At about seven P.M. people began arriving at the house to offer their condolences to Tony and Teresa Scarnato. Many arrived in black Cadillacs or Chryslers, and the men who emerged from the limos were dark-haired, well-groomed people who carried themselves with an easy sense of power. Their women, however, ranged from housewives to showgirls, with an accent on showgirls among the wives of the younger men.

They were greeted at the door by Vincent Malle, a short, bull-necked, balding man who served as Tony Scar's butler, chauffer and personal bodyguard. His wasn't the kind of job one applied for. Malle, a former numbers collector, had won his position the way generals won their stars—on the field of battle.

Malle had earned his job one Sunday afternoon in 1976. Tony Scarnato had decided to take in a ball game at Yankee Stadium that Sunday and had invited Vincent Malle along because the Yanks were playing Boston, Malle's home town.

The Yankees had taken the lead early and held it until the eighth inning when their pitcher, a black righthander named Shaw, lost his fast ball and let the Red Sox load the bases on him.

"Get that nigger out of there," Scarnato had yelled.

Four young black men sitting in the next box had lowered their beers and frowned at Scarnato. "Watch your fuckin' mouth," one of them warned.

"Listen," Scarnato had said, "Shaw's not a nigger because he's black. He's a nigger because he can't *pitch.*"

"We don' like that word," said another of the black men. "So stuff it. Right now."

Scarnato wasn't accustomed to taking orders, especially from blacks. He swung around and yelled out, "Bench the nigger, get him outta there . . ."

The man who had warned Scarnato rose but was held in check by one of his friends. "Not here," the friend whispered. "Later, after the game, we give shithead somethin' special."

Scarnato was too intent on the play to hear that remark, but Vincent Malle had been paying close attention. He knew there would be trouble. Neither he nor Tony Scar was armed, but he'd give ten to one the blacks were packing something. Guns. Knives. Whatever. They were dangerous.

The Red Sox scored and led by one run at the top of the ninth. But the Yankees put a man on first, and then Reggie Jackson hit a towering homer into the top deck in right field to win the game. "Now there's a *good* nigger," Scarnato announced, making even Vincent Malle cringe.

The forty-three thousand people in Yankee Stadium moved en masse for the exits. Scarnato and Malle joined in with the crowd from the mezzanine boxes and pushed their way toward exit number twenty. The four black men fell in several feet behind them. They didn't dispute each other about the distance on Jackson's ninth-inning homer, as many of the fans were doing. They remained quiet, stayed close together and kept their eyes on Scarnato and Malle.

Scarnato, always attuned to danger, sensed the problem and poked Malle with his elbow. "Trouble?"

"Probably."

"Four of them, huh?"

"Right behind us."

"Are they talkers or what?"

"I don't think so. If they were talkers they'd start trouble in the stands where someone would stop it for them. No, these guys are out for blood."

Scarnato sighed. "You can't even say 'nigger' any more without having some asshole on your back. Let's try to beat them to the car."

The crowd made it difficult to put any distance between themselves and the four blacks, especially on the circular ramp that led down to street level. They emerged onto the street with the four men directly behind them. "To hell with the car," Scarnato said. "We can send someone for it. Let's grab a cab."

There were no cabs. By the time they discovered that all the available taxis had already taken on passengers and left, the four men had disappeared.

"They were talkers after all." Scarnato laughed.

"Maybe."

They went into the parking garage and up a narrow spiral stairway to the second level. Three of the men were waiting at the top of the stairway. The fourth blocked them at the bottom, a knife held in front of him.

Malle pressed the car keys into Scarnato's hand. "Go on, I'll handle them."

"No. I'm the one they got the argument with."

"This is what you pay me for."

Scarnato looked at his employee with frank admiration. "You're a good man, Vincent." He walked quickly away as Malle placed himself between the three blacks and his employer.

"Move aside, butterball," one of them taunted. "It's your pal we want."

"It's me you got." On the way out of the stadium Malle had picked up a piece of scrap steel lying near a refreshment stand where construction work was being done. He swung the steel upward, driving it into the nearest man's throat. The flesh under his assailant's jaw peeled back like a banana skin and he collapsed with a yelp of surprise.

The others lunged for Malle, who danced away. The one with the knife came up the steps, saw what was happening and ran for Scarnato. He caught up with him at his car, just as Scarnato was putting the key in his door.

"Back off," Tony Scar told him.

The young black stabbed at him with a swift underhand movement, but Scarnato was faster. He caught the wrist and twisted it back and under. The wrist snapped. Scarnato drove his knee into the man's face and let go of the wrist as his attacker catapulted backward.

Scarnato climbed into his car and drove off. The tires of his Cadillac ran over both legs of the fallen man, crushing the bones into small pieces with a sickening sound. As he drove down the ramp Scarnato could see Vincent Malle through his rear-view mirror struggling with the two other blacks. One of them appeared to have a knife, too. Passersby in the garage were running from the tableau like terrified children.

On the drive home to Short Hills Scarnato listened to the news on station WNEW. He heard that the day's Yankee victory had been marred by "A violent post-game melee in which a fan leaving the stadium was knifed to death and several others were reported to be seriously injured."

He hoped Vincent wasn't the one who had died. Men with his kind of balls were hard to find.

When he arrived home he asked Catherine and his wife to stay off the phone, he was expecting an important call. By early evening he was beginning to worry; there had been no word from Vincent, or about him. It wasn't until almost eight o'clock that Malle phoned.

"You're okay, Vincent? I was worried about you. They said on the news that someone died back there."

"I'm fine, Mr. Scarnato, but I had to make one of those guys eat his switchblade. Don't worry, they won't tie me into that. I walked away before the cops got there. Took the subway home."

"You should have called sooner."

"I stopped for dinner at the Oyster Bar in Grand Central."

Scarnato was impressed with Malle's ability to enjoy a nice dinner after killing a man. "I'm sorry I put you on the spot, Vincent. My big mouth gets the best of me sometimes." He added with real feeling, "Can you move your things into the guest house? I need a guy like you around here."

Malle knew he was being accorded a unique honor. No other business associate of Tony Scarnato had ever become a permanent member of his household. "I'll bring my stuff over tomorrow, Mr. Scarnato."

"From now on call me Tony. See you in the morning."

From that day Vincent Malle had been part of the Scarnato family. So it was natural that on this particular evening the guests would put their arms around Malle too, and offer him the same words of condolence they would give to Tony and Teresa.

Malle needed their solace. He was as shattered as his employer by Catherine's death. She had grown up under his protection. He had thought of her as a godchild, and she had readily accepted his burly acts of affection—the hamster given to her on a birthday, rides to school, advice on how to deal with boyfriends, his opinion on a new dress. She was the only girl who had ever thought of Vincent Malle as something more than a thug.

"The boss is like a tiger," he would tell each pair of guests in his hoarse voice, "so walk careful."

And they would nod knowingly to Malle, because Tony Scar's temper was a thing of legend.

There was a ritual flavor to the evening. Although this was not a formal wake, the women gathered near a figurine of Jesus on the mantel to pray and cry while the men met in somber conference in the library. In there, bottles of whiskey had been placed on a table along with a bucket of ice and a tray of Waterford tumblers. The curtains were drawn and the lights kept low so that the sick palor of Scarnato's face would be less noticeable.

Malle's warning that his boss was "like a tiger" captured Scarnato's mood exactly. He paced the length of the library with a cat's restlessness, pausing only to greet each new visitor with a few choked words of welcome and a brutish hug. Occasionally his eyes swept the group of men who stood together at one end of the room, measuring each in some secret way. Scarnato's guests were all employees as well as close personal friends. He had no friends outside his business, nor did he want any. His concept of a friend was someone who was useful to him. When a friend ceased to be useful, he ceased being a friend.

The last to arrive was Sal Genovese. He came into the library with outstretched arms and embraced Scarnato mightily. "May God be with you on this terrible day." He patted the glossy black hair at the back of Scarnato's head. "Catherine was a jewel, Tony. A jewel! I feel as if I've lost one of my own daughters."

"Thanks for coming, Sal." Scarnato disengaged himself from Genovese's grip. "Fix yourself a drink and sit down. We'll have a short meeting. All of you find chairs for yourselves. Freshen your drinks first."

As the guests milled around the table pouring out whiskey and adding ice to their glasses, Genovese announced in a loud voice, "I don't understand why the cops can't round up all the goddamn perverts and shoot them down like animals. That's the only way to put a stop to this sort of thing."

Several glances were exchanged, but no one had the temerity to remind Genovese that as a young man he had spent three years in Attica for robbing, beating and then sodomizing an eighty-five-year-old woman. Genovese had lived down that unfortunate beginning and gone into labor organizing after Attica and was now president of a pipe-fitters local, although many people claimed that all Sal

109

Genovese knew about pipes was how to wield a twelve-inch piece for busting heads.

Genovese had risen to power in New Jersey by using his union as a conduit for payoffs to the vast network of state and local public officials on Scarnato's payroll. He was a tall, aquiline man in his thirty-ninth year. Clothes were his passion. His suits came from a small shop in New Bond Street, London, where his measurements were on permanent file. Those measurements never varied because Sal Genovese ate carefully and exercised daily. He had a wife who quietly despised him and three daughters who lived in perpetual fear of his bad humor. He was a success.

Some people believed that Sal Genovese harbored secret plans to usurp Tony Scar's place on the mob's ruling council. The big question on those minds was whether Scarnato realized the scope of his friend's ambitions.

People quietly settled into their chairs, the only sounds coming from the clink of ice cubes in their glasses. Scarnato occupied the center chair, with Genovese on his right. Peter Wells sat to Scarnato's left, an open notebook on his lap. The other guests were Jack Torre, Phil Costello, Murray Bloom, Danny Frederico and Lou Ponte. Wells and Bloom were the only ones present who did not have Sicilian blood. They were specialists who took part in all major decisions, though it was understood that neither could ever rise to positions of genuine power.

Wells looked after the organization's legal interests. Murray Bloom, a slight, spry man who always seemed to be fighting some kind of allergy, was Scarnato's financial advisor. In an age when even schoolteachers used calculators, Bloom could still add and store a long column of figures in his head. He also possessed an unerring instinct for moving Scarnato's money in ways that the platoons of Justice Department lawyers and accountants couldn't trace.

Torre and Costello controlled the gambling action in Newark and Jersey City, with Frederico and Ponte having the license for gambling in the rest of the state. The four men were so close to each other in size and coloring that they might have been brothers. They were all in their forties, hefty men who carried their weight well, all with dark eyes set into square faces. Scarnato liked having pairs of men sharing the responsibility for a single territory. It was a system that tended to keep people in check. Only Sal Genovese had a single area of authority—political management—which he had shrewdly used to build his power base.

"First," Scarnato began, "I want to thank you fellas and your wives for coming over tonight. It's a comfort to have the company of friends on a night like this, especially for Teresa."

As if on cue Teresa Scarnato let out a wail of despair that would have frozen the blood of a less hardy group. Scarnato waited patiently until the other women in the living room had calmed his wife. "The wake will be tomorrow night at the DiMato Funeral Home in Newark and the service will be at eleven A.M. the next day. Instead of flowers we're asking our friends to send donations to The Neptune Society, that save-the-whale outfit. It was Catherine's favorite cause.

"Now . . ." Scarnato sighed out the word. "My number-one concern is to find the son of a bitch who killed my daughter. The cops don't have much, and even when they do have something they'll move slow. I don't have to move slow. When they pin down the man, he's gonna be mine."

No one had to be told what Tony Scar meant by that.

"Since I won't be able to concentrate on the business for a while, I'm shifting some responsibilities." The level of attention in the room rose dramatically, as Scarnato knew it would. "Peter has been doing most of the negotiating for the Atlantic City casino license, so he'll take full charge of that project for now. Murray will make the weekly close of the books for me and Danny will handle the political payoffs."

No one looked directly at Sal Genovese, but there was a stir as his sympathetic expression altered to accommodate his self-concern. "What about me, Tony? What's my job while you're gone?" His manner just barely avoided an outright challenge to Scarnato's decision.

"Sal, I need your help to find Catherine's killer."

Genovese began to scowl, then realized what his only response could be. "You honor me."

Jack Torre gave Lou Ponte a wink that was imperceptible to the others and Phil Costello nudged Danny Frederico with his elbow. They were silently applauding Scarnato's decision. Leave it to the boss! Only Tony Scar could use his own daughter's death as a tool

III

to cut Genovese loose from his power base. Even more impressive, he was handling Genovese in a way no one could fault—not even Genovese himself. Genovese could hardly refuse to help Tony find his daughter's killer. Such a refusal would be as good as signing his own death warrant, as far as the ruling council would be concerned.

Danny Frederico was having as difficult a time as Genovese in concealing his emotions . . . Sal would never move back into his old spot, he was thinking. Not if Danny Frederico played his cards right . . .

The others knew exactly what Danny was thinking because that would be their reaction if they had been tapped for Genovese's spot.

Scarnato adjourned the meeting. "Okay, that's enough business for now. I'll be in touch with all of you tomorrow."

He opened the library doors and led everyone into the living room, thinking that Genovese was taking the news well. This wouldn't be the end of it, of course. Sal was a good man, but he was trying to move up too fast. If he couldn't be made to understand that, if he wouldn't control his personal ambition for the good of the organization, he would have to go.

"Teresa, come sit down." He went to his wife, who was kneeling before the crucifix on the mantel praying aloud, and helped her to a chair. Immediately the other wives surrounded him to offer sympathy with identical sets of clichés. Their words sickened Scarnato. He wanted to tell everyone to get out, but that would leave him alone with Teresa. An unbearable thought.

He turned to Genovese. "Sal, could your Maria stay overnight? Teresa needs someone . . . another woman."

"Sure, Tony." Genovese took his wife aside and issued terse instructions. They returned and Genovese said, "It's settled. Maria will be happy to stay."

Scarnato took Maria's hand and squeezed it. "Thank you, dear. I'm very grateful." He tried to look grateful, but it wasn't a look that came easily to him.

"I'm glad to help out," Maria Genovese muttered.

"Vincent will get you anything you need. Sal, let's talk some more." He took Genovese's arm and led him to a pair of wingback chairs in one corner. They sat down and Scarnato came straight to the point. "You're sore about the way I handled things in there."

"You took away my toys," Genovese admitted with a rueful smile. "How could I enjoy that?"

"Temporarily." He gave Genovese a comradely pat on the back.

"Is it, Tony? Temporary, I mean? I get the feeling you think I'm coming on too strong. Hell, I'm only doing the job you gave me to do, ain't that right?"

Scarnato clucked in disbelief. "I never thought that, Sal. Ask anyone. They'll say I've been bragging on how well you handle the fatbellies."

"Well, thanks, Tony. I appreciate that."

Scarnato removed the top from a humidor and offered Genovese a cigar. "Okay, this is what we do: I want you to contact a cop named Trelska . . . Sergeant Trelska . . . Connecticut State Police. I don't know his first name. He took me to the morgue today to identify Catherine's body. Big cop. Built like a weight-lifter. Wears a tailored uniform and hundred-dollar shoes. Carries a custom handgun. You know his type. He was *very* polite to me and Peter, more polite than he had to be. Get my meaning?"

"Sure. He's got his hand out."

"Absolutely. Trelska was sending out signals like a Forty-second Street hooker. I could've fucked him in the ass in his police car if I'd wanted."

"Yeah, I deal with his kind every day."

"That's why I picked you to help me, Sal. You know how to steer these guys better than anyone. What I want from him, I want to know everything about Catherine's death that the cops know. Get to Trelska and bring him on our team. I don't care what it costs."

"Five figures?"

"Sure. Go as high as fifty grand if you have to."

Genovese's eyes bulged.

"Sal, let's not lose this guy over money. He can be bought, we know that, so hit him with a big buck right away. Let's not haggle."

"Don't worry, Tony. He'll be in your pocket. But a sergeant? He can't be running the case. If you're willing to pay top dollar, why not go after the number-one cop? Do you know who he is?"

"Lieutenant Conde." Scarnato screwed up his face. "I wouldn't make a move on Conde. He's got that no deal look."

"I'll run the usual line on him anyway. See how big a mortgage he has. Whether he owes anyone money. Has a sick kid who needs an operation. The whole drill." Genovese took a small notebook and a gold Cross pen from an inside pocket. "How do you spell their names?"

Scarnato spelled Conde's and Trelska's names as Genovese wrote them in his book.

"I'm very careful about names," Genovese said. "My first year at this, I was told a building inspector named Hopper would okay a building-site variance for one of your restaurants if he got three grand. I took Hopper's name out of the City Hall directory, his address from the phone book and dropped three grand in the mail to him. That was how he wanted his payoff—thirty crisp new one-hundred-dollar bills in a plain envelope." Genovese scratched his chin and smiled. "The variance was denied. I was so steamed I wanted to hit the son of a bitch. Then I discovered the guy I was supposed to sweeten was named *Hooper,* not Hopper. Hopper was a goddamn dogcatcher! I'd bribed the wrong fucking public official."

Despite his sadness Scarnato was drawn into the story and found himself chuckling along with Genovese.

"So now I write down the names. Don't worry, that's only to get them in my head. I'll burn this piece of paper before I go to bed tonight. It's good you can still laugh, Tony."

"Did Hopper ever turn in the three grand to the cops?"

"Hell, no. He pocketed it, like anyone would. But Tony, I swear I'd have given another three grand to have been there and watched Hopper's face when he opened that envelope. He was one lucky dogcatcher."

Scarnato rose. "Thanks for making me laugh, Sal. I needed it. You'll get to Trelska right away?"

"Tonight, if I can. I know a guy in the Connecticut State Police who'd be willing to make the first contact for me. I'll set up a meeting with Trelska for tomorrow."

"Good. Keep me informed." He shook Genovese's hand and motioned to Vincent Malle. "Sal is leaving, Vincent. Walk him to his car, will you?"

"See you tomorrow, Tony." Genovese left without bothering to say goodnight to his wife.

Scarnato began to circulate through the living room, drawing aside each of his lieutenants and thanking them again for coming. He also used the occasion to pass on confidential instructions to a few.

To Bloom he said in a very low voice, "With Danny out of the numbers operation, I want you to give more attention to Lou's books. Not that I don't trust Lou, but I know what temptation can do to a man. Got it?"

Bloom's eyes slid casually over Lou Ponte. "He won't short you, Tony. I'll make sure of that." His reply ended with a wheezing cough.

"Watch that cold," Scarnato warned.

"It's my sinuses." Bloom massaged his forehead. "They go crazy this time of year."

Later, talking sotto voce to Danny Frederico, Scarnato whispered, "Keep an eye on Bloom, will you? He's a damned good man, but I've never let him close the books without me. You never know, he might get a fatal attack of greed. A man with his allergies is liable to catch anything."

"You never saw a Jew who could shortcount an Italian," Frederico whispered back. "I'll make sure he stays kosher."

And to Lou Ponte he said in the same confidential way, "I need a man I can trust to watch the store while I'm busy. Let me know if any of these guys looks like he might try something cute. I especially want to know if anyone acts like he's in business for himself. You're the only one I can depend on, really. You and me go way back."

"I know what you're saying." Ponte nodded slightly. "I'll be on the horn to you fast if I see anything like that developing."

"Thanks, pal." Scarnato squeezed Ponte's arm.

Soon afterward the men gathered up their wives and left, still repeating the familiar phrases of condolence. He closed the door behind them and returned wearily to the living room.

Teresa was still there, sitting in trancelike silence with Maria Genovese's plump arm around her shoulders.

"Take her upstairs," he told Maria. "See if she'll sleep." Teresa allowed herself to be helped up the steps. Scarnato was so relieved to see her go that he almost lapsed into a childhood prayer.

Sighing, he poured himself a brandy and collapsed into a chair. With no one except Vincent Malle to see him, Scarnato allowed himself to weep. He wept for Catherine's beauty and innocence. He wept for all the years of life she had lost. Finally he wept for himself, because he would never again see that sweet smiling face. "Catherine . . . Catherine . . . my rose . . ."

Malle came to his side and removed the glass from his hand. Vaguely, he saw that most of the brandy had spilled on the carpet. This was no good. He had to be strong.

He rallied and found his voice. "Vincent! First thing tomorrow, go out and buy me a meathook."

Malle, totally alert, nodded decisively. "Right, Tony. And I'll sharpen it myself."

The two men looked at each other in perfect understanding.

CHAPTER 7

HARRY PICKED his way down the hillside with fresh spray cans of Garden Bug Killer and Off tucked under one arm. A nice breeze was still coming off the sound, for which he was grateful. Any stir of air made it difficult for the mosquitos to fly.

He had no idea whether anyone was in the house. It was then just past seven P.M. so there should have been, but neither Ben's nor Donna's car was in the driveway. Harry took his transceiver from under the bush where he had concealed it, stripped off the protective plastic cover and plugged in earphones.

After dialing through all four channels he was convinced the house was empty. He detected no sounds in any of the rooms where his bugs were planted. He was tempted to go into the house immediately and take the button off Ben's shirt. Then he could call the police any time he wanted and say that the killer of the young girl in New Canaan just might be living in a certain house on Clapboard Hill Road, Westport. But it would be risky to go into the house when someone might arrive home at any minute, so he waited.

That afternoon, on the train back to Connecticut, he had picked up a *New York Post* and was startled to see the face of the girl he had killed staring at him from the front page. He learned that her name was Catherine Anne Scarnato and that her father was a well-known hoodlum, a member of the Mafia.

Imagine that!

No wonder she hadn't been enthusiastic about going home to New Jersey. Who'd want to spend the summer with some old garlic-soaked greaseball. I knew she was Italian, he thought. That hot Mediterranean blood stands out every time. A beautiful girl.

He actually felt a stab of remorse about the deaths of Catherine Anne Scarnato, and the others. Now and then an unsettling feeling of guilt came at him out of nowhere. His hands would tremble and his eyes water and his face sting as though it had been slapped, as the faces flashed past. The "blue shakes," he called them. In a minute they would be gone and he could think of the girls calmly again, even with amusement. They'd been whores anyway, lucky he'd even bothered with them. Sure as hell, they didn't deserve him, giving themselves to any cock with money to pay.

Harry's attention returned to the house as Ben's car came up the drive. The car halted in the turn-around area and Ben climbed out, dragging his briefcase with him. His coat was thrown over his shoulder. He looked tired. His mouth sagged at the corners and worry lines creased his forehead.

It was a beautiful sight.

Harry also observed Ben's alarm when he realized that Donna's car was not in the driveway as it should have been at this hour. Ben hurried to the front door and studied a piece of paper tacked there. He looked relieved as he pulled it from the door and went inside.

Interesting, Harry decided. Any change in pattern makes Ben jump. Brother Ben, precious Brother Ben, is starting to crack.

BEN CRUMPLED THE note from Donna saying she had gone to Stop and Shop and dropped it in the kitchen trashcan. After shedding his coat and briefcase, he went to his study and dug out the folder marked Family Finances.

A few days ago . . . was it only Sunday? . . . his financial position had looked solid. Now he wondered just how long he could hold on without the income from the two big accounts Harry had cost him.

Okay, there was the IBM stock and the municipal bonds, almost twenty-two thousand dollars' worth. Plus something over fifteen hundred in the checking account and a certificate of deposit for seven thousand five hundred. Half the interest would be lost if he cashed in the certificate early, but screw the interest. Accounts receivable? Another two K, perhaps. That amounted to about thirty-five thousand dollars, enough to live on for a full year without changing their lifestyle. Longer, if they tightened their belts.

Those were liquid assets. There were items of value that could be sold, if necessary. He loved his collection of antique silver boxes, mostly Georgian silver plus a few American pieces like the beautiful old cigar case that had once belonged to Diamond Jim Brady. He estimated the collection's value at ten thousand, though it might take weeks, or even months, to sell. And his estimate could be off.

Miscellaneous stuff: sterling silver dinner service, Olympus camera with extra lenses, five or six good pieces of jewelry that belonged to Donna, furniture, the second car, the piano. There might be twenty-five thousand in all that junk.

Ben grimaced. *All that junk.* The things you spend a lifetime collecting become junk mighty fast when your back is to the wall. And make no mistake, my boy, your back *is* to the wall.

He heard Donna's car drive up. Quickly he gathered together the papers and slipped the financial file back into the deep drawer of his desk. No use worrying Donna with money problems yet. She had enough to think about.

"Hi, babe." He took a grocery bag from her arms as she came in the door. "I got your note. How'd it go today?"

"Good, I have lots to tell you. What about you? Did you finish the model for the bus? I'm dying to see it."

Ben thought of the sleek lines he had carved from wood with his Exacto knife and his idea for video games built into every seat. The design might have transformed a dull, uncomfortable bus trip into a downright enjoyable experience for millions of people. With great difficulty he shook off the image. It was no longer relevant.

"Where are the kids?"

"They've had dinner. Oop took Sharon and Jeff down to Baskin Robbins for ice cream. He's really a nice boy. I hope Sharon keeps him around for a while." A glance at the kitchen clock reminded her of the hour. "Why are you so late? Was the work going too well to stop?"

She knew that an interesting design idea would sometimes blot everything else from his mind. Often when Ben was late she would learn that he had simply forgotten to look at his watch.

He answered with a strange slowness, "No, I was thinking things through."

"Well, sir, you'll be happy to learn I've maybe solved a few of our problems. I talked to Crane Security Services about installing one of their systems in the house. Some men will be here Friday to make a survey and give us a price. Besides that, I hired three investigators from their New York office to canvas the good hotels in Fairfield County and Westchester. They'll locate brother Harry, if anyone can." She smiled at him, ready to be complimented for her resourcefulness.

"That was a good idea," he said cautiously.

"And then," she went on, "I told the man there, a very earnest chap named Carter Phillips . . . a Princeton private eye, if you can believe his class ring . . . that Harry seems to know an awful lot about us. He suggested Harry might have bugged our house, and your office too. Isn't that wild? I don't believe it, but I did agree to let him send men with electronic gear to look for bugs tomorrow. Wasn't that a good idea?"

While she talked, Ben had taken a carton of milk from the refrigerator. He poured himself a glass and took a long gulp. He hadn't eaten any lunch and the milk tasted sweet and filling. "Yes, it was. While I was thinking out things this afternoon, I came to that same conclusion. That's why I'm late. I've been looking all through the office for a bug. Turned the place inside out, in fact."

"Did you find anything?"

"No." Ben shrugged. "Of course, I didn't really know what I was looking for. That's why you were right to hire the Crane people. Let's have them change all the door locks, too."

"Yes, they'll do that on Friday as part of the survey. Phillips also suggested we install a new type of lock on our doors, a French design. It takes a four-sided key that he says is impossible to pick." She shivered and hugged herself. "It's creepy to think Harry might have been in here. I really don't believe it, not yet. But this should stop him if he's still around."

"Oh, Harry's still around. Yes, indeed."

120

The way Ben said that made Donna catch her breath. "What's he done this time?"

Ben repeated to her the highlights of his conversations with Walter Stanton at Allied and Art Manning at Warner-Bengelheim. "Harry must have been damned convincing. Walter Stanton is sharp, nothing phony gets past that old boy. If Harry had enough information about the bus project to talk about it with Stanton, he could only have gotten it from my office." He hesitated, then decided Donna had a right to know everything. "I lost the project. The Warner-Bengelheim job is gone too. We've got some financial problems, hon, if we can't put an end to this thing soon."

"Ouch!" Donna smacked her forehead with the heel of her hand. "I committed us to about four thousand dollars' worth of services from Crane. That doesn't include the alarm system for the house, which would cost five to seven thousand if we went through with it."

Ben gave a low whistle. "It's cheaper these days to get burglarized than to protect yourself against the burglars. But then . . . Harry's no ordinary burglar. We'd better go ahead and have the system installed."

"Can we afford it?"

"No. But we can't afford not to do it, either."

Donna gestured wanly at the grocery bag Ben had just carried in for her. "Do you want some dinner? I picked up a package of those big shrimp you like."

"I'm not too hungry. Later I'll have another glass of milk, maybe a cup of soup. Right now all I want is a shower."

"What makes him like this?" Donna burst out. "Harry! Why is he like this? Why doesn't he just *go away?*" And then she was in tears, the taut self-discipline of the day vanished.

Ben gathered her into his arms, understanding that she needed reassurances and knowing that he had none to give. "I don't *know* why he's like this, hon. I *never* knew why." He kept on patting her until Oop's car could be heard coming up the driveway.

Donna wiped her face with the dish towel. "Let's get out of here. Suddenly I hate kitchens."

Jeff came pounding into the house ahead of Sharon and Oop.

"What's that on your face?" Donna said.

"Chocolate fudge with marshmallow. *Triple* scoop! Oop's the best boyfriend Sharon ever had."

"Wash it off," Donna commanded gently.

"Sure, mom. Upstairs bathroom, and I won't get the towel dirty." He took the steps two at a time.

Ben watched him with admiration. "I suppose he'll learn how to walk up a flight of stairs someday, and by then I'll miss the sound of him pounding those steps."

"He wouldn't be Jeff if he walked upstairs."

Oop and Sharon came in, Oop dropping his hand from around her waist at the doorway. "Good evening, Mrs. Ryder. Mr. Ryder."

"Hello, Oop." Ben was impressed once again by the maturity of the young man's presence. "Thanks for taking Jeff along today. That was nice of you."

"My pleasure, sir. I was wondering, do you mind if I take Sharon to a movie tonight? I mean, is everything all right?"

"Everything is fine." Ben thought his voice sounded hollow and tense, but no one else seemed to notice it.

"We're only going to the Fine Arts," Sharon said. "We'll be home by eleven."

"Okay."

"Any news on Uncle . . . on your brother?" Sharon laughed self-consciously. "Isn't that funny, I can't call him Uncle Harry."

"No news. Which Fine Arts are you going to?"

"Cinema One."

"Have a good time."

They went out the front door and Ben walked quickly to the window out of fatherly curiosity. Sure enough, Oop's hand slid around Sharon's waist and he drew her tightly to him as soon as they were outside. He decided that Oop was a very wise kid. Say "sir" and "ma'am" to the parents and buy the little brother triple-scoop ice-cream cones. Then you can do what you want with the daughter. Oop would bear some watching.

"Take your shower," Donna said. "I'll put away the groceries and warm some soup for you. Cream of mushroom?"

"What? Oh, sure . . ."

"I'm sorry I bawled." She set her mouth in a firm line, which somehow made her even more beautiful. "It won't happen again."

122

"Yes, it will. Only next time I'll join you." He waved away her smile. "This nightmare is driving me crazy too. I've been a zombie today."

"At least we're going crazy together. Take your shower, I'll put on the soup in about fifteen minutes."

JEFF RYDER HAD been listening to their conversation from the top of the stairs. When his father started upstairs he retreated to his room and closed the door.

Uncle Harry was still in town and he was making mom cry . . .

His father's footsteps passed his room. Jeff heard him go into the master bedroom and close the door. In a minute or two he'd be in the shower.

Jeff wanted to wait until he heard the shower door close and the water start, but he was too anxious. The secret bundle at the rear of his closet was practically calling out to him.

He went to the closet and burrowed for the bundle beneath all the junk he had artfully used as camouflage. There it was! An old yellow beach towel wrapped around a long object. He carried it to the bed and laid it out lovingly.

Wow! Super!

The walnut stock was revealed first as he began unwrapping the .22 Remington rifle he had borrowed that morning from Tony. Then he uncovered the barrel and reached into his pocket for the six .22 Peters center-fire cartridges Tony, after much argument, had given him.

Tony had demonstrated how to operate the weapon too. They had gone through several "dry fire" exercises, as Tony's father had done with him, before putting any live ammo into the chamber.

Loading the weapon was a snap. Pull back the bolt. Slide the rounds one by one into the grooved spaces in the chamber. Close the bolt, which automatically drives the top round into the chamber. Easy.

Wait! The safety catch. Oh, wow! It was off!

Jeff's hand shook as he slid the safety lever forward. Can't let that happen again.

He heard the shower and went to his window, which looked out on the woods fronting the house. Uncle Harry might be out there somewhere right now thinking up new ways to make mom cry.

His bedroom window provided a view of a piece of Clapboard Hill Road, a stretch about a hundred yards long. A light-colored station wagon was parked under the trees off the road, and it seemed to Jeff he had seen it there before. More than once? He raised the rifle and aimed at the station wagon over the .22's open sights.

Pow! Pow! Pow! I could hit it from here. I'll *bet* I could.

BEN STOOD IN the shower with his eyes closed letting the blast of water flow directly into his face. Donna's question was still in his mind. *What makes him like this?*

No one had ever come up with a satisfactory answer. At the trial the psychiatrists for the prosecution and defense had dueled over it in a professional way, trading worn phrases: "Pathological misogynist" . . . "Oedipal complex" . . . "sado-masochistic psychotic . . ." Until the words lost any meaning.

All Ben knew was that Harry had always seemed contemptuous of women, vaguely hostile, and maybe even a little afraid, but such a simple explanation would hardly satisfy anyone. They would have wanted details, the uglier the better, and he hadn't wanted to do that to his brother, his family. Still, maybe he should have told the psychiatrists about poor Natalie Winder . . .

NATALIE WINDER HADN'T been the prettiest girl in their junior class in high school, but she held an attraction for the boys that transcended her plain face and dumpy figure. In the language of that time and place, Natalie Winder "put out." She was overweight, myopic, given to shrieks and giggles, and fond of horror movies. There weren't many other Jewish girls in Pasadena High. Those there were did not "put out." They studied hard and dated A students. Natalie, on the other hand, favored boys who wore chinos or yellow cords, combed their hair in "ducktails" and cut class.

Natalie never had to look far for a date. She could have gone out every night of the week, if she'd had the stamina. But now and then a different type of boy caught her eye, someone unusual enough to go after.

The idea of screwing twin brothers had immense appeal to Natalie. It was something a heroine in a movie might do. Ben and Harry Ryder were alike in every other way; she had naturally wondered whether the two brothers did it the same way too. And they were good-looking guys with wide shoulders, narrow waists, great smiles and ready laughs. She didn't have any boyfriends as handsome and popular as the Ryder brothers.

One day Natalie managed to bump into Ben as he came out of the biology lab, making sure her breasts caught him square in the chest. "Oof! Careful, Benny, you'll break 'em!" She giggled behind her hand. "Say, how come I don't see you after school?"

"I don't know." Ben blushed and was furious with himself. "Where do you hang out?"

"The bowling alley across from the Academy Theater. Come around some time, I'll show you how to make a strike." She wasn't sure Ben caught her double meaning so she nudged him again.

Harry came out of the lab frowning into a book. "I don't understand this question about bacillus. What the hell's a bacillus anyway? Oh, hi, Nat. What's doing?"

"I was just wondering when you guys were going to take me out?"

Harry and Ben looked at each other as if they'd just been handed a fabulous Christmas present.

"Take you out?" Harry pressed. "Both of us?"

"Sure, why not? I've never dated twins before. It might be a kick."

"When?" Ben said immediately.

Natalie pulled the books in her arms up over her breasts in a coquettish movement. "I don't know. I'll be at the bowling alley tonight. Maybe I'll see you guys there." She walked away, swinging her hips.

Ben was excited. "I think she wants to do us, Harry. *Both* of us. Really."

"Yeah," Harry grunted, watching her hips.

"We need a car. She'll never go out with us if we don't have a

125

car." Ben snapped his fingers. "Artie Wilson! We can borrow his Plymouth."

"Naw, that old junker's too small and the seats are torn. We need something with a big back seat. A pussy wagon, like Bobby Lang's Pontiac. He owes me a favor. I slipped him a few answers in the geometry mid-term."

"Talk to him." Ben took his brother's arm and led him away from the biology lab doorway. "Harry; we've never had a girl before, either of us. Do we need anything? Rubbers?"

"I don't think so. If one of Natalie's guys caught the clap everyone would know. You can't keep a secret in this school."

"I was thinking about something else. Suppose she gets, you know, knocked up."

Harry laughed. "What if she did? They'd never know which of us was the father. We've got the same blood. That's one of the good things about being twins, Ben. Let's take advantage of it. Hey, let's make a pact. We'll always go out with the same girls, okay?"

Ben agreed, a bit uneasily.

That night they dropped by the bowling alley in Bobby Lang's Pontiac, both smelling of Old Spice and wearing clean undershorts. Natalie was there, but she wasn't quite ready to give herself to the Ryder brothers. First she flirted with a couple of other boys. Only after making Ben and Harry squirm for a sufficiently long time did she agree to bowl a line with them. Afterward they went to Gwinn's for milkshakes. When they were near the bottom of their shakes Ben suggested a drive. "Have you ever seen the view from the top of Lake Avenue?"

Natalie gave a throaty laugh. "Only about a hundred times. But sure, let's go up there."

Harry drove. Natalie sat in the front seat between the brothers, distributing pats and squeezes to work them up. She liked her guys hungry for it.

At the top of Lake Avenue Harry found a cutoff leading to one of the Mount Wilson fire roads and parked the car facing toward the San Gabriel Valley. Below, the valley sparkled with lights all the way to Whittier. Natalie took Ben's face in both her hands and kissed him more passionately than he'd ever been kissed, shoving her tongue hard against his. At the same time she pressed her left leg against

126

Harry; inviting him to do what he liked. Harry buried his face in her breasts and shoved a hand up Natalie's skirt. She responded with gyrations that trapped his hand between her legs.

Neither brother, of course, had ever experienced anyone, anything like Natalie. They probably would have gone on kissing and groping the rest of the night if she hadn't pushed them away and, with one of her childlike bursts of the giggles, said, "Come on, one of you take me in the back seat. It's too crowded up here."

Ben was surprised to see a sheen of nervous sweat across Harry's face. Harry hardly ever showed nervousness about anything.

"Go ahead," Harry whispered. "You first."

Ben swallowed hard and climbed into the back seat with Natalie, who sighed romantically as she helped Ben unloosen his pants. Her panties were already off and her skirt hiked above her waist. She began making moaning sounds even before he entered her.

The sensation surprised him. The muscles inside her were powerful and practiced; they seized his cock like a warm, moist hand. He had expected something else, but surely wasn't disappointed by this. He gave himself to her rhythms until they were moving together in cadence.

Ben shuddered his way to the final contraction, finished by leaning into Natalie and kissing her throat. She crooned a high sound and said, "That was great, Benny. You're a sweet boy. A sweet, sweet boy."

"My turn." Harry scrambled over, exchanging places with Ben.

As Ben was putting on his pants in the front seat Harry began whispering obscenities to Natalie. She giggled again, nervously, and thumped around, getting ready for him. "Ow, *easy,* Harry." Harry laughed, not a laugh of pleasure. The car began to shake with his movements and Natalie continued to protest. "Easy, honey . . . let me do it for you . . ."

"Shut up," Harry said. "Just shut up and hold still."

"No, you're hurting me. Ouch, *stop.* You don't have to be so damned rough—"

Harry slapped her. The sound made Ben ashamed, shocked him, not just for Harry but for himself. This wasn't the way it was supposed to be. He had *liked* it. He liked Natalie's wanton eagerness, though it still wasn't really what he wanted. But it was worse now that Harry was mistreating her. And for no reason . . .

"Little whore," Harry was saying, almost like a litany, over and over.

"Don't call me that—"

Harry continued riding her, thrusting home, rocking the big Pontiac with his exertions. His grunts and heaves were unrelated to her. He seemed to have no sense of the rhythm of the act. They had stopped arguing, but Natalie's submission was obviously no pleasure for her. The silly giggles and romantic sighs had dissolved into pained whimpering.

"There," Harry shouted. "There, there, *there,* goddamn you."

"Get away from me." Natalie struggled with her clothing. "That was a mess. You're nothing like your brother. You're a pig, Harry Ryder. A rotten rough old pig—"

Harry slapped her again.

"Don't," Ben called out, cringing from the sound. "For God's sake, leave her alone."

"Sure. We got what we wanted, didn't we, Ben? And believe me, so did she." Harry opened the door and put his foot against Natalie's ample rear end. "Get out, you fat cunt." He kicked her through the door, then pulled it shut and jabbed down the locking button.

"What the hell are you doing?" Ben demanded.

Harry jumped over the seat and turned the ignition key. The engine started with a roar. "Getting the *hell* out of here. Let the bitch walk home, or find another ride. She'll find someone, you can bet on it."

Natalie was on her feet pounding at the window. "Let me in, you can't leave me out here—"

Harry laughed at her through the glass.

"You're a lousy fuck, Harry Ryder, that's what's wrong with you! Ben knows how to treat a girl, but you're lousy, just *lousy* . . ." She began to cry and pull at her hair.

Harry, his face set, threw the car into gear and drove away.

"Bastards," Natalie called after him.

Ben slumped in his corner while Harry found Lake Avenue in the darkness and turned toward Pasadena. He didn't know what had gone wrong back there. Harry had treated Natalie badly, but for some reason he felt sorry for his brother too.

128

"What the hell happened?"

"Nothing." Harry shrugged. "Forget it. She was just no good, that's all. Used up. We won't make that mistake again." And what he didn't say was that it was the last time he'd share with his chicken brother. To hell with him too.

BEN STEPPED FROM the shower and began toweling himself dry with a big, shaggy Martex that always made him tingle as if he'd just had a massage.

After that night he and Harry had gone their own ways as far as girls were concerned; their pact tacitly forgotten.

Maybe, he thought, Harry would have learned to treat girls differently if I'd helped him. I didn't stick with him there. We kept on doing everything else together, but I never even double-dated with Harry after that night.

And the strange thing was that Natalie went out with Harry several more times. For some reason she continued to let Harry hurt and humiliate her. He knew about women who enjoyed that sort of treatment, but what made Harry want to go along with it, to hurt them in the first place? It had been and he guessed would always be a mystery to him. . . .

He dressed swiftly and went out into the hall to bang on Jeff's door. "Jeff? Come on, I'm taking you and your mom out for the evening."

"Okay, dad. Be right down."

Ben went downstairs and straight to the kitchen, just in time to stop Donna from opening a can of Campbell's cream of mushroom. "Never mind the damn soup. Let's get out of the house for a while, take a drive over to White Plains and poke around The Galleria. Maybe have a hot cinnamon bagel, or some other gourmet delight. We deserve it."

Jeff came downstairs, the shadow of secret knowledge in his eyes, and they locked up the house securely before leaving.

HARRY WATCHED IN puzzlement as they drove away. Stupid. How could they be stupid enough to leave their house when they suspected it might be bugged? Didn't they realize that if he heard their conversation about hiring Crane he might remove the equipment while they were gone?

For several minutes Harry sat in frozen concentration while he considered whether this might be a trap. Ben could have hired someone . . . Crane Security? . . . to stake out the house. There could be men waiting as silently inside the house as he waited here among the trees. Sharon and her boyfriend had left first, then the rest of the family. The whole thing could have been an elaborately staged charade to make him believe the house was empty.

Gradually, after careful thought, Harry began to relax. Ben and Donna were too straightforward to be able to play such a clever game. And they weren't really stupid, just, as Ben always had been, naive and self-deluded. In theory they might consider the possibility of their house being bugged, but they hadn't yet accepted the idea, hadn't yet been able to believe it. They'd been too safe for too long. Too bad for them . . .

All right then. Go into the house and remove the listening devices before Crane's experts can find them. Take the button off the shirt too . . . this could be your last chance, they're changing the door locks on Friday. Gather up all this equipment and take it away. Next, go to Ben's office and retrieve the tiny transmitter he hadn't found because it was too well hidden inside the tubular leg of his work table.

He began packing up equipment, slipping everything except the bug sprays and binoculars into a green plastic trash bag. Those items he left hidden in the underbrush. Tomorrow morning, he decided, I'll watch the experts from Crane sweep the house. That should be amusing. I'll also want to know when Sharon leaves. With luck that dumb-looking boyfriend will take her somewhere, and I'll be right behind them.

Harry went silently through the woods to the rear of the house, waited there for several minutes, listening intently. When he detected no sounds from inside he unlocked the side door to the garage and entered his brother's house.

The spring-blade knife was ready in his hand as he went through the kitchen. Thoroughly satisfied at last that he was alone, Harry went through the house room by room, recovering his miniaturized transmitters. Held in the palm of his hand the devices resembled four loose coins—small change. Perhaps he could return to plant them again after the electronics wizards from Crane swept the house.

No matter. He'd already gotten his money's worth from the listening devices.

Ben's dress shirts hung at one end of his bedroom closet, but his soft sport shirts were kept in a deep drawer of a long pine bureau. Harry opened the drawer carefully and removed a stack of shirts. He laid the neatly folded shirts on the bed and searched through them for the mate to the soft tan sports shirt he had been wearing the night he killed the Scarnato girl. Was it in the laundry? Ah . . . no . . . here it is.

The button on the pocket flap was identical to the one he had torn off his own shirt and tossed down by the girl's body. He had no idea whether the police had found it. The story in the *Post* had said that a large number of police were being assigned to the case. Well, together they at least should be able to find one small button near a corpse.

With a single motion he ripped away the button, leaving only loose threads dangling from the shirt pocket.

Try talking your way out of this one, Ben. You'll find out what it's like to have a bunch of animal cops jumping on every word you say, ridiculing your masculinity, pushing you around . . . You'll scream at them to go away, leave you alone. But they won't go away. They'll stay at it until you're wondering if maybe you did kill the girl. Until you're ready to say you did just to get the bastards off your back . . .

Harry returned the shirts to the drawer and slipped the loose button into his pocket with a hand that faintly trembled. Your hands will tremble, too, Ben. I damn well guarantee it, dear brother.

Wednesday

CHAPTER 8

SERGEANT EDDY Trelska, dressed in civilian clothes and yawning widely, drove along Route 9W into Nyack, New York, looking for a Teddy Bear coffee shop. It was six A.M. and already over eighty degrees, a steamy eighty at that. A ten-foot-high stylized Teddy Bear's face appeared on his right. He turned into the coffee shop's parking lot, still yawning and blinking the sleep from his eyes.

"Teddy Bears at six A.M. I must be nuts."

There were only a few customers in the shop: a pair of truck drivers arguing baseball over hotcakes, an old woman, three kids on their way to Jones Beach, and a squat, dark man in a gray suit who was nursing a cup of coffee.

The squat man, Vincent Malle, gestured at Trelska to join him.

Trelska slid into his booth. "You the guy who wants to see me?"

"No," Malle answered, "I'm the guy who's gonna take you to the guy who wants to see you."

"Screw that. I don't have all day to drive around Rockland County. My duty starts at eight and it's an hour's drive from here to Westport."

"You didn't want to meet us in your own backyard, did you?" Malle shoved aside his coffee. "We don't have to go far. Come on."

He pushed himself out of the booth and walked to the swinging doors leading to the kitchen.

Trelska followed slowly, still not sure he wanted to be here. An old buddy now working at the Southbury barracks had called him at midnight, told him a "mutual friend" wanted to have a chat at six A.M. in Nyack. The chat would be "worth your while" his buddy had said. Who was the mutual friend? The buddy had replied, "I can't say. But I'll tell you this, Eddy—I'm getting a grand just to call you."

So that's why I'm here, Trelska thought. If someone got a grand just for making the call, there must be a lot more in it for me.

The cook at the grill didn't look up as Malle led Trelska through the kitchen to a small table set up in an empty storeroom next to a meat locker. Sitting at the table was one of the most elegantly dressed men Trelska had ever seen. Clothes were his hobby, so he recognized the custom tailoring as English. Gracious touches had been provided for the table: good linen and silver, fine china and a slim crystal vase that held a single rose.

Holy shit, Trelska thought. I know this guy's face. He's Sal Genovese—The Fixer.

"Hello, Eddy. Sorry to bring you all the way over to this side of the Hudson so early." Genovese didn't rise, but he did offer Trelska the other chair at the table.

Trelska dropped into it, a smile inching across his face. "Good morning, Mr. Genovese."

"You know me? That's good, saves time. Here, try some orange slices. They're delicious." He saw the skepticism on Trelska's face. "You're wondering why they're red? Because these oranges are from *Sicily,* my friend. The red oranges of Sicily are the best damned fruit in the world. You don't think I'd eat the shit they serve in this place, do you?"

"Why not? Everyone knows you people own the Teddy Bear coffee shops."

"Yeah, that's why we don't eat here," the squat man said. "This breakfast is catered." He held out a battery-operated instrument the size and shape of a portable radio. "I gotta do this. No offense meant."

"Help yourself." Trelska lifted his arms while the squat man moved the instrument, a device for detecting both high and low frequency sound waves, around his body. "I'm not wired."

"We didn't think you would be," Genovese said. "That's to remind you we're careful people. You won't go wrong doing business with us."

"I'm not doing business with you." Trelska spoke in a particularly loud voice in case Genovese himself was wired.

"Sure, I understand. Here, Eddy, have some breakfast. There's plenty."

Trelska helped himself to eggs and toast, ignoring the strange Sicilian oranges. Guinea food. He wanted no part of it. "What's this all about?" he asked, digging into the eggs.

"I've got a certain friend whose only beloved daughter has been murdered. You know who I'm talking about."

"Maybe."

"My friend isn't popular with your boss, Lieutenant Conde."

"Conde's a good man," Trelska said for the record.

"Sure he is. Just a little conservative. Look . . ." Genovese put aside his fork and molded his face into a mask of sincerity. "My friend wants to know what the police are doing to find his daughter's killer. You can understand that, can't you? I mean, isn't that a reasonable request? But Conde believes in official channels and rules of evidence and all that shit."

"Yeah, true." Trelska noticed that the squat man had gone away.

"So all I'm asking," Genovese went on, "is that my friend gets cut in on whatever information you guys have. Nothing more."

"You'll get it—through proper channels."

Genovese knew what that meant. It was another way of saying no money, no information. His eyes raked the policeman, noting the greed in his manner. Trelska was a familiar type, the flashy hotshot who can't live on his salary. Look at that crumby leisure suit. The jerk probably thinks it's stylish. A fucking rag is what it is. The asshole's in debt to someone, I can smell it. He probably let some slut wangle a Bloomingdale's credit card out of him and now he feels like a big man because she's got him three or four grand in debt. God, I hate doing business with small-timers. "Proper channels? Nah . . . too slow. I want to know everything about this case, and I want it *before* Conde gets it."

137

Trelska ate his eggs and toast and said nothing. He was still too leery of the setup to talk money. *Let the guinea mention dough, if he really wants to do business.*

"You haven't had any tea." Genovese took a sterling silver teapot from a trolley next to the table.

"I don't drink tea."

"This is a special brand." He took off the top and tilted the pot so Trelska could see the envelope inside.

Trelska's enormous shoulder muscles bulged inside the gabardine leisure jacket. He wanted to reach for the envelope, wanted to so very much, but was afraid. *This is happening too fast,* he thought. *There should be another meeting in a place I pick. We should come to an agreement about money beforehand. No reason why I should take whatever Genovese feels like giving me.*

But his mouth was dry and his fingers itched to dip into the envelope. So after a short interval he reached into the cool darkness of the silver teapot and withdrew it. A moment later he knew he had done the right thing. There were *thousands* in there. He leafed through the bills. Ten. Twenty! Twenty-five thousand! All in used fifty- and hundred-dollar bills. The thickest, loveliest envelope he had ever seen.

He thought of Ginger, the girl whose bed he had left at five A.M., thought of her hard, compact body. Ginger had already cost him a bundle in dinners, gifts, clothes and weekends at the Playboy Club in Great Gorge. The cash in this envelope would settle those debts and pay for a vacation in the Bahamas, plus that red BMW he had looked at the other day.

Trelska gave Genovese an answer clear enough for his purposes, but too terse to be useful to anyone listening to a tape recording: "Okay." A phone number was written across the envelope in large block letters. He ran his finger across the number so Genovese would know he understood what the number was to be used for.

Genovese nodded. "You're smart, Eddy. Stay that way."

"Good eggs." Trelska used his last bit of toast to sponge up the yoke on his plate, then popped it into his mouth. "You'll hear from me, *through channels.*"

"Well, thanks for coming anyway."

Trelska walked out of the kitchen, taking care to avoid getting

138

grease splatters from the grill on his suit.

"A punk"—Genovese sighed—"but he'll do the job."

Vincent Malle came around the partition separating the storeroom from the rest of the kitchen. He was working the rewind lever on a Nikon 35-millimeter camera. "Got it, Sal. Only five frames, but they were good ones; Trelska thumbing through that wad of cash with a big shit-eating grin on his face."

"I hope you didn't catch me in any of those shots," Genovese said sharply.

"Naw." Malle had been taking his pictures through a hidden slot in the wall. He opened the back of the camera and tossed the roll of film to Genovese. "Just the cop, like you said."

"Good. Now we own the jerk." Genovese put one of the oranges in his coat pocket and threw down his napkin. "Let's get outta here. The smell from the grill is giving me a headache."

"In a minute." Malle opened the door to the meat locker and went inside. He emerged seconds later with his breath coming in white puffs of condensation. In his hand was a long curved meathook. "A present for Tony."

TRELSKA DROVE OVER the Tappan Zee Bridge toward Connecticut feeling better than he'd ever felt in his life. Even the rush-hour traffic didn't bother him, or the strange new *p'ting . . . p'ting . . . p'ting* coming from the engine of his worn-out Toyota. *Two more days, that's all this junker has to last. Just long enough for me to take delivery on the red BMW.*

His hand kept straying to the bulky envelope in his inside jacket pocket. *Twenty-five thousand dollars . . . got to spend it carefully . . . mustn't do anything to make Jim Conde suspicious. In fact, I'll do the best damned job I've ever done for him. The only difference is that Scarnato and his pals will know everything we know. So who's hurt . . . ?*

A chill touched him. *When you take the mob's money, you have to produce. That's a given. Let's hope we nail the asshole that killed Scarnato's daughter, or at least get a line on him. All Scarnato wants is a name. And if push comes to shove, well, the name doesn't* necessarily *have to be the right one. Scarnato's no D.A. He isn't*

139

looking for evidence. He just wants somebody to kill.

Just a name, Trelska repeated. A plausible name . . .

The traffic continued to be heavy all the way up the Connecticut Turnpike. Even so, Trelska arrived at Troop G headquarters well before eight A.M. He went straight to the squad room and studied with fresh interest the blackboard covering the west wall. At the progress meeting the night before all information gathered by the investigators had been listed on the blackboard under five headings: *Victim. Killer. Physical evidence. Witnesses. Assumptions.*

The longest list of information came under the "Victim" heading. Quite a lot was known about Catherine Anne Scarnato, enough to convince everyone she had been picked up on the Merritt and killed near one of the turnoffs from the parkway. Under "Witnesses" was one entry; a woman living on a side road near Exit 36 had reported seeing a light-colored car parked near her house at about the time the Scarnato girl must have been killed. There had appeared to be two people in the car, but they hadn't stayed long.

The only listing under "Physical Evidence" was a small brown button found by the criminal science team near the spot where the body was found. The button wasn't at all weathered. Nor did it come from the girl's clothing. The assumption was that the girl tore it from the killer's clothing while they were struggling, or that he lost it when he dumped her body.

"Hello, Eddy."

Trelska turned to find Lieutenant Jim Conde standing in the squad room doorway. "Good morning, sir. Doesn't look good, does it?"

"No," Conde said slowly. "I was hoping we'd have more to work on by now. What the hell are you doing in that getup anyway? Going to a cocktail party? Where's your uniform?"

"Haven't changed yet. I don't go on duty for half an hour."

"Yeah . . . come into my office soon as you change."

"Sure, lieutenant."

Conde went down the hall to his office and felt the usual sense of grateful release when he tossed away his hat. He picked up the phone and called his home. His wife, Betty, answered. "Hi, Betty. Say, I'm sorry I snapped at you."

"That's all right, Jim." Her voice was warm, but it retained a trace of hurt feelings. "I know you're under a lot of pressure right now—"

"The kids got off to your sister's all right?"

"Yes, Jean picked them up. They'll be home around ten tonight. Jim, can we go out for dinner tonight, just the two of us?"

"No, sorry, this is going to be another late night, I'm afraid."

The hurt feelings surged to the surface. "They're *all* late nights. It's not right, Jim, and it's bad for us."

"When this case is over—"

"There'll be another. Enjoy yourself." The phone clicked off.

So much for apologies. Conde put aside his personal problems and tried to concentrate on this case. "This damned case," he had started to call it. Like "that damned hat" it was becoming a sore point with him, and for good reasons. Suspects: none. Witnesses: none. Physical evidence: one brown button.

There had been other murder cases like this, cases that had begun with no witnesses and very little evidence. Conde had taken his time on those cases. Chipped away at them. Picked up a stray fact here, a motive there. Talked to people who knew the victim. Made charts and lists. And sooner or later the puzzle would usually come together.

But there wasn't the luxury of time with this case. Bob Spence had told him not to worry, that the mob didn't own Connecticut the way they did New Jersey. Maybe Commander Bob Spence, sitting in his plush office up in Hartford, didn't know the state as well as he thought.

Conde had already received some interesting calls regarding the Catherine Anne Scarnato case. He had expected calls from City Hall types, as Bob Spence had suggested, and one did come from a councilman in one of Connecticut's larger cities. But there had been five others from a surprising spread of people: an industrialist whose name was synonymous with power and civic progress, a member of the governor's staff, *two* state senators and—most surprising of all —a member of the Connecticut State Police Advisory Board.

Each had used different words, but the message was the same: find the Scarnato girl's killer—fast. The message was so consistent that it could only have been programmed by one man, Tony Scar. Scarnato had moved quickly and he had known exactly which buttons to push.

Conde looked at the stack of material in his "Action" basket, all of which he would have to wade through before he could concentrate on the Scarnato girl. They were primarily reports from community police departments in his district. Most could be simply filed, but some of the cases would require follow-up by the state police.

He plunged into those files without enthusiasm. Ten minutes later he was still deep in the process of routing the cases and feeling a growing irritation with the mass of trivia they represented, when someone said, "Excuse me, Jim. I thought I'd check with you about those fingerprints before you get too busy."

Conde raised his eyes to find Ben Ryder once again in his office. His initial surprise turned to anger and then to gratitude. Here was someone he could legitimately chew out. "What the hell is this, *A Christmas Carol?* Every time I look up you're standing there like Marley's ghost. Don't you have a family to raise? A business to run? Someone else, in short, to fuck with this morning?"

"Yes, I do," Ben said in a measured voice. "The Crane Security people are due at my office in just a few minutes. They'll be checking it for listening devices. My house, too."

"Ah. Then I assume your evil brother Harry is still lurking about."

Ben Ryder nodded slowly. "Yesterday he visited two of my best clients. He pretended to be drunk and cost me both of those accounts. I don't suppose you'd be interested in following up on that."

"Drunken ghosts aren't police business. I suggest you try an exorcist."

"What about the FBI report on that card I gave you? Has it come in? Were any of Harry's prints on it?"

"What? Wait a minute." Near the bottom of the pile of documents in his "Action" basket was a red-bordered envelope from the FBI crime lab. He rummaged and pulled it free. "These are delivered by courier, when requested. I put a top priority on this file just to get you off my back. Okay, let's see what we have, or don't have . . ."

Conde slit the envelope and dumped the contents on his desk:

the card, a typed report and several large blowups of fingerprints. He examined the report with a series of grunts and sighs. "There were fingerprints on the card, all right. Yours, for one. And your wife's. Evidently she was fingerprinted years ago when the federal government hired her for some kind of summer program. But there were *no* prints of your brother."

Disappointment carved harsh lines on Ben's features. "You got what you wanted, Jim. I won't bother you again."

Conde tossed the card across his desk. "Take that with you. Sure, I'm glad there were no other prints on the card, and you should be, too. The guy's dead. I can understand your not wanting to believe a brother, especially a twin, has died. It's sort of like a piece of you has gone. I've seen that reaction before. My advice is go home and have a drink. Have several drinks. You'll feel better and probably see things more clearly—"

"Bullshit." Ben stalked out, almost knocking Sergeant Eddy Trelska off his feet outside the door.

"Who's the loose canon?" Trelska asked.

"Name's Ben Ryder. He claims his dead twin brother is following him around, spying on his family."

"A psycho."

"Not exactly." Conde tried for a better description of Ben Ryder. "He's a very worried man. The kind of guy who's never had a serious problem, never even been threatened in any way. Suddenly he's sold himself on the idea that he and his nice cozy family are in danger, and now he won't give it up."

"This is what . . . the third time I've seen him here in the last three days?" Trelska watched through the window as Ben climbed into his car and drove away.

"Yes, that's right." Conde made a gesture of dismissal. "Forget him. I've gone over your list of known sexual offenders. There are twenty-two names here that I want investigated completely. Bring in these people for questioning. Interview their families and friends. Check alibis. Give lie-detector tests when you can get permission. And remember, the local police in the towns where these people live can do most of the legwork, pare down the possibles. So use them. Doublecheck their results, but *use* them. We can't close this case in a vacuum."

"I understand." Trelska was thinking that one of these names, some schlump without an alibi, could be fed to Scarnato if necessary. "I'll get right on it."

THERE WAS A pull-in area on Clapboard Hill Road, a place where a car could be parked off the road in the protection of the trees. Harry didn't like to leave his car there too often. Predictability could be dangerous. On the other hand it was convenient to the route he took through the woods to his brother's house.

He parked and checked the road in both directions before stepping from his rented station wagon. The heat was oppressive and the mosquitos so thick that he almost gave up his plan to watch the house. Only the intense pleasure of watching Ben's electronic experts strike out could have brought him into the sweltering heat.

Beads of sweat glittered along his brow before he had climbed fifty feet up the hillside. He was licking the salty moisture from his upper lip when a young voice said with loud bravado: "Stop right there, Mister Harry Ryder."

Harry came to an abrupt halt. The sweat seemed to freeze on his lip and brow. Slowly, with an attempt at good-natured nonchalance, he turned toward the voice. Ten yards away stood young Jeff Ryder. The boy held a rifle pointed directly into Harry's midsection, his finger resting lightly on the trigger—just like John Wayne.

"I beg your pardon?" He was wearing the false mustache and glasses, so there was still the remote chance of confusing a kid like Jeff.

"I told you to stand still. Don't move an inch or I'll shoot."

More John Wayne. The rifle was only a .22, but plenty of people had been killed by small-bore weapons. Harry decided his best chance was to stall for time, keep the brat talking while he worked out a way to handle him. "Who are you, young man? What's this all about?"

"You know me. I'm Jeff Ryder, and you're my father's twin brother."

"You're mistaken. My name is Henderson. I live over on Pond Road. My dog ran off this morning and I chased him in this direc-

144

tion." Harry pointed up the hill. "He's a golden retriever, answers to the name of Champ. Did you see him?"

"That's a lot of bull."

"Put down that gun," Harry said sharply. "I know your father, and yes, we do look something alike. But I'm *not* his brother, for God's sake. So put away your gun." He paused, then: "Do it!"

The barrel had wavered, but on Harry's command Jeff steadied it and smiled. "You even sound like my dad. Whenever he's sore he snaps at me the way you did just now. He even uses those same words . . . 'do it!' "

"I'm not going to stand here and waste my time with you, young man. All I care about right now is finding Champ, but the police will hear about this, you can bet on that." Harry turned and began to walk away. Not downhill, that would have been too obvious, but on a slant across the hill.

Crack.

A bullet whacked into the tree two feet from Harry's head. He flinched and drew back. The shot hadn't been especially loud. It had sounded very much like a branch snapping loose from a tree, a common sound in these woods. Harry hoped that's what it would be taken for, if anyone had heard.

"Nice shot," he said calmly.

Jeff worked the bolt to drive a fresh round into the chamber. "There's five more in here, *Uncle* Harry."

Harry took a fresh look at the boy. At close quarters Jeff's resemblance to himself at the age of eleven was startling. Jeff's lively brown eyes and pugnacious expression were duplicates of his own, as were the strong straight nose and wide mouth. The resemblance didn't stop at physical characteristics. Jeff carried himself with a confidence beyond his years. He had nerve, plenty of it, and a devilish presence. Right now there was no fear in him that Harry could see, only a tense pleasure at having trapped his quarry.

He's bright and nervy and independent, Harry thought. Much more like me than his father. He could have been my son . . . if I hadn't been locked away for seventeen years . . .

"How'd you know where to find me, Jeff?"

The boy was eager to brag. "I can see part of the road from my room. Last night I noticed a cream-colored station wagon parked in

145

that turn-around spot. We own a cream-colored station wagon too. I figured if you're pretending to be my dad, you'd have a car like his. So this morning I came here and waited."

"Where'd you get the gun?" Harry guessed at the answer. "From your friend Tony?"

Jeff's eyes narrowed. "How did you know about Tony?"

"I know everything about you."

"Yeah, you're a big snoop, all right." Jeff raised the rifle to his shoulder. "You're making my mom cry with all the dumb things you've been doing."

"I'm sorry, Jeff. I was just having some fun, you know. Your dad and I used to do this all the time. Maybe it got a little out of hand—"

"I don't believe you."

No dummy, this kid. Harry was listening for sounds from the road or from Ben's house on the other side of the hill, anxious to get out yet hungry for more contact with this boy who reminded him so much of himself.

"I don't see why people think you're my dad," Jeff said. "He doesn't wear glasses, or have a mustache."

Harry laughed as he peeled off the fake mustache and glasses. "I only wear them when I don't want to look like Ben." It occurred to him that the more he looked like Ben the harder it would be for Jeff to pull that trigger. To shoot at the image of his own father. He sat down on a fallen tree and slipped the mustache and glasses into his pocket. Look relaxed, he told himself. Put the kid at ease.

"Now you're *exactly* like my dad." Jeff's eyes were wide with astonishment. "Wow!"

"When I was eleven years old I looked very much like you, Jeff. Except that you're, oh, an inch taller than I was then. You'll be a big man. Six foot two, at least."

"Probably," Jeff agreed, flattered despite himself. He lowered the rifle from his shoulder. It was still aimed directly into Harry's midsection, but he held it in a more relaxed manner. "Did you really kill a lot of girls?"

"Of course not," Harry said. "You're a smart boy. I'm sure you've heard about people going to prison for crimes they didn't commit. It happens every day. You know that. I could show you

146

people in prison right now, men I met there, who are completely innocent."

Jeff nodded knowingly. "I've seen that on TV . . ."

"Sure you have. That's why I never confessed to those crimes. You can ask your dad, he'll tell you I never confessed to anything. Don't you think I would have if I was guilty, to get a lighter sentence?"

"Maybe. But dad believes you killed people and that you want to hurt us too. He's not wrong about important things like that."

"Not often," Harry replied mildly, "but sometimes he is. For instance, I know Ben thinks you're too young to handle guns. Obviously he's wrong about that. You put your slug just where you wanted it in that tree."

Jeff blushed.

"If you were my son I'd take you hunting. We'd go up into Pennsylvania in November and track deer, maybe even hunt one of those big mountain cats. I loved to hunt when I was a boy but I could never get Ben to come with me. It was the only thing we didn't do together."

"Well, that's not dad's kind of thing . . . he's an artist, sort of."

"Sure he is. Who do you think gave him his first sketch pad. I did. I saw his talent right away. I wanted Ben to make something of himself, and he did. I'm proud of my brother. As proud of him as you are."

Harry saw it then, that wisp of doubt he'd been looking for.

"Then why are you doing all this?"

"I told you. And besides, have I hurt anyone?" Harry made a production out of shrugging his shoulders. "All right, I'll let you in on something else, because you're a very smart boy and you deserve to be treated like one. I'll confide in you. Back in Los Angeles your father for some reason didn't seem to believe in my innocence. So I decided that one day I'd show him how it felt to tell the truth and have people think you're a liar, or worse yet that you're crazy. That's the truth, Jeff." And, by God, it was, Harry thought, or at least part of it.

"I don't know, you made my mom cry," Jeff repeated. "She never did anything to you—"

"I said I'm sorry." Harry realized he'd spoken in a sharper tone

147

than he'd intended. Moderating his voice, he said, "I'll apologize to her, and make it up in some way. I promise." He groped for another angle. "I'd like to talk to Ben about all this. Make peace with him, if I can. Maybe your father and I can even be friends again. I'd like to come over for dinner sometimes, go to a ball game with you and Ben. I'll bet you're a Yankee fan."

"Red Sox." Jeff stepped back a pace as Harry got to his feet. "Don't move!"

"Why not? You believe me, don't you?"

"We'll see. Maybe you didn't kill anyone, and maybe what you said about my dad is right, but I don't know. I *do* know you've been bothering us and making my mom afraid. I'm taking you to the police, Uncle Harry. They can figure out whether you've done anything wrong. At least they'll know my dad isn't lying, that you're alive, like he says . . ."

Harry tried to act resigned. "Whatever you say, Jeff." He stepped over the fallen tree and began walking toward the road. Jeff followed. The tree was a giant old hickory with a trunk measuring at least two feet in diameter. He'd been able to step over the trunk easily, but Jeff would have to climb over. For an instant the boy would be off-balance.

When he heard Jeff clambering over the tree trunk Harry spun and jumped to his left.

"Stop!" The rifle cracked and Harry felt a tug at his sleeve, followed by a burning sensation along the underside of his left arm. The goddamn brat had actually shot him!

"Stay back!" But Jeff was still off-balance and having trouble with the bolt of his rifle.

The springblade knife was open in Harry's hand as he swiftly moved to the boy. Jeff tried to work the bolt, which had jammed in an open position. His foot slipped as he backed away. He fell. "Stay back—"

Harry lunged and landed with his knee on the boy's chest. He slashed out, before he saw that Jeff had dropped the rifle. It would have made no difference.

Jeff gasped as the breath was driven from his lungs so that he could not cry out when the blade sliced his right arm from the shoulder down to the elbow. The sight of his own white bone under

148

the red blood stunned him more than the pain. He gulped for air, his eyes fluttered weakly, and he fainted.

Harry climbed to his feet, watching the boy's small chest rise and fall in shallow breaths. The artery wasn't cut, there was no rhythmic flow of blood, but Jeff was losing a good deal of blood, more than someone his age and size could spare for very long. Those breaths would become increasingly shallow until he wouldn't be able to draw any breath at all.

He wiped the blade on Jeff's trouser leg and slipped it into his pocket, listening calmly for any sounds. A single shot could be ignored or mistaken for something else. A second would be more likely to draw attention.

His upper arm ached, but the bleeding was slight. Before going down the hill to his car he cast a look at the small crumpled figure. "I'm sorry about this, Jeff. You were my favorite nephew."

CHAPTER 9

DONNA HAD allowed Oop to take Sharon out for the morning, but kept Jeff home. Jeff had surprised her by not objecting. In fact, he had been positively cooperative. "I want to work on my stamp collection anyhow," he had said, and went upstairs to his room. His stamps had always been a winter diversion, something to do when the weather became too foul for outdoor sports.

At nine thirty Ben phoned, sounding curiously strained. "I'm at the office. The people from Crane are here, two men and three aluminum cases packed with more electronic gadgets than James Bond ever saw. Jeff's going to love it. For a thousand dollars someone should have fun."

"Have they found anything?"

"Not yet."

She knew Ben would have said something if the police had identified Harry's fingerprints on the card, but she couldn't help asking, "What about the card? Was there any word from the FBI?"

"I'm afraid the only prints on the card were yours and mine." He now sounded not only strained, but bitter.

Donna ground her teeth together, something she did only under extreme tension. "I never thought I'd hope that your office, or our home, would be bugged, of all things. But I want the technicians from Crane to find at least *one* device. That would prove *something.*"

"I'll have to hang up, they want to check the phone. We'll be there in an hour or so. Keep the faith."

Keep the faith. Yes, faith was definitely needed. She was almost beginning to doubt Harry's existence herself. No, that was ridiculous. She banished the idea from her mind and went into the living room.

As she entered the room a raw nervousness took possession of her, the same fearful mood that had begun making sporadic visitations on her earlier in the year. Its effect was peculiar. Commonplace things, like the bright orange tiger lilies along the driveway and a favorite brass floor lamp, seemed to leap at her in dangerous fashion. At the same time her other senses had become more acute; she could hear the distant warring of blue jays, taste the bitter salt air from the sound, smell the rot of last year's leaves beneath the brush.

Those sensations produced an overwhelming sense of danger, a warning that her time and place in the sun might have passed. She felt giddy with panic as various words that might describe her condition passed through her mind: depression, hysteria, anxiety. But none of them answered the essential question of why she felt danger at this particular moment.

Gradually it came to Donna that for several months, even before Ben had told her that he suspected Harry of being in Westport, she had on occasion sensed the presence of something that threatened her and everyone she loved. Harry was *here,* no question. Her moods of spring had been a subconscious early warning, a litmus reaction to the presence of Harry. And why had it hit her just now?

She went back to the kitchen and ran her fingers over the cool yellow telephone. She could phone Ben, ask him to come home. But what reason could she give?

A foolish pride stopped her from calling. Ben had always admired her strength, congratulating her every time she dealt singlehandedly with an emergency—Jeff's broken arm, the four-foot-long blacksnake that had found its way into the house one morning, the little girl she had dragged from the water at Compo Beach last summer and revived with artificial respiration. After all that she could hardly call for help because of a *mood,* for God's sake.

Moods. She had been in a similarly depressed mood on the very day she met Ben . . .

The meeting had occurred on a Tuesday afternoon in October in the second-floor lounge of the Student Union at the University of Southern California. They were both seniors. She was a recent transfer from the University of Kansas and he was in his last year at U.S.C.'s School of Industrial Arts.

The lounge was a cavernous room filled with enormous old brown-leather couches and chairs. The walls were decorated with six-foot-high oil paintings of former Trojan football coaches. Their names meant nothing to Donna, but the men in the portraits were obviously held in great reverence by the school.

Donna had transferred on an athletic scholarship. For some reason her first quarterly check had not arrived. A mysterious Mr. Meeker, who worked for the Director of Athletic Programs, was rumored to have the check. He had not returned her phone calls, so she was lying in sullen wait for him in a chair that offered a view of his office door across the hall from the lounge.

A tall young man plopped down in the next chair, arms filled with books and magazines. He rummaged through them, separated one heavy text from the others, and appeared to settle down to study. After a few minutes Donna became aware that he was staring at her. There was nothing subtle about it—he might have been ogling a nude centerfold in *Playboy.*

"Take a picture," she snapped. "It'll last longer."

The young man mumbled an apology. "I'm sorry. I know I've seen you, I was just wondering where."

"A very unimaginative line," she said coolly, and went back to watching the door to Mr. Meeker's office.

"*The Daily Trojan.*"

"I beg your pardon?"

"That's where I saw your picture, in *The Daily Trojan.* You're Donna Neal."

There had been a photo and story on her in the sports section of U.S.C.'s daily newspaper under the headline: KANSAS GYM QUEEN DEFECTS TO CALIFORNIA.

"I couldn't help wondering why a person who has accomplished so much at one school would transfer out here in her senior year.

153

Especially when you're 'Kansas born and bred' as the *Trojan* said in its original way."

Donna had been asked that question several times. She usually gave the same precise reply in the belief it was best to face tragedy squarely and honestly. "The boy I was engaged to died in an accident on the Kansas Turnpike, near the first Topeka exit, which can be treacherous in winter. We'd been going together since our freshman year and I didn't care to finish at Kansas State after that. Too many memories."

The color drained from his face. "Oh, God, I'm sorry. I didn't mean . . . I had no idea it was anything like that. Please forgive me."

He was so miserable that Donna regretted her candor. When he began to awkwardly gather up his books she said, "Don't go. I shouldn't have been so blunt. I was rude."

"No, I pried. It's just that you're more beautiful than your picture. Usually it's the other way around, and I got carried away."

Donna was shocked to find herself delighted with the compliment. It seemed disloyal to be flattered by someone else's words only nine months after Jack's death. She felt doubly disloyal to realize she was attracted to this young man. He was tall and slim, yet so wide and heavily muscled through the shoulders and upper body that he might have been a gymnast himself. He had the handsome, regular features of a born Californian, yet there was none of the vacant expression often found on very handsome faces. Under straight brown hair he had hazel eyes that were lively, warm and intensely interested in her. And although his clothes were inexpensive and simple . . . jeans, a corduroy shirt and sneakers . . . they appeared to have been carefully selected. An unusual young man. "Thank you. And please don't leave. I've been sitting in this damned chair for three hours and I'm so depressed I want to scream."

"Three hours. Why?"

She explained about the late check and why she had picked that particular chair.

He smiled. "Sure, I understand. I'm on a scholarship, too. Not an athletic scholarship, but there's a finance committee that administers all the scholarship money. For some reason, they never seem to get the checks out on time. It'll probably come in the next two or three days."

"By then I'll be dead from starvation, a cold corpse with great lats."

They laughed together. "My name is Ben Ryder and you won't starve if you let me buy you dinner. By dinner, I mean a hamburger and fries. My check hasn't come yet, either."

"Throw in a Coke and it's a deal."

They went downstairs to the canteen, collected burgers, fries and Cokes and found a booth under a huge photo of a key play from one of the U.S.C.-Notre Dame games.

"Everything here is *football*," Donna said. "That's not good for a gymnast's ego."

"I hear they play the game in Kansas, too."

"Play it, yes. At U.S.C. people live it."

"Not me. I haven't been to a single game since my freshman year. Not that I don't like football, but I work on Friday nights and Saturdays at a coffee shop on Jefferson Boulevard. That's how I keep from starving when my check is late—dinner goes with the job."

"Do you live on campus?"

He paled. "I did. But I moved to a rooming house last year after . . . in April."

They lingered over their burgers until Ben glanced at his watch. "It's almost six. I also pick up extra money tutoring history, and I have to meet someone who can't remember any important dates except the Fourth of July—he thinks that was the day Pearl Harbor was bombed." He paused. "Can I see you again?"

Before she could think of Jack she said, "Yes, I'd like that."

"Okay! I'll call you soon." He scooped up his books and started away. At the door he stopped, shook his head and came back to the table. "It might help if I knew which dorm you live in . . ."

He called the very next day and invited her to see an old movie, the Marx Brothers in *Duck Soup,* which was being shown in Founder's Hall auditorium. The day after that he came to the gym and watched her work out on the high and low parallel bars. By the following Monday they were seeing a lot of each other, snatching spare hours away from their studies just to walk together off campus or sit on a bench near the statue of Tommy Trojan and enjoy the sun.

They talked about hundreds of subjects. Books they loved or hated. Politics. Favorite professors. The differences between California and Kansas. Scholarships and budgets. Surfing. Music. Italian restaurants. Fashions. *Everything.*

No, not quite everything. Donna poured out her life's story, but she was unable to get much out of Ben. She knew only that he had been brought up fifteen or twenty miles away in Pasadena. That his father had died when he was nine years old and his mother only two years ago. He seemed oddly reluctant to say more about his family, or his life outside the campus.

At first that didn't matter. Later, when it became clear to her that she was falling in love with him, it became important. But each time she tried in a gentle way to start Ben talking about himself, he nervously turned to another subject. She sensed he was hiding something, but what?

She decided to ask a friend of Ben's, Ray Kennedy, exactly what was behind Ben's reluctance to talk about himself. A few days later she arranged to run into Ray outside the Student Union and fall in step with him on the way to Founder's Hall, where they both had a ten-o'clock. After some idle preliminary conversation, she said, "Ray, will you tell me something? What's Ben's big secret?"

Ray Kennedy was also an industrial-arts major, a roly-poly pipe smoker with a reputation for wild practical jokes. His greatest coup had been sneaking into the U.C.L.A. locker room the night before the big game with U.S.C. and stealing the Bruins' football jerseys. Beneath that, he was a serious student of art and design. He and Ben had gone all the way through I.A. School together and admired each other's design ideas and styles. So she was surprised when Ray gave her a searching and not altogether friendly look. "Why do you want to know? To satisfy your curiosity about an ugly piece of gossip, or for a more serious reason?"

Stung by his hostility, she answered, "I think I'm in love with the guy."

"I see." His suspicion melted. "Can you cut your ten-o'clock? What you want to know will take some explaining."

They went across the street to Coffee Dan's and found an empty booth way at the back. After their coffee had been served, Ray said, "Lots of people have asked me about Ben. You're the only one I've talked to because I think you might be good for him." He laughed.

"I *know* you're good for him. He's smiling again, and I thought that might never happen."

"I don't understand."

"Has Ben told you that he has a twin brother?"

"A *twin?* Ben? No! Why wouldn't he tell me something so . . . so . . . special about himself?"

"Because Harry, his brother, is in prison. You've heard of Camarillo? It's a place up north for the criminally insane. That's where Harry is—where he'll be for the rest of his life." Toying with his coffee and speaking in terse sentences, Ray Kennedy told her everything he knew about Harry, the murder he had committed and Ben's reaction to the whole chain of events.

He concluded by saying: "Ben has been almost a hermit since then. I was the only person he'd socialize with, until you. You know, those two brothers are as different as two sides of a coin. I didn't like Harry even before it came out that he was a psychopath. Oh, he was loaded with charm and he could be very funny. But he looked at people, especially women, as if they were bugs. It's funny. Ben is perceptive and intelligent, but he had a blind spot about Harry. He thought Harry was a great guy. Now, through some twisted logic, Ben thinks he somehow failed Harry. Nothing could be further from the truth."

She squeezed Ray's hand across the table. "Thanks for telling me. I thought it might be something worse."

"Worse!"

"Yes, I thought he might not love me."

Ray sat back. "No way. I like you, Donna. And I want the chance to play best man at a wedding. So don't let him get away from you."

"I don't intend to."

Soon afterwards Donna found her chance to tell Ben that she knew about his brother and give him a more explicit message about her feelings for him. They had pooled their extra funds and come up with fifteen dollars, enough for both of them to ride for an hour at the Griffith Park stables. After a ride that took them through hills just beginning to change from soft brown to winter green, they walked up a path to some picnic benches and found themselves with a magnificent view of Los Angeles.

157

She intended to tell him then. But before she could speak Ben put his hands around her waist and drew her into the hard comfort of his arms. She went to him hungrily. There was a long, sweet silence as they kissed fiercely, then tenderly, then fiercely again before collapsing, laughing and breathless, on the grass.

"About time," Donna said. "Another week and I'd have been driven to drink."

"And me into a padded cell." Ben kissed her again, with a new kind of hunger that caused her to pull away.

He groaned and stroked her hair. "My padded cell awaits."

"Padded cell," Donna repeated in a disquieted voice that caused Ben to look sharply at her. "Yes, I know about Harry."

Ben tried to disentangle himself from her.

"It doesn't *matter*. That was *him* . . . not *you.*"

"We're *identical* twins. Did you know that?"

"Yes, Ray Kennedy told me." She saw anger flare in his eyes. "Now don't get sore at Ray, he's too good a friend."

"Donna, I'm—"

"You're *Ben* Ryder, and you have to learn to live with the loss of a brother. I know exactly what you're going through. Don't you think it hurts to bury Jack in a remote corner of my mind? We both feel guilty about doing that to someone we love. But we have to."

Ben said, "We're a couple of walking wounded. It's a damned good thing we found each other."

"A *damned* good thing," she agreed.

They kissed again, more leisurely.

Eight months later, right after graduation, they were married. Ray Kennedy got his wish: he was Ben's best man. A month later they switched places as Ben stood up for Ray at his wedding to Carol Leahy, a nurse at the U.S.C. Medical Center.

Job offers had drawn them to Connecticut, and a good life— until now. Until the return of Harry . . .

THE PHONE RANG, startling Donna out of her reminiscences. She snatched it up hoping for good news. "Ben?"

"You're warm."

"What's happened? Have they found something?"

"Who, the Crane techs? That's unlikely."

"What's wrong? You sound strange—"

"And you sound delicious. How would you like a real man to take care of your little clit—"

Oh, God . . . "Harry!" She said the name aloud without meaning to.

"No, dear, this is Harry's ghost. Can't you hear my bones rattle?"

It was terrible, eerie . . . the voice was Ben's, but the words were Harry's. What to do. Hang up on him? Try reasoning with him? She opted to try to play his own cool game. "You sound too lively for a spook. Where are you?"

"Close by, darling."

"Why are you calling? I thought your act was to hover in the wings, dashing onstage just often enough to confuse the audience."

"I'm calling about Jeff."

The bottom dropped out of Donna's stomach. No more cool. "Jeff? Don't you dare touch him—"

"I already have."

She looked toward the stairs. "You're trying to scare me, this is just another of your rotten tricks. Jeff is upstairs working on his stamp collection—"

Harry laughed. "The kid's a born liar, like his uncle. He sneaked out and actually tried to set a trap for his old uncle . . . I just called to say you can count on me for a spray of carnations at his funeral."

The line went dead.

"Jeff!" Donna wheeled and slammed down the phone. "Jeff, come here this minute!"

When there was no answer, she began to tremble. "Please, God, let it be a lie." She ran upstairs calling Jeff's name, knowing in her heart that he was not in his room. At the top of the steps she threw open his door. Empty.

She went quickly to the phone in the master bedroom and dialed the number of Ben's office, praying that the Crane people weren't dismantling the phone at that moment.

"Ryder Industrial Design."

Thank God. "Ben, Harry called and—"

"Harry phoned you?"

159

"Yes, and he's done something to Jeff."

"*What?*"

"Call an ambulance and come home as fast as you can." She dropped the phone and ran downstairs and out the front door. The logical part of her mind registered the possibility that this might be a ploy to draw her outside the house. She didn't care. Jeff was gone. "*Jeff,* can you hear me?" Oh God, he could be anywhere.

She thought she heard something . . . a voice . . . up on the hill, and ran in that direction, taking pathways where she could find them and breaking through the heavy undergrowth where she couldn't, all the time calling out Jeff's name.

Weakly, a voice finally came to her . . . "Mom?"

The top of the hill. She heard a car pass on the road a hundred yards below. Stumbling, she found herself on the opposite slope in a small clearing. Jeff's voice had come from somewhere around here. There! Jeff's bright yellow T-shirt with the Puma logo. She ran across the clearing and threw herself down next to him.

Blood everywhere. Dark and brackish. Sticky. The entire right side of his body was covered in blood. Even his tousled brown hair was matted with it.

"Mom," he said again, and closed his eyes.

Girl Scout life-saving classes . . . *find the wound, stop the bleeding* . . . her fingers probed something hard, almost metallic. Oh God! His bone! It's exposed. Eyes stinging, she wiped away enough blood to see the wound clearly. It was horribly clean and deep.

She ripped the belt from Jeff's jeans and picked up a sturdy stick, for the first time noticing a rifle that lay nearby. The small, familiar body was so still, so limp. And his face had become almost colorless.

His baby name came to her lips. "Jeffy . . . Jeffy . . ."

Swiftly Donna slipped the belt around Jeff's arm and moved it as high as possible, all the way to the shoulder. She pulled tight and cinched it, then shoved the stick between the belt and the flesh and began twisting.

The flow of blood stopped. She wrapped the slack around the stick to hold the belt in place and stood up, pulling Jeff's sagging body with her.

She marveled at how heavy an eleven-year-old boy could be as she pushed downhill, not able to protect Jeff from sharp branches.

In a matter of seconds she was out of the woods, solid asphalt under her feet. A car had just passed the spot where she emerged. "Help, stop, please . . ."

The car continued down Clapboard Hill Road.

"Please," Donna moaned.

She turned uncertainly toward their driveway, suddenly weary and confused. Reaching the road had been her goal. Everything would be all right when she reached the road, she had thought.

Brakes screeched behind her and she turned to see Ben jump from his car.

"Donna! God, what's happened?"

"Hurt . . . up there in the woods . . . blood all over. Ben, I can't feel him breathing any more . . ."

Ben took their son from her arms. "No, he's breathing, hon. I swear he is."

"The ambulance?"

"Coming. They said they'd be right here." His face was ashen. "Harry did this? He admitted it?"

"Yes."

"I'll kill him, I promise you."

She had never heard Ben speak so matter-of-factly about such an act. It made her shiver. The high, rude wail of a siren cut through her fear. The ambulance came around the curve at high speed, stopping barely in time to avoid a collision with Ben's station wagon. The driver and paramedic got out and came quickly toward them.

"What happened to him?" the driver asked.

"He's bleeding to death, I think he was shot or stabbed . . ." Donna found herself talking in sobs.

They took Jeff from his father's arms and carried him to the back of the ambulance. Ben and Donna stood back while they carefully lifted Jeff into the ambulance and strapped him to a stretcher.

When Donna slid in next to Jeff, the paramedic took her arm. "I'm sorry, passengers aren't allowed—"

Ben's hand closed on the man's shoulder.

"Hey!"

"My wife will ride in the ambulance. I'll follow in my car. Now move!"

"Listen, you can't—"

The driver cut him off. "Let's roll, Charlie."

"If the dispatcher hears about this . . ."

"To hell with the dispatcher. He doesn't have a kid who's bleeding all over the place." The driver jumped out the rear door, leaving Donna alone in the ambulance with Jeff and the paramedic, who quickly put aside his annoyance as he checked Jeff's vital signs. "He's breathing, and the bleeding has stopped. I'll have to loosen that tourniquet just a skosh, he could lose the arm otherwise . . ."

The driver was behind the wheel by then and the ambulance took off, siren screeching. The sound crescendoed as a Westport police car caught up with them. Donna heard the ambulance driver talking over his radio. She realized he was speaking to the officer behind the wheel of the police car when they waved to each other and the car zoomed in front of them.

They made a three-car convoy: the police leading the way, the ambulance following and Ben's car bringing up the rear. Within a minute they had reached the Sherwood Island ramp to the Connecticut Turnpike and were heading south toward Norwalk hospital in a scream of speed.

At that point Donna began to have difficulty breathing. She found herself fighting for air, swallowing it down to no effect.

"You're hyperventilating." The paramedic gripped her shoulders with both hands. "Sit back, try to relax."

"I can't." She gulped, desperate for air. "Not until Jeff . . ." Her balance went and she felt herself tumble away into a private fog.

CHAPTER 10

SERGEANT EDDY Trelska, carrying a clipboard in one hand and a cup of steaming coffee in the other, used his shoulder to push open the door to Troop G's interrogation room.

A young Bridgeport Police Department plainclothes officer came quickly to his feet. "Sergeant Trelska?"

"Right. You must be Detective Hayes."

"Joe Hayes."

"And this is . . ."

"Gregory Anderson." Hayes indicated an even younger man, a boy of nineteen or twenty who sat at the end of a gray metal table that occupied most of the interrogation room. Greg Anderson stared at Trelska in nervous concentration. He was neatly dressed, with dark shoulder-length hair and a puffy pretty-boy face marred by a mild case of acne.

Trelska put his cup on the table and shook hands with Detective Hayes. "Nice to meet you. D'you want some coffee? There's a Silex next door, and extra cups. Help yourself."

"Thanks." Hayes's eyes went to Anderson. "Can I sit in on the interview?"

"Sure, I could use your help."

Hayes looked grateful. "Be right back."

Trelska sat down across from the suspect and studied a file that had come to him by messenger from the Bridgeport PD. When he looked up, Anderson was still staring at him nervously. "Did Detective Hayes read you your rights?"

"No, some other guy did." Anderson cocked his head. "Am I under arrest or something?"

"Of course not," Trelska said. "But you were Catherine Scarnato's boyfriend. Naturally we're interested in talking to you."

"Then why all this stuff about 'rights'?"

"In a murder case we tend to do that automatically. I'm sorry if you were offended. You're entitled to have an attorney here while I'm interviewing you. I'm sure you were told that." He carefully avoided the word *questioning.*

Anderson tossed his long hair and drummed his fingers on the table. Trelska could see he was debating whether it might look better, and make things move faster, to decline an attorney.

"I don't need one, I've got nothing to hide."

Trelska let out his breath. "Whatever you say, Gregory. Do they call you Gregory, or Greg?"

"Greg."

Hayes came back into the room with two cups of coffee, one of which he offered to Anderson. "This is black. There's cream and sugar if you need it."

"Black is fine," Anderson said, visibly relaxing.

Trelska was pleased with Hayes's contribution to settling down the suspect. "We're going to tape-record this conversation, Greg. You may know something about the killer without realizing it, and we wouldn't want to miss anything. Now, when did you hear about the Scarnato girl's murder?"

"Yesterday morning, on the news. It was terrible. I ran upstairs and threw up, just made it to the toilet."

"You live with your parents?"

"Summer and holidays I'm home. Most of the year I'm in school."

"You and the girl were in the same year at Holy Cross?"

"Yes, Cathy and I were juniors this year."

"When did you last see the Scarnato girl?" Trelska noticed a

164

muscle jump along Anderson's neck. "I'm sorry, would it be better if I called her Cathy?"

"Yes."

"All right, when were you last with Cathy?"

Anderson squirmed a bit. "Sunday up on the Cape. And then while I drove her down here."

"You mean Cape Cod?"

"Sure."

"At The Red Snapper in Truro?"

Anderson pursed his lips. "Who told you that? Molly?"

"Yes, we've been in touch with Miss Henderson."

He laughed nervously. "I get it, she told you Cathy and me were arguing."

Trelska said nothing.

"I suppose she told you I slapped Cathy, too." Anderson threw up his hands. "Yeah, I guess I did. But it didn't mean anything. Little disagreement, that's all."

"She wanted to go home," Trelska said. "You wanted her to stay on the Cape for a few more days."

"Umm," Anderson murmured, squirming again.

"The two of you occupied a single room at the Holiday Inn in Hyannis, is that right?"

"Umm."

"Molly was staying in Truro?"

"Yeah, she has a cousin there."

"Greg, I have here a copy of a report filed last February eighth by a campus security guard at Holy Cross. You and Cathy had a loud argument in the lobby of her dormitory, so loud that the security office had to be called. You hit her that time, too."

"No!" Anderson leaned forward, his face flushed and the pretty-boy face twisted in a pout. "I gave her a push, that's all. The security guard overreacted. You know those guys, frustrated FBI agents."

"Cathy had a black eye the next day. That's a matter of record, she was treated at the campus infirmary."

"It wasn't that simple."

"What about Sunday night, Greg?"

"I *knew* it. You guys are so incompetent . . . that's the

word . . . you'll try to blame these things on the nearest person. Well, I sure didn't kill Cathy. She was my *girl.* Okay, we had a lot of fights. She thought I was 'immature,' her favorite word. After the argument at The Red Snapper, I agreed to drive her home to New Jersey. But on the way she got on my case again. *You shouldn't be so moody. You should study harder, get better grades.* I told her I wanted a girl, not a mother. Finally she said to drop her off on the Merritt, she'd hitchhike the rest of the way home. I know, I shouldn't have, but I was bugged. So that's what I did."

Trelska was feeling it. This kid fit the profile of a rapist-killer almost perfectly. He knew the victim. He had a history of violence and a previous criminal record for sexual assault. And according to the administration office at Holy Cross, he was seeing the school psychiatrist for "severe adjustment problems."

"Exactly where did you drop her off, Greg?"

"The Trumbull exit."

"What time?"

"About ten o'clock."

Trelska could feel Detective Hayes straining to get into the act. "Hayes, anything you want to ask?"

The young cop was like a Doberman going for a throat. "You were arrested for child molesting a few years ago, Greg. Is that what Cathy meant by *immature?*"

"*No.* She didn't know anything about that." Anderson laid his chin on his chest. "No one's supposed to know. I was only thirteen, a 'youthful offender.' The arrest wasn't supposed to go on my record."

"It didn't," Trelska assured him, "but people remember those things. One other question, Greg. Where did you go after you dropped Cathy on the Merritt, and what time did you get home?"

"I went straight home. Got in at ten thirty. You can ask my folks, we watched TV together." The sullenness fell away as he remembered he was safe. He had an alibi. "Our neighbor, Mrs. Wilowiskz, was there. We all watched that extra-innings Mets game until twelve thirty, then had some coffee and cake. She'll remember."

Hayes made the mistake of looking disappointed, which cheered Anderson even more.

"Yeah, she'll remember. Ask her. Say, can I get out of here

now? There's a wake for Cathy over in New Jersey. I want to go."

The door opened and Lieutenant Jim Conde stuck his head into the interrogation room. "Excuse me, can I see you for a minute, Eddy?"

"Sure." Trelska stopped the tape recorder. "Relax, Greg. We're just about wrapped up here." He joined Conde and Max Harris, the state prosecutor, in an adjoining room equipped with a two-way glass through which Greg Anderson and Detective Hayes could be seen drinking coffee together. "What do you think?"

"You don't have enough to hold him," Harris said. The state's attorney pulled apart his pipe, blew through the stem and shoved the two pieces back together. "Turn him loose right now. And if you bring him in again later, *insist* that he consult an attorney."

Conde responded to the disappointment in Trelska's face. "The Bridgeport PD talked to Anderson's parents and their neighbor. All three confirm that the boy got home from Cape Cod about ten thirty Sunday night and watched television with them for a couple of hours. Then they had a snack together. The Scarnato girl died during that time period."

"If the coroner was mistaken by only one hour, Anderson could have killed her," Trelska pointed out.

"Even then," Harris said, "there's no evidence he did. Only that he would have had the opportunity. And I don't think the coroner is wrong. She was found too soon for him to be wrong. If she'd been lying in the park for several days . . . but she was found Monday morning."

Trelska shrugged. "Okay, I'll kick him loose. That rookie detective—Hayes—will have a heart attack. He thought he was Bringing In The Killer."

"Maybe he was"—Harris sighed—"but you can't prove it, and I don't want Anderson interrogated for one more minute without evidence he's implicated."

"Keep turning the suspects," Conde said. "Let me know when someone else starts to look dirty."

"Will do."

Conde looked at his sergeant approvingly. "You're really hustling on this case, Eddy."

Trelska adopted a modest pose. "A pretty young girl like that,

I just want to nail the bastard who killed her." He hitched up his belt and, like a man, stepped next door to tell Anderson he was free to go.

AT THE DIMATO Funeral Home in Newark, Teresa Scarnato sat hunched in the front row of chairs making the guttural sounds of a wild animal. The same women from the previous night took turns offering words that gave no comfort and hugs that did not warm.

Catherine's body had arrived at the funeral home at six A.M. The most skillful mortician in New Jersey had been standing by to disguise the bruises on her neck and mold the shrunken mouth into a serene smile.

A stream of people entered and left DiMato's. To Tony Scarnato's surprise, he knew less than half of them. The others were Catherine's high school and college friends and people who knew her from the community work she had done in the Newark ghetto in past summers.

Because he couldn't bear to look at the dead shell of his daughter, Tony Scar stood at the back of the room greeting each new visitor and thanking them for coming as they left. It was exhausting work. He had been pleasant to more people in this one day than in all the previous years of his life. The funeral the next morning would be almost a relief from this everlasting hand-shaking.

After lunch the crowd thinned to primarily close family and friends. Scarnato asked his brother Fredo, a hat manufacturer who lived in Philadelphia, to take his place greeting people while he relaxed for a few minutes.

In a room that had been set aside for him, Scarnato made a few business calls that wouldn't keep. While he was talking, Sal Genovese and Vincent Malle returned from their appointments. As soon as he put down the phone Scarnato asked about Trelska.

"He's ours," Genovese reported. "You were right about him, Tony. A punk, but well-placed. The reason we're late, Trelska has already called the number I gave him. He told my man he's got a live one. We'll find out what that means tonight. I'm meeting Trelska at six o'clock in Connecticut."

Tony Scar grunted. "Pictures?"

Malle took a set of eight-by-ten-inch black and white photos from a manila envelope and handed them to his boss.

Scarnato leafed through them. Each photo showed Trelska grinning over a wad of currency. You could even see the denomination of the bills. "You missed your calling, Vincent. This is award-winning photography."

"Is my family here?" Genovese asked.

"Yes, Maria and your daughters are sitting with Teresa. Go and see them. I want a few words with Vincent anyway."

When Genovese had left, Scarnato said. "Did you get the second set of pictures?"

Malle took from his pocket an Olympus 35-millimeter camera small enough to fit in the palm of his hand. "Right here. I haven't had a chance to develop them; I've been with Sal all morning. But I snapped a few of Trelska, the money *and* Sal."

"No hurry, they'll just go in the kitty with the others."

Scarnato knew Genovese would someday make a move against him. Toward that day he had been putting away in the personal vault in his home a file containing photos, tape recordings and documents that could be used to send Genovese to prison for life.

Malle slipped the camera back into his pocket. "Tony, how does Catherine look? I mean . . . can you tell what happened to her?"

"No." Scarnato massaged his temples. "They did a good job with her. Did you see the people out there? We've had a couple hundred visitors, even niggers and P.R.s. I'll tell ya, Vincent, it makes me proud to know my girl had so many friends."

"She was always doing for others," Malle said, choking up. "I want to look at her, but I'm afraid."

Scarnato patted Malle's arm. "Go ahead. She'd want you to say goodbye." Malle left and Scarnato went over to a table where a cold buffet had been set up for him. He realized he'd had nothing to eat for more than thirty-six hours. That didn't make him any hungrier, but he felt he must maintain his strength. Listlessly, he made himself a roast beef sandwich with Swiss cheese and opened a bottle of beer. He was surprised to find that taking some nourishment immediately raised his energy level.

Later, after washing his face and splashing on some lotion, he went out to find that the crowd had built up again. Vincent sat in a chair near the coffin, weeping silently into his hands. A good man, Scarnato thought. Bringing him into the family was the best idea I ever had.

Resuming his post by the door, he again began welcoming people. The only visitors he failed to acknowledge were cops; there were two of them, one a detective Scarnato knew from the Newark Police Department and the other a federal officer of some kind. They were just standing around scanning faces.

At about two o'clock a young man with long dark hair appeared, halted indecisively at the doorway, then approached Scarnato. "Excuse me, you're Cathy's father, aren't you?"

"Yes."

"I'm a friend of hers from school. I just wanted to tell you, sir, how terrible I feel about this. It's just awful, a complete waste of a beautiful person. Cathy was very special."

It was a moment before Scarnato could speak. The young man's words had unsettled his carefully controlled emotions. Ordinarily he couldn't stand long-haired kids, or men whose features were pretty. But he felt grudging affection for someone who could so perfectly sum up his own feelings. "Thanks for saying that. You were in school with Catherine? Maybe she mentioned your name."

"Greg Anderson. I was . . . we'd known each other since last year." He looked around. "There'd be more Holy Cross people here if this wasn't the summer break. They're scattered all over the East Coast."

"I'm glad you could come, Greg. It's good to know Catherine was so well liked." A nice boy, he thought, turning his attention to others.

IT WAS MIDAFTERNOON before Trelska found an opportunity to run a Xerox copy of the reports on Greg Anderson and dupe the tape of the interview. Anderson probably wasn't the killer, but Scarnato would certainly be interested to know that the kid had roughed up his daughter and then dropped her on the Merritt instead of driving her all the way home. He might even pay a bonus for this stuff.

As thoughts of money came into his mind. Trelska reached into his desk drawer and pulled out a stack of unopened bills. They'd been sitting there for days while he thought about how he was going to pay his debts. Now that he had money, he might as well run a total.

He quickly opened each envelope and set out the bills in a stack. Several were marked *Second Notice* or *Final Notice.* He tossed away the duplicates and used a calculator to add them up.

The final sum made him sick. More than eleven thousand dollars. Shitfire. Ginger must be crazy. Look at the crap she's bought —dresses and coats and shoes and nightgowns and beauty treatments and gold chains and gourmet food and videotapes and figure-skating lessons and a string of pearls and a dog. A dog? A blooded Yorkshire terrier, the bill said, though Trelska had never seen the damned thing. It must have been a present for someone. And figure-skating lessons? Those were charged to his bank card in May. Who the hell took ice-skating lessons in *May?*

His twenty-five thousand dollars had shrunk to fourteen thousand. Maybe less, if there were still more of Ginger's bills to come in. He still had enough to buy the BMW, but the Bahamas trip was definitely off.

He swept the bills into his drawer and vowed to retrieve his charge cards from Ginger that very night, even if he had to break her goddamn arm to get them.

HARRY SAT IN a Stamford bar drinking Wild Turkey bourbon by the shot and thinking about Jeff. If only Jeff had been less gutsy, a little snot with buck teeth and pimples. If only he hadn't been *me.*

So the kid wasn't dead. He'd seen the ambulance streaking down Clapboard Hill Road and later he'd phoned all the hospitals in the area. Jeffrey Ryder was in Norwalk hospital "in serious condition." Harry didn't know whether he was relieved or disappointed.

"Bartender, some telephone change, please."

Harry exchanged a dollar bill for quarters and dimes and retreated to a phone booth. With the door firmly closed, he dialed the number of the New Canaan Police Department and asked to speak to the chief of police. The chief had left for a meeting, but the watch captain was available. "I would like to speak with him," Harry said.

A moment later a strong voice said: "Captain Rice speaking."

Harry replied in what he hoped was a convincing European-type accent, "Hello, sir. I am pleased that you are speaking with me. I have an urgent communication."

"Yes, what can I do for you?"

"The poor child who is found dead in the park. You know of whom I am meaning?"

"The Scarnato girl," Rice said with more interest. "What about her?"

"I am living in this area. And I am seeing something the night the child was killed. A gray station wagon automobile. Connecticut license SF 1877. You are understanding?"

"Yes, I have the number. SF 1877. What about the car? What does it have to do with the girl's death?"

"I am driving by the park late Sunday night and that car is almost hitting me. It is coming out of the park fast. Too fast, which is why I make sure to write down the number. I am angry, I think I may report him. But I do not. Then I read about the terrible crime."

"What's your name, sir?"

"No. I must not be involved. I am working, sir, for my citizenship. This is important to me, to be a U.S. citizen. I must not jeopardize that, above all, with involvement in this unhappy affair."

"Sir, there's no reason—"

Harry hung up the phone. Smiling, he returned to his stool at the bar.

The bartender came over with the bottle of Wild Turkey. "Another one?"

"I drink Wild Turkey only when I'm depressed. At the moment, my spirits are revived. Bring me a champagne cocktail."

Chapter II

THE DOCTOR who had cared for Jeff in the emergency room was named Hollis. Emergency wasn't his responsibility. He had just happened to be there when Jeff came in and had stepped into the case. At Ben's request, he was continuing to treat the boy.

He took Ben down the hall into a small, sparsely furnished conference room and ordered him to sit down. "Try to relax, Mr. Ryder. You probably don't realize that your teeth are chattering and your skin is cold to the touch. You're on the verge of going into shock."

Dr. Hollis pressed two tablets into Ben's hand. "Take these. Chew them, that's it." He draped a blanket around Ben's shoulders. Although Dr. Hollis was dour and overly precise, he managed to convey a genuine sense of concern. "Sit quietly. I'll return in half an hour. While I'm gone a nurse will look in on you. Don't worry, I'll answer all your questions. For now, be assured your son is going to be all right." He smiled and left the room.

Ben's mind was a whirlwind of images. The paramount one was of Jeff *and* Donna being lifted from the ambulance on stretchers. Apparently she had fainted in the ambulance. Only one thought remained constant: *I'll kill Harry for this.* Never before had he seriously considered taking a life, but he now knew there was no other way to rid himself of his brother.

After a few minutes the tablets began having an effect. The iron ball in his stomach grew lighter. His shoulder muscles loosened. His arms lost some of their rigidity. A nurse occasionally looked into the room and smiled reassuringly. After about forty-five minutes of that, Ben decided to go looking for Donna and Jeff and to give a lot of trouble to anyone who tried to stop him. His determination became academic with the return of Dr. Hollis.

"Sorry," he said, "I was checking your wife's X rays for a possible hairline fracture." He subdued Ben's alarm with a wave of his hand. "Don't worry, the X rays were only a precaution. Mrs. Ryder passed out in the ambulance and cracked her forehead on an oxygen tank. That's one good reason passengers aren't allowed to ride in the ambulance . . . they're always fainting or throwing up. Keeps the paramedics from attending to the patient. Of course I can understand why she wanted to be with your son—"

"How is Jeff?"

"He's in serious condition, but he'll recover. The loss of blood was substantial, so he's very weak right now. Fortunately the cut was clean and missed both the cephalic and basilic veins. He would certainly have died if either of those major veins had been severed. The wound went straight down the length of his biceps. It's too early to be certain, but I doubt that he'll lose any function in that arm."

"So he was stabbed. Is that what you're saying?"

"Yes." He looked at Ben closely. "Feel strong enough to see him?"

Ben got to his feet. "Sure, let's go."

"We'll pick up Mrs. Ryder on the way."

They rode an elevator back down to the emergency area, where Dr. Hollis ushered Ben into a treatment room. Donna was sitting on an examination table looking pale but otherwise healthy except for a butterfly bandage on her forehead. "Ben . . . how is Jeff? No one's said anything . . ."

"He's doing well," Dr. Hollis cut in. "In fact, you'll be surprised at how lively he is. Come along, you'll both feel better when you've talked to him."

Ben helped Donna to her feet and they kissed. She looked completely self-possessed, but he could feel the tension humming

174

through her. "Dr. Hollis says Jeff will recover completely. He won't even lose any mobility in that arm," he told her.

"That's not a certainty," Dr. Hollis cautioned. "Here we are."

They went into a private room where Jeff was lying with his right arm propped up on a pillow. It was heavily bandaged from elbow to shoulder. There was still no color in his face, but his bold eyes snapped with pleasure at the sight of his parents. "Hey, look at me, *The Mummy's Hand.* Remember that old movie?" He exhibited his wounded arm with pride.

"You little jerk." Donna's laugh shortened to a sob as she pressed herself gingerly against Jeff's small form and pelted his face with kisses.

"Aw, cut it out."

"He looks . . . good." Ben was amazed. The last time he had seen Jeff, his son appeared to be dying.

"Youth," Dr. Hollis said. "It's amazing what those tough young bodies can take. As soon as we put some blood into him, he came back very quickly. Well, I'll leave you now. We'll talk again later. Have a good visit, then let Jeff get his rest. He's weaker than he looks."

"Thanks, doctor."

Jeff's eyes were going back and forth between his parents in awed fascination. "Wow! Is all that *mine?*"

Ben and Donna were suddenly made aware of the ugly bloodstains on the front of their clothing. An emergency-room nurse had swabbed the blood from Donna's bare arms but not from Ben's. He could only admire the cool professionalism of the hospital staff; no one had made them feel uncomfortable about the way they looked.

"Yes, it is. Jeff, do you feel like talking about what happened?"

"You *bet.*"

There was a short *pro forma* knock on the door and Lieutenant Jim Conde came in, his hat held behind him as if he were ashamed of it. "Excuse me, Dr. Hollis said it would be all right if I came in."

"What the hell for?" Ben said in a rising voice. "This didn't happen." His arm swept toward Jeff. "This is a figment of my imagination . . . like Harry."

"I'm sorry your son has been hurt," Conde said evenly. "When I saw the report, I went straight to your house." He smiled at Jeff and moved closer. "Hello, I'm glad to see you looking so chipper. My name is Jim Conde. Lieutenant Conde." He turned to Ben again. "I found your front door open and two technicians from Crane Security on the premises. They had a work order showing they'd been hired to check your home for listening devices. In the interest of . . ." He dropped his cop's "official report" manner. "Well, let's just say I wanted to know whether you were bugged too, so I told them to go ahead and sweep the house. Afterwards I locked up and asked the Westport PD to leave a man there until this incident is cleared up." He gave Donna a look. "Don't you want to know what the Crane people found?"

Ben shrugged. "I'm sure they found nothing. It doesn't matter." He ignored Conde. "You were going to tell us what happened, Jeff."

"This concerns me too." Conde brought out his notebook, annoyed that no one was paying much attention to him.

Jeff was enormously pleased to be the central figure in a melodrama. Though he seemed more tired than just a few minutes before, he launched enthusiastically into his story. "Well, I figured out what Uncle Harry was up to. He has a car just like ours, a cream station wagon. I saw it parked on the road last night and guessed he was watching our house from somewhere on the hill." He licked his lips, which were dry from dehydration. His expression became wary. "I'm sorry, but I borrowed Tony's .22 and took it there this morning. I waited, and after a while Uncle Harry came up the hill."

Donna was the only other person in the room who had been on that hill. The scene came back to her with nightmare clarity—the fallen tree, blood-soaked leaves, a .22 rifle on the ground, Jeff lying there like a broken toy. She wanted to add her own observations but couldn't find the words.

Jeff had paused to sip from the water glass on his tray. He pushed away the straw and continued eagerly, but there was a feverish haste to his words and his eyes were glassy. "I caught him, all right . . . got the *drop* on him too. Wasn't sure at first . . . he was wearing a . . . fake mustache and glasses . . . but when he took them off, dad . . . when he took them off . . . it was you! I swear it. And then he jumped me." Jeff's eyes began to flutter and he began to have trouble holding up his head. "I shot at him . . . twice . . . and scared him good. Wait'll Tony hears. One of the bullets hit a tree . . . gonna

176

dig it out and drill a hole through it, wear the bullet around my neck on a chain. That'll be neat. Okay, mom? Didn't know Uncle Harry had a knife until . . ." In mid-sentence Jeff's voice trailed off and his eyes closed completely.

Donna snatched up the call cord and punched the button to ring for a nurse.

Ben moved to soothe her. "It's okay. Exhaustion, loss of blood. He just fell asleep."

"I know, but I want a nurse to look at him." Donna fidgeted until the nurse came to check Jeff's blood pressure and pronounce him resting comfortably.

"Let's step outside," Conde suggested. They went into the hall and down the corridor to an outdoor patio where patients sometimes sunned themselves. It was empty except for an elderly man in pajamas and robe who was asleep in a wheelchair in a far corner.

Conde asked Donna if she'd like to sit down, offering her a nearby bench. When she refused he became almost curt. "I thought you might still be shaky." He paused, flipping through the pages of his notebook. "Look, you're sore because you kept telling me something was wrong and I brushed you off. Well, your story was flaky. No good cop would have bought it. For one thing, there was no evidence of a crime. Now there is. So try to forget our disagreements and tell me what happened this morning."

Donna sighed. "Ben had gone to his office and I was at home when the phone rang. I picked it up—"

"What time did it ring?"

"About ten thirty. Perhaps a quarter to eleven."

"You can't pin down the time any closer?"

"Nearer to ten forty-five. I'm sorry, that's the best I can do."

"Go on."

"At first I thought I was talking to Ben. Then I realized it was *Harry* on the phone—"

"Excuse me, why did you think you were talking to your husband?"

"Because he sounds just like Ben."

"Had you ever talked to Harry before today?"

Donna shook her head. "No, never."

"Then how do you know it *wasn't* your husband?"

Ben started to say something but Donna waved him off. "Because of *what* he said." She repeated Harry's obscene invitation. "Ben doesn't talk that way. Then he told me he'd hurt Jeff, talked about sending flowers to his funeral. God . . . he was so cold . . . I ran upstairs—"

"Why do you think he'd attack your son and then call to tell you about it?"

"To rub it in," Ben snapped. "That's his *game.* I've told you that."

"I ran outside and called for Jeff," Donna went on. "Thank God he heard me and still had the strength to answer." She touched the butterfly bandage on her forehead. "The rest you know."

Conde shifted his questions to Ben. "Do you recall what time your wife phoned you?"

"As she said, about a quarter to eleven."

"You can't place it any closer either?"

"No."

"Were the technicians from Crane still at your office?"

"You've already talked to them. Isn't the answer right there in your little book? Anyway, the answer is no. There were two of them . . . Leary and Marchand . . . and they left a little before Donna called me, said they needed additional equipment from their office. I was supposed to meet them at eleven at my house."

Conde put away his book. He was no longer after facts. What he wanted now was a reaction, and he wouldn't see it with his nose buried in a notebook. "Do you own a false mustache? Or a pair of plain glasses?"

"You're *crazy,* " Donna said.

"No, I don't own either of those things," Ben said, fighting for calm.

"I must tell you that you have the right to remain silent. You also have the right to consult an attorney. If you can't afford an attorney, the court will appoint one to represent you. Do you understand?"

"Yes." Ben didn't blink, wouldn't give the s.o.b. the satisfaction.

"Did you leave your office and return home, Ben? Did you park on Clapboard Hill Road and go up the hill wearing some sort of theatrical disguise? Did you meet your son on the hill? Did he think,

178

after all the ugly stories you must have told him about your brother, that *you* were Harry? Did he try to stop you with that borrowed rifle? Did you, accidentally or otherwise, inflict a knife wound on Jeff? Did you then drive the three miles back to your office and call your wife, warning her that your son had been hurt, but talking in a way that would make her think it was your brother?"

The questions came in a flat, staccato style, to provoke an emotional outburst from Ben. Instead Donna went after him. "You blind, stupid idiot. You're saying *Ben* stabbed Jeff? His own son? You're crazy . . ."

Conde stepped back smartly as Ben took hold of his wife's shoulders. "Sshh, hon. Let him say and think what he wants. It's us against Harry. We're on our own. So be it . . ."

"Mrs. Ryder, I have to tell you I think your husband is a sick man," Conde said.

Donna's angry reaction to that awakened the elderly man in the wheelchair, who blinked around in confusion. "Is it dinner, or only time for one of those damned enemas? Lord, how I hate those things."

Ben continued to try to restrain Donna. "Forget him," he said. "I've got to find Sharon. She doesn't know what's happened."

"Sharon! Oh God, yes, she's probably still at the beach. Go ahead while I watch Jeff."

"All right. I'll bring you some clean clothes from home." To Conde: "I'm free to go?"

"Yes." He'd tried for a reaction, and the one he'd gotten was revealing. Ben Ryder was too calm. He was a man accused of trying to kill his own son and was completely calm. Which said two things: guilty, and crazy as a March hare. His accusations had been shots in the dark, but now he really believed in Ben's guilt. He'd seen plenty, too many, cases of mentally ill fathers hurting, even killing their kids.

But did he have a case? State's Attorney Max Harris would tell him.

"COME HERE." Oop put his arm around Sharon's waist and drew her across the beach towel. "Closer."

"Not here." Sharon eased away. They were on Compo Beach, having just returned from sailing the sound in Buzz Mann's Sunfish.

"Then tonight." Oop grinned, nuzzling her. "Maybe we'll play that game with the beads again."

Sharon laughed into her hand. "Where'd you learn it? From some other girl, I'll bet."

"No," Oop said seriously, "from a book a friend brought back from Japan. Sort of a picture book. The idea is to give people our age a way to enjoy each other, without actually having sex. The Japanese are much more realistic about those things."

"I'd like to hear you explain that to my parents."

"There are some things parents shouldn't know." Oop kissed her lightly on the neck. "It just makes them crazy."

Sharon closed her eyes and lay back, enjoying to the full Oop's attentions and the sun's warmth. There were so many contradictions to Oop. To many people he looked muscle-bound and dumb, but to her those primitive features were somehow very sexy. He impressed adults as a responsible young man, and that too was true. What adults usually didn't suspect was that Oop also possessed a tremendous sexual drive which he had learned to satisfy in highly imaginative ways.

"How are your parents today?" Oop asked.

They hadn't talked about "the problem" all day. It was a subject Sharon avoided because she was beginning to doubt that there was a problem. "Nervous, and testy with each other. I don't know, my dad may be going off the deep end on this thing."

Oop nodded judiciously. "I've wondered about that myself. He doesn't seem the unstable type, though. And someone had to send those ski suits and the champagne. Those things weren't imaginary."

"And there is . . . or was . . . an Uncle Harry." Sharon arched her neck. "But it's so wild to think of someone *going after* your own father, and so far we haven't seen or heard anything of Uncle Harry."

Oop leaned forward, staring across the beach. "Sharon, here comes your father. Hey, *look* at him."

She sat up and peered over Oop's shoulder. Her father had left the car double-parked on the street and was jogging toward them. His face was twisted from fatigue and his shirtfront splattered with blood.

She jumped up and ran toward him, Oop trotting at her side. "What *happened?*"

Ben stopped and waited for her, breathing heavily. "I'm sorry, I didn't mean to scare you. I should have gone home and changed first—"

"Are you hurt, Mr. Ryder?"

"No, Oop, I'm fine. But Jeff has been stabbed. His arm was cut and he's lost a lot of blood. He's in Norwalk hospital."

Sharon grabbed her father, too frightened to speak.

"Was it . . . your brother?" Oop asked.

"Yes. Jeff identified him."

"Did the police catch him yet?"

"No, only Jeff saw him. It happened on the hill by our house. Sharon, I'm going home to clean up and find fresh clothes for your mother. Pick up your beach stuff and come with me."

"Wait!" Oop said. "I don't mean to be disrespectful, Mr. Ryder, but there's the matter of the signal."

"Signal?"

"Yes, sir. I won't let you take Sharon away until you've given her the signal you set up. It was your rule. You could be . . . well, *you* could be Sharon's Uncle Harry."

"Oop," Sharon said, "this is no time for—"

"He's right," Ben said. "I'm glad you're thinking so straight, Oop." He tugged at his right ear. "Okay?"

Oop stepped back, his face red. "I'm sorry."

"Don't be. Just keep on using that brain of yours."

Sharon ran back to the spot where she and Oop had been sprawled and began stuffing things into her beach bag.

"I'll take Sharon to the hospital," Oop said, "she'll be safe with me, sir."

Ben looked at the thick cords of muscle along Oop's arms and shoulders. "Yes, I can see that. All right, and thank you." Sharon rejoined them. "Oop's taking you to the hospital. Tell your mother I'll be there soon."

"Yes, dad." Her eyes were bright, and wet. "Jeff had better be all right. I love that little creep."

"I know." Ben stared over her shoulder into the past. At your age, he thought, I felt the same way about my brother.

CHAPTER 12

THE PARKING lot at the Westport train station was Trelska's choice
for his second meeting that day with Sal Genovese. He would have
preferred a spot many more miles from Troop G, but things were
moving so fast that he could spare only an hour for dinner. Half a
dozen new suspects were being brought to Troop G for interviews.
They were all longshots, but longshots seemed to pay off more frequently in police work than at the race track.

He had specified that his contact should arrive at five thirty P.M.
in a car with a white flower fixed to the top of its aerial. He figured
Sal Genovese would be the contact again . . . this was too important
to Tony Scar, he wouldn't send an errand boy. Which was why
Trelska had selected a place where an extremely well-dressed man
wouldn't look out of place. At five thirty in the afternoon hundreds
of well-dressed men would be stepping off trains from New York at
the Westport station.

At five twenty Trelska was finishing a large slab of apple pie at
a small restaurant across from the station. The front window gave
him a perfect view of the parking lot. When he saw a blue Chevy with
a white flower on its aerial drive into the lot, he put down his fork,
asked for and paid his check.

He walked across the street watching casually for familiar faces,

183

saw none. The blue Chevy had parked in an area jammed with cars, a good spot for their purpose. Sure enough, Sal Genovese was behind the wheel. Trelska opened the door on the passenger side and slid in next to him.

"Hello, again, Mr. Genovese."

Genovese nodded curtly. "Eddy, what have you got?"

"Not the killer, but something your 'friend' will want anyway."

"You got me all the way over here for nothing? How many times do you think we can meet before someone spots us together? I thought you were smart, Eddy. Not brilliant, I never hoped for brilliant. But I thought you were a guy who could at least find his asshole with both hands."

Trelska ignored the outburst. He took a tape recorder out of a paper bag and pressed the play button. His interview with Greg Anderson began to play. Within seconds Genovese's scowl had disappeared. The Fixer listened intently. While he listened, Trelska showed him the documents he had brought—the Holy Cross security guard's report on Anderson's argument with Catherine Scarnato at her dormitory and Molly Henderson's statement.

When the tape finished playing, Trelska said, "Your friend's daughter would still be alive if Anderson had taken her all the way home, like he promised. Isn't that worth something?"

Genovese gave him a look. "You know what you've done to this Anderson kid, don't you?"

"No. I don't know, and I like it that way. All I'm doing is giving you a tape and some papers. Whatever happens, hey, it's none of my business, right?"

"The original innocent bystander." Genovese—a man capable of disgust, he'd have you know. "Give me the tape."

Trelska ejected the tape and dropped it into Genovese's hand. "This will cost you more money."

Genovese said nothing, waited.

"Another eleven thousand. The way I see it, this has nothing to do with fingering the girl's killer. The Anderson kid is extra."

"I gave you twenty-five thousand dollars this morning. What'd you do, paper your walls with it?"

"I want another eleven thousand," Trelska said.

No one ever jacked up the price on Genovese. That was the one unbreakable rule, the single taboo. He considered throwing the creep out of his car and sending three collectors to take back the twenty-five thou with baseball bats. But he needed Trelska—for the moment.

"You live in an apartment, don't you, Eddy?"

"Yeah, why?"

"Got a mailbox that locks?"

"Sure."

"Give me your key. Tonight I'll have someone put an envelope in your mailbox. In the morning you'll find the key under your doormat."

Trelska smiled, greed overcoming his better judgment. "That sounds okay." He brought out his key ring and separated the mailbox key from it. "Here you are."

As he accepted the key, Genovese thought how simple it would be to plant a bomb in the mailbox instead of an envelope full of cash.

Another time.

TRELSKA RETURNED TO headquarters in an expansive mood. The bluff, he convinced himself, had worked. Tomorrow morning his kitty would be up to twenty-five thousand dollars again.

He went at his work with new enthusiasm. One of the suspects was brought in, a computer salesman who lived in New Canaan and who had once served a deuce for rape. It took only a few minutes to establish that the salesman couldn't possibly have committed the crime; he had eyewitnesses to prove he was in Pennsylvania that night. The suspect was released.

His paperwork had been piling up, but one item caught his eye. He had asked one of the Southbury investigators to run a make on a license-plate number given to him by Captain Ed Rice of the New Canaan PD. Rice had gotten the number from an anonymous informant who claimed to have seen late Sunday night a station wagon pull out of the park where the girl was found. Connecticut MVD showed that the car was an Oldsmobile owned by Benjamin Ryder of Clapboard Hill Road, Westport.

The name seemed familiar, but Trelska had gone over so many names in the past two days that for a moment he couldn't place it. Ryder. Ryder. *Sure,* Ben Ryder . . . the guy who'd been bothering

Troop G the last few days. Since Monday morning, in fact—the morning after the murder.

Trelska started for Conde's office with the MVD report, but stopped before he reached the door. Genovese would want this information ahead of Conde, and producing the killer for him in a single day would really be a spectacular coup. But where would the profit be? If he called now, Genovese might decide to cancel that late-night deposit to his mailbox. No point in paying out eleven grand when you've already got the information you want. No, his best move was to give this to Conde first. Build up brownie points. He and Max Harris would move slow, deliberate, like always, still giving him plenty of time to sell Ben Ryder to Genovese . . . Who knows, I might milk me another bonus out of those wops.

He knocked briefly and went in to find the lieutenant and state prosecutor Max Harris in conference. Harris was fiddling with his pipe, as usual, while Conde sat with his large hands clasped thoughtfully on the desk.

"What is it, Eddy?"

Trelska stepped inside and closed the door behind him. "I think I know who killed the Scarnato girl, that's all."

Harris stopped playing with his pipe. "Go on, sergeant."

Conde looked at him suspiciously.

Trelska threw down the name like a gauntlet. "Ben Ryder."

"Where the hell did you come up with that?" Conde said. "He might have cut up his son, but how does that pin the Scarnato job on him?" He hid his ideas, but he wanted to draw Trelska out.

"Son?" Trelska shrugged. "I don't know anything about his son. Someone spotted Ryder's car coming out of the park Sunday night, and Ryder's been sniffing around here since Monday morning. That story about a crazy brother was a snow job. He wanted to find out what we knew. Didn't you see him in the squad room yesterday? He was eyeballing the evidence board."

"Slow down," Conde said. "Who saw Ryder's car coming out of the park?"

Trelska drew up a chair across from Conde and Harris and summarized Captain Ed Rice's conversation with the informant and the results of the MVD report on the license number. And then he asked, "What's this about Ryder's kid?"

"Someone stabbed his eleven-year-old son this morning. I think Ben Ryder did it himself," Conde said. "I talked to the boy in the hospital and he said it was Uncle Harry. Except he also said the man who cut him looked just like his dad. *It was you,* I heard him tell his father. I think the kid was closer to the truth than he knew."

All of which made Trelska even more excited. "Ryder's been feeding his son that bullshit about his twin brother coming after him, right? So the kid bought it. And now we know why Ryder's been insisting that his brother is alive. He needed someone to blame for the Scarnato girl's killing, in case we got too close. What a great alibi. *My twin brother did it.* When you told him the brother was dead, he should have dropped the story. Probably would have, but he was committed to it by then."

In spite of his built-in conservatism, Conde was caught up in Trelska's scenario. "It fits . . . Ryder'd told his family the brother was around. He even sent himself ski equipment and champagne and tried to make it look as if 'Harry' had bought them. No . . . he couldn't change his story after all that . . ."

Harris leaned forward. "Slow down, fellas. Legally, you haven't got a case. The boy says his uncle attacked him, and the informant who called Ed Rice didn't give his name. The caller could have been someone with a grudge against Ryder, a hatchet job to embarrass him. If the informant had come forward and given us a chance to question him, then we'd have some evidence. Anonymous calls aren't evidence, you know that."

"There's probably evidence in Ryder's house," Conde said, looking at Harris in a hopeful way.

Harris rubbed his bald head as if it were a talisman. "You want a search warrant? There's not a judge in Connecticut who'd give you a warrant on the basis of one anonymous call. If it was that easy, every cop who wants to search a home would only need to drop a dime. Forget it. You need something more, and it's called 'probable cause.' "

There was silence as each man regrouped his thoughts. Trelska poured himself a cup of coffee while Max Harris scraped at the bowl of his pipe with a tiny penknife. Conde knew that Harris wanted to go after a search warrant for him, but the prosecutor had rules to live by. That was okay with Conde. Mostly he believed in those rules.

"Well, I'd bet money," Conde said deliberately, "that the button we found by the girl's body came off a shirt of Ryder's. I wonder if it's still in his house."

"Maybe he threw it away," Trelska said, "or burned it. That's what I'd do."

"Or maybe," Conde said, "he doesn't even realize he lost a button that night. How many times have you sent a shirt to the laundry and discovered a week later, when you went to put it on, that there was a button missing?"

"Plenty," Trelska said.

And it occurred to Conde that maybe whatever had gone haywire in Harry Ryder's mind eighteen years ago might somehow have come alive in Ben Ryder today. Maybe it had been there all the time, a sort of virus of insanity, waiting to get out, be released. Twin brothers, twin mental disorders . . . "We need a psychiatrist," he said.

The way he said it made Harris laugh. "You sound like we're the ones who are crazy."

"I hope not, my hospitalization doesn't cover psychiatric care." Conde reached behind him and resurrected the printout he'd gotten from the California Law Enforcement Survey Center. "We need a psychiatrist to tell us how to approach Ryder, to understand him. Who's the best man for that sort of thing, Max?"

"Dr. Forrest Mendel," Harris answered. "I've used him as an expert witness a dozen times. He's not one of those shrinks who likes to show off his jargon. Mendel talks straight, thinks like a lawyer . . . don't tell him I said that, he'd consider it an insult."

"Can you get him?"

Harris jumped up, went to his battered old briefcase, from which he removed an address book that was even more aged. He tried to call Dr. Forrest Mendel at his home in Greenwich, but he was out. It took two more calls to reach him at a reception for the new director of the Yale School of Medicine. At first Mendel declined, saying his case load was already too high. But when Harris explained the nature of the case, he agreed to be at Troop G headquarters at nine the next morning.

"We've got him," Harris said triumphantly. "We'll work out a strategy in the morning, then bring in Ryder for questioning."

Conde nodded toward Trelska. "Eddy, keep the men churning

188

on other suspects. We could be wrong about Ryder. He might be pure as honey."

"Yes, sir. But what do we do about Ryder tonight?"

Conde looked to Max Harris, who shrugged his stooped shoulders. "We don't have a shred of admissable evidence. I want to see a transcript of the testimony from his brother's trial, and I'll contact the Los Angeles D.A.'s office for that myself. With luck we can have it here tomorrow morning by Federal Express."

"Meanwhile Ryder just sits?" Trelska asked.

Conde looked slantways at his sergeant. "Let's hope that's all he does."

THEY SAT IN the lounge at Norwalk hospital making awkward attempts at small talk. Donna looked feeble and exhausted. Sharon clutched Oop's large hand, her eyes red and frightened; her doubts about the danger from Harry had vanished with her first look at Jeff.

"It's no use all of us sitting around here," Ben said. "We should do this in shifts." He struggled to sound businesslike. "Donna, I'll take you home as soon as Dr. Hollis finishes with Jeff." She started to object, and he quashed it. "You're about to keel over, hon."

Dr. Hollis came out of Jeff's room and they all stood up. He waved them impatiently back into their chairs. "I've instructed the floor nurse that someone from the family will be allowed to sit up with Jeff all night, as you asked. The boy's strength and overall condition have improved dramatically, but it certainly won't hurt to have someone at his bedside."

"How long will Jeff have to stay in the hospital?" Donna asked.

"He can probably go home in two or three days."

"That soon?"

"Jeff is strong and the wound is a simple one. Loss of blood was his big problem, and we've offset that. He'll have to come back for regular examinations and to have his stitches removed. But he'll be up and around soon." Suddenly Dr. Hollis dropped his precise professional manner and said with real feeling, "I don't know who did this to your son, but I hope they send him away for as long as the law allows. One thing I've never learned to accept is the savaging of a child."

"Unfortunately," Ben said, "the police seem to think I did it."

"*You?* That's preposterous. If they'd seen you when the boy was brought in they'd never talk such rubbish. Send them to me, I'll straighten them out." He looked at his watch. "I have other patients to see. I'll look in on Jeff again tomorrow morning. Meanwhile, he should sleep the night through. I have him on a mild painkiller and tranquilizer. And antibiotics, to make certain that arm doesn't become infected. Goodnight, and let me suggest that both of you need rest as much as Jeff does."

"Why don't you two go home and try to rest," Oop suggested. "Sharon and I can stay with Jeff."

Ben shook his head. "We can't let you do that."

"I called my parents and told them what's happened. They said I could stay as late as I'm needed."

"Go on," Sharon urged.

Ben pressed his fingertips to his forehead, suddenly allowing himself to be aware of how tired he was. "It's seven o'clock. We'll be back at midnight. Oop, you've been great, we owe you."

Ben first went to the nursing station and introduced himself to the floor nurse, Mrs. Price. He explained that his daughter and her boyfriend would be staying with Jeff until midnight, when he and his wife would return to spend the rest of the night. Mrs. Price didn't appear happy with the arrangement but she had her instructions from Dr. Hollis.

He went back and collected Donna. "We'll see you kids at midnight. Call us at home if Jeff's condition changes in *any* way."

"I will," Oop promised.

CARTER PHILLIPS HAD been torn all his life between his desire for adventure and his need for security. Once in Princeton he and some friends had answered a newspaper ad for mercenary soldiers to fight in the Congo. When weeks drifted by without any reply Carter Phillips was secretly relieved. He wanted adventure, but he didn't want to die in some fly-infested outpost. After Princeton he had considered joining the army, or perhaps becoming a policeman, but neither occupation paid especially well.

Crane Security was the ideal compromise. He was highly paid

for his management and sales skills and, though he wasn't a field investigator, he was often associated with cases involving blackmail, fraud, industrial espionage and arson.

Sometimes, as he reviewed the file on one of those cases, he would find himself slipping into the role of a Sam Spade or Phillip Marlowe. For a few delicious minutes his imagination would take him down some dark street with his collar turned up and a snub-nosed .38 tucked in his belt. Fortunately, corporate headquarters considered him too valuable as an office manager to actually send him into such risky situations.

He was at home reading such a report from a field investigator when his phone rang. "Yeah . . . this is Phillips," he answered in his Sam Spade voice.

"Lieutenant Jim Conde, Connecticut State Police. I'm the commander of Troop G here in Westport. I think we've met."

Phillips quickly abandoned his Sam Spade persona. "Yes, sir. I believe we have. What can I do for you?"

"You're working for Ben Ryder. Reason I know that is I bumped into two of your men at his house."

"They told me you were there. Something about a boy being slashed?"

"Yes, Ben Ryder's son."

"I'm sorry to hear that." He wondered what this had to do with Crane Security. "You don't think any of our men were involved, do you? We're a reputable, bonded firm."

"No, I don't think that. I want to know if your technicians found any indication at all that Ryder's house has been bugged. I also want to know what other work you might be doing for him."

The question gave Phillips a queasy feeling. "I'm sure you know our relationship with a client is privileged."

"Tell me," Conde said. His voice held an implied threat.

Phillips didn't care for the tone. Sam Spade would tell him to go to hell, he thought. Phillip Marlowe would laugh and hang up the phone.

On the other hand, Conde would make it difficult for Crane Security to do business. Prospects were always calling the police to inquire about Crane's reputation, and there were state codes regarding agencies like Crane Security that could be enforced with a velvet glove—or an iron hand. Phillips cleared his throat. "We found no evidence of listening devices. No abandoned installations. Nothing. That applies to Ryder's office as well as his home. We also have investigators looking for a brother name Harold Raymond Ryder, whom Mrs. Ryder believes to be in Connecticut."

"Have you found any traces of him?"

"No, he's dead."

"But you're taking money to look for him." Conde snorted and hung up the phone.

Carter Phillips put down his own receiver with a bang. Arrogant damn cop, I ought to go down there and punch that wise-ass mouth of his. That's what Sam Spade would do.

With a regretful non-Sam Spade sigh he picked up the field investigator's report. It really made very exciting reading.

TONY SCAR COULDN'T stand another minute of it. He decided that the next person who said to him "She's with God now" would soon see God for himself. "Come on," he told Malle, "let's go across the street."

"Across the street" meant Nunzio's, a narrow little bar catering to truck drivers and laborers from a nearby chemical plant. Scarnato walked across the busy boulevard without looking to the right or left, and into Nunzio's.

Nunzio's eyes bulged when Tony Scar walked into his place. "Hello, Mr. Scarnato, nice to have you here, sir. I was planning to pay my respects later tonight. Your daughter was a beautiful girl, Mr. Scarnato. Beautiful. She's with . . ." He hastily changed the subject when Scarnato gave him a murderous look. "What can I get for you? On the house, of course."

Scarnato walked to the rear of the establishment without speaking and threw himself down onto the bench of the last booth.

"Johnnie Walker black label with ice on the side," Malle said, "and a draft beer for me. Miller's, if you've got it."

"Yessir, Mr. Malle."

Malle followed his employer to the back of Nunzio's and joined him in the booth. He studied the knuckles of his stumpy left hand while Nunzio bustled up and put a full bottle of Johnnie Walker, a glass, a bowl of ice and one draft beer on the table. When the proprietor left Malle said, "It's almost over, Tony. Another couple of hours, you can get some rest."

"It's like being whipped with chains, seeing Catherine dead and listening to those assholes talk about her. They act like they owned her, or something. She was *mine.*"

And mine, Malle thought, in a way you could never understand. "Two more hours. And the funeral tomorrow morning. Then it'll be over, Tony." He dropped some of the ice cubes into the glass and poured Scotch over them. "Have a drink, it'll help relax you."

They were still working on their first drink when Sal Genovese joined them. He sat down next to Malle, put a brown paper bag on the table and gave Nunzio's menu a cursory once-over. "Tony, there's a better place down the street. A French joint, frog's legs and everything. Let me take you over there, buy you a nice hot meal."

Scarnato looked pointedly at the paper bag. "Aren't you brown-bagging it tonight?"

"This is what our friend in Westport gave me."

"Oh? Is it what we need?"

"Not exactly. You'll be interested, though," Genovese glanced over his shoulder. "Nunzio, Campari and soda, in a clean glass."

"Yessir." Nunzio jumped for the Campari like a rabbit.

"The cops brought in a boyfriend of Catherine's this morning, sweated him and let him go. He didn't kill her, they're sure of that. But I gotta tell you, Tony, he was responsible for Catherine being on the Merritt Sunday night."

"Responsible? How? And who is this 'boyfriend' anyway?"

"His name is Gregory Anderson."

Genovese shut up when Nunzio appeared with his drink.

"Anderson . . . I know the name." The too-delicate face appeared in his mind. "Sure, he was at the wake this afternoon. Just what did he do to my Catherine?"

Genovese took a tape recorder out of the paper bag and inserted the cassette Trelska had given him. "I got to keep it low, we don't want these jerks to hear." He switched on the recorder and turned the volume down so that it would be audible only to those in the booth. The tape began with Eddy Trelska saying, "We're going to tape record this conversation, Greg . . ."

193

As the questions and answers droned on, Scarnato's expression went from blank incomprehension to red-faced rage to stony determination. He flipped through the documents Trelska had provided, and when the tape ended, punched the stop button so hard the machine broke.

His eyes fixed on Malle. "I want this person gone, Vincent. Tonight."

Malle glanced around the bar. "Not so loud, Tony."

"The bastard shook my hand this afternoon," Scarnato said. "He walked right into DiMato's and told me how terrible he felt, and all the time he knew he'd left my little girl on a dark highway to be killed." He poured another glass of Scotch and drank it down, wiping his mouth with the back of a hand. "Do it," he whispered, "and make sure he knows it's coming from me."

"You got it." Malle felt deeply guilty that Anderson had been able to treat Catherine so badly without immediate punishment. One of the documents on the table caught his eye, the suspect profile which listed Anderson's home address in Bridgeport. He picked up the sheet of paper and left Nunzio's with his face flushed with shame.

CHAPTER 13

HARRY PACED his apartment as he had paced the locked room at Camarillo for all those years. The luxurious condominium had begun to seem as confining as that small room. He had pushed too hard, gone through those woods once too often and thereby destroyed his advantage. His call fingering Ben to the police had been premature too. It should have been his parting shot after accomplishing everything else he had set out to do.

He had returned home depressed. A small boy had trapped and almost shot him. The bullet had only scarred the fleshy part of his underarm, but he would prize the scar as a reminder to do better.

What next, then?

At any moment now Ben would have his hands full with the police, which might provide an opportunity to put his hands on little Sharon. Ben's daughter intrigued him. He took her virginal looks as a personal challenge. Donna? A secondary goal. It would be a nice touch to use Donna's athletic body to humiliate Ben, but that wouldn't be a terminal blow. Their marriage looked too solid. However, Ben would come apart at the seams if Sharon were hurt. To have a daughter soiled . . . Sharon. Sharon. Sharon. The name rang out in his mind like a bell. A tocsin. It called. He visualized Sharon naked, terrified. The scene pleased him.

He reached for the telephone and dialed the number for Norwalk hospital. Might as well find out how Jeff was doing. The strange affection . . . attraction? . . . identification? . . . he felt for the boy was a weakness, he decided, like a craving for sweets. He questioned his own motives for calling Donna after he had slashed Jeff. At the time he thought it might be sport to taunt her with the knowledge of what he'd done. But was that his real reason for calling? Or was it to give her a chance to find the boy before he died? It was bothersome to think he might have such a *soft* spot.

"I'm calling about a patient, Jeffrey Ryder," he told the hospital switchboard operator. "Can you tell me what his condition is?"

"We don't give out that information over the phone."

"This is Dr. Edward Nelson."

"Oh, I'm sorry, sir. I'll connect you with the second-floor nursing station."

Moments later someone answered, "Miss Myerson."

Harry summoned up the officious voice doctors so often use with nurses. "This is Dr. Edward Nelson. I'm Jeffrey Ryder's pediatrician and I've just been told what's happened to him. What's the boy's condition?"

"He's stable, sir. Completely out of danger."

"Good, I'm relieved to hear that. Um . . . are Jeff's parents still there?"

"No, sir. They've gone home. They'll be back about twelve, I understand."

"Is anyone with the boy now?"

"Yes, his sister and a young man. Her boyfriend, I think."

Harry's pulse quickened. "Oh? And they'll be there until twelve?"

"Yes, doctor. I believe so."

"Well, I'll stop in and see Jeff in the morning. What room is he in?"

"Room 206."

"Thank you. Good night."

Harry softly put down the phone. So Sharon and her ape-man were alone at the hospital. Convenient. The boy wouldn't be a problem. He was obviously a low-grade moron. And Sharon would be in an emotional state over Jeff.

196

He got up and walked quickly into the bedroom, where he slid open the door to the closet holding his duplicate set of Ben's wardrobe. What would Ben wear for a late-night hospital visit? Something casual, clothes that could be thrown on.

After careful consideration he put on a pair of lightweight summer slacks, a blue pullover shirt identical to the one Sharon had given Ben on his last birthday, and loafers. He regarded himself. "Sharon, say hello to daddy."

EDDY TRELSKA LIVED in an apartment house in South Norwalk near the Connecticut Turnpike, a featureless two-story structure with minimum rent and maximum noise provided by the trucks that hauled along the turnpike at wide-open throttle twenty-four hours a day. One thing Trelska intended to change very soon was his apartment. His next place would be small but very tasteful. Westport, just off Post Road. That was the ticket.

He looked through the slots in his mailbox, but it was too early for Genovese's messenger to have left an envelope for him. He decided to set his alarm clock for three A.M. There was never an inconvenient time to collect eleven thousand dollars. But first he planned to take those damned credit cards back from Ginger.

The driving beat of rock music led him to his apartment. He went in and stooped just inside the door to pick up a pair of sandals and a brassiere from the floor. There was a cold half-eaten pizza on the couch and crumbs all over the carpet. The other half of the couch was littered with fashion and movie magazines. A pile of dirty clothes lay in one corner, wet towels and a sopping blue bikini could be seen on the floor just inside the bedroom and the dinette table was covered with lipsticks, face creams, nail polish, cuticle pushers, eyeliners, mascaras and other beauty aids. The funny thing was, she didn't need any of them.

Trelska turned down the blasting stereo. "Ginger, I'm home!"

"Hi, baby!" she called from the bedroom. "Be right out. Don't go away, I've got a surprise."

"A clean house would surprise me," he muttered, and began to straighten up. He dumped the stale pizza in the kitchen trash, swept the crumbs into a dustpan and wiped the Formica table where a bottle of nail polish had tipped over.

His temper rose with every small clean-up chore. Ginger was the worst slob in the world. Her own place looked like ground zero after an atomic blast, and now his apartment was getting just as bad. Look at that, *toenails* all over the chair. There was nothing so disgusting as a pile of cut toenails. He swept them onto a copy of *Soap Opera Digest* and tossed the whole mess into the trash.

Ginger's purse lay open on the coffee table. He was about to look through it for his credit cards when she came out of the bedroom.

"Hi, Eddy."

He swallowed hard. She was wearing a skin-tight lime-green blouse and slacks. Her red hair was tumbling and she smelled of oils and perfumes. Her face had the perfect blank beauty of a fashion model's, but her body glowed with a special power. Only her breasts were voluptuous; the other lines of her body were sleekly angular.

"D'ya like it? I made a special trip to B. Altman's today, in honor of the occasion."

"What occasion?"

The delicately painted lips formed a pout. "Two months ago today we met at Papa G's." She swung her hips in evocation of the music from the neon-lit disco. "Remember?"

"Yeah. You can sure move, baby." He pulled her to him. "Want to go dancing tonight?"

"If you do. I thought you might be tired, you were up so early this morning."

"Naw, it's been a great day." He thought of Sal Genovese, the packet of money, the bills resting in his desk drawer, the credit cards in Ginger's purse. "Papa G's?"

She nodded and stroked his cheek. "Afterwards, I've got something different planned. For starters."

"Different?"

"When I was a little girl I just loved to lick whipped cream off a long spoon." She nuzzled his neck. "So I was thinking today, I was thinking *yum,* wouldn't it be *delicious* to lick whipped cream off that fabulous cock of Eddy's? It'd be just like being a kid again, only better. So I went right out and bought myself a pint of Reddiwhip."

Trelska began to overheat. "And that's only for starters?"

"Oh, yes, Eddy. You know I always eat my dessert first."

The determination to retrieve his credit cards, which Trelska had been holding firmly in his mind, slipped away into whipped cream.

GREG ANDERSON HAD spent the early part of the evening watching television. Cathy's death had made him feel obligated to spend a quiet night at home, but after a while he became restless and decided to go out. He told himself it was useless to spend twenty-four hours a day mourning someone. Life was for the living, wasn't it?

He put on a pair of clean cords and a sports jacket and headed south on the Connecticut Turnpike for a disco in Port Chester that was supposed to be the new "in" place, a spot where lots of single chicks hung out. On the way down the turnpike he noticed a pair of headlights behind him all the way from Bridgeport to Stamford, which made him wonder if the police were still suspicious of him. He slowed down and moved over into the middle lane. The lights disappeared and he breathed easier.

The disco was located in a sprawling shopping center across the street from a Catholic hospital. He could hear the music as soon as he turned into the parking lot and wondered who the disco paid off to be allowed to make that much noise near a hospital. Lights, music, women. Greg Anderson felt better already. Cathy's gamin face appeared in his mind. He pushed it away. Maybe he wouldn't even go to the funeral. The wake had been enough.

He went into a barnlike building with a dance floor in the center, a bar along one wall and a balcony with tables overlooking the dance floor. The music was deafening. Red, yellow and blue lights flashed in rhythm with the music. Greg Anderson snapped his fingers and moved into the crowd, his mood on the rise.

"Hey, Roy!" he shouted, catching sight of a high-school pal from Bridgeport.

"Greg! Come on over!"

He pushed his way over to Roy Pease and they shook hands. "Hey, Roy, how ya doing, kid?"

"Good, Greg. Home from Holy Cross? You college guys have the life, on vacation half the year."

"I might be on permanent vacation soon. I didn't exactly make the dean's list this year."

"Flunked out?"

"Not quite. I'm on 'trial extension' next fall, which means I get kicked out if my grades don't come up in the first quarter."

"Tough." Roy Pease studied the women at the tables. "See anything you like?"

"I like everything I see. You made a move on anyone yet?"

"No, but I'm about to." Roy Pease made his way to a nearby table, where he asked a girl to dance. Greg ordered a stinger and sat back to study the talent. Plenty of foxy ladies, but not as many singles as he'd been led to expect and about a hundred horny guys trying to hit on those few who were alone. It would take real work to line something up here, and he wasn't partial to real work.

The waitress brought his drink. When he reached into his pocket she said, "All paid for, courtesy of the gentleman behind you. He said to make yours a double—on him."

"Paid for?" Greg Anderson twisted around to see a tall, good-looking guy in a white suit raise his drink in salute. At first he didn't recognize the face. Then he placed it—Sergeant Trelska, the cop who had interviewed him in Westport that morning.

He raised his glass and pantomimed a "thank you" over the music, then turned back to the dance floor. Weird, having a cop buy you a drink. He wondered why Trelska did that. The cop sure looked different in civies. Sharp. And that redhead with him—Va-voom.

Roy Pease didn't come back, and the waitress gave his chair to someone in a bigger party. It was irritating to watch Roy connect so quickly. Greg felt isolated and out of place. Even the loud music didn't help. He asked two girls to dance, but for some reason they both refused. Cows. He wouldn't even talk to them up at Holy Cross.

A hand clamped on his shoulder. "How are you, Greg? You like Papa G's?"

"Sure." It was Sergeant Trelska and his girl, stopping at his table on their way to the dance floor. "Hey, thanks for the drink."

"My pleasure." He pulled his girl closer. "Greg, this is Ginger. Ginger, say hello to my pal."

"Delighted," Ginger said.

"Say, how come you bought me the drink? I didn't think police did that for guys . . . well, guys they meet professionally."

"I owe you, Greg."

"Owe me? I don't get it."

"You will." Trelska squeezed his shoulder. "See you around."

They moved onto the floor and began dancing, Ginger throwing her sleek body around and Trelska following her with precision. They danced well together. Greg drank the stinger Trelska had bought him and wished he could connect with someone like Ginger. But more and more it seemed like just too much trouble. You talked and danced and bought them drinks and then they went off with someone like Trelska, some big jerk stud who took whatever he wanted. And they seemed to want it.

"Another drink?" the waitress asked.

"No, I'm leaving. Not enough action here."

The waitress shrugged and took away his empty glass. Greg Anderson gave up his table and made his way outside.

The night air had the heaviness of a steam bath. He walked toward his car, whistling a melody from an old Bee Gees album and fumbling through his pockets for car keys. At least he hadn't spent any money in there. As he was unlocking his car he somehow felt a presence behind him. Before he could turn, something hit him directly in the center of his back. He was driven into the car door and rebounded to fall to the asphalt.

He tried to cry for help, but the blow had temporarily deadened his senses. Numbness attacked his rib cage and limbs in radiating waves. Something was slapped over his mouth. He was rolled onto his stomach, his hands and ankles were swiftly bound and he was lifted and tossed into the back seat of a car parked next to his. A blanket was thrown over him. A door slammed and the car he was in began to move.

At first Greg was afraid he would suffocate. He could only breathe through his nose, his empty lungs demanded air. Eventually he inhaled enough so that he could breathe normally, but by then the pain in his back had become fierce. He struggled, seeking relief, found none. No question he was being kidnapped. But why? His father wasn't rich. And by whom?

A thick piece of tape had been put across his mouth and around his wrists and ankles. No matter how much he tugged and worked his mouth, the tape wouldn't budge. After a few minutes of struggle Greg fell into his usual attitude—he laid back and felt sorry for himself.

The car moved at a moderate speed for a long time, perhaps an hour. Then it slowed and went over heavily rutted streets. At one particularly bumpy stretch he heard a train rumble past and guessed he was being driven through an industrial area, the kind of section criss-crossed with old, poorly maintained railroad spurs.

He didn't know what to think when the car stopped. He badly needed to stretch his aching muscles, yet it was chilling to have no idea where he had been taken or by whom.

The blanket snapped back and he had the impression of a gnome-like creature above him. He was lifted and carried through the darkness across a meaty back. There was nothing to see, only gradations of darkness and indistinct shapes.

A heavy metal door was pushed back on rollers. They entered a building and the door rolled shut behind them. Greg began to shiver. He was being carried through a frigid building permeated by a fetid aroma.

Without warning they were in the center of a crowd of people. He could make out the shapes of twenty or more dark forms, people just standing around. He shouted through the tape, but no one moved to help him.

His abductor dropped him on a concrete floor. He yelped, wondered if any bones had broken. The tape was ripped from his mouth and he began talking at once: "Who the hell are you? You'd better let me go right now. My father is a *CPA,* mister. He's got friends *all over.* If you let me go right now, everything will be all right. Otherwise I can't answer for what might happen to you. Ahh . . . no . . . *don't . . .*"

The man's heavy foot had shot out, catching him square in the stomach.

"Don't . . . please, I won't say anything, honest I won't. Just let me go . . ."

A light was switched on. Greg blinked rapidly as his eyes adjusted. Finally he saw that the forms around him weren't people at all, they were sides of beef swinging from hooks. The smell was meat.

"What am I doing here? Who are you?"

"Take a good look, kid. Ever seen me before?"

Greg Anderson fastened his eyes on the man's wide, pock-marked face. Yes, he had seen him somewhere. "DiMato's! You were at the wake today."

"My name is Vincent Malle. Have you heard of me?"

"*You're* Vincent? Cathy talked about you a lot. She said you were her only friend at home. Jesus, what's this all about?"

The face softened. "She said I was her only friend? You don't know how glad I am to hear that, Greg. Catherine didn't think of me as a mug. I was sort of an uncle to her."

"Please . . ." Greg again began to struggle against the tape on his wrists. "Look, I want to go home, I'll do whatever you say but—"

"You can't go home. You're gonna die here, kid. You let Catherine down. You dumped her on the Merritt in the middle of the night and some freak came along and killed her. Everyone pays for their mistakes. It's your turn. Take it from me."

Greg shook his head violently, at first no words came . . . and then . . . "You can't . . . please . . . I loved Cathy, I swear I did—"

"That's why you were out looking for cunt at Papa G's."

"No, it wasn't like that. I was depressed, I needed to get out. Please, you can understand that . . ."

"Yeah, I'm depressed about Catherine myself." Vincent Malle reached down and circled his thick arms around Greg Anderson's waist. "Tony Scarnato wants me to say this is from him, so I'm saying it. But actually, this is my pleasure."

"What are you doing? Let me *go.*"

"Hold still, kid."

Greg Anderson tried to fight, but his arms and legs were pinned in the vice of Malle's arms. He was thrust up as high as the sides of beef. His face brushed one of the hooks fastened to the low ceiling, and Malle's intent became clear. "Oh, God, *no.*"

The tip of the hook caught him under the chin. At that moment Malle let go and Greg Anderson dropped. He fell only inches. The hook pierced his mandible and exited through his mouth. His jugular vein was cut, sending blood spewing, and the entire crushing weight of his body came to rest on his jawbone.

Malle jumped back to avoid being splattered. He watched with a mirthless smile as the boy gagged and coughed on the meathook, his bound feet kicking the air frantically. "Gimme a disco step, kid. That's your style, isn't it?"

With his head arched back, Greg Anderson's eyes were cast straight up toward the ceiling. Malle's words seemed to come from very far below. He tried to plead for mercy, to beg forgiveness, but the steel shaft filled his mouth and pain flowed through him like an electric charge. The last thing he saw as he choked to death on his own blood was the tip of the meathook suspended four inches above his eyes.

Malle studied the swinging corpse with professional detachment. In that attitude Greg Anderson looked as if he might have died praying, but Malle didn't think so. That definitely was not the kid's style.

HARRY DROVE AROUND Norwalk hospital three times before he satisfied himself there was no trap set. What had made him nervous was the police car in front of Ben's house. He had gone to Westport first to make sure Ben and Donna were really at home. There could be a couple of reasons for that car: the cops were already onto Ben for the Scarnato girl's death, or because of what happened to Jeff. Either way he was glad he'd rented a different car for the night.

He parked near the emergency entrance and entered the hospital along with an elderly woman who was being rushed in with her arm canted at a strange angle. A display in the main hall provided a diagram of the hospital floor by floor. Harry studied the diagram for a long time, noting the locations of all exits and the relationships of the corridors. Only when he felt completely oriented to his surroundings did he continue on.

Harry passed up the elevator in favor of the stairs. At the second-floor landing he peeked through the small door in the window. He was near Room 202, just as the display had indicated. Room 206 should be only a few yards to his right.

He stepped into the hall and saw that the door to Jeff's room was open. Harry took a deep breath and walked down the corridor and through the door, half expecting the room to be full of police. Police and Ben. Wouldn't I look like a prize idiot then, he thought.

"Hi, daddy."

"Hello, Mr. Ryder. You look rested."

Harry released his breath slowly. "Hi, kids, How's Jeff?"

"He's been sleeping since you left."

Harry looked down at his nephew and felt uneasy. An emotion he couldn't define, and so didn't know how to act. With a start he realized Sharon and her boyfriend were watching him. What should he do? Oh . . . sure . . . he went to the bed and leaned over Jeff. Kissed him gently on the cheek. Rumpled his hair. A fatherly gesture, that's what was expected. Well, wasn't he the father in a way? And a better man by far than the official father.

"Where's mom?" Sharon asked.

"At home. She's not feeling well, throwing up and can't seem to get her breath. I'm really worried about her. I need your help at home."

He saw the instant concern in Sharon's eyes and knew she had bought the story, she and the ape-man both. His eyes strayed to her breasts. They were so young, bouncy like two cats in a bag. This was going to be a four-star night.

"I'll stay with Jeff," Oop said.

"Thanks. It'll only be for a few minutes. I've asked for a private nurse to sit with Jeff for the rest of the night. She'll be here at eleven." He smiled in a kindly way at Oop, thinking that the boy had the ugliest face he'd ever seen. He couldn't understand what a piece like Sharon wanted with him.

Sharon ran a hand over Jeff's forehead. "Little squirt. Get well fast, you hear?" Then she kissed Oop and told him to call her in the morning.

"First thing," he promised.

Harry still worried that Ben might show up early so he took Sharon's arm and steered her toward the door. "Let's go, I don't want to leave your mom alone too long. Oop, thanks again."

"Glad to help." The boy had been all smiles, but his forehead wrinkled in a tentative frown as they left the room.

Harry took Sharon past the nursing station to the elevator. They had to wait for an elevator for what seemed to Harry a millennium. Outwardly he maintained a father-in-charge calm. Inwardly, he was a storm. He wanted to take her down the stairs, but that might have looked suspicious. Mustn't rush, he told himself. Mustn't look tense.

The elevator *finally* arrived. He shoved Sharon inside and pressed the first floor button.

"Have you called a doctor for mom?"

"Not yet, but we'll have to if she keeps on like this for the rest of the night."

"I'm surprised. You're always the first to want the doctor when someone's sick. Even with a stomach ache. Old Doc Ryder."

Harry smiled. "I must be outgrowing it."

When the elevator stopped on the first floor he said, "I'm in the emergency lot, in a rented car."

"Rented?"

"In case Harry's close by. He knows our Olds by now."

"Oh."

A syringe loaded with a fast-acting sedative, knockout drops, bartenders called it, was on the front seat of the car. He planned to sedate her as soon as he got her in the car, then take her to a quiet place. Not the condo. A spot where she could scream her head off without anyone to hear. He knew a state park near Ridgefield that would be perfect.

They were halfway across the parking lot when Oop came trotting up behind them. "Mr. Ryder! Sharon!" He came to a stop. "I thought you'd want to know that Jeff just woke up."

Harry forced himself to show concern. "How does he feel?"

"Pretty good, that's what I wanted to tell you. He asked if tomorrow someone could bring his electronic football game."

"Sure, tell him I'll bring it right after breakfast. And that I said he should go back to sleep. He won't want to, but insist."

"You bet." Oop scratched his head and grinned, embarrassed. "Another thing, and I feel silly about it again . . . the signal?"

"Signal?"

"Yes, sir. You didn't give us the signal in the hospital room. I thought . . . well, this afternoon I got the impression you wanted to stick with the system."

System. What was he talking about? "Yes, I suppose so. But I'm in a hurry right now. Let's talk about it later."

"Daddy, it was your idea. Just give Oop your signal and let's go."

"We don't have time for games, kids. Sharon, your mom's waiting." He took Sharon's arm and pulled her along. So that was it. Ben had set up some kind of recognition signal so they could tell one brother from the other. Nothing to do but brazen it out.

"Mr. Ryder!" Oop hurried along behind him. "We *can't* just forget the system after what happened to Jeff. It was your own rule . . ."

"Daddy, you're hurting my arm."

They were almost to the car.

Oop ran forward and jumped between them. "I can't let you do this, sir. I thought it was silly at first. Now I want to see that signal, if you know it."

"Damn you, get out of my way."

Harry struck at Oop, but the boy moved out of reach.

Sharon tried to pull away. "Oh, my God, you're not my father, you're *him.*"

"Sharon, your mother is sick, she needs you, and you're acting like a little fool—"

"Help, somebody please—"

"Shut up." Harry slapped her across the mouth.

Oop jumped at him now, fingers extended stiffly. One hand caught Harry below the heart. He staggered back and Sharon's arm slipped from his grasp.

Harry threw a punch and connected this time. Oop's head snapped back, blood dribbling from the side of his mouth. He fell back a step and went into a karate position, feet balanced and hands moving with calculated flourishes. His foot whipped out, catching Harry's right knee and spinning him around. Harry managed to keep his balance as Oop moved in and caught hold of his shirt.

Harry knew little about karate, but he did understand that the essence of all martial art was to make your enemy turn his movements and weight against himself. So he knew instinctively when Oop shoved him backward that this was a feint, that in a split second Oop would reverse the movement and throw him forward onto the ground.

The movement came as Harry checked his backward motion by leaning into Oop. At that opening Oop pivoted on the ball of one foot and tried to catapult Harry past him. He used his foot to sweep

Harry's legs off the ground, then thrust him back and downward.

Harry grabbed Oop's belt and hung on, determined to drag Oop down with him.

"Help us," Sharon yelled. "Someone please help . . ."

Harry landed hard. He thought his arm had been yanked from its socket, but somehow he held onto Oop's leather belt. The boy grunted and fell with him. Harry wrapped his legs around Oop's waist and drove a fist into the side of the boy's face. Once. Twice. Three times he hit him. Each time Oop only grunted and continued to rise.

An elbow smash jarred Harry, blurring his vision. He fought back the pain and struck out again. This time Oop's head lowered an inch. Harry applied more pressure with his legs and snaked an arm around Oop's muscular neck. He knew he was finished if the boy got to his feet. The little ape had too many tricks, was too fast and young.

Sweating and writhing on the hard black tarmac, they struggled for advantage. Oop attacked Harry's throat, using reserves of strength to break Harry's grip long enough to deliver a blow to his throat. The side of Oop's hand glanced off Harry's chin instead.

Something pelted Harry's head. Sharon, leaning down, was hitting him with her own balled-up fist. Which distracted Oop more than Harry.

"Sharon, get away . . . run . . ."

Harry took advantage of the diversion to drive the heel of his hand square into Oop's face. The bridge of Oop's nose disintegrated with a crackling sound, and again his head dropped an inch. Sharon kept on hitting at him and crying out, now incoherently.

Suddenly Oop broke Harry's grip and was almost free. The boy's lightning-fast movement also sent Sharon flying. Harry grabbed the belt again, this time to no effect. Oop tore himself free.

Harry jumped up on shaky legs. The boy's eyes went to Sharon, checking her safety. It was a crucial hesitation. Only a moment, but in it Harry managed to reach his pocket, find the springblade knife. There was no time for skill. He launched himself, driving into Oop. As they came together Harry thrust his knife upward. It found flesh. He pulled it down and drove it upward again.

Oop sagged, groaned quietly.

People were at last responding to Sharon's screams. Several attendants and nurses from the emergency room were running toward them. Someone had even grabbed a flashlight. The beam picked up Sharon's huddled form, bent over the still body of Oop MacRae.

Harry stumbled away into the darkness.

Thursday

CHAPTER 14

BEN SAT with his head between his hands trying to comprehend what had happened. He uncovered his face and looked at the Seiko on his wrist. Only eight A.M. It seemed a lifetime since he and Donna had returned to the hospital, but it had been only eight hours.

"Mr. Ryder?"

He reacted slowly. "Uh . . . yes?"

"I'm Sergeant Trelska, Connecticut State Police. I'd like you to come with me."

"I'm very tired."

"I can see that. You'll have to come with me anyway."

"All right. What about my daughter?"

"Dr. Hollis has sedated her and we've put guards on her room and your son's. Your wife will be taken home by one of our men. This is for you, by the way." Trelska handed Ben an official document.

"What is it?"

"A search warrant for your home and office."

"Now that's almost funny. I've been trying to get you guys to search my house all week. Had to hire—"

"It's a legal requirement. I believe Lieutenant Conde explained your rights to you yesterday, but I'll do it again." Trelska recited Ben's legal rights in the same monotone Conde had used.

"Am I really under arrest?"

"No, but Lieutenant Conde wants to interview you. I suggest you call an attorney. Tell him we're taking you home first, and then to Troop G."

Ben shook his head, still dazed by the terrible craziness of it all . . . Harry scores again . . .

"I'll ask my wife to make the call, if you'll let me see her before we leave."

"Okay."

They went to the room where Sharon had been taken and Ben was ushered past a Norwalk policeman posted at the door. Sergeant Trelska said he'd wait outside and told Ben to stay inside the room.

Donna was in a chair next to Sharon's bed. Their daughter lay with the open-mouthed stillness of someone who has been heavily drugged. Ben noted that Donna was alert and calm, her depression visible only in the uncharacteristic slump of her shoulders.

Ben leaned down and kissed her. "Hon, the police will take you home in a few minutes. When you get there, pack some clothes for all of us. We're leaving."

"Leaving? For where?"

"I don't know yet."

"The children . . ."

"We'll collect them this evening. I've talked to Dr. Hollis. He's not keen on the idea, but he seems to understand better than the police that we're all in danger. He says Jeff can travel. Jeff's awake now and asking for more breakfast, a good sign. Sharon should be better by this evening. Dr. Hollis has given me medication and instructions for both of them."

"Will the police let us? They think *you* killed Oop, I can hear it the way they talk to you."

"I know. But they're just theorizing. There's no proof." (He hoped. He didn't even have an alibi—except his wife saying they were home.) "Call Bobby Colangelo, will you? Tell him the police are taking me to the state police barracks for questioning."

"Let me make sure I have his number." Donna dug an address book out of her purse. "Yes, I'll call him right away. Ben, have you seen Oop's parents yet?"

Ben nodded. "An hour ago. I tried to talk to Mr. MacRae, but you might as well know that he blames us for Oop's death too. I think the police hinted that they suspect me of stabbing his son because he tried to get his hands around my throat."

"Those *idiots.* You were right yesterday, we're all alone. Harry has everything his way."

Ben braced his shoulders in an attempt to undo the knots in his muscles. "I keep thinking about Oop, the promise of that kid . . ."

"Oh, Ben. The MacRaes have lost *two* sons now."

Donna's carefully constructed composure began to slip. She reached far into herself and found something to hold onto—hate. "Harry has got to pay for Oop, if not for anything else. That boy saved Sharon's life."

With a show of energy he didn't feel, Ben slapped his kneetops and stood up. "Well, I'd better go along with the sergeant now. I'll see you at home."

Donna let her greatest fear surface now. "What if they don't let you go?"

Ben smiled. "They will. I guarantee it."

They took each other's hands and exchanged a wordless pledge of love, which was what they both needed most at that moment. Ben went to the door and told the policeman stationed outside that he was ready to go.

"You'll have to wait a minute," he was told. "Sergeant Trelska is making a phone call. He'll be right back."

IN THE PHONE booth at the end of the hall Trelska had finally managed to reach Sal Genovese. "Listen good, Genovese. I can't talk for long."

"What'sa matter? You got your envelope, didn't you? I had someone make the drop last night."

"Yeah, I got it. I'm not calling about that." He glanced down the hallway. "We know who killed your friend's daughter."

"You sure?"

"I'm sure. His name is Ben Ryder. He lives on Clapboard Hill Road in Westport. Are you getting this?"

"I'm writing it down. Spell the name."

"R-Y-D-E-R. Benjamin. He's an industrial designer and a full-fledged whacko. Way off the deep end. Yesterday he sliced up his own son, and last night he may have killed his daughter's boyfriend. I'm bringing him in for questioning myself. Hardly had time to get on the horn to you."

"You stupid bastard, you were supposed to get this information to me *before* the cops pulled him in. How the hell can I deliver this guy to my friend if he's already in the can?"

"That's your problem. Ryder's a one-man bloodbath, been leaving bodies all over the place. Conde says bring in Ryder, so I'm bringing him in. You've got what you wanted—the name. We're square."

Genovese ignored that last. "Where's he going to be?"

"Troop G, Westport."

"Troop G," Genovese mimicked. "Sounds like the Boy Scouts."

"Up yours." Trelska hung up on him. No need to crawl now that he'd given Genovese the name. No more bonus money, either. And suddenly he realized he still hadn't taken back his credit cards from Ginger. Oh well, how much more could she spend in one day? Maybe he'd get lucky and she'd have a bad cold.

He pushed himself out of the phone booth and went for Ben Ryder.

JIM CONDE BROUGHT a team of five investigators to search the Ryder house. They were prepared to force an entry, but that had been unnecessary. A neighbor had a key for emergency purposes and nervously agreed to let them into the house when she was shown a copy of the search warrant.

Conde instructed his men to collect all knives and to look for any mementos Ryder may have taken from the body of the Scarnato girl. In Conde's experience rapists often took something from their victims as a keepsake. He also told his team to leave the master bedroom alone, he wanted to search that room himself.

Despite his intense interest in Ben Ryder's wardrobe Conde forced himself to tour the other rooms first to get an overall impression of the Ryder household.

Donna Ryder kept a very clean, orderly house. Even the children's rooms were neat. The only cluttered space was a study obviously used by Ben Ryder. It held a drawing board positioned under a small bubble skylight, colored pens in profusion, Exacto knives, stacks of books on art and architecture, samples of building materials, and hundreds of pieces of soft balsa wood.

"Take special care with this room," he told one of his men. "It's the kind of place Ryder would hide his private things. Lots of sharp blades in here too."

"Nice house," the investigator commented.

"Too bad his wife couldn't keep him inside it at night," Conde said. "Westport would be a safer place."

The investigator nodded as he slipped on a pair of surgical gloves.

Conde went to the master bedroom and opened the closet door. Rows of nice clothes, as he'd expected. He went through Ryder's shirts one by one without finding what he was looking for. His luck changed when he opened the drawer of a pine bureau. It was filled with soft cotton sport shirts, all colors. Yes, indeed, Ben Ryder was a well-dressed gentleman even in his leisure hours.

He flipped through the shirts, exhaling a terse gasp of satisfaction when he came on his prize. The shirt was a beige pullover, two buttons, one missing. The remaining button looked exactly like the one found near the girl's body.

Conde allowed himself a private little smile. "Gotcha." He took a plastic evidence bag from his pocket, shook it out and carefully slipped the shirt inside.

He was too excited to finish his search of the room. Instead he delegated the task and went downstairs. In the foyer he met Eddy Trelska, who had just returned from Norwalk hospital with Ryder in custody.

"Hello, Ben. You're wasting that good-citizen-outraged look. We have a warrant to search your house, I'm sure Sergeant Trelska has served it."

Ben stared at him. "Just keep an eye on your 'investigators,' will you? I don't want any of my property to 'get lost' in the trunk of some cop's car."

Conde's face tightened. He thrust out the plastic bag. "Do you recognize this shirt? Is it one of yours?"

"Yes, that's mine. Why?"

"When was the last time you wore it?"

"I don't remember."

"Sunday night?"

"Sunday? No, I don't think so. Ask Donna, she pays more attention to things like that. I still want to know why you're so interested in my sartorial splendor."

"Eddy, take Mr. Ryder to our shop. I'll be along soon."

"Right. Let's go, mister."

"GOOD MORNING, TONY. How do you feel?"

"Not bad, Sal—considering I got about ten minutes' sleep last night."

Genovese glanced around. He had never been in Scarnato's bedroom and was interested in what it might reveal about his *capo*. First, it was exclusively a man's bedroom. He wasn't surprised that Tony slept alone; everyone knew he had lost interest in Teresa years ago. The furniture was heavy and dark. And expensive, of course. He was surprised only by the mini-bar in the corner. Was Tony a secret drinker? He'd always suspected that, but The Man kept his secrets well. If so, it was a weakness he might some day turn to his own advantage. Tony's breath did smell slightly minty this morning, as if he'd had a drinker's breakfast—a shot of whiskey and a package of Clorets.

He watched Scarnato fitting the studs into his French cuffs and held back a smile. French cuffs were long out of date. Was Tony getting there too?

Vincent Malle entered the bedroom. "The limo is here." He took a black suit coat from the closet and helped his boss into it, then whisked clean the coattails and lapels with a small brush. "You look first-rate, Tony."

Scarnato patted Malle's back. "Did you see the papers this morning, Sal? Vincent took good care of that punk. He didn't look so pretty when you finished with him, did he, Vincent?"

"He looked like a side of beef," Malle acknowledged without a smile.

Genovese made a noncommital noise. He thought that killing

218

the kid so soon was stupid. Anderson could have been taken care of later, when the cops wouldn't be so sure to tie the mob to his death.

"You want to ride with us to the cemetery, Sal? There's plenty of room."

"I'm not going to the funeral, Tony."

"Oh? Why is that, Sal?"

"I found out this morning who killed Catherine. Unfortunately the cops know too. They've picked up the guy already. I'll have to move fast to get him sprung—"

"*Who* is he?"

"His name's Ben Ryder. He's some kind of designer, lives up there in Westport. The thing is, he's gone bananas. Besides killing Catherine, he stabbed his own son and some other kid yesterday. There was no way to make a quiet move on the guy. He's got police all over him."

"After all that you can still pop him loose?"

Genovese was pleased at the odds. Showed his class. "I've got a gimmick. But I wanted to explain in person why I won't be at the funeral."

"Do whatever you have to, Sal. Just bring him to me. Wait, we need a place." Scarnato snapped his fingers. "There's a garage in Paterson where we service the delivery trucks for the Mr. Speedo shops. You know it?"

"Sure."

"Bring Ryder there tonight, after business hours. I'll want him for myself, so make sure he's in one piece." Scarnato's eyes took on a vision and sparkle for the first time in days. "The garage is a good place. Thick walls. Steel doors. No one'll hear a thing."

"I'll bring him," Genovese said, "*if* I can put my hands on him. That's not a *sure* thing, Tony."

"No ifs. You're my number-one man, Sal, so long as you deliver. No more 'The Fixer,' Sal. Back on the streets with the dirty-finger-nail boys, checking collectors' pockets for loose change, eating spaghetti with the runners in Trenton. Get the picture, Sal?"

Genovese got the picture. Go back to working the alleys and side streets of all those crummy cities in New Jersey? Not Sal Genovese. "I'll see you tonight, Tony. Bring your hook."

CONDE ARRIVED AT Troop G in high spirits. He called Trelska into the office and told him to stand by for a report from the criminal science lab on Ryder's shirt. "They're scrambling right now to see whether that button came from Ryder's shirt. Actually I don't think there's much doubt. Where did you put Ryder?"

"Locked him in the interrogation room. Let the bastard sweat for a while. Also, Dr. Mendel wants to observe him through the two-way glass. Mendel seems a good Joe, not tight-assed like most shrinks."

"Is Max here?"

"With Mendel."

"Okay, we'll begin the interrogation when Ryder's lawyer arrives. Eddy, stay on top of the lab. I want their results as soon as possible."

Conde went to join the prosecutor and psychiatrist. Ordinarily he despised shrinks and their mumbo jumbo. He expected to dislike Dr. Forrest Mendel too, in spite of Max's endorsement, but he found himself warming to the psychiatrist on sight. Mendel was a huge Santa Claus figure, down to the requisite white hair and pink face. Only the flowing beard was missing. Even his voice boomed cheerily as he introduced himself and complimented the state police for moving so fast on the case.

He'll make a great expert witness, Conde thought. Juries love big, confident men with strong voices. No wonder Max swears by him. "Thanks, Dr. Mendel. But we've got a long way to go in making a case. Everything we have right now is circumstantial. That's why your help is so important. We know he's mentally disturbed, and we don't want to come at him from the wrong direction."

"Yes, I can appreciate that. I've spent the last hour reading the files that arrived from California this morning, and the police reports on the two stabbings. Do you want my snap judgment, or would you prefer the fifteen-minute Freudian analysis complete with bullshit?"

"We've got plenty of bullshit, doctor, it comes with our jobs," Harris said. "Just tell us how to reach this man."

"And whether you agree that he's capable of murder," Conde added.

"Oh, I believe he's capable of it. Without even talking to him, just from his brother's record, I believe the germ . . . who knows, maybe the gene . . . of disorder may be there." Dr. Mendel removed his glasses and began polishing them with a spotless linen handkerchief. "We know that Ben Ryder is one of a pair of twin brothers and that the other brother, Harold, had a violent psychopathic personality. Now, some mental disorders can be traced to chemical imbalances in the brain. It's my belief that those imbalances are related to hormones secreted by the pituitary gland, but that's beside the point. What's significant is that after all these years that imbalance may have finally occurred in Ben Ryder's brain. Nature lying in ambush, so to speak. Identical twins often contract the same diseases, but not necessarily at the same time. One twin might develop cancer at the age of twenty. Ten or fifteen years later the other twin might develop cancer in the same organ." He replaced his glasses.

Conde whistled softly through his teeth. "Jesus, what a fate."

Dr. Mendel agreed. "Yes, Ben Ryder has apparently led a stable and productive life until now. I doubt that he understands what's happening to his mind. His insistence that his dead brother is committing these acts of violence may not be a total ruse. He may actually believe it. Oh, one side of him knows what he's doing. But the other side must deny it. A classic schizophrenic reaction. Your job is to break through the elaborate defenses he's set up in his mind against his bad self. That may not be as difficult as it sounds. His behavior in coming here at all hours, ostensibly about his brother, was, I suspect, a thinly disguised cry for help."

"So what should our approach be?"

"Present him with facts and the conclusions you've drawn. Don't argue with him, you'll only push him deeper into his defensive fantasies. Just open the door for him to confess."

"Thanks, doctor."

Harris took Conde's arm. "Will you excuse us, Forrest?" They stepped into the hallway. "I know you've got a lot on your mind, Jim, but there's something you should know. While you were at Ryder's house I learned that the boy you brought in for questioning yesterday, Greg Anderson, was found dead early this morning."

"Anderson? . . . How did it happen?"

"His body was found in a wholesale meat warehouse in the Bronx. Someone had hung the poor bastard by the throat on a meathook."

"Tony Scar. That's his trademark—"

"Of course. What I'd like to know is how Scarnato learned about Anderson slapping around his daughter and leaving her on the Merritt. That's obviously why the boy was killed."

"A leak? From one of my people?"

"Or mine," Harris admitted with distaste. "Someone around here has sure as hell been talking to Scarnato."

Trelska came up the hallway escorting Bobby Colangelo, a well-known Westport attorney.

"Hello, Jim." Colangelo shook hands with the lieutenant. "Max, how are you this morning?"

"Hello, Bobby." Dr. Mendel came out of the observation room and Harris introduced him to Colangelo.

"So much for professional courtesies, gentlemen," Colangelo said. "Now tell me why you're holding Ben Ryder."

Harris took the lead. "Bobby, the state police have evidence that Ryder is the man who murdered Tony Scarnato's daughter last Sunday night and a boy named John MacRae last night."

"Ben? That's the most ridiculous charge I've ever heard. I've handled Ben's legal affairs for years. He's a fine man. There must be a mistake."

"I don't believe so," Conde said. "Let me bring you up to date," and he outlined the events of the week and the evidence against Ryder in each of the cases under investigation.

Colangelo remained skeptical. He shook his head of salt-and-pepper hair vehemently. "Every damned thing you've got is purely circumstantial."

"Except for the button found near the girl's body," Harris put in.

"And you have yet to prove that it came from Ben's shirt."

"We hope you'll advise Ryder to talk to us," Harris said.

Colangelo considered the request. "Okay, but I'll also advise Ben that he needn't answer your questions if he doesn't want to."

"Fair enough," Conde agreed.

"May I join you?" Dr. Mendel asked.

Colangelo gave his approval only because he knew that psychiatrists often drew conclusions that hurt the cases of the very police who hired them.

They went next door to the interrogation room, where Ben jumped up and smiled nervously. "Bobby, I'm sure glad to see you. They've kept me locked up in here for an hour. Can they *do* that? I haven't even been charged with anything, so far as I know."

"Relax, Ben, you haven't been charged with a crime. They only want to ask you some questions. And yes, they must charge you soon or let you go. I'm sure you'll be free very shortly."

Colangelo sat down next to Ben. Conde and Harris took chairs at the opposite end of the table and Dr. Mandel placed himself in neutral territory.

"Ben, this is Max Harris, the State's Attorney for this district, and Dr. Forrest Mendel. He's a psychiatrist who's a consultant to the state.

"You don't have to answer any questions," Colangelo continued in a measured voice. "Not a single one, Ben. Legally, it's probably best to stand mute. On the other hand, you may be able to clear up this misunderstanding right now—"

"I'll talk to them."

Colangelo looked to Conde and Harris, nodded.

Harris began, keeping his voice conversational. "John MacRae was knifed to death in the parking lot at Norwalk hospital a few minutes before eleven last night. You claim that you arrived there about midnight with your wife. Is that correct?"

"Yes."

"And yet Mrs. Price, the floor nurse, saw you leave with your daughter at ten forty-five. And a minute later the MacRae boy followed you outside."

"That wasn't me," Ben said wearily. "It was my brother, Harry. He killed Oop MacRae. My daughter told the police that."

"Where were you between ten forty-five and eleven last night?"

"At home," Ben said. "My wife and I were asleep. We got up about eleven thirty and went to the hospital. That's when we learned what had happened to Oop." Ben turned to Colangelo. "Say, there was a police car outside my house last night. They must have seen what time I left for the hospital."

Colangelo turned quickly to Conde. "Is that true, Jim?"

Conde cleared his throat. "There was a patrol car there for part of the evening. About ten thirty they were called to a three-car accident on the turnpike, terrible mess. So they couldn't say what time you went to the hospital. The way I see it, Ben, you could have left your wife asleep at the house, gone to the hospital, killed that boy after some kind of argument and returned home without your wife even being aware that you were gone."

"That's not what happened."

"Okay . . . Ben, have you heard about the murder of a young girl named Catherine Anne Scarnato?"

"Yes, but what's that got to do with—?"

"We found a button at the scene of that crime. It appears to have come from your sports shirt, the one I showed you earlier. Did you notice that a button was missing from that shirt?"

Ben's expression went from anger to shocked understanding. "Wait a minute. That girl was strangled and raped, wasn't she? My God, Harry may have done that too, and, of course, left a button from my shirt to implicate me . . ." He pushed himself back from the table. "I'm not saying one more word. Get me out of here, Bobby. Just get . . . me . . . *out.*"

Conde's right hand moved toward his rear pocket, where a flat blackjack rested in a special grooved pocket. Before it became necessary to use it, Bobby Colangelo had calmed his client.

"I'd like you to be aware of one more item." Conde wanted one more reaction. "An informant has identified your car as being in the area where the girl was killed on Sunday night."

"An informant? What informant?"

"We don't have his name. It was an anonymous call."

"*Harry* again." Ben pounded the table in frustration. "You people are willing to believe anything but the obvious—Harry is out to *destroy* me."

"Take it easy, Ben." Colangelo put a hand on his shoulder. "Max, your case is crap. You really don't intend to hold my client any longer, do you?"

"I do," Harris said. "We'll keep him until the search of his house is complete and the results are back from the lab on that button. There's ample precedent for holding a suspect on such grounds."

Colangelo stood up and closed the curtain in front of the two-way glass. "Then I'd like to confer with my client alone. And he's not answering any more questions unless he's charged. This interrogation is over."

"SERGEANT NOON?"

Sergeant Tom Noon, desk officer at the New York City Police Department's 120th Precinct on Richmond Terrace, Staten Island, looked up from his paperwork to find a thin, spectacled face staring at him. The face was vaguely familiar. Actually, Noon recalled the physique more than the face. The man's shoulders were so hunched that his body in profile resembled a question mark. "Yes? Can I help you?"

"I'm George Elgin."

"So?"

Elgin looked hurt that he wasn't remembered. "I work around the corner at the Mr. Speedo dry-cleaners. Sometimes I deliver clean uniforms to you and the other guys."

"Oh, yeah. Now I remember. Sorry, we see so many faces around here that it's hard to place them all. What can I do for you, George?"

"I'm here to give myself up."

"What for? I mean, have you done something *in particular?*"

It was a hot, busy day and Tom Noon's temper was beginning to run short.

Elgin was astounded by the question. "Oh, yes. I've committed murder."

Noon put down his pencil and loosened the leather thong over the hammer of the .38 revolver on his belt. You never knew what to expect these days. A psycho had walked into Manhattan South three weeks ago and for no known reason opened up on the desk officer and two other policemen with a sawed-off shotgun. "Before you say any more, you'd better tell me if this is a joke."

"It's no joke," Elgin said sadly.

"Then put your hands up here on the counter, George. And keep them there."

George Elgin did as he was told.

"I'm coming around the desk. Don't make any sudden moves." Noon drew his pistol, stood up and walked around the desk. He

225

stepped behind Elgin and patted him down. He then took out a pair of handcuffs and manacled Elgin's hands behind his back. As he did so he informed him of his rights.

"Now," he said, "who did you kill?"

"Some people up in Connecticut."

"How many is *some?*"

"Three."

"Why?"

"Robbery. I robbed them, or tried to, and I can't stand thinking about it any more. That's why I'm giving myself up. Oh, and I raped the girl I killed too."

Noon didn't believe him. There was a false ring to Elgin's words, a rehearsed quality. "Who were those people?"

"There was a liquor-store clerk in Stamford. A girl I picked up hitchhiking on the Merritt Parkway. And a young guy last night in a parking lot at Norwalk hospital."

"Connecticut? What were you doing all the way up . . ." The words "Merritt Parkway" clicked in Noon's mind. "Are you telling me you killed the Scarnato girl?"

George Elgin appeared pleased that Noon had made the connection. "That's right, I raped and killed her. Do you believe me now?"

He didn't, but he took Elgin firmly by the arm and began leading him toward the captain's office. "George, I'll give you this, you've sure as hell captured my attention. Let's go see Captain Dunleavy. I've got a feeling he's going to *love* your story."

Chapter 15

A PLEASANT young policeman drove Donna home at about ten A.M. Although Donna knew her house was being searched, she was shocked to find men actually poking among her belongings. There was something indecent about the way they fingered her clothing and rummaged through the cupboards and closets. She could see they were trying to do their jobs without making a mess, but whatever they picked up was put back at least enough out of place to upset her. She felt as if a giant hand had lifted one corner of the house and made everything inside slide two inches off-center.

She fumed silently and followed the worst offenders around, giving them hostile looks. The tactic seemed to work. The investigators went quickly through the final stages of their job and cleared out by eleven.

Whenever she needed to blow off steam, Donna called Joan Southman, her next-door neighbor. She and Joan used each other as escape valves; they traded complaints like old recipes and knew a great deal about each other, from menstrual cycles to their secret fantasies about Mikhail Baryshnikov. With a cup of tea at hand, Donna settled into her favorite chair and dialed Joan's number.

"Hullo?" Joan's voice signified an upbringing very close to the Mason-Dixon line.

"Hi, Joanie. Got time to talk?"

"Oh, I was just going out, Donna. I have the Junior League today—"

"But this is Thursday. You always go to Junior League on Friday. Joanie, I really need to talk to you. The last few days have been horrible. You'd never believe the things that have been going on."

"Well, I *did* see the police there yesterday, and an officer in a funny hat made Jack turn over your spare key this morning, so we've realized that something strange has been happening . . ."

"Can you come over? I really need to talk to you."

"Ah, not right now."

"I've just brewed a fresh pot of Twining's."

"Darlin', let me ask you straight out—is Ben in trouble? It's all over town that he's been *arrested.*"

"No, that's not true."

"Miriam saw him taken away."

Donna bristled. "Miriam is a myopic bitch. Ben is at the state police barracks straightening things out. You may not know, but Jeff is in the hospital. He was badly hurt yesterday."

"Yes, I heard. I also know the MacRae boy was killed last night. Donna, people are saying *Ben* did that."

"Oh, God, that's so *unfair.* Joanie, I *must* talk to someone before I go crazy."

"I'm sorry, honey . . . Jack and I were talking about this at breakfast, just after that policeman was here, and we decided, actually Jack decided, that since he's on the Westport Police Commission . . . you knew that, didn't you? . . . well, it could be a conflict of interest for us to get involved—"

"Joanie, how the hell could having a cup of tea with me constitute a 'conflict of interest'?"

"Darlin', I'm truly sorry."

"So am I . . . *darlin'.*" Donna broke the connection and turned to her tea. She discovered she needed both hands to hold the cup. Later, when she had better control of herself, she rinsed the cup and teapot and went upstairs to pack. Ben was absolutely right. They had to get away from here.

She was putting Jeff's things in a suitcase when she heard the

228

front door open and Ben's voice call out: "Hello? Donna? Are you home?"

His upbeat tone lifted her spirits. "Ben, what's happened?" She hurried downstairs to find Ben opening a bottle of champagne in the living room.

He laughed as the cork popped, sending a gusher of bubbly onto the carpet. Two champagne glasses were set out on the coffee table. He filled them and handed one to Donna. "Hon, it looks like our nightmare is finally ending."

"How? What's going on?"

"Well, first they asked me a lot of questions . . ."

"Was Bobby Colangelo there?"

"What? Oh sure, he was there. Anyway, after treating me like The Beast of Westport all morning, the cops suddenly did an about-face. Out of the blue they apologized for the *inconvenience,* and told me I was free to go. They gave me a ride home in a police car, in fact."

"What about Harry? Have they found him? Are they at least *looking* for him?"

He draped an arm around her shoulders. "Everyone was evasive on the subject. They still think Harry is dead, so far as I can tell. But they now agree *someone* is after us, and they're putting a twenty-four-hour guard on the house for the next few days. That'll give us breathing room for a change."

"Then we still have to worry about Harry."

"Come on, drink up. We've finally had some good luck. Let's enjoy it."

"You're right." Wanting to match Ben's enthusiasm, she determinedly pushed all of their problems from her mind and gave herself over to a sensation of relief.

His lips brushed her neck. "Jesus, I feel alive again. You'll laugh, but I had a premonition that I'd never see you again outside a jail or a courtroom."

"Thank God your ESP is lousy."

"Is it? I just had a revelation you'd like to put away all bad thoughts and go to bed with your husband."

Donna affected a Groucho Marx voice. "That was no revelation —that was your wife."

"Take my wife . . . please."

Groucho Marx and Henny Youngman were earning their keep overtime. He put down his glass, swept her up in his arms and carried her upstairs, Cary Grant style. Donna smoothly disposed of her empty champagne glass as they passed the mantel, à la Irene Dunne.

The moment they entered the bedroom their jokey play-acting ended. They moved together in a dreamlike cadence. Slowly, with deliberate pleasure, he deposited her on the bed and drew the drapes. She waited without moving, her hair moist and tangled. The bedroom seemed cooler than the rest of the house, but the flesh of her under-thighs felt on fire. She held her breath as he leaned down. There was a tearing sound as he pulled open her jeans at the waist. The violent movement took her breath away. She said nothing, though he had surprised her. Ben was usually so gentle. He took hold of her face with both hands and kissed her, hard. There was a curiously gamey taste to him. Never mind, she responded to him eagerly. His teeth fastened to her neck, making her groan in pained surprise.

His hands never stopped moving as they explored her vagina and the small of her back, fussed over her breasts, pinched her nipples, squeezed and caressed everything they found. They seemed to possess the curiosity of a blind man's hands, the aggressiveness of a pickpocket's.

Donna's eyes closed while she tried to accommodate Ben's preoccupation with the familiar contours of her body. It wasn't that this athletic approach was not enjoyable, just unusual . . .

Maybe I'm too tense, she thought. Too wrapped up in myself—

His hand moved roughly. She gasped, but held back from asking him to be more careful. There was a signal she often used to let him know when she was moist enough inside for him to begin his exploration of her. It was a playful thing . . . she would put her finger on an old faded scar at his neck and rub in a circular motion. For some reason neither had ever figured out, that gesture always aroused Ben, sent his hand directly between her legs. She moved her finger to the spot . . . found that she couldn't locate the scar . . . .

A tiny alarm sounded at the back of her head. Where was it? Where the *hell* was it?

She braced her hands against his shoulders and pushed back, searching his eyes. They were Ben's eyes, of course. Bright hazel ovals. But where there should have been warmth and passion she saw only pinpoints of steel.

"No." She pushed hard, not able to budge him. "No . . . you can't be . . . dear *God* . . . you're *Harry?*"

"I'm a *Ryder*. Does it matter which one?" He sat back on his knees, swiftly shucking off the rest of his clothing.

Donna tried to slither away, but he hit the side of her head. "Where's *Ben?*"

"Ben? In jail, of course. They won't let him out for a long time, Donna honey, Donna sweetheart, Donna cunt, Donna whore—"

"Please . . ."

"They think he killed the Scarnato girl. You've seen her picture in the newspapers, haven't you? A sweet child, but she shouldn't have hitchhiked. Hitchhiking girls are my weakness. I left a little clue pointing to Ben, and another one today that should convince the police that Ben killed that boy last night. Dear brother Ben is finished, Donna. Old true-blue beloved Ben is now marked as an insane murderer. Isn't that a howl?"

"Why are you telling me?"

"Why not? I'm on my way home to California, back to my nest among the roses. But I couldn't leave Connecticut without sampling at least one of Ben's women, though frankly, no offense, Sharon would have been preferable."

Donna felt sick at the reference to her daughter, and then realized her immediate fear should be for herself. "You're going to kill me."

"I'm sorry, but there it is."

"Good. I'm *glad*. At least then they'll have to believe you're alive. They'll have to let Ben go. So go ahead, you miserable sick bastard . . ."

Harry shook his head. "Well, well, Ben picked himself a tough one, I'll say that for him. I almost hate to disappoint you, but good things in good time. The police, or neighbors, are going to find you swinging by a rope from one of those charming exposed oak beams in your living room, a victim of suicidal depression. The police ought to buy it, after all you've been through. But Ben will know what

231

really happened. That's what I want. For Ben to know, and not be able to do one damned thing about it."

She slapped him then with all her strength. His head snapped back, but he only smiled and pinned her arms. She kicked and thrashed her legs, tried to bite his shoulders. Useless. Harry jammed himself between her legs. Up down up down up down, like a pile driver. Donna felt more like a boulder being reduced to rubble than a woman being raped. Even this grunts had the rhythm of a laboring engine.

She did her best to negate his presence inside by closing her eyes tight and summoning up images of other places, other times. They went through her mind now like tableaus revealed in flashes of lightning . . . birthday parties, anniversaries, days at the beach, a table beautifully set for Thanksgiving dinner, Ben's face, relaxed in sleep . . .

As Harry grunted to a climax, his hands closed around her neck. Almost calmly, she prepared for death. What came were shouts and threats, and she realized that Harry's hands were gone from her throat. He was no longer straddling her. Instead he was grappling with three men who had thrown him to the bedroom floor. They were holding guns, and one had struck Harry across the side of the face with the barrel.

"Up," one of the men ordered.

Another pointed his gun at Donna. "Just stay there and shut up, lady." He grinned. "Sorry to interrupt the matinee, but we want your husband."

"Husband?"

The gunman ripped the cord loose from the telephone on her bedstand. "Put on your pants," he told Harry.

"I'm not her husband," Harry said thickly.

The gunman used the barrel of his pistol to smash a framed photograph of Ben on the bureau. "That's you, Mister Ben Ryder. Now just get dressed—"

"No . . . not me, you've got the wrong—"

He kicked Harry in the ribs. *Move.*"

The gunman who gave the orders was a tall, dark-complexioned man. Because she was staring at the gun in his hand, Donna noticed that his fingernails were carefully manicured and polished to a high gloss. He and the others were dressed in gray coveralls, the kind worn by moving men. She couldn't guess who they were, only knew they couldn't be police . . .

While he got dressed, Harry glared at Donna as if the gunmen were friends of hers who had unfairly trapped him. Apparently he didn't know who they were either. Well, Donna was just grateful that they'd arrived when they did.

"The phones are dead," said the man who did most of the talking. "You will be, too, Mrs. Ryder, if you try to leave the house until we're well gone. Understand me?"

Donna nodded.

The other two grabbed Harry's arms and pushed him out of the bedroom, pistols jammed in his ribs.

"Remember—stay put." The third gunman left.

She heard Harry apparently try to break free on the stairway. Shouts, a nasty thumping sound, followed by a rolling body coming to rest on the foyer floor.

Ha! . . . whoever they were, they didn't mean Harry any good. So hurray for them. The front door opened and a minute later she heard a car accelerating up the road. She was alone.

She pushed herself off the bed, and immediately collapsed on the gold shag carpeting. The lower half of her body was heavy with pain and her thighs were smeared with her own blood. She knew she should try to get up. There were things to be done. But somehow she could not move, and then, blessedly, everything went black.

A FEW MINUTES before noon a courier from the criminal science lab delivered an envelope to Jim Conde. "Here it is," he announced, holding the envelope aloft. "The results of the tests on that button."

Colangelo fidgeted in his chair. "This isn't the Academy Awards ceremony, Jim. You don't have to pose for the cameras. Just open it."

Conde realized with some embarrassment that he was indeed guilty of posturing. He opened the envelope in a more businesslike fashion and skipped through three pages of technical jargon to the conclusions in the final paragraph. He felt a rush of triumph, followed by a disappointment.

"Well?" Colangelo snapped. "Is the winner Fonda or Streisand?"

Positive facts first, Conde decided. "The lab says the button found at the crime scene is identical to those on the shirt we found at Ryder's house."

Sam Harris sat back, impressed. Maybe there was a case . . .

"However," Conde continued, "the threads from that button don't seem to match those from Ryder's shirt."

"So you haven't got anything," Colangelo said.

"It's not as conclusive as I'd hoped," Conde admitted, "but taken along with all the other facts, I'd say we still have a case." He looked to Harris. "Sam, it's your call. Do we charge him, or not?"

Harris looked somewhat deflated, but perhaps that was because his ever-present pipe had been stuffed into a pocket. "I think we may have enough for an indictment, at least as regards the MacRae boy."

There was a knock at the door and Trelska came in. "Well, I've got good news and bad news."

"Why is every cop suddenly in show business?" Colangelo asked of no one in particular.

"The search team found this in Ryder's car." Trelska showed them a plastic evidence bag that held a switchblade knife still streaked with bloodstains.

"That does it for me," Harris announced. "If the blood on that knife matches the MacRae boy's blood type, I'm going for an indictment."

"The bad news?" Colangelo said.

"Some guy walked into a police station on Staten Island this morning and confessed to killing the Scarnato girl . . . *and* John MacRae . . . *and* a liquor-store clerk in Stamford. He had a pair of pearl earrings that belonged to the Scarnato girl. They think robbery was the motive in all three killings."

Colangelo's breath came out in a rush. "Still going for that indictment, Sam?"

Harris stared at the blood-streaked knife without answering.

"This is too damn convenient," Conde said, "too coincidental—"

"Not for me." Colangelo straightened his shirt cuffs. "You'll have to let Ben go . . . or the man on Staten Island. Can't hold two suspects for the same killing."

Conde looked hard at the lawyer. "Lunatics come out of the woodwork whenever there's a killing in the headlines. You know that, Bobby. What if this guy from Staten Island recants his confession tomorrow?"

Colangelo shrugged. "All I know is that right now my client is being wrongfully held."

"I'm sending that knife to the lab."

"Go ahead, do whatever you want, so long as you set my client free."

Conde looked at Harris, who could give him no help. Then: "Eddy, turn Ryder loose."

At that moment Trelska felt like a poker player who knew what cards everyone at the table was holding . . . he knew that Sal Genovese had paid the chump on Staten Island to confess to those crimes. And Conde was right. Tomorrow the guy would recant his confession and come up with a dozen witnesses to prove he couldn't possibly have committed those murders. But by then Ben Ryder would be in Scarnato's hands, and probably dead. "Whatever you say, lieutenant."

BOBBY COLANGELO DROPPED Ben at the foot of his driveway. Driving him home he'd told Ben about the case Conde had been assembling against him and the timely confession by the man on Staten Island. "I'll try to get your car out of impound by tomorrow morning," he promised as Ben stepped from his car.

"Thanks for everything, Bobby."

Ben walked up his driveway without the relief he should have felt. He was far from free. He was, in fact, more determined than ever to get his family out of Connecticut. This wasn't the end of it, not with the police, or Harry. Especially not with Harry.

He stopped abruptly when he saw his front door standing wide open, then broke into a run. A man's belt lying on the doorstep, drapes drawn across the windows of the master bedroom, a flowerpot knocked over at the front entranceway . . . ? He stopped just inside

235

the door, where the first thing he noticed was the living-room phone lying on the floor, its cord torn loose from the socket.

He stayed downstairs long enough to pick up one of Jeff's baseball bats from the garage, then climbed to the second floor as silently as possible. When he looked through the door to the master bedroom, the bat slipped from his hand. "Donna . . ." She was lying on the floor, naked from the waist down.

He went to her and saw with a sick rage that her legs were smeared with blood.

He lifted her gently to sitting position, and she opened her eyes. "Ben . . . yes, *Ben,* oh God, please, it's all right . . . I'm not . . . Ben, please start the shower, help me . . ."

"For God's sake, what happened?"

"Harry was here. I thought it was you, at first. Then, when it was too late . . . Ben, he raped me. Ben, don't say anything, just hold me."

And he did, for a long time, stroking and kissing her hair, until finally she patted his shoulder. "Go on, dear . . . the shower."

He helped her up and went in to start the water. By the time he had adjusted the temperature, Donna had stripped the bed of sheets and blankets and wrapped herself in a terry-cloth robe. She moved stiffly, but seemed well enough otherwise. "I guess I blacked out at first but I wasn't unconscious when you came in," she said, trying to assure him. "I was just having trouble functioning. Will you make me a drink, darling?"

While Donna showered, Ben went downstairs and brought back two large brandy and sodas. She came out of the bathroom looking fresher and stronger. He handed her one of the glasses and asked if she felt like talking.

"Yes." She sat down on her dressing chair and glanced uneasily at their bed. "It would be better to talk now, before this begins to fester inside me."

As Donna quickly told him what had happened, Ben felt sickened but tried to match Donna's matter-of-fact way of dealing with it. It was her way, he knew, of trying to keep the horror of it at arm's length, and make it easier for him too.

When she stopped to puzzle over the identity of the men who had taken Harry off, Ben thought he had the answer. "The father of

236

that girl Harry killed is Tony Scarnato—Tony Scar. You've seen his pictures in the newspapers too. Harry killed her and left a trail leading to me, just like he said. Those men were probably Scarnato's. They were after me and took Harry by mistake. How's that for irony?"

"Then they'll kill him, won't they?" she said hopefully.

"Maybe. I wouldn't count on it, though. Harry's awfully tough, slippery. Those guys don't know what they've got on their hands. And what if they do? What if they make him disappear? I'm still on the spot for killing Scarnato's daughter and Oop. It's obvious now that someone faked a confession to those murders just to get me out of jail. Well, they think they've got me. Whoever confessed will take it back and the police will be coming after me again." He moved restlessly around the room. "Finish packing."

"Where will we go?"

"Harry said he was on his way to California? To his 'nest among the roses'?"

"That's right."

"Then I know where he's going. If we can get there first, we might be able to give Harry a very unpleasant dose of his own medicine."

HARRY'S HEAD THROBBED. He was furious with himself for being taken so easily. And by wops, at that. He hadn't had time to think this through. He knew only that he was riding in the windowless rear of a blue Ford van with his hands tied behind his back and two men with guns watching him.

"Relax, Ben," said the one who seemed to be the boss. "We don't have far to go."

"I tried to tell you back there, I'm *not* Ben. My name is Harry Ryder. I'm Ben's twin brother."

Both men laughed.

"Watch him, Danny, while I get out of this thing."

"Right, Sal."

The boss unzipped the gray coveralls and kicked them off, revealing a tailored blue pinstripe suit.

"English?" Harry asked.

237

"Yeah."

"I like the way the lapels fall. How much?"

"Two hundred. And that's pounds, not dollars."

"Nice."

"I'm Sal Genovese. You heard of me?"

"I don't keep track of every greaseball in New Jersey. Isn't that where you're from? Aren't you one of Scarnato's hoods?"

Genovese studied Harry with quickened interest. "You got a mouth, Ben. You're not what I expected. I was looking for some wimp with calluses on his hand from jerking off, not a stud who bangs his wife in the afternoon. And right after getting sprung from jail."

"That wasn't my wife. If you know anything about Ben Ryder, you should know he has a twin brother. You're making a hell of a mistake, Genovese."

"I don't make mistakes. I correct them."

The partition between the cab and the back of the van slid open. The driver asked, "What route shall I take, Sal?"

"Avoid as many tollbooths as you can. Take the 139th Street Bridge into Manhattan and the George Washington Bridge to Jersey." Genovese slapped the heavy barrel of a Colt .45 against the palm of his hand. "Ben, you keep your mouth shut going through town or I'll have to put you to sleep. Got it?"

Harry settled back against the steel wall of the van. He would be very quiet. These people were obviously under orders to deliver him alive to Scarnato, but not necessarily undamaged. In spite of himself, he couldn't overlook the irony. All the trouble he'd taken to convince people he was Ben had sure as hell backfired this time.

Well, what was done could be undone.

They'd tied his wrists with tight, competent square knots. What they didn't know was that he'd spent many years of his life in "restraint suits," straight jackets, and that his hobby during those times had been to work on the complicated system of straps, buckles and knots at the rear of the suits. Twice he'd almost worked himself loose before an attendant noticed.

He went at these knots with practiced fingers, working them slowly and patiently, feeling for the soft spots, using the tips of his fingers to tug and probe. He didn't know exactly how much time he had, but it would take at least an hour to get to New Jersey from Westport. Plenty of time, even for a square knot.

FORTY MINUTES LATER the partition slid open again and the driver, Johnny, announced, "The 139th Street Bridge is coming up, Sal."

"Okay."

Harry felt the van make the turn, heard a rumble as they went over a stretch of old cobblestones. The knot was almost loose. He had a fingernail worked into a crack and was gently rotating against the grain of the knot. There. His finger penetrated the heart of the knot. He pulled it out and used the thick pads of his fingertips to unravel the strands. Seconds later the rope started to fall away. He held onto them and rubbed his hands together to work out the numbness.

They were over the bridge, which meant they were where— Harlem? That sounded better than New Jersey, Scarnato's home ground.

Both Genovese and his pal Danny had relaxed their vigilance. Genovese still held his gun, but Danny's was stuck in his belt. Harry decided to hit Genovese first.

He braced, let the rope fall and launched himself. Genovese jerked back in surprise and raised the pistol, but not in time. Harry went inside his arm and drove him to the wall. The gun went off, tearing a hole in the roof of the van.

Danny yelled out, "Sal!" and pulled out his pistol.

Harry tried to shove Genovese between himself and Danny's weapon but Genovese was solid muscle under his expensive suit and refused to be moved.

"Shoot him, Danny, the leg, *shoot . . .*"

Harry tried to break for the door. Genovese grappled with him, holding tight and trying to bring his own .45 into play. Danny lined up his sights on Harry's leg. He was squeezing the trigger when the driver, reacting to the shot, hit his brakes.

They all flew forward toward the cab. In the melee Genovese lost his grip on Harry. Harry was instantly on his feet. He hit the rear doors of the van with his shoulder. They burst open and he tumbled onto the street, automatically rolling to his right to dodge out of sight.

The driver of an old Ford coming from the opposite direction popped his brakes, managing to stop just short of Harry's sprawling legs. Harry jumped up and clambered over the Ford's hood. He hit the pavement running, still not focusing on his surroundings. His priority was to put distance between himself and Genovese.

Harry veered past another car and found the sidewalk. Without slowing down he looked around, and what he saw looked for all the world like a devastated war zone—Berlin after the saturation bombing of World War II. The streets were deserted, no pedestrian traffic. Around him were rows of abandoned, crumbling three- and four-story brick apartment buildings, their windows and doors covered with sheets of metal or plywood. Broken glass littered the sidewalks. Garbage lay in the gutter. A no-man's-land.

He cursed himself for not yanking the driver of the Ford from behind his wheel and taking the car. There was no damned place to go here. And behind him, feet pounded along the sidewalk.

CHAPTER 16

AT THEIR home in Concord, Massachusetts, Ray Kennedy and his family were enjoying a pre-dinner swim in their backyard pool when a car pulled into the driveway.

"I'll be damned." Ray pointed at the car. "Hey, Carol, kids, it's the Ryders!"

The family piled out of the pool and raced for the car. The two boys, Ed and Boomer (alias Ray, Jr.), reached its first. "Hi, Uncle Ben," Boomer boomed. "Why didn't you tell us you were coming?"

Ray and Carol came up at a jog, hastily toweling themselves dry. "You guys are a welcome surprise," Ray said. "We just acquired a fresh fifth of Myers's rum and we haven't a clue how to get it open. Now, with your legendary experience—"

"Ray . . ." Carol shut off his chatter by placing her hand on his arm in a familiar gesture of warning.

"Yes, I see," Ray said quietly. "Come on in, folks."

The Kennedys had gone from a reaction of open pleasure to puzzled apprehension. The Ryders looked awful. Little Jeff's arm was heavily bandaged and Sharon, usually the most outgoing member of the family, seemed hardly to recognize them. She entered the house in stone silence. Donna looked pleased to be with them, but was almost as withdrawn as Sharon. Ben, at the other extreme, carried an air of fierce determination, completely at odds with his usual manner.

"Can I give the children something to eat and put them to bed?" Donna asked. "We can talk afterwards."

"Sure, honey." Carol went to work on the arrangements with Ray and the kids. A cot was set up for Jeff in Ray's study and fresh sheets were put on the guest-room bed for Sharon. Jeff and Sharon silently ate a bowl of soup and a sandwich and allowed themselves to be put to bed. Jeff had lost his previous bravado on learning of Oop's death. The news had cut deep; he'd begun to think of Oop as an older brother.

The kitchen table was cleared and a second round of soup and sandwiches set out for the adults. Ed and Boomer, full of curiosity, were shooed out of the house with money for burgers at the neighborhood McDonald's.

Since their U.S.C. years, the Kennedys and Ryders had remained close friends. Both familys had moved to the East Coast. Ray was now director of design for a large Boston computer manufacturer. They'd visited each other often and those occasions were always full of spicy foods, lively conversation and plenty of laughter.

"Look, I don't know what's wrong," Ray said, "but it's obvious that something is and we're damn glad you came to us. End of speech."

Ben dipped his spoon into the soup. "You and Carol were the first people we thought of . . . We'd like to leave Jeff and Sharon here for a few days, if it's okay . . ."

"Of course," Carol said quickly.

"We're going to Los Angeles," Ben said. "It's about my brother Harry, I have reservations on the eleven P.M. plane out of Boston."

"Harry!" Ray put his arm around Carol as if to protect her. "But he's in prison."

"No, he's out. And he's been doing some terrible things."

"Jeff's arm?" Carol said, not believing her own speculation.

Donna told her that she was right, Harry was responsible for what had happened to Jeff, and then told them the whole story. By the time she'd finished, Carol was in tears and Ray had pushed away his soup in favor of a bottle of brandy.

"Oh, the bastard," Carol said. "He hasn't changed at all."

Ben was caught by surprise. He hadn't been aware that Carol knew Harry, only that she knew of him.

"Know him? That's one way to put it." Carol patted Ray's cheek. "It's all right, love, I don't mind talking about it. Not now." She pulled a cigarette from a pack of Virginia Slims and lit it nervously. "Back at U.S.C., when I was working at the Medical Center, Harry asked me for a date. That was before I met Ray. Anyhow, we went out for drinks and Dixieland music at the Beverly Caverns, then he drove us up to one of those roads off Mulholland Drive. I thought, a little necking, why not? He was a good-looking guy. I was young and feisty. But Harry wasn't satisfied with a few kisses. He forced me to . . . well, let's just say he forced me. It was awful. He was like . . . like . . ."

"A machine," Donna supplied.

"*Yes.*"

The two women looked at each other briefly.

"Why didn't you ever tell me?" Ben said. "Or go to someone? The police."

Ray poured out four glasses of brandy. "Girls go up to Mulholland Drive for only one thing, as far as the police are concerned. And when you're a nurse besides, the cops just don't want to hear about it. As for you, well, neither of us wanted what Harry did to affect our friendship with you. So it was never mentioned."

Ben felt a too-familiar helpless rage. "I don't know what to say—"

"Don't say anything." Ray sipped at his brandy. "Jeff and Sharon will be fine here. Go to Los Angeles and find Harry. And I hope you can find some way to pay him back. For all of us."

A BLACK LIMO with New Jersey plates moved through the streets of Harlem with an escort of two plainer cars. A few blocks north of 125th Street they turned east and came to a halt in a deserted block of dirty, boarded-up buildings.

Vincent Malle hustled out from behind the wheel of the limo and opened the door for Scarnato, who emerged unsteadily onto the sidewalk. "Where . . . are we . . .?"

"Harlem," Malle answered.

Scarnato sniffed the air. "Should'a known. Go find Sal."

Before Malle had to look for him, Sal Genovese came through the door of an empty storefront. Dusk was settling over New York, its gray light doing damage to Genovese's swarthy features, making them darker and even more malevolent than usual. He nodded to Malle and said, "Hello, Tony."

"You got him?"

"Yeah, he's bottled up somewhere on that block." Genovese pointed at the row of abandoned buildings across the street.

"Then you don't have him."

Genovese wasn't about to admit that he had Ryder, then lost him. "I got him sprung from the cops, tracked him down and bottled him up. Another hour . . . two hours, tops . . . we'll have him. I thought you'd want to be part of this. That's why I called you."

"Yeah, sure." Scarnato leaned against the limo, bracing himself. "Fill me in."

Genovese now realized Tony Scar was drunk. Not just high, but really in the bag. "Like I said, he's trapped in that block of buildings. As soon as we pinned him down I called in Willie Jones. Willie sent a dozen boys over and they've got the block ringed. Ryder can't leave the block without being spotted. Willie's rounding up more guns, then we'll make a building-by-building search. Flush out the bastard."

"Willie Jones?" Scarnato made a face. "Why're we using niggers? We got men of our own."

"This is Willie's territory," Genovese reminded him. "No one makes a move down here without Willie." He hesitated, then decided to give Scarnato the whole picture. "I promised him fifty big ones to help us take Ryder."

"Fifty! You're throwing my money around like bird feed, Sal."

"You told me not to quibble over dough. You want this guy, I'll deliver him. But I need Willie's help. Hey, I don't like Willie any more than you do. But this is Harlem, Tony."

"Fifty grand for niggers," Scarnato grumbled. "What's the world comin' to?"

A maroon Rolls Royce touring sedan turned into the filthy street and slid majestically to a stop. Willie Jones, resplendent in a white suit and oversized red hat, and carrying a cane with a pure

244

silver handle, stepped from the car like the royalty he was. He was built on the dimensions of a middle-linebacker, tall and very wide with arms that could reach forever.

"So it's the Scar man, is it?" he said, grinning and throwing his impressive arms wide open in greeting. Then, remembering what he'd been reading in the newspapers about Scarnato, he modified his smile. "Oh, man, I'm sorry about your gal. Hey, I got ten or twelve kids of my own, y'know, and I'd be a real mess if one o' them got popped."

He put out his hand for Scarnato to shake, and Genovese and Malle held their breaths. To their certain knowledge Tony Scarnato had never in his life taken the hand of a black man. Genovese worried that Scarnato's drunken belligerance might overcome his good sense. But Scarnato was no fool, even in his cups. He shook the big hand limply. "Thanks, Willie."

"Well, I'm glad to be o' help, Tony. And about the dough, I wouldn't even take it for somethin' like this, 'cept I gotta lay some bread on my troops."

"Boss." Malle jerked his head toward a police car that had turned onto the street and was approaching at a crawl. When the patrol car drew opposite them, Willie Jones stepped under a street light and raised his silver-handled cane in salute. The officer behind the wheel nodded to Willie and proceeded up the avenue at accelerated speed.

"Shit, don't worry about them boys. They just makin' sure nobody bothers us. 'Poolside service' we call it around here. We pay for it."

Additional cars began arriving and men were dropped off in groups of three and four.

Willie waved his hand at the opposite block of buildings. "Now them abandoned tenements over there, Tony, they're like a goddamn maze, y'understand? This Ryder cat is maybe on a roof, maybe in an air vent, lyin' low like, and hopin' we'll ease out after a while. He's got an ace, 'cause he can move real easy. There's holes through the walls from one buildin' to another, basement passages, or he can go over the roofs.

"What I'm gonna do is start two teams, one at that end of the block and the second one down there. They'll work toward the

245

center, dig? He can move, but we'll drive him ahead of us." He laughed heartily. "Just like the tiger in *Bwana Devil*. Remember that one? Hell of a flick."

"Sounds okay," Scarnato said thickly. "Get at it."

"Just keep your boys out of the way, Sal. My troops are lookin' for a honky and they're liable to whack out anyone your shade."

"I want him alive."

Willie told him to relax and went off to organize the search.

"You can wait in there, Tony." Genovese indicated the empty storefront he had been using as a headquarters.

Scarnato wrinkled his nose. "I'll stay in my car." He opened the door, then whirled around. "Sal, this better work or it's your ass."

To avoid showing his anger, Genovese walked away from the limo. Talking to me that way in public, it's not right. These bums see Tony dress me down and it gives them ideas. Makes it look like I'm slipping. He stopped shoulder to shoulder with Malle. "Vincent, how'd the funeral go?"

"Okay," Malle said, scanning the rooftops.

I won't get anything out of this bum, Genovese decided. He walked farther down the sidewalk and stood next to another of Scarnato's men. "What happened at the funeral, Lou?"

The man peeped at the limo to make sure Scarnato wasn't watching him. "The boss came apart. Cried like a baby and threw up behind a tree. The guys were really surprised."

"Was Tony drunk?"

"Let's say he wasn't sober. His legs weren't working, that's all I know. Vincent practically had to hold him up."

Genovese shook his head and moved off. So Tony had been tanked at the funeral, in front of everyone. A mistake. The boys didn't like public displays of weakness. He felt better. He was one step closer to Tony's job, and Tony was two steps closer to the grave.

HARRY LAY ON a rooftop looking down at the street and wondering what the hell to do next. When he had crashed into this empty building through the plywood sheet over the front door he'd thought his troubles were over. The building was a funhouse of hidey-holes and stairways going nowhere. He had hidden in an airshaft for half an hour, certain Genovese would give up looking for him and decide he'd skipped out through another exit. But now there were at least fifty people down there and they appeared to be organizing a search.

He crossed the roof and examined the street on the opposite side of the block. Men had been stationed down there too. The block was ringed. While he watched, groups of men were dispatched to the buildings at either end of the block.

Not many options. He could find a nook and hope they missed him, but those men would know all the best hiding places in these old buildings. He could jump one of them. Grab a gun. Shoot his way out. Except there were probably forty other guns down there in the hands of men who knew how to use them. And there was no one to turn to for help, this neighborhood had been abandoned to the arsonists and junkies long ago. Now, apparently, even they'd moved on. Leaving option number four—find a weak spot and make a break.

A metal door clanged on another roof. Each building was at a slightly different height, so that the roofs didn't join in a continuous line. So he couldn't see far. Thank God it was finally dark. He was sure that someone had come onto the roof of the last building on the block.

Time to move.

Harry took the fire stairs down one floor and crossed to the rear of the building. There was a trash- and glass-littered concrete back-yard down there. There were patrols on the street on the other side of the fence, but maybe he could get a jump on them.

Someone groaned behind him.

Harry spun around.

"Umm. Oh, man, I'm sick, so sick . . ."

In a dim corner on the skeleton of an old bed lay a dirty, stick figure of a man in tattered clothes. To Harry he was beautiful—he was white.

"Help me, man. I need a fix. You holding?"

"No."

"Spare me some money?"

Harry moved closer to him.

"Hey, I'll give you a blow job for five bucks. Okay?"

Harry picked up a heavy piece of wood from the floor, the leg of someone's long-forgotten bedside table. He raised it above his head and struck down. The stick figure's skull shattered on impact, his eyes rolled up under their lids.

He hoisted the junkie's slight body from the bed to his shoulder and retraced his steps to the roof, where he quietly laid his burden down and crouched behind a brick cornice that crowned the building.

The searchers were making a good job of it down there, going slowly and, he was sure, thoroughly. Too soon to make a break. Wait, go when they're worn out and frustrated and ready to believe.

He felt a sneeze coming on, clapped a hand over his mouth and nose just in time. What a way to go, with a big, boogery sneeze.

Damn it, he hoped he wasn't catching cold. Summer colds were the worst, went against the grain of the season, made you feel not only sick but foolish. Colds . . . the subject triggered a memory of one particular cold that had made him sick for a long, long time . . .

HE WAS TEN years old, a fifth-grader in the grammar school on Del Mar Avenue in Pasadena. His cold had started in April and hung on through the second week of May, when it became more serious. In the middle of his English class he felt feverish and dizzy. Automatically, he looked at Ben. They usually caught the same viruses at about the same time, but Ben was writing in his notebook with no sign of feeling ill.

"Ben," Harry whispered across the aisle, "I'm sick. I feel lousy."

Ben stared at Harry in surprise. "You look awful. What's wrong?"

"Mr. Ryder," said Mrs. Meecham from the front of the room, "you're supposed to be diagramming sentences, not speaking them." (She called both of them "Mr. Ryder" because she couldn't tell them apart.)

"My brother's sick," Ben said.

"Oh?" Mrs. Meecham, a flinty spinster who took nothing for granted, came to the back of the room and put an ice-cold hand on Harry's forehead. "My, I guess he is. Mr. Ryder, go straight to the nurse's office. Tell her I think you should be sent home. There's too much flu going around, we can't have you infecting the whole school."

"Yes, ma'am." Harry gathered up his books and touched Ben's shoulder. "See you at home."

"You planned this to miss the history quiz," Ben hissed.

Harry giggled and left for the nurse's office, where his temperature was found to be 101 degrees. The nurse wanted to phone his mother and have him picked up, but Harry said, "She's working. I can go home myself, it's only a couple of blocks away."

"Well . . . all right." She gave Harry a pass to leave the school grounds and ordered him to go straight home, no shortcuts.

In spite of the fever and the achey feeling in his bones, Harry was delighted to be out of school. There was a delicious sense of freedom in being on the streets at ten A.M. when everyone else he knew was in school.

On his route home was a small store where kids hung out after school and the elderly people in the neighborhood who didn't care to walk to the supermarkets on Green Street bought their groceries. Harry dug into his pocket and found two dimes, went in, bought a strawberry soda and stepped outside to drink it and admire three huge Harley-Davidson motorcycles parked at the curb, mammoth machines with yards of chrome striping and wheels larger than automobile tires.

"Do you like bikes, kiddo?"

There had been three people in the store arguing with the proprietor about the price of a six-pack of Hamm's. Now they stood behind him, two men in their late twenties and a pretty red-haired girl who looked slightly younger. They were all dressed in chino pants, T-shirts and boots. It was the girl who had spoken to Harry.

"Yeah, they're neat."

"This one's mine." She went to a silver Harley-Davidson and strapped a six-pack of beer to the luggage carrier. Her eyes lingered on Harry. "You're a nice-looking kid. What's your name?"

"Harry. Harry Ryder."

One of her companions, a bearded, bloated man whose belly looped down over his belt, said, "I'm a hairy rider myself," and laughed in appreciation of his own wit.

"That's Chick," the girl said. "This is Randy. And I'm Tina."

Randy was smaller and marginally neater, with a shy smile and teeth that could hardly be seen beneath nicotine stains.

"You don't look so good," Randy said.

"I've got the flu." Harry drained the last ounce of strawberry pop. "The nurse sent me home from school."

"Where do you live?" Chick asked.

"Couple of blocks away." Harry pointed toward Marengo Avenue.

Tina smiled brightly. "I'll bet your mom is waiting for you with a big bowl of hot soup."

"Naw, she's at work."

"Let's go, Tina." Randy hopped on his motorcycle and threw back the kickstand, impatient to be on his way.

"Tell you what," Tina went on, "we'll give you a ride and then take you home. Right to your door."

"Tina—"

"Shut up, Randy," Chick said.

Harry's achey feeling was worse and he knew he was not supposed to go anywhere with strangers. But the girl was so pretty and friendly . . . he trusted her . . . and besides, the chance to ride one of those big "hogs" (he knew what the gangs called their machines) was too much to resist. "Sure, I'd like to. Thanks a lot."

Tina threw a leg over her bike. "Jump on behind me, Harry. That's it, hold tight."

They roared away with Harry feeling as if he was in the center of a squadron of fighter planes. From inside the triangle the sound of the three bikes was magnificent, a full-throated blast of primitive power.

At Los Robles Avenue they turned north. "We'll go up into the hills," Tina said over her shoulder. "It's not far." Her right hand twisted the throttle and they gained speed toward the Mount Wilson foothills. At Colorado Boulevard they veered northeast to Sierra Madre, up into a region of barren, unpopulated canyons that reached for the throat of the mountain like bony fingers. When the roads ended they followed a firebreak to a box canyon strewn with boulders six feet high, the residue of some ancient flood.

Tina, leading, circled one of the boulders and cut her engine. The depressing terrain reminded Harry of how rotten he felt. His fever was higher, he didn't need a thermometer to tell him that. "Can we go back now? I liked the ride, but I don't feel so good."

"Not yet, kiddo," Tina said.

Randy parked his bike and took the six-pack from Tina's luggage carrier. "I'm going up the hill. Call me when you're through."

"Hey, man! Don't take all the beer!" Chick yanked the six-pack from Randy's hands and twisted four cans loose. Randy walked away. Chick pulled a fifth of whiskey from his bike's saddlebag, took a long swallow, passed it to Tina, who first drank from the bottle and then chug-a-lugged a beer.

Harry sat down on one of the smaller rocks, dizzy and confused. "Please take me home, I'm afraid I'm gonna throw up."

"Go ahead." Chick laughed. "Ain't nothing around here to ruin."

"Take off your clothes, kiddo," Tina told him.

"What?"

"She wants you to strip. Our Tina's got a thing for kiddos. Come to think of it, so do I."

"No, I won't do that . . ." Harry tried to run, but his legs were wobbly. Chick grabbed him by the collar before he'd taken two steps and started to pull his shirt off.

"Please . . . don't." Harry was shaking now.

Chick dropped the bottle, threw Harry on the ground and proceeded to pull off the rest of his clothes. His breath was sour and heavy. His bloated belly jiggled while he worked off Harry's pants and shoes. And all the while he whistled in a cheerful monotone, serenading his own fantasies.

"Don't let him—" Harry begged Tina, but Chick's big hands were spinning him around and throwing him face down in the sand. As Chick drove into him from behind, Harry made tiny fists and beat them against the ground. The pain was awful. It seemed to go on forever. He was crying, begging Chick to stop, but got only a renewed burst of passion from Chick in reply.

When Chick finally was finished and had hoisted up his pants, Harry rolled over on his back, tears in his eyes. Randy had come back from the hillside and was observing the scene in disgust. But to Harry's cries for help, Randy only shrugged and turned away.

Tina squatted next to him, a can of beer dangling from her hand, her eyes unnaturally bright. "You're okay. My turn, pretty boy."

By then the fever had a firm hold on him. He was only dimly aware of a loud argument beginning between Randy and Tina, heard them shouting, but little meaning penetrated the fog that had closed in around him. He did sense, though, that Randy had finally helped him in some way. The argument went on until he was pulled to his feet and his clothes were roughly put back on him.

The roar of the motorcycle engines broke through to him. He was sitting on a machine again, Randy's this time, in front of Randy with his weakened legs straddling the gas tank.

Randy held him upright with one hand and maneuvered the bike with his other as they wound down the mountainside into Pasadena. The fever converted to chills so that the soothing breeze soon began to feel like an arctic gale.

They dropped him on the corner of Los Robles and Del Mar. "Just forget this ever happened," Randy advised. "That's best for all of us. And don't look so drag-ass. It could've been worse. Those two are nuts, you know. Sweet Tina wanted to kill you. Well, there's no way I'd go along with that. I got enough cops looking for me already . . ."

They roared off, leaving Harry alone and dazed, with only a haze of blue exhaust smoke to prove they had ever existed. And within seconds that slight trace had disappeared too.

Somehow Harry managed to get home and crawl into bed. When Ben came home from school he found his brother delirious with fever. He called his mother and their doctor. The doctor couldn't come to the house but from the symptoms Ben described he diagnosed Harry's problem as Asian flu and prescribed a mild antibiotic.

For three days Harry suffered through periods of fever, chills and stretches of delirium that his mother attributed to high temperature. In moments of clarity he was determined to tell no one about his experience, not even Ben. He'd learned that there were dragons out there. Not fairy-tale dragons, real-life monsters.

What shocked him most was the revelation that girls were the worst of all. The least worthy of his trust. The most vicious. Especially pretty girls like Tina. He had liked her. Trusted her. Expected her to help him even after she had stood back and let Chick do what he wanted. He had trusted her at the very moment she must have been trying to talk the others into killing him.

He'd come right up to the point of death on account of a girl. A girl he'd liked and trusted. He made a pact with himself there and then. Never again. He'd never ever again trust a pretty girl, or let himself like one. It was a pact he would keep.

DOWN ON THE street a huge black man in a white suit was urging on the others with the promise of money. People were stomping around the rooftops of the buildings on either side of him. Someone tripped on loose tarpaper and swore.

You can't wait any longer, Harry told himself. Do it, *do* it. He settled the butterflies in his stomach, then lifted the junkie's body above the cornice and heaved it over the side, accompanied by a contrived scream that sounded phony even to his own ears.

He scuttled across the roof in a crouch and tucked himself into the shadows of a rusted watertank.

Two men scrambled over the dividing walls onto the rooftop where he was hiding.

"Damn . . . bastid went off the roof."

"Prob'ly tried the fire escape, lost his balance."

"I want my money anyways."

"Hey, so do I! This rooftop jive don't go down. Look here, new pair of Calvin Kleins all fucked up."

Harry crept silently away, climbed the divider onto the next roof and headed for the last rooftop on the block, listening for other voices as he glided through the darkness.

At the corner rooftop he looked down into the dimly lighted street and was pleased to see people gathering where the junkie had hit the sidewalk. As he'd hoped, everyone's attention had shifted there. Nothing attracted a crowd like a corpse. Harry went onto the fire escape and hand over hand started down.

GENOVESE HAD BEGUN to sweat. After almost an hour Willie Jones' men hadn't found a trace of Ben Ryder. The possibility that Ryder had somehow slipped away now had to be considered. He might have

broken free during that first half-hour, before they'd gotten organized.

On the surface Genovese stayed confident. He even accepted
Scarnato's gruff invitation to join him inside the limo. More to shore
up his own spirits than Scarnato's he said, "The boys are closing in,
Tony. I told Willie to bring that creep over here and spreadeagle him
on the hood of your car."

"Don't you have to find him first, Sal?" Scarnato brought out
a flask and offered it to Genovese.

"No, thanks, Tony, not right now."

Scarnato took a drink himself. He tried to make it look like a
sip, but Genovese could tell he had swallowed half the contents of
the flask. Drink up, he said silently. Pickle your goddamn liver—

A scream from somewhere high up, followed by a crash as two
curbside garbage cans flew ten feet in the air and bounced down the
street like a pair of huge dice.

"There he is!"

Genovese hit the door handle and propelled himself out of the
limo.

"I want him alive," Scarnato called after him.

Genovese ran toward the commotion. He knew Tony would be
wild if Ryder had taken a swan dive off the roof, but that would be
a hundred times better than losing the prick altogether. "Let me
through."

Willie Jones was at his side. He caught one of the men around
the neck with his cane handle and yanked him aside. "Get outta
there, Sammy. Let's see what we got."

The circle expanded to make room for Genovese and Willie
Jones.

"Whooee!" Willie laughed. "That boy has paid his ticket, Sal."

The body of a white man lay twisted and flattened in the gutter.
It was not Ryder. Genovese quickly weighed the possibility of passing off this dead man as Ryder. He had only seconds to make that
decision, because Scarnato was pushing toward them.

Scarnato lunged to his side and stared down at the corpse.
"*Damn* you, Sal. I told you I wanted him delivered alive—"

"Relax, it's not Ryder." He'd decided that lying to Scarnato
would be stupid. The lie might hold up for days, even weeks, but

sooner or later Ben Ryder would turn up and then what . . .

"Then where *is* he?"

"Still in there." Genovese took hold of Willie Jones' arm. "Get your men back on the job, Willie."

"You sure that's not him?" Willie said. "We don't hardly find two honkies to a block around here."

Genovese nodded vigorously. "I'm sure. He's still up there. Find him, damn it."

LUCK WAS WITH him, Harry decided. The street light in front of the building he descended had long ago been broken and never repaired. He lowered himself to the bottom rung of the fire escape and let go, dropping about seven feet to the sidewalk.

Ordinarily he was snobbish about the kind of car he drove, but just then all he wanted was a set of wheels, any kind of wheels. The worst old junker in Harlem would do just fine. The cars the searchers had arrived in were parked directly across the street, and unless the law of averages had been repealed, at least one should have keys in the ignition.

He left the shadows and sprinted across the open street, heart pounding. No way to avoid being spotted now. Just run and hope.

"Hey, you . . . *stop* . . ."

Harry was headed for a nondescript old Dodge when a gorgeous maroon Rolls Royce caught his eye. He swerved for it without hesitation. The damned thing was just too beautiful to pass up, even though he would need a few extra steps to reach it.

"There he is—"

Men with drawn guns ran toward him. Harry threw open the door of the Rolls Royce, pushed himself behind the wheel, fumbling along the steering column for the ignition key. Bound to be one . . . a Rolls owner wouldn't lock up his car like some peasant . . .

Someone yelled out, "Don't shoot, goddamn it, I'll kill the fucker puts a bullet hole in my Rolls. Jackie, block the street . . . get them cars turned around . . ."

Harry, figuring right, found the key. The motor caught instantly with a quiet power that pleased him greatly. His pleasure was cut short, though, when he discovered that the Rolls Royce was a motor car not built for quick acceleration, rather it picked up speed with the smooth, unhurried grace of an ocean liner. Ahead of him three cars were being swung around to block the street.

He kept his foot hard to the pedal and aimed the sleek automobile straight at the narrowing gap between two of the cars. None of the black men had fired at him, but Genovese's men began opening up. Bullets thudded into the Rolls, which absorbed them into its heavy-gauge steel as it plunged on. He almost but didn't quite make it to the end of the street ahead of the blocking cars . . . the Rolls smashing into the front end of a Ford, sending it flying in a shower of sparks, one of which hit a ruptured gas line. The Ford exploded, fireballing into the air. An ugly gash had been torn along the right front fender of the Rolls, but the machine continued to gather speed with imperious calm.

Harry threw back his head and laughed like a carefree boy. He'd gone into Harlem as a prisoner under guard and had come out driving a Rolls Royce.

It could only happen in America, Harry my boy. Only in America.

Friday

CHAPTER 17

"As a boy I loved California," Ben said. "In those days you could camp out on the beach with only a bonfire for company and not have to worry about being mugged. A movie at Grauman's Chinese cost only fifty-five cents. Out around Tustin you'd see fruit trees by the thousands, and the grove owners didn't get upset if you helped yourself to one free orange for the special pleasure of eating it off a tree. California was a playground.

"Harry and I"—he stopped to rephrase the sentence—"I used to travel all the way to San Diego just for a pizza because the drive was so beautiful. Now it's all freeways and supermarkets."

"At least it's still got great weather," Donna said.

"They'll find a way to ruin that too. Already have with the smog."

He and Donna were sitting in the reception area of Honeyhill Properties on Wilshire Boulevard in Los Angeles. Honeyhill Properties was a real-estate development company owned by Harry's father-in-law, Sean Rafferty. All Ben knew about Rafferty was what Jim Conde had said—that Rafferty had hated Harry. Which was enough to make Rafferty a possible ally.

A secretary came out of Rafferty's office shaking her head. "I'm so sorry, Mr. Hollis. Mr. Rafferty is extremely busy this morning.

Since you don't have an appointment, he's asked if you can come back another time. May I make an appointment for you?"

Ben had borrowed Dr. Hollis' name for the morning. He hadn't wanted to use his own name, figuring that Rafferty might well refuse to see the brother of Harry Ryder. "Please tell him this is an urgent personal matter. Urgent for both of us."

"I'll tell him, but I can't promise it will make any difference."

She returned to Rafferty's office, quickly came back looking bemused. "You can go right in."

They entered the office to find a florid, long-legged man with white hair fussing over some papers on a French Provincial desk. "What's this about an urgent personal matter?" He glanced up at Ben and paled. The papers slipped from his hands. He got up from his chair, swayed and started around the desk, his face twisted in anger.

"You . . . bastard . . . I'll kill you, how did you . . .?" Halfway around the desk he put both hands to his throat and began struggling for breath. His florid face became an even deeper shade of red.

Donna reached him as he began to collapse. She and Ben helped him to his chair and loosened his tie.

"Top drawer . . ."

Donna instantly went to it and found a pill bottle. Rafferty, barely able to speak, held up two fingers. She shook two of the pills into her hand and forced them between his lips. Rafferty swallowed, closed his eyes. Gradually his color improved. He pulled a handkerchief from his breast pocket and wiped his forehead.

"I'm terribly sorry," Ben said. "We shouldn't have barged in like this without warning. I'm *not* Harry, Mr. Rafferty. I'm Ben Ryder, his twin brother."

"Shall we call your doctor?" Donna asked, still anxious about his condition.

"No." Rafferty put away the handkerchief and squared his shoulders. He was a big man with large freckled hands that bore the marks of heavy manual labor. His face, too, had the rough texture of a man who had spent his youth working out of doors. "I have these attacks sometimes . . . the nitro tablets clear them up." He turned shrewd eyes on Ben. "No . . . you aren't Harry. He would have thrown my pills across the room and watched me crawl for them. With a smile."

He pushed himself out of the chair. "There, you see? Lazarus didn't have a damned thing on me. Care for a drink?"

"Should you?"

Rafferty shrugged. "No, of course not. Come on, join me. It's almost ten A.M. I always told Melinda . . . my wife . . . she died five years ago, God rest her . . . I always told her a man who won't drink before noon is missing one of the most purely wicked pleasures of life."

He went to a bar at the other end of the office and splashed several ounces of Jack Daniels into a glass. With grumbles about the loneliness of solitary drinking he filled Donna's request for Perrier water and gave Ben a ginger ale. "You're certainly different from your brother. Harry would have asked for champagne. Now, what can I do for you?"

Ben got straight to the point. "We came to tell you that Harry is alive, and to ask your help in finding him."

"That's *impossible*. Harry and my daughter Ellen died together in a car crash up in Ventura. I *saw* his body. In fact I identified both bodies—"

"I understand they were badly burned, that the ID was made through personal items found on the bodies. I don't know who the man in that car was, but Harry planned the crash so he could take on a new identity."

"My God, you're saying Harry faked his death? That he killed my daughter?"

"Yes, sir, I'm afraid so."

"And he's still alive? You're *absolutely certain?*"

"Earlier this week he gave our son a twelve-inch knife wound that almost cost him his life, and killed our daughter's boyfriend," Donna said. "Ben's a fugitive because of what Harry has done." She added as an afterthought, determined not to spare herself in this effort, "He raped me, so I can personally confirm that Harry is alive—"

Rafferty shook his head. "I should have known. When I found out how much money was gone I should have guessed it was something like this." He shrugged apologetically. "I'm sorry, I shouldn't dwell on my problems when you've obviously been having such a rough time of your own."

"Will you help us?" Ben asked again. "You've surely got a stake in finding Harry too."

Rafferty trudged back to the bar and poured himself another four ounces of Jack Daniels. "I'm afraid Melinda and I made a lot of mistakes with Ellen, we were too anxious to give her a better start in life than we'd had. It's an old story . . . Melinda and I came from dirt-poor beginnings. She kept us going in the early years teaching school while I was learning the construction business.

"Anyway, I settled a big hunk of money on Ellen when she was eighteen. Also an old and not very noble story . . . tax purposes, avoiding probate. The money made her a target for men like Harry. We also goofed by sending her to a very exclusive private school that turned her into a lonely introvert. Yes . . . she was ripe for Harry, a set-up for a good-looking stud with charm to spare and a smile you could pour over waffles. They met at some party and Harry swept her off her feet, if you'll pardon an old man's expression. Two weeks later they were married. Eloped. Las Vegas, for Christ's sake."

Rafferty raised his glass, then thought better of it. "I always liked the grape, but I've been drinking more since Ellen died. She was all I had left. Anyway, they were married and at first I tried to be happy about it. Tried hard. And Harry *seemed* all right, always had a big smile for me, I was welcome for dinner any night. That sort of thing." His face tightened. "Then I noticed that Ellen was changing. She'd always been quiet, but after six months with Harry she was hardly talking at all. Went around white-lipped, scared-looking. Finally I couldn't make up any more excuses for it . . . was convinced that Harry was terrorizing her in some way. A sex thing, I guessed, otherwise she'd have talked to me about it . . . she was shy, but we were very close. So I did some serious research on Harry and discovered he wasn't a wealthy commodities trader, which is what he claimed to be. He was a graduate of the nut factory up in Camarillo. That scared me. By then I knew he'd married Ellen for the money and when I looked into her trust fund I got one hell of a jolt—most of it was gone. Two million dollars."

He finally downed the Jack Daniels. "Harry had been looting Ellen's estate from the very first day of their marriage. I was talking with my lawyers about the best way to shoot the bastard down in flames when the so-called accident happened." He shrugged. "The rest you know."

"I wondered how Harry came by his money," Ben said. "But you still haven't said whether you'll help us."

"You're damned right I will. Just tell me where you want to start."

"I think Harry set up his new identity somewhere in the Pasadena area," Ben began. "When he was . . . with Donna, Harry said he was on his way back to California. As kids we used to ride our bikes through the best sections of Pasadena drooling over the big houses and expensive condos. San Marino. Orange Grove Boulevard. Flintridge. Those were the areas Harry liked most."

Rafferty leaned back, reacting out loud. "Pasadena . . . that's interesting. I once ran into Harry in Pasadena. A friend had invited me to lunch at the Huntington-Sheraton. Harry was there, too, having drinks with someone I'd never seen. I went over to their table and said hello, to be polite. Harry seemed reluctant to introduce us. Finally the fellow introduced himself. Said he was a stockbroker. What was his name? Anyway, Harry threw down some money on the table and took his friend away. I didn't make anything of it at the time, it was right after he married Ellen and before I learned what kind of a man he was." Donna asked him if he could remember the broker's name. "No, but I remember there was something different about the way he dressed. Was his name Orville? No, it was Ollie . . . and he wore a bow tie. You don't see many of those these days."

"Can I use a phone?" Donna asked. "And the Yellow Pages for the northeast area of L.A.? I'm going to call every broker in the San Gabriel Valley until I find one named Ollie."

"Sure." Rafferty buzzed his secretary to set up "Mrs. Hollis" in a vacant office with what she needed. He watched Donna leave the office with unconcealed admiration. "Hell of a woman you've got there, Ben. Can I call you Ben?"

"Sure, and thanks for continuing the 'Hollis' fiction."

"Your wife said Harry has made you a fugitive. I didn't think you'd want your real name bandied around." He opened a drawer and removed an elastic armband and other paraphernalia for taking blood pressure. Rolling up his shirtsleeve, he said, "I'm supposed to do this whenever I have one of those incidents." He winked. "That's what the sawbones call them. Actually, it was a heart attack of sorts. Trust a doctor to find a mealy-mouthed word for it."

Rafferty took his blood pressure, saying, "I wish the Dow was this high." After making a note of the numbers and stuffing the paraphernalia back into the drawer, he said, "Now tell me about yourself and your problems with Harry. I'd like to know exactly what he's been up to since he supposedly died."

Something about Rafferty, perhaps his plain outspokenness and weathered old face, made it possible for Ben not only to give the facts about the events of the week but to bring out his emotions as well. He accepted a powerful Bloody Mary from Rafferty and, with the vodka loosening his tongue, reached deep into himself. "Harry was always the strong one. The confident one. When he was put away I was almost grateful because I wouldn't be in his shadow any more. I could be my own person. Now that he's back, it's the same damn thing all over again . . . Harry dominating me, playing the game his way. I guess it's especially important for me to beat him here, on his own ground." He drank some more of the Bloody Mary and remembered he hated tomato juice. "The problem is . . ."

When Ben couldn't go on, Rafferty tentatively, perceptively, suggested, "You still feel something for the pissant, in a way."

"I guess I do," Ben said, "deep down. God knows I've no good reason to, not any more . . ."

"Hell, I can understand . . . I had a brother who was a son of a bitch too. Bob was his name. I called him Bobby. God, how we used to fight. I hated him with all my heart, or at least I thought I did. Bobby worked down in Texas, a roughneck in the oil fields. One day I got a telegram that he was dead. He'd been working the top of a rig when subterranean pressure blew the drill string straight up out of the hole. Took Bobby's head right off. I passed out cold, and for two days I could hardly do anything but bawl. Brothers. It's a damned complicated relationship, for sure."

"You're quite a philosopher, Rafferty," Ben said, and it occurred to him that maybe Rafferty's comment about hating his brother "with all my heart" was a clue to his heart problems . . .

"Call me Sean. No, I'm not a philosopher. But I'm one hell of a gambler, and a gambler has to know people. Now look here, how can you be so sure Harry's still alive? Those thugs you told me about, the ones who took Harry out of your house yesterday, could have killed him by now. Have you thought of that?"

"Yes . . . but I believe I'd know if Harry were dead. We're identical twins, Sean. That means more than that we look alike. Our senses are mingled . . . there're scientific, genetic grounds for this . . . I won't give you a lot of mystical mumbo jumbo, but if Harry died, I'd *feel* it. Do you believe that?"

Rafferty stared at Ben. "I guess I think I do. I guess I'll have to . . . besides, I want to . . . for my own reasons . . ."

They talked on, Rafferty tossing off anecdotes about his early years of scratching for contracting jobs until his jump into the pressure-cooker world of high-stake land deals, where a one-point shift in interest rates or a wildcat strike by a small union could mean the difference between making a fortune or losing your shirt. He seemed to know every politician and banker in southern California on a first-name basis and he didn't mind saying so. He was proud of his achievements, yet also melancholy that he no longer had a family to share his success with.

Like most successful men he was interested in what others did for a living. He questioned Ben closely about work he had done for various companies, and as a real-estate developer he was especially interested in one of Ben's stories about a contractor in Hartford who built a ten-story office building with only two small elevators.

"A payoff to some zoning board," Rafferty said. "Go on."

"The tenants who moved into the building," Ben said, "naturally found themselves waiting a long time for an elevator, and the building began to get a bad reputation. Well, one thing you can't do with an office building is to add more elevators, so the owner called me in to look for some sort of design solution to his problem. It was pretty simple, really. I just put large mirrors on every floor next to the elevators. People love to look at themselves. Comb their hair. Straighten their ties. Check their makeup. The complaints stopped almost immediately. People were waiting just as long for an elevator, but it no longer bothered them because they had something to do."

Rafferty loved the story. "I could've used you on some of my jobs that went sour. A brainy guy who can stand back and see a problem with a fresh mind can make all the difference. Maybe we can do some business together, I mean, when this thing about Harry is finished. You're smart, Ben, and it's obvious you've got imagination and guts. Hell, you don't have to stand in anyone's shadow, especially Harry's."

Donna interrupted them, waving a slip of paper. "Does the name Ollie Crandall sound familiar? He's a stockbroker at Patterson, Hill and Wyman in Pasadena."

"*Yes* . . . that's the guy . . . the one Harry was lunching with . . . Ollie Crandall, about forty, face like an over-aged Boy Scout. A heavy drinker." He grinned wryly. "It takes one to spot one."

Ben planted a kiss on Donna's cheek. "Nice work, honey. Is this Crandall's phone number?"

"Yes." Donna checked her watch. "Why don't you call Crandall now. If he can be convinced that you're Harry, you might be able to get some information out of him."

Ben dialed the number of Patterson, Hill and Wyman in Pasadena. While he waited to be connected Sean Rafferty switched on his speaker system so that he and Donna could hear both sides of the conversation.

"Ollie Crandall."

"Hello, Ollie. This is—"

"Harry! Are you calling from New York?"

"No, I'm back in California and thought I'd touch base."

"You want to crow about the St. Regis and Honeywell buys. Well, go ahead. Those were shrewd moves, Harry. Frankly, I don't believe you used the darts that time. Someone gave you a tip on those stocks. Am I right?"

"Maybe . . ." Ben looked at Rafferty and Donna in puzzlement. *Darts?* "How does my account look?"

"Well, let's see." After a brief silence Crandall said, "Damned good. You could get out with two hundred and eighty thousand and change, if you wanted."

And now Ben realized he'd found a way to strike back at Harry. He said quickly, "That's why I called. I need some quick cash for a deal I'm into. What I'd like to do, Ollie, is liquidate and pick up a cashier's check today. This is a short-term move. I'll only need the money for a couple of weeks. You won't be losing a customer, you'll be gaining a commission."

"You know the standard brokerage-house terms, Harry. You get a check within seven days after a transaction. Asking for an amount that large on a few hours' notice is rather unusual."

"Sure, but you can bend the rules for a good client. Leave a thousand in the account. We'll be doing business again by the end of the month. That's a promise."

"Tell you what. I'll have a cashier's check for you in one hour if you promise to throw away those damned darts. Deal?"

However Harry used those darts, they certainly bothered Crandall. "Deal," Ben said.

"Okay, I'll start liquidating your holdings right now. There'll be a check here for you around noontime."

"Thanks, Ollie."

"What about that envelope you left with our trust officer? Do you want it back now?"

"Oh . . . the envelope. Yes, I'll pick it up along with the check. See you soon."

Ben put down the phone and said to Rafferty, "I just got some of your money back for you, Sean."

Rafferty nodded. "Thanks, Ben, but the money's not so important. What counts is that we're a little closer to Harry. You played Crandall just right." He tapped his desktop with a fingertip. "That's one greedy brother you've got. He'll do a Mount St. Helens when he learns you've stolen some of his marbles."

Ben agreed, and was glad of it . . . "You know, I think this is the first time I've ever taken anything away from Harry."

"I wonder," Donna put in, "what's in the envelope Crandall is holding for Harry."

"Let's find out." Rafferty got up and came around the desk, then led them toward the door. "I'm going to Pasadena with you."

CHAPTER 18

JIM CONDE had spent an hour poking around the Ryder home. It was a pointless exercise, but he was too angry and frustrated to stay in his office. The night before George Elgin of Staten Island had recanted his confession and produced witnesses to prove he couldn't have killed the Scarnato girl. *Or* John MacRae. *Or* the liquor-store clerk in Stamford.

A warrant had been issued for Ben Ryder, charging him with the murders of Catherine Anne Scarnato and John MacRae. But by that time Ryder and his wife had taken their children out of the hospital and disappeared. Conde was disappointed that Ryder had been able to continue conning his wife. She had to know that Ben was mentally sick. He was continually surprised at how many wives stuck by husbands who'd gone off the deep end. They thought it was the honorable thing to do. Even when the guy was a murderer. "Till death do us part" could be taken too damn literally . . .

He went into the living room and examined a collection of antique silver boxes displayed in a glass case. The boxes and other valuables—sterling silver, clothing, jewelry, a file box full of IBM stock—weren't the kinds of things people normally abandoned. On the surface it appeared that Ryder intended to return, yet he must know the case against him was strong.

The doorbell rang. Conde opened the front door to find himself facing a well-groomed man who was vaguely familiar. He looked surprised, a little alarmed, to be facing Conde.

"Excuse me, aren't you Lieutenant Conde?"

"Yes."

"I'm Carter Phillips, Crane Security."

"What do you want?"

Phillips seemed to be looking over Conde's shoulder. "I was shocked to read in this morning's paper that Mr. Ryder is wanted for murder. I never met him, but his wife is a lovely lady . . . is she at home?"

"No, they've skipped."

"Oh . . . well, I've been trying to contact her with our final report . . . and invoice. She owes our company a substantial sum for the work we've done. My district manager in New York was rather annoyed, furious, in fact, to think we might not be paid for that work."

A grin took over Conde's face. "Mr. Phillips, thank you."

"For what?"

"The thought of you vultures getting stiffed is the only bright spot in my day."

Carter Phillips straightened his glasses. "That's a strange attitude for a law officer. You can be sure—"

Conde slammed the door in Phillips' face and resumed his tour of the house. Everything he saw further convinced him that Ryder intended to return, so he locked up and drove back to Troop G, where he issued orders for a round-the-clock stakeout of the Ryder home.

He pulled out a manila folder that had no connection with Ben Ryder and brooded over it until Eddy Trelska came in.

"You wanted to see me, lieutenant?"

"Yes, Eddy, I wanted to see you."

"Any feedback from the APB on Ryder?"

"Yes. In fact, I have a pretty good idea where Ryder went."

"So soon? That's great. Where is he?"

Conde tucked the file he'd been studying under his arm. "Come with me." He went out through the squad room to the rear entrance. Trelska followed uneasily as Conde walked around the corner of the building to a deserted alleyway containing only a metal trash bin.

Without warning, Conde turned and drove his knee into Trelska's groin, then chopped at his face with a short right hook that sent his sergeant staggering against the trash bin.

Trelska, holding his groin, tried without success to straighten up. "*Hey,* what the hell . . . I can't walk—"

"You'd better walk, you crud, because I want you out of this headquarters within fifteen minutes. Leave your resignation on my desk."

"Resignation? Why the hell should I resign—?"

"Come off it, Trelska." Conde opened the file. "I took a phone call for you from Powell Motors last night. They said to tell you they'd knock down the price on the red BMW to seventy-five hundred dollars, seeing as how you were paying cash. I wondered where you got that kind of money, everyone knows you're broke. So I took the liberty of going through your desk."

"You had no right—"

He brandished a fistful of charge-account statements in Trelska's face. "Eleven thousand dollars in bills, and you're paying cash for a BMW. Where'd you get the money, Eddy? Did you sell Greg Anderson to Scarnato?"

"*No,* I wouldn't do a thing like that—"

"I should bring you up on charges, but it would only hurt the department and you're not worth that. Just get out of my sight." Conde pulled the badge off Trelska's tailored linen uniform, ripping a jagged hole in the shirt as he did so.

Trelska looked at the hole as if it was a bullet wound. "I didn't mean any harm, I've been working hard on this case, lieutenant, really hard—"

"Yeah. But not for me." Conde tucked the file back under his arm and walked away.

IT WAS DIFFICULT for Trelska to stand up straight. He eased his hand inside his pants and found a swelling damn near the size of a baseball just above his penis. He hobbled inside the building and lowered himself gently into the chair behind his desk. No one in the squad room seemed to notice his discomfort or the jagged hole in his shirt. He pawed angrily through the desk, but there was nothing he wanted to take away. The idea of bringing Conde before a review board occurred to him, but only briefly. He scribbled a letter of resignation and was putting it into an envelope when his phone rang. He answered it only to avoid drawing attention to himself.

"Trelska."

"Hello, Eddy," Sal Genovese said.

"We got trouble, Eddy. Ryder got away from us last night."

"*You* got trouble?" Trelska further dropped his voice to a whisper. "Conde found out about the dough. I'm out, I have to resign—"

"Tough titty—"

Trelska, ever alert for an angle, said, "I want another ten grand or I'll tell Conde that you're out to find the girl's killer ahead of him."

Genovese laughed. "Sounds like he's figured that out for himself. Tell him or anybody else what you want. You can't prove anything. But I've got a set of pictures from our breakfast meeting. Great stuff. You slobbering over a big wad of cash."

"Goddamn you—"

"Relax, those pictures will stay in the deep freeze as long as you behave. If you really want to make some more dough, tell me where Ryder is. I know there's a warrant out on him."

"Yeah, Conde claims he knows where Ryder went, but he sure as hell won't tell either of us. Ryder got away? You must be in shit up to your armpits for that one. I'll bet Scarnato's mixing up a concrete bathing suit for you right now. Tough titty yourself, wop."

He put down the phone in a better mood. After all, things could be worse. Conde wasn't going to have him prosecuted, and there was thirty-six thousand dollars stashed away in the spare coffeepot in his apartment. And he was no longer tied to his lousy job. Or, for that matter, Connecticut.

A plan took form . . . why bother paying off those debts? Why not stiff the creditors and head for California or Florida? With Ginger, of course. Spend part of the bundle on a nice vacation, then buy into some kind of business. A bar, maybe. Plenty of money in liquor.

Trelska was feeling almost cheerful, until he tried to stand up and discovered that the swelling in his groin had grown to the dimensions of a small grapefruit.

"WELL, SAL?"

Genovese steadied his nerves. He was in Scarnato's study and Tony was looking at him as if he were already a corpse. Vincent Malle stood by the door, his oak arms folded across his chest. If I don't handle this just right, Genovese told himself, I'm not gonna walk out of here alive. "Good news, Tony. Conde has a solid line on Ryder."

Scarnato sat at his desk playing with a carved ivory letter-opener. He was sober, the whiskey and volatile anger of the previous evening having long since worn away. "That doesn't sound like such good news to me, Sal. Conde is no canary."

"Remember that I told you I was looking for a hook on Conde?" Genovese heard desperation in his voice and hated himself for it. "Well, I found something that'll make Conde give us Ben Ryder on a silver platter."

"That was a forty-carat fuckup last night, Sal. You can't afford another. Now get out and don't come back until you can tell me where my daughter's killer is. Vincent, stick with him."

Vincent Malle gave Genovese a death's-head smile and followed him out the door.

CHAPTER 19

IT HAD been fifteen years since Ben last visited Pasadena. To most people the city meant the Rose Bowl and Rose Parade, but Ben always thought of Pasadena's palm-lined boulevards, the academic atmosphere fostered by Caltech, the elegance of Lake Avenue's exclusive shops, the looming presence of Mount Wilson to the north. He was almost sure his brother would have returned here. Harry had loved this bustling little city more than any other place.

Patterson, Hill and Wyman had offices in a Lake Avenue office building occupied by firms connected with Pasadena's old moneyed families. Sean Rafferty parked nearby and suggested they meet in Andre's, a restaurant just across the street, after Ben had seen Ollie Crandall.

Donna kissed him lightly. "Good luck, honey."

"I'll see you in about twenty minutes." Ben walked across the street and into the offices of Patterson, Hill and Wyman. It resembled every other brokerage operation he'd ever seen . . . account executives working at desks facing an electronic board that displayed the changing prices of stocks, at their fingertips computer terminals that could call up at a touch information on individual companies, customers lounging in chairs at the rear of the large, open room watching the big board with pleasure or in misery, depending on their portfolios.

Ben spotted Ollie Crandall from his bow tie and Rafferty's description of him . . . "a face like an over-aged Boy Scout."

"Harry!" Crandall called out. "Welcome home, old son."

"Hello, Ollie."

"How does Smogville look to you?"

Ben took the chair next to Crandall's desk and shook hands with the broker. "Damned good." He looked at the board. "What's the market doing today?"

"Making a technical correction, which means it's dropping like a rock and wiping out people's life savings." He laughed merrily over the image. "Not yours, of course." He pulled a check from his desk drawer. "Here's what you asked for, Harry, a cashier's check for the balance of your account, minus a thousand to keep the account open. Be careful with that, it's negotiable anywhere."

Ben glanced at the amount. More than a quarter of a million dollars. Not a bad morning's work. And Ollie Crandall had accepted him on sight. "Can I see my statement?"

"Sure." Crandall riffled through a stack of client statements. "Here you go."

Ben ignored the columns of buy-and-sell figures. His eyes fell instead on the heading at the top of the page: HARRY BOND. 16 WAVERLY PLACE. SAN MARINO. Harry's new name, and his address. San Marino . . . cloistered, rich, national headquarters for the John Birch Society, community of stately Spanish-style homes surrounded by adobe walls and shielded from neighboring eyes by giant flowering bougainvillea bushes. Ellen Rafferty's money would have bought Harry a lot of privacy in San Marino.

Crandall misinterpreted Ben's tight smile. "I'd grin too, with a portfolio that outperformed the market by thirty percent."

"You've done a great job for me, Ollie."

"I suppose your crazy darts have to get some of the credit."

Ben was still curious about what darts had to do with buying and selling stocks, but of course didn't dare ask. "Where's the envelope you were holding for me?"

"Still in our safe, I'll get it." Crandall left his desk and went upstairs, where the firm's accounting and trust departments were located. While he was gone Ben jotted down Harry's new name and address and the Social Security number he had used to open the brokerage account. Harry Bond. Nice and simple. All-American. Eagle Scout. God . . .

Crandall came back and dropped a bulky legal-sized manila envelope on the desk. "Okay, now that we're done with business, how about some lunch? You and I haven't lifted a glass together in months."

"I'd love to Ollie, but business comes first. I have to get back to L.A."

"I understand, old son. Anyone with that much money in his pocket has things to do and places to go."

Despite the breezy reply, Crandall looked dejected at the refusal. Ben glimpsed a likeable and rather lonely personality behind the loud bow tie and regretted having to turn down the invitation. Besides, Ollie Crandall might know a great deal about Harry Bond. "Soon, Ollie, maybe Monday, okay?"

Crandall brightened. "I'll hold you to that."

Ben lingered for a while answering Crandall's questions about New York women and exchanging chitchat about the market. He was curious to see whether Crandall might notice any difference between himself and Harry and remark on the change. But Crandall just went on in his breezy fashion, apparently convinced that Ben was the man he knew as Harry Bond.

Ben was surprised at how easily the impersonation came to him. He found himself speaking in Harry's sardonic way and even dredging up from his memory some of Harry's small mannerisms, such as the way he occasionally stroked his chin with a thumb. He was almost sorry when he saw they'd been talking for much longer than twenty minutes, but he had to break away . . . Donna would be starting to worry.

"I really have to go, Ollie. But I'll call you Monday morning. First thing."

He patted Crandall's shoulder, another gesture Harry had often used, and walked from the brokerage office feeling that the account of Harry and Ben was finally beginning to balance out.

IN A BOOTH at Andre's, Donna toyed restlessly with a glass of white wine and glanced repeatedly at her watch.

"He's all right," Rafferty said, trying to reassure her.

She pushed away the glass. "I know, it's just so nerve-wracking to sit here and do nothing."

The waitress came with menus, but Rafferty shook his head. "We'll wait. We have someone else coming." His polite smile expanded into a grin. "Leave the menus. Here he is."

Ben joined them in the booth and gave Donna a loud kiss that attracted smiles.

"You nut," she said fondly. "It must have gone well."

"Better than well." He looked at her wine and Rafferty's martini and shook his head. "Hey, that stuff's for peasants. Let's fit the drink to the occasion . . . waitress, a bottle of champagne."

Ben put the cashier's check on the table and pushed it over to Rafferty. "There you are, Sean. All yours."

"Ellen's, you mean." He downed the dregs of his martini and left the check where it was.

"What *happened?*" Donna asked. "Did Crandall show any doubts at all about you?"

"None. He looked at me and he saw Harry . . . heard Harry . . . believed Harry. I had a ball . . ."

Donna, a bit uneasily, was aware of a striking shift in Ben's mood. He certainly was up. Flying, in fact. Part of it, she realized, was the exhilaration of having finally given Harry a dose of his own medicine—revenge could be sweet, especially after all they'd been through. But somehow there was more to it than that. Ben's *manner* had changed. He'd become uncharacteristically demonstrative, waving his hands and talking too loud, as if to an audience instead of his immediate table.

Now he was saying in what could only be called a strident voice, "Good! Here's the bubbly." He let the waitress show him the label and pour him the host's sip. "Yes, that's very good. Fill 'em up."

"My liver recoils, but my heart sings." Rafferty lifted his glass in toast. "To the end of Harry."

"Amen," Ben said, still in a loud voice.

Donna joined the toast, reluctantly. Somehow the sentiment

depressed her. God knew she loathed Harry, but wallowing in hate, toasting death . . .

Her hesitation didn't go unnoticed.

"I apologize," Rafferty said. "That was crude."

"Me too," Ben said, not able to mean it.

She smiled at both of them, took a sip of champagne. "What was in the envelope they were holding for Harry?"

"I haven't looked." Ben took the envelope from his inside coat pocket, tore off one end and dumped the contents in the center of the table.

Rafferty gave a low whistle.

The table was covered with bank deposit books. They began picking them up and reading the bank names and deposit amounts aloud to each other.

"Security National Bank, five hundred and twenty thousand dollars."

"Bank of Southern California, four hundred and ninety-five thousand dollars."

"Bank of America, six hundred and twenty thousand dollars."

"California Trust, two hundred and eighteen thousand dollars."

Donna, awestruck said, "This must be the money Harry stole from your daughter."

Rafferty stared at the bank deposit books as though in a daze. His craggy face collapsed into leathery folds. "He killed Ellen for this, bank books. My God, I'd have *given* him this much, more, just to go away and leave her alone. Sweet Jesus, the waste."

They sat quietly while Rafferty slowly regained his control. The champagne suddenly tasted flat. The pile of bank books was too grisly a reminder of the man who had brought them together. After a few minutes Rafferty set aside his champagne and ordered another martini. "Sorry, folks . . ."

"There's nothing for *you* to be sorry about." Donna picked up several other documents that were bundled together with an old rubber band. "Did you see this? It looks like a complete set of identification in the name of Harold Bond—California driver's license, Social Security card, credit cards, everything needed to be Harry Bond."

279

Ben was sorting through the deposit books. "Suppose I were to withdraw all this money from these banks and transfer the funds to a new account. An account Harry couldn't know about. In one afternoon I could strip Harry of every dollar he took from your daughter, Sean. That surely would draw him back to California. Harry isn't going to let a couple of million dollars slip away without a fight."

"You're right, Harry would come on the run when he learned his money had disappeared." Rafferty looked at his watch. "The sooner the better. It's a quarter after one. The banks stay open until six on Friday, so we have time to make those withdrawals. Let's see . . . yes, all these banks are here in the San Gabriel Valley. Say, Ernie Deems at California Mutual is an old drinking buddy of mine. That's only three blocks away, up on Colorado Boulevard. Open an account at California Mutual, using this ID, in the name of Harry Bond." He thumped the table with a heavy index finger. "You can transfer funds electronically, you know. Leave it to me. I'll do the talking, you do the signing."

"Signing?" Donna questioned. "Ben, is your signature close enough to Harry's to pass a bank's inspection?"

"Our handwriting was almost identical when we were kids . . . I don't see why that should have changed." He took out his pen and signed "Harold Bond" on the paper place mat under his glass.

They compared Ben's "Harold Bond" with the one on the driver's license.

"Close," Rafferty said, "but not perfect. It'd be pretty sure to get by if we were dealing with smaller sums, but in this case the signature will be checked *very* closely."

"Let me practice for a few minutes."

Harry's signature was more flamboyant than Ben's and characterized by larger loops and whorls. Ben continued practicing it on the place mat, trying for a smoothly effortless sweep that was basically an expanded version of his own natural script. After some twenty tries he began to achieve a very passable imitation of Harry's signature.

"You're getting it," Donna said, meaning to encourage him.

Ben didn't need it. Actually he was experiencing a strange

sensation . . . at times his hand seemed to move across the paper on its own, and the signatures he produced then were the closest to Harry's. He wanted to tell Donna and Sean what was happening but was afraid it would sound silly to them—or odd. "Can I sign deposit slips ahead of time, or will I have to do it there?"

"I'm afraid they'll want to verify your signature on the spot," Rafferty said. "The money involved is just too big for banks to take any chances. They use those damned 'pattern recognition' machines to verify signatures in electronic transfers. They're supposed to be able to spot the difference between a genuine signature and a forgery, though I don't really know how accurate they are."

"Maybe we should forget the whole idea. It sounds too dangerous," Donna said, worried now.

"No problem," Ben said, continuing to sign "Harry Bond" with an increasing smooth flow. "I've got this down so cold that I'm almost looking forward to going up against the machine."

And there it was again, she thought. That, for Ben, unnatural . . . arrogance. It made her increasingly uneasy, mixing as it did with her concern over the danger of what they were trying, what Ben was trying . . .

Rafferty dug the olive out of his martini, set it aside. "Folks, think about this for a minute. If Ben's idea works, and I think it's got a damn good chance, Harry will make a beeline for California —assuming he got away from those goons you told me about. And you think it's likely he did. In any case, we'll know soon enough . . . All right then, what do we do with him? We might have enough evidence right here to prove Harry isn't dead, but would that take you off the hook with the police in Connecticut? I mean, will the fact that Harry is alive prove to them you didn't kill anyone?"

Ben had been turning that same question over in his mind. "No, it wouldn't. I'm not sure I could convince the police Harry has ever been in Connecticut, much less that he killed Oop and the Scarnato girl."

"Even if Harry were arrested and sent away to another hospital," Donna said, "how do we know he wouldn't be released *again* some day. I don't want to spend the rest of my life dreading the day Harry is set free."

"Then we're in agreement," Ben ventured. "We don't want to

bring in the police. Our plan is to trap Harry ourselves. Trap . . . and kill him."

"Yes," Donna said, nodding her head, telling herself her earlier squeamishness was just what the Harrys of the world counted on.

"Damned right." Rafferty made it unanimous, a pact.

THE DINGBAT HAD much less élan than Andre's. It perched perilously close to the railroad tracks in Norwalk, the south wall leaning to within two feet of the right-of-way. Some day it would lean an inch too far and a fast-moving freight train would take off the corner of the building.

Jim Conde walked into The Dingbat in midafternoon and heard a familiar voice call out: "Jim . . . over here."

"Bob? It's like the inside of a boot in here." He finally recognized Commander Bob Spence at the rear table and made his way across the sawdust-covered floor to join him.

"Thanks for coming, Jim. Want a beer?"

"Sure."

"Bartender, a beer for my friend and another of these for me." Spence raised his glass and rattled the ice cubes.

"Kind of a funny place for a meeting, isn't it?"

"Nothing like a beer joint for privacy," Spence said.

Conde's eyes had adjusted to the dim light so that he could now clearly see the considerable bulk of his old friend Bob Spence, chairman of the Connecticut Organized Crime Investigative Task Force. Spence was in civilian clothes, which didn't surprise Conde. The racketeering investigators had to keep a low profile. What did surprise him was Spence's condition. He was slightly drunk. His massive body swayed in his chair. His eyes looked wet. The drink the bartender put in front of him was a double.

"Cheers," Spence said, picking it up too quickly.

"Cheers," Conde replied without touching his beer. "What's this all about, Bob?"

"I need your help."

"I'll . . . do whatever I can for you."

"It's this damned Scarnato thing, Jim. Why did you put the lid on the case?"

"We've had some leaks. I think I've taken care of that, but I don't want it to happen again."

"That explains a lot," Spence muttered, more to himself than Conde. "They lost their ear, their pipeline, so they needed someone else. Dirty mothers."

Conde was now genuinely worried. Bob Spence was one of the toughest, smartest cops in the state police. He had risen faster than anyone in their age bracket, and Conde was counting on Spence's rise to help him gain his own captaincy. Spence was tough, politically savvy and as hard on himself as on the men who worked for him. He was not the kind of man who sat around taverns in midafternoon drinking doubles and muttering to himself, unless something had gone very wrong for him.

"Bob, why did you want to see me?"

"My neck's on the chopping block. I need a big favor, Jim. I want to know where Ben Ryder has gone, and then I want you to ease off. Put the investigation on the back burner."

"What? You're telling me to let Ryder get away?"

Spence shook his head. "He won't get away. Scarnato will have his ass for breakfast. The poor sick bastard doesn't have a chance."

Everything became clear to Conde. "Scarnato sent you?"

Spence became evasive. "Maybe. Oh, crap, I won't lie to you. It was Genovese."

"The Fixer? Why didn't you tell him to go to hell? Bust his damned head?"

Spence laughed derisively. "Do you remember what I told you last Monday? I said the mob doesn't own Connecticut, the way they do New Jersey. Well, I was wrong. I've been up there in Hartford kidding myself that I'm doing a real job. Bob Spence, boy crime-buster. What a crock. Yeah, I snagged a few Mafia butterballs who were so dumb they practically sent themselves to jail, but until today I never knew how well organized the mob is up here. If I don't produce for Genovese, I'll be working speed traps on Route 84 for the rest of my life. Or worse."

"I'm sorry, Bob. Disgusted but sorry. And I won't help you."

Spence looked at him pityingly. "Do you think you have a choice? Haven't you been listening? You're finished too unless you do as you're told—"

"The hell I am. I'm reporting every word of this to the state Attorney General's office."

"Jim . . . Jim . . ." Spence drew a notebook from his inside coat pocket and consulted it. "They told me to remind you of an Exacta you hit at Aqueduct raceway three years ago. You walked away from the track with twenty-five hundred dollars that day."

"So what? It's legal to bet at the track and I had a lucky day. That was only the third time in my life I'd ever been to a race track."

"Yeah, but you didn't declare that money as income on your tax form."

"Sure I did." But even as the words left his mouth, Conde was trying to remember. He'd won the money in the spring, March or April. A year later at tax time had he remembered to declare it? "If I didn't I certainly meant to."

Spence silently finished his drink.

"So if I forgot I'll declare it now and pay the penalty. No big deal."

"Tax *evasion* is a big deal, Jim."

"There are people who forget to declare millions of dollars and nothing happens to them. Who's going to care about an overlooked twenty-five hundred?"

"Buddy boy, Genovese has one of his tame Congressmen primed to contact Internal Revenue. The tax people tend to jump when a Congressman fingers someone . . . Congress votes their appropriations. The mob will see that you're prosecuted for tax evasion. Sure, you'll probably get off with a fine and probation, but even if you win a court case your reputation will be shot as far as the state police is concerned, and you'll be thousands of dollars in debt for attorney's fees. If you lose big, you go to jail. It's a no-win situation."

So this is how it happens, Conde thought. They find one mistake and ride the hell out of it. But wait . . . I'm not sure I didn't declare that money. "I'm not doing anything until I check my tax return. Genovese may be bluffing."

"No, he's not. He showed me a copy of your return for that year. You forgot to declare it. I'm sorry, Jim."

"Genovese has a copy of *my* tax return. Where the hell . . . ?"

"They've got people everywhere, pal."

284

Conde's normal cool was edging toward panic. I can't let Scarnato do it to me . . . I've fought those people all my life, I can't end up *working* for them. "Bob, I can't do it."

"Look, do you think *I* like this? Years ago, when I was a kid, I made one lousy mistake. One. I'd almost forgotten it myself, until today."

Conde had seen other men broken, disgraced by the mob, and seldom had felt pity because invariably they'd brought it on themselves. He would never have believed it could happen to him. And over a mistake, a technicality, a lapse of memory . . . "Why did Genovese send you? Why didn't he come himself?"

"Why should he? Besides, he figures I'd do better with you." Spence paused. "Well?"

The words had to be forced out, but once started, after the resistance, it was as though Conde's professionalism took over, he wouldn't do less than a thorough job, no matter what it was . . . "Ben Ryder is in California. He must not have taken much money, he left a credit-card trail a mile wide. He and his wife flew from Boston to Los Angeles last night. They probably left their kids with someone up there, because they're traveling alone. At L.A. International they rented an Avis car, again with a credit card. An APB was put out on the license numbers throughout the L.A. basin. Then, a couple of hours ago, the L.A. police spotted the car in a lot behind an office building on Wilshire Boulevard. The Rafferty Building, which is owned by Sean Rafferty, the late Harry Ryder's father-in-law. LAPD contacted Rafferty's office and learned that he went out this morning with a couple who answer the description of the Ryders. Sooner or later the Ryders will return for the car, and be arrested."

"Get on the phone as fast as you can, Jim. Call off that stakeout. Tell the LAPD that Ryder is no longer under suspicion, the warrant's been withdrawn. Tell them anything. But keep the police *away* from that car."

Conde said nothing.

"Jim?"

"One time. Tell The Fixer that. *One time.* If he tries this again —ever—I'll kill him. You tell him that. I'm not sure, maybe I can convince myself that a lifetime, my family, are worth that. But that's it."

"ERNIE DEEMS. How the hell are you?"

Deems swung around in his chair and smiled at Sean Rafferty. "Hello there, Sean. What brings you out to the San Gabriel Valley? Trying to steal land from some poor old widow lady?"

They smiled over the ritualized insults as Deems stood up and shook Rafferty's hand.

"Ernie, I'd like you to meet some friends of mine, Harry and Donna Bond. Believe it or not, they actually want to do business with this bank. Oh, I've warned them about you, but they won't listen. That's the younger generation."

Deems was a heavy, balding man with an open face and firm handshake. "Nice to meet you. Don't pay any attention to Sean. He hasn't had a good word to say about California Mutual since we helped make him rich. What can I do for you?"

"I'd like to open an account and consolidate some funds from other banks here," Ben explained. "I want it done this afternoon, if possible."

"In the electronic age anything is possible." Deems arranged chairs in front of his desk for them, and personally seated Donna.

Ben explained that he wanted to open a commercial account that could be used as the basis for letters of credit he would need for a business trip abroad. Deems was happy to open such an account, and understood the need for urgency when Ben told him he would be leaving for London on Monday. The account was opened in the name of Harold Bond. For tax and reference purposes he showed Deems the driver's license and charge cards from the envelope Ollie Crandall had been holding. The ID satisfied Deems completely. On the application form Ben listed his occupation as "investment counselor." When he gave Deems the deposit books, the banker looked suitably impressed. "It seems I owe you a dinner at Scandia," he said to Rafferty.

"With drinks at Anselmo's," Rafferty added.

There were additional forms to be filled out in order for a transfer of funds to be made electronically from the other banks to California Mutual. When the forms were completed, Deems said, "I'll have to ask you to step over here, Mr. Bond."

"Harry," Ben said. "Call me Harry."

"All right, Harry. Mrs. Bond, our electronic transfer system might be of interest to you too."

Donna and Sean Rafferty followed Deems and Ben across the bank floor to an area behind the teller windows occupied by a small data-processing system.

"I'll key this transaction myself," Deems said to a teller who came over to assist him. He sat down at the keyboard and typed a series of words, numbers and symbols into the computer. "I'm putting your new account number into the computer and contacting the other banks through their computers. That little gizmo on the screen is the universal banking code for a withdrawal. Right now assistant vice-presidents in those four banks are being informed that a *sizable withdrawal* has been requested."

A flat screen had been built into the desktop of the computer. Attached to the system by a power cord was a strange-looking pen. "This is a light pen. Just sign your name on the electronic pad. Your signature will be transmitted to the other banks and verified by their computers."

Donna hoped nobody saw her at that moment, her suddenly clenched fists, the tightness around her mouth like steel bands. Practicing Harry's signature in a restaurant was one thing . . . fooling a sophisticated computer system was another.

Ben seemed unperturbed. He was. In fact, he actually felt a rush of excitement as he picked up the light pen. It was a rather awkward instrument to hold because of the power cord, and ways to improve its design automatically went through his mind.

"Just use it as you would an ordinary pen or pencil," Deems said. "Nothing to it. You're just writing with a beam of light instead of a penpoint."

Ben knew he'd have a better chance if he didn't overly concentrate on the signature. He applied the tip of the pen to the screen and dashed it off with a few quick strokes. "That's all there is to it?" he asked Deems.

"Just about. The computers in the other banks are scanning your signature right now. When they make the verification, the funds will be transferred here in a matter of milliseconds."

"Incredible," Donna said, meaning it more than one way.

"I haven't totally adapted to it myself," Deems said.

"Ernie comes from the old school of banking," Rafferty said. "I remember when he wore a green eyeshade and garters to hold up his sleeves."

"That was my daddy, Sean. In your declining years you tend to confuse us."

Donna suspected Rafferty's banter was a nervous reaction to his tension. What in God's name would they do if the computer said Ben's signature was a forgery . . . ?

A star-shaped symbol appeared on the electronic pad next to the signature.

"There's the first verification," Deems said.

They watched as, one by one, three additional star-shaped symbols appeared. An instant later the signature disappeared from the screen and a series of figures appeared indicating the transfers had been made.

Deems, unaware of the deflating tension around him, said, "We're delighted to have you as a customer, Harry. Let me know if I can be of help to you. I'll have those letters of credit for you by ten A.M. Monday. And if you need a loan, that's what we're here for."

"Ernie will accept any of your major vital organs as collateral," Rafferty added, his face glistening with sweat.

Ben joined in the polite laughter, taking care not to show his truly wild joy. At last he was ahead of Harry, in control of events.

Now the trick would be to stay there.

"TONY, THIS IS Sal."

"What is it?"

"Ryder is in Los Angeles."

"L.A. is a big city."

"He's with a guy named Rafferty. I called out there to Ray Parisi and told him to put some people on Rafferty's home and office. I told them to locate Ryder, but to keep their distance until we get there."

"How the hell will they know him?"

"I sent a picture of Ryder to the coast over my banker's telecopier."

"Charter a plane, we'll leave tonight. You. Me. Vincent. Is Vincent with you now?"

"Sure."

"Tell him to bring the hook."

HARRY WAS PACKING for his return to Los Angeles. The *New York Post* lay open on the coffee table to page three, where a headline read: WESTPORT EXEC HUNTED IN SCARNATO GIRL KILLING. That was a laugh. Anyone who wore a suit and tie was an "Exec" as far as the *Post* was concerned.

His eyes frequently strayed to the headline as he sorted through the few possessions he'd accummulated during his stay in Connecticut. The fact that Ben had managed to get a jump on the police didn't bother him. Ben was a babe in the woods when it came to out-foxing the law. The police would pick him up in a day or two, maximum.

"Junk," Harry said, dumping the contents of his desk drawer into a garbage can. There was very little in the apartment he wanted to take, least of all his duplicate set of Ben's wardrobe. Ben's taste was much too conservative for him.

He planned to board a TWA flight to Los Angeles in the morning with his fake glasses and mustache in place, and wearing rumpled Levis, a cowboy shirt and an authentic Stetson purchased at Billy Martin's western togs store on Madison Avenue. Anyone who bothered with a second glance at him would see only a played-out rhinestone cowboy on his way home. There were half a dozen of those on every flight from New York to L.A.

Ben's wardrobe went into a large cardboard box. He would dump the box in a Goodwill donation center on the way to the airport. What the hell, he was a good citizen. Help the less fortunate.

What else?

The one thing he truly regretted leaving behind was the beautiful Rolls Royce he had ditched on his way home from Harlem the night before. Even with a crumpled fender, it was a gorgeous machine. A smile crossed his lips as he replayed in his mind the escape from Harlem. Moments like that came once in a lifetime. They deserved to be savored. He wondered who the Rolls belonged to. Scarnato, he hoped.

The smile grew wider as he considered all the unpleasant things that would happen to Ben if Scarnato found his brother before the police did.

"Darts!"

Harry opened the endtable drawer and removed the six red steel-tipped darts he used for making his stock-market picks. Can't leave these behind. How else can a man make a few dollars in such a crazy market?

CHAPTER 20

THE HOUSE on Waverly Place was exactly what Ben had expected. Spanish-style with a red-tiled roof. Flowering trees in the outer yard. Secluded behind a high white wall. It was the house Harry had talked about having when he was a kid delivering newspapers to places just like this one.

Ben pushed open the wrought-iron gate and stepped into the courtyard. The house seemed lived in. The drapes were open and someone had watered the plants outside the front door. Could Harry have beaten him back to California? He was still certain Harry had escaped from Scarnato's thugs—they thought they were kidnapping a simple industrial designer and Harry and his tricks would have come as a nasty surprise—but even Harry would need time to free himself from a man like Scarnato.

Still, someone was inside. He pushed the doorbell and waited tensely, glad he had been able to convince Donna and Rafferty that he should come here alone.

The door was opened by a beautiful young woman with long red hair that fell to her shoulders. She wore a tank-top with the name "Tina" embroidered over the heart and blue bikini bottoms. She was barefoot. Her dimpled jaw dropped at the sight of Ben's face.

"Harry? What are you doing here? You didn't call . . . I thought . . ."

Ben walked past her into the house. Who was the girl? Why was she here? Was anyone else in the house? Those questions and others caromed through his head. He couldn't rely totally on his physical appearance. He'd have to start acting and talking like Harry right away, know what Harry knew . . . including who this Tina was.

The house was furnished in Mediterranean style. Impressionist prints decorated the walls along with one or two original oils by artists of a newer school. Dark oak floors were brightened by colorful area rugs. He noticed a gun cabinet stocked with rifles and shotguns and a staircase leading to a second floor. Ben took it all in as quickly as possible as he tried to project the image of a man returning home.

"How are you, Tina?" Thank God her name was stitched on her tank-top.

"Okay. Why didn't you use your key?"

"I lost it somewhere." He strolled around, ostensibly examining the condition of the house while looking and listening for evidence of other people. The house appeared to be empty except for the girl. He did see a lot of dishes in the sink and dirty clothes piled up in the laundry room. And many of the windows were streaked with dirt, from a recent Santa Ana.

The girl had followed him around, nervously rubbing her palms and trying to distract him from the occasional messy area. "I'm sorry, Harry. I'd have cleaned up better if I'd known you were coming home today. Really I would. The house isn't usually like this, I swear it isn't."

Her voice told Ben she was terrified. What would Harry do to her for a messy house? He wouldn't just shrug it off. Not brother Harry.

Ben turned and slapped Tina's face.

She fell against the breakfast counter. She didn't cry. Didn't say a word. The woman really was terrified.

"This place is a garbage heap. I'm going upstairs to change. I want to see things in better shape when I come back down or you'll get better than a slap."

"Yes, Harry." Her first words since the slap.

Ben left her hurrying off for the vacuum cleaner and went up to the second floor. The girl had been so scared she could hardly move. Her hands shook. Why in God's name did she stay? He felt guilty about hitting her, and was a little surprised that he had instinctively known exactly what Harry would do.

There were two bedrooms upstairs, each with its own bath. The huge master bedroom had a vaulted ceiling that gave the room a marvelous sense of openness. Ben remembered the tiny cubicle they had shared as children. Barely enough space for two narrow beds and a bureau. The dressing room for this bedroom was larger than their old cubicle.

He opened the closet and found rows of suits and sports clothes. Harry obviously intended to make up for the years he had spent wearing only the gray twill uniforms issued in mental institutions. Ben slowly stripped off his own clothing and chose a pair of yellow slacks, a white sportshirt and tan loafers from Harry's wardrobe. He dressed, he admitted to himself, with a certain sense of revenge. At U.S.C. Harry would share anything with him except his clothes. To Harry clothes were a way of advertising a prosperity he didn't have. Harry's clothes, Harry's skin. His own had a strangely tingling sensation all over . . .

The bedroom also contained a locked desk. Ben used a letter-opener to force it open. Examining what he found was a crash course in deception . . . a death certificate for a man named Harold Bond who had died two years ago of a heart attack. This original Harold Bond had been an appliance salesman from Fresno, a bachelor with no close relatives. Harry had adopted the name and carefully rebuilt the identity before all the computer systems of the business and government worlds could learn that the real Harry Bond was dead. Ben also found a sales agreement for the new Mercedes he had seen in the driveway and a tidy file of receipts for all the major purchases Harry had made since beginning his new identity. One of the receipts indicated Harry was renting this house at a cost of three thousand dollars a month.

He also decided he'd better go through the girl's belongings in the second bedroom. There wasn't much of interest, just clothes and a few letters from the girl's mother. He almost missed the peculiar thing about the letters because it was so obvious . . . the girl's mother called her Rosemary and the letters were addressed to Rosemary

Davis, 52 Waverly Place, San Marino. Ben looked through her purse and discovered that all of her identification was also in the name of Rosemary Davis. Yet the name "Tina" was embroidered on every one of the blouses, T-shirts and tank-tops in her closet.

Strange.

He went downstairs and found the girl busily stuffing plates and silverware into the kitchen dishwasher.

"How's the Mercedes running?"

"What? Oh, there was an oil leak, but it was only a loose gasket. I had it fixed."

"Good . . ." He wished he had a clever way to ask the next question but couldn't think of one on the spot and figured he'd better know the answer quick. He'd risk it . . . "Tell me something, why the hell do you have Tina on your clothes when your name is Rosemary?"

She looked at him in astonishment. "Is this a joke? You *told* me to put Tina on all my clothes. You *insist* on calling me Tina but never tell me why. Please, Harry, no more games."

He was elated, he'd gotten away with it.

Tina returned to the stack of dirty dishes. "Do you want something to eat? There's cold turkey and salad in the refrigerator, or I can make you something hot."

"No, I'm not hungry."

"Do you want to have sex?"

"Not right now."

Tina hadn't dropped a beat in the rhythm of her work to ask that question. She might have been inquiring whether he wanted a cup of coffee. Aside from her initial surprise when they met at the door, the only emotion she'd shown was fear. Her manner was like a bond slave, but he suspected her cold and aloof servility was a mask for hatred. She'd service any whim of Harry's, from a turkey sandwich to sex, like an automaton. But why? Why in God's name would a woman with her exquisite figure and face to match submit to Harry's demands, to his demeaning of her? Hell, Harry wasn't even a movie producer.

"Have there been any calls for me? Mail?"

"No calls, and no mail except for bills. I paid them out of the money you left. If you want to check the receipts, they're in that drawer."

Time for another gamble . . . "Did you get a call from *me* recently?"

She looked at him. "Harry . . . ?"

"Don't sweat it . . . I've been drinking too damn much lately . . . some things have slipped my mind."

"You called last week," she said, still looking closely at him, "and told me you'd be home soon. You said you'd phone first so I could pick you up at the airport. That's why I was so surprised to see you." She looked away from him, as though hiding something.

"There was something else. What was it?"

"You *know,* you know exactly what you said. This is just another of your sick games."

Ben moved just slightly and she flinched, expecting to be hit again.

"Relax, I'm in a good mood. How about some champagne?"

"All right."

He'd guessed champagne would be a staple in Harry's pantry. "Bring it on. I'll be in the living room."

Ben proceeded into the spacious main room, sat down in a comfortable chair next to the telephone, and had committed the number to memory by the time Tina arrived with a split of Dom Perignon and glass on a silver tray. He noticed how stiffly she held herself. Experience had apparently taught her that Harry might do anything to her at any time.

Tina. The name was so important to Harry that he had taken the extraordinary step of having it labeled on all of this girl's clothes. Where had the name come from? Why did Harry want a girl with that specific name?

For a moment he was tempted to tell her who he was, she so obviously hated Harry . . . but quickly decided against it. She might despise and fear Harry, but that didn't preclude some sort of sadomasochistic relationship that could be mighty dangerous to disrupt. Given Harry's sadism with women, it certainly followed. And, on a practical level, being Harry had advantages here . . . Tina was conditioned to carry out whatever instructions Harry gave her, never mind the reason. That was too useful an asset to throw away. He'd need every edge he could get to pull off what he was up to. And . . . was he also liking his role too much to give it up, even with one person? It had been a curiously exhilarating day. He seemed to have found a new source of energy, a greater awareness of . . . what? . . . his own powers? Being Harry was a culture shock, and like most such shocks it released energy, stimulated. In one stroke, literally, he had acquired two million dollars, a house in San Marino, a new Mercedes and a mistress—of sorts. He felt cunning, stronger, even dangerous. Like a new person . . . yet one who was familiar, even if in a removed sort of way. He'd need to learn to handle this new person.

He picked up the champagne and nearly drained the glass. Had he ever had champagne in the afternoon before? Not that he could remember. No question, this was a day of firsts.

Tina was bent over a magazine rack next to the couch, straightening the large pile of back issues. In an attempt to break through her cocoon, he said in what he thought was a conventional voice: "How's your mother getting along?"

She turned around, face chalk-white. "Harry, you haven't hurt her? I said I'd do anything you wanted. Please, for God's sake, she's an old lady, she thinks I'm a *secretary*. Please, just leave her *alone*." She came toward him like a supplicant.

"Don't worry," Ben said quickly. "I saw some letters from your mother in your room and wondered about her, that's all."

"You promised you wouldn't go near her."

"I haven't. Now forget it."

"Can I call her?"

"Be my guest."

"From upstairs?"

"You can call from Seattle, for all I care."

She left the living room hesitantly, still afraid of some trick.

So that's how he controls her, Ben thought. In his unique way, Harry probably explained all the "accidents" that could happen to a vulnerable old lady. Explanations would be only a beginning, of course. Harry would have had a demonstration, something to leave Tina too terrified to resist him or risk going to the police.

It seems I owe one to Harry for Rosemary Davis too.

"WHAT ARE THOSE men doing?" Donna said.

Sean Rafferty looked around. "Where?"

"The blue Chevy." Donna pointed across the parking lot. "Two men in that Chevy are watching the car Ben rented at the airport. Don't stop. Drive right past."

After, at his request, leaving Ben in Pasadena, they had returned to Rafferty's office on Wilshire Boulevard so that Donna could retrieve the car Ben had rented. That was clearly impossible now, with two men watching it. Donna said she was sure they were police.

"But what makes you think they're police?" Rafferty said. "They could be just . . . two men."

"No, they're the police, and now they're looking this way. Drive on past, Sean."

Rafferty maneuvered his Cadillac through the parking lot and swung around the block into the private garage beneath his building. As they took the elevator to Rafferty's penthouse office, they talked about their predicament. The plan had been for Ben to enter and search the house on Waverly Place. Meanwhile Donna would collect their suitcases from the car and wait in Rafferty's office for Ben's phone call. If the house in San Marino was safe, they would go back there to set their trap for Harry. But now their luggage was under the eyes of the police and if they left, they might lead the police to Ben.

Rafferty picked up a fistful of messages from his secretary. "Were there any calls besides these, Rita? Anything out of the ordinary?"

"In a way, yes. Someone called to ask where you were. I didn't know, so I only said you'd gone out with Mr. and Mrs. Hollis. For some reason the caller found that interesting . . . asked if the Hollises were a couple in their thirties, if he had dark hair, that sort of thing."

"Who was he?"

"I don't know. He hung up before I could ask. Mr. Rafferty . . ." she looked at Donna with suspicion, and concern for her employer. "Are you all right?"

"Yes, Rita. Don't worry, I'm just doing some fancy footwork on a business deal. Put it out of your mind."

Rafferty took Donna into his office and closed the odor. "You were right. Those people must be the police. How did they find you?"

"Through the car, I suppose. We had to use a credit card to rent it. Well, we can't go back to San Marino tonight. That would be too dangerous for Ben."

Rafferty paced the floor, the business messages in his hand forgotten. "We'll use *The Melinda.*"

"What's that?"

"My boat, a cabin cruiser berthed at Marina del Rey. After Ben calls, we'll drive to the marina. Let the police follow if they want. It won't do them any good. We'll cast off and move the boat down to Newport Beach, where I have another berth. We can pick up a car and drive to San Marino from there."

"You're starting to think like a fugitive too. I'm sorry we've brought so much trouble into your life—"

"Nonsense. It's Harry who caused the trouble. And Harry who has to pay. I'll risk plenty for that. And besides, I like you people."

Donna smiled, but his words triggered thoughts of Sharon and Jeff, the pain and terror they'd gone through because of Harry . . . "May I use your phone to call Boston? I'd like to talk to my children."

"Sure, I'll clear out and give you some privacy." He took note of the droop of Donna's shoulders and her dour expression and put an arm around her. "You'll see them soon, Donna. This is almost over. Harry is going to fall right into our trap, don't you worry . . ." He wished he were as sure as he hoped he sounded.

Rafferty's secretary buzzed them from the outer office. "Sir, Mr. Hollis is calling."

"Put him on." Rafferty handed Donna the phone and switched on his speaker system.

"Hello?" Ben's voice boomed from the speaker.

"Ben? We're here. Sean has his speaker open so we can both talk to you."

"I'm in the house, everything is quiet."

"Any sign of Harry?" Rafferty asked.

"Apparently he's still in Connecticut. There's a . . . housekeeper here. Thinks I'm Harry, of course. She was expecting him home soon, so apparently we've got just a little time to make our plans. I'm not too happy about the idea of tangling with Harry here. The house is too big, too many ways to enter it. If Harry suspects we're onto him, he certainly won't walk through the front door—"

Donna broke in. "Ben, the police are watching the car we rented. I think they saw us drive through the parking lot. We didn't stop at the car, but they looked us over. So they'll probably follow when we leave here. Sean has a boat at Marina del Rey. He thinks we can lose the police by driving to the marina, then taking the boat down the coast to Newport Beach."

"Sounds all right. Hey, why don't we set our trap on your boat, Sean? There are damned few ways he could get onto a boat without being seen. I could leave a message for him here, tell him the only way he'll see that money again is to take it away from me. If we taunt him enough I think he'll come to us." He paused. "Sean?"

"Suits me," Rafferty said with a nod. "My slip at Newport is way out at the end of a dock. Couldn't be better for our purposes. It's the Trade Winds marina, slip A-12, Newport Beach. Can you find it?"

"Sure."

"How will you get there?" Donna asked.

"Harry has a Mercedes sitting in the driveway. I'll take it. That'll sure fuel his fire." He cleared his throat. "There are all sorts of weapons in the house. I'm no marksman, so I've picked a shotgun for myself. Can you handle a gun, Sean?"

"I was raised on a farm, son. Hunted jackrabbits for dinner. Bring me a rifle. Thirty-caliber would be best. Lever action, if you can find one. If not, use your own judgment. Just make sure you bring the right type of ammunition for whatever iron you choose."

"Will do. Donna, have you talked to the kids yet?"

"I was just about to call Boston."

"Give them my love . . . tell them we'll be there soon."

"I will. Be careful, Ben."

"You, too. I'll see you in Newport Beach later tonight. Bye."

Donna put down the phone as if it were a strange new technology she mistrusted.

"What is it, Donna? Does the idea of taking on Harry still bother you—?"

"No, it's not that. But did Ben sound strange to you?"

"Strange? No. He's under a strain, of course."

"Yes, sure . . . that must be it. The strain."

She wanted very badly to be convinced. But deep down she had the nagging feeling that Ben . . . his tone, his mood swings . . . was not entirely Ben any more.

BEN SELECTED A 12-gauge shotgun for himself and a Winchester lever-action rifle for Sean Rafferty. He found the correct ammunition for both weapons in the bottom drawer of the gun cabinet, wrapped the weapons and ammo in a blanket and locked it all in the trunk of the Mercedes. As an afterthought he added a pistol to his armory, a small Walther PPK for Donna. He doubted she would use it, but was determined that she should have some kind of weapon available to her.

These preparations alarmed Tina. She hovered nearby, obviously looking for an opportunity to speak.

"You want something, Tina?"

"You said that when you came back to California you might let me go. Remember? You said it twice. Can I leave now, Harry? Will you let me out of this? I don't know what you're up to with those guns, and I don't *want* to know. Just let me go. I've done everything you wanted. You haven't had any more trouble with me. I took care of your house. Did what you liked in bed. You never heard me complain, did you? Not since the beginning—"

She flinched when the phone rang. Before Ben could stop her, she'd picked up the phone and said hello. She looked confused, her free hand moved languidly to her cheek. And she looked at Ben wide-eyed. "Harry? No, it can't be. You're here, right here—"

Ben grabbed the phone from her hand. "Go upstairs, Tina. Stay in your room until I call you." He waited until she had gone, staring blankly at him over her shoulder, before putting the receiver to his ear. "Hello there, Harry. How's the weather in Connecticut?"

"*Ben?*"

It had been eighteen years since Ben had heard that voice. Despite everything it produced a flash of warmth in him. "Yes, it's me."

"What the hell are *you* doing there? How did you—"

"You've got a nice house, I've always liked San Marino myself.

But you should be buying, not renting. Property values in San Marino can only go up."

Harry recovered enough to give out a burst of laughter. "So you found my little hideaway. I figured you were on the run. You surprise me. In fact, I'm impressed. Congratulations."

"*Thanks,* brother."

"I'll do you a favor, Ben—for old time's sake. Keep the house until September. The rent's paid. The refrigerator and wine cellar are stocked. Keep Tina, too. She's pretty good in the sack. Not as good as Donna, but she'll do. You should have met the original Tina— what a bitch *she* was."

Ben's hand tightened on the phone. The warmth from the past was abruptly gone. "I have more than the house, Harry. I dropped in on Ollie Crandall this morning. On my instructions he liquidated your stock and gave me a check for the balance."

"By God, I'll kill that—"

"I also picked up the envelope you left with their trust office. Lots of goodies in there too, Harry. I've co-opted your new identity. I'm now Harry Bond. Those four banks transferred your money to me without a question."

"My money—"

"No, *my* money. You're broke, Harry. Remember how poor we were as kids? Well, you're back to square one."

"Goddamn you. You've always been such a smug little—"

"Get yourself a job in a gas station, Harry. No, a supermarket. Bag boy, that's for you. Stuffing cartons of milk and cans of tomato juice into brown paper bags all day long. There's good money in that, Harry. Four bucks an hour, maybe more. Get yourself a union card. Find a solid company and work your way up from the bottom—"

"You're dead," Harry said in a near-choked voice. "You *and* your whole family."

Ben continued to apply the pressure. "You can't hurt us any more. We're going to disappear, Harry—with your money. Get yourself a monkey and a music box. Kids love to throw dimes to monkeys." And continued over Harry's threats . . . "Or come on back to California and take the money away from me. If you can."

"What?"

301

"Catch one of the red-eye flights. You can be here in a few hours."

"And you'll have the police watching every one of those flights for me."

"The police aren't exactly in my corner, thanks to you. You did a good job there, Harry. Besides, this is personal. You're mine, Harry."

"Bull. You haven't got the guts to frighten me. You never did."

"I had enough to strip you of every dollar you stole from your wife's estate."

"So you latched onto my dear ex-father-in-law. Old Sean Rafferty. Don't you know he's the biggest land vulture in California? You probably fell for that country boy act. And . . . oh yeah . . . Sean ran into Ollie and me at the Huntington once, but just for a second. I didn't think Sean even caught Ollie's name. Well, to hell with it. I still don't believe you won't call the cops, try to convince them you're True-Blue Ben, just like you did in Connecticut."

Ben looked at his watch. "It's almost four o'clock here. Seven in Connecticut. You can be in Los Angeles between midnight and three A.M., depending on which flight you take. I'll be waiting for you, Harry. If you aren't here by dawn, I'm leaving with the money. And you'll never find me, Harry. I'm learning your game, and it seems I'm a fast learner."

A tense beat while Harry made up his mind. "I'll be there," he said. "Oh yes, brother Ben, I'll *be* there . . ."

Ben pulled out of his pocket the scrap of paper on which he had written the name of the marina where he would meet Rafferty and Donna. "I'll be on board *The Melinda*. She's berthed at the Trade Winds marina, slip A-12, Newport Beach."

"So I was right, Rafferty is in on this."

There was no reason to deny that. "Yes, Rafferty will be there, Harry. It seems he has some settling up to do with you too."

"Settling up? Come off the cornpone, Ben . . . Ellen was a nuisance, and damned if she didn't look exactly like Sean. Can you think of a better reason to get rid of a woman?"

He said it without a trace of humor, and suddenly Ben felt very depressed. "Why, Harry?"

"Why what?"

302

"Why do you hate women—?"

"I don't hate women, Ben. I love them." His voice became silky. "I just love them to death. Hell, I'm a very tragic figure . . . ask the damned shrinks."

Ben's depression turned to anger . . . "Be at Newport Beach by dawn or kiss your two million dollars goodbye." He broke the connection, reached down and pulled the phone cord loose from its wall jack.

He no longer craved champagne. Hard liquor was more appropriate to his new mood. He found a bottle of fine bonded bourbon in the liquor cabinet, poured a generous drink and dropped a handful of ice cubes into the glass.

Settling again into the comfortable living room chair, he sought relief in the raw, burning power of the whiskey. No luck. Liquor had never been much of a release for him. A jog down a quiet country road or a fast game of racketball had always provided more relaxation than a drink. Regretfully, he set the whiskey aside.

Tina had come back to the living room. Her approach was like a cat's. She came slinking around a corner and halted by the wall, then moved a few feet closer and stopped, moved again on a slant, finally coming to rest on the edge of the couch.

"So you aren't Harry. That was Harry on the phone . . . you're the brother—Ben."

"Yes."

"He hates you, Ben. He went east to deal with you, as he put it. I knew what that meant. You're lucky you're alive. I'm surprised. Is he coming back here?"

Ben nodded. "He'll be in Los Angeles in a few hours. Look, I'm sorry I slapped you. I've been playing a part today, pretending to be Harry to get my hands on his money and get him back here. It was weird, I must say. I felt . . . more myself . . . smarter, unbeatable, powerful." He looked away. "I told myself that my only reason for doing these things was to get back at Harry. But there was more to it . . . I wanted to know for once in my life what it was like *to be Harry*. To do whatever I wanted, to have no second thoughts or conscience about anything."

Tina wasn't really taking it in. She had her own troubles . . .

303

"What am *I* going to do? He'll blame me for letting you in the house."

"Tell me why you're here, maybe I can help you."

"Well, I met Harry last fall at a singles bar in the valley. He seemed like a nice guy. He said he was looking for a red-headed girl named Tina but I'd do. He was really charming, bought me presents, took me to the best places. I told him everything about myself, even that I'd once been in a mental institution, years ago, when I was seventeen. I went through the acid thing, you know? It burned out my brain for a while. Harry was all sympathy about that—at first.

"One night he brought me here, locked me in a tiny attic room without any windows and went to work on me. He's no good at sex. Awful. He tries to make up for it with his cruelty. I was in that room for weeks, I think. Never mind what he did. I don't want to repeat it. When I came out I'd given up any idea of fighting him. I have a history of . . . hallucinating. Do you know what that means? If you have a wild story, you can never convince people you're telling the truth. I know. One of the orderlies at the hospital made me have sex with him once. I tried to complain . . . have him fired . . . no one would even listen to me. I knew the same thing would happen if I went to the police about Harry. They'd take one look at my record, and at the address of this house, and tell me to go away. Harry had picked me very carefully.

"He told me I'd be his Tina or he'd take my mother somewhere and give her the same treatment he'd given me . . . God, my mother's nothing like me . . . a sweet, simple woman. My only family. And she stuck by me through all my troubles. She's the one person I'd never do anything to hurt. Harry knew that too. And even if I'd gone to somebody, made them believe me, how long would they have kept Harry locked up? He'd soon be out and make good on his threat." Tears started. "Oh, what difference does it make? He's coming now—"

"And I intend to stop him from hurting you or your mother or anybody else. Ever."

She looked dubious. "You said yourself how smart Harry is. How nobody beats him . . ."

"Maybe. Maybe not." Ben remembered the brand-new check-book from California Mutual. He took it from his hip pocket and fumbled for a pen. "Where does your mother live?"

"San Diego."

"Can she travel?"

"Yes, I suppose so."

He picked a figure out of thin air—fifty thousand dollars—and wrote out a check for that amount, hoping Rafferty would approve. "Take this to California Mutual and turn it into traveler's checks. I'll call the bank to make sure they don't question the check. Pick up your mother and take her as far away from here as you can get."

"Fifty thousand dollars?" She rubbed the check between her fingers. "God, that's a fortune."

"It's not mine. Or Harry's, although he thinks it is."

"You're crazier than your brother, but in a much nicer way." She leaned forward and kissed him. "Can I go right now?"

"Tina . . . Rosemary . . . you don't need anyone's permission to leave. Just go."

She scrambled to her feet, really animated for the first time since he'd met her. "I won't even take anything. All my clothes have *this* on them anyway." She flicked a finger at the embroidered name on his tank-top as if it were a poisonous insect.

"Good luck, Rosemary."

"Ben, I'm afraid you're the one who's going to need the luck." She kissed him again, and paused only long enough to collect her purse and put on a pair of sneakers before leaving.

Ben sat alone now in brooding silence. The dice were rolling. In a few hours, if Harry kept his word, they would be reunited for the first time in eighteen years—for the sole purpose of trying to kill each other.

"BETTY?" CONDE ENTERED his kitchen through the breezeway and quickly ditched his hat on top of the refrigerator.

"In here."

He went into the dining room, where his family was in the middle of their dinner. "Ah, macaroni and cheese. My favorite. Hope you saved some for the old man."

"There may not be enough," Betty said in icy tones. "We didn't expect you this early."

305

Laury, their eight-year-old, said, "You haven't been home for dinner all week, daddy."

"I know, and I'm sorry." Conde slipped into his seat at the head of the table and opened a napkin. "From now on I'll be home at six o'clock every night. That's a promise." He spoke to Laury, but the promise was directed at his wife.

"That'll be the day."

"I mean it. Six o'clock every evening."

When Betty realized he was serious, she put down her fork. "What's wrong, Jim? What's happened?"

"Nothing." Conde gave himself a small portion of macaroni and cheese. "I'm just not going to put so much time into my job any more. It's not worth it."

"Job? You've always called it a career."

"That was before I knew better." He forced a smile to mask his feelings. "Say, this is good macaroni. You're a genius."

THERE WERE FOURTEEN steps from the ground floor of Eddy Trelska's apartment house to the second-floor hallway. He ascended each step in agony. The doctor he had seen that afternoon had diagnosed "swelling of the sigmoid colon." Son-of-a-bitch Conde. He'd considered suing him but didn't have the heart for it. Too many things could come out in court.

So forget Conde. Forget the Connecticut State Police. Forget this crummy apartment house. Think only of the thirty-six thousand dollars in the spare coffee pot and a new life in a warmer climate. He limped to the door of his apartment and unlocked it.

"Ginger?"

She was out. Trelska went into the kitchen and began looking for the heating pad he'd used the time he wrenched his back. The doctor had told him to move around as little as possible and to apply heat until the swelling on his colon went down.

Sigmoid colon. Sounded like a fag psychiatrist.

Eventually he realized that his apartment was as neat as a hospital ward. No dirty dishes. No perfume or hair rollers on the dinette table. No crumbs or magazines on the floor. That wasn't like Ginger.

Giving up his search for the heating pad, Trelska dragged himself to the bedroom. "Ginger?" The closet and bureau drawers had been left open. Only his clothes were there.

He sat down on the bed. Ginger had her own apartment, and she hadn't gone there to do the laundry. Ginger never cleaned anything. She threw things away when they got dirty. Stockings. Blouses. Underwear. Shoes.

He picked up the bedstand phone and dialed her number. No answer. Ginger had been in the bedroom when he'd stashed the two envelopes from Genovese, but she couldn't have known what was in them. Could she?

Trelska hobbled to the kitchen as rapidly as his swollen groin would allow. The spare coffee pot was hidden behind a row of old Mason jars and a package of chocolate-chip cookies. He threw open the cupboard door, swept aside the cookies and jars, several of which broke at his feet. He snatched down the coffee pot, plunged his hand inside.

Gone, of course. Thirty-six thousand dollars. Just . . . *gone.*

The pot fell from his hand as he sank onto a dinette chair. Ginger-peachy. Ever-lovin' Ginger. He used to say she had no understanding of money. Bad joke. Runs up eleven thousand dollars on my credit cards, then takes off with every cent I have. I'll ruin that pretty face.

If I can find her.

He knew with a sickening certainty that he would not find her. Never. A girl like Ginger, living in the shadows of society on someone else's credit cards, could, and would, disappear without a trace.

Eddy Trelska put his head on the dinette table and began to cry like a baby.

"YOUR FLIGHT LEAVES in an hour, sir. Would you like a window seat or aisle?"

"Aisle," Harry said.

"Smoking or non-smoking?"

"Non-smoking."

The clerk at the United Airlines ticket desk entered the information on his computer terminal. "You'll be in seat 24-C, sir." He wrote the information on a boarding pass and slipped the pass into the ticket envelope. "That will be four hundred and sixty dollars."

Harry pulled out a money clip and separated five one-hundred-dollar bills from it. The bankroll was shrinking fast. Only twelve or fifteen hundred left. Even so, he had bought a first-class ticket because he couldn't bear to ride economy with the tourists and traveling salesmen.

"What times does the flight arrive in L.A.?"

"One ten A.M. Have a good trip, sir."

Harry headed for the bar, still shaky from his conversation with Ben. He had sounded so damn sure of himself, so in control. Ben had never talked to him like that. Never dared to. He'd moved fast, no question. All that money, and now it was out of reach. Stashed away in some other bank. It would take months, maybe years, to find another pigeon like the late Ellen Rafferty. And what would he live on until then?

He had to get back to Los Angeles, and not just for the money. There was no way in this world he would let Ben beat him this way. *Any* way.

And Ben had made a mistake today. He'd been too quick to choose *The Melinda* as a meeting place. Ellen had once shown him the boat when it was berthed at Newport Beach. A-12 was the last slip on the quay, very convenient to the channel. Nothing but the best for old Sean Rafferty. Isolated. Anyone walking up that narrow fingerdock would be dead meat. Well, there was more than one way to board a boat.

Harry ordered a scotch and soda, light, and proceeded to form his plan.

Saturday

Chapter 21

Scarnato had delayed his departure from New Jersey until late
Friday evening to lessen the possibility of the police finding out he
was traveling west. His chartered Cessna Citation slipped unnoticed
into The Orange County airport forty miles south of Los Angeles a
few minutes before one o'clock Saturday morning. At that hour few
people were about to watch Tony Scarnato, Sal Genovese and Vincent Malle deplane.

They were met by Ray Parisi, *capo* for the Southern California
area and an old friend of Scarnato's. Parisi had begun his career in
New Jersey as a runner for Scarnato and owed his success largely to
Tony Scar's patronage. He greeted Scarnato with a firm embrace and
kisses on both cheeks. "Tony, my friend, I'm so sorry about Catherine. It's an honor to help you settle this terrible matter."

"Thanks, Ray. I appreciated your letter of condolence. You're
a good friend."

They embraced again.

Parisi shook hands warmly with Genovese and nodded perfunc-
torily to Malle, who acknowledged the greeting just as coldly. Parisi
resented Malle's access to Tony Scar, and Malle disliked Parisi's
tanned good looks, his socialite friends and the damned gold chains
around his neck. A "Hollywood gangster," Malle called him. Not

that the man lacked balls. Parisi had personally carried out several important jobs for Tony Scar. He had, for example, hit Hymie Wertz in the middle of his dinner at the Stage Delicatessen on Seventh Avenue, taking out his two bodyguards at the same time. You had to respect that, never mind what else you thought of the guy.

"Have you found Ryder?" Genovese asked.

Parisi nodded happily. "I've got him high and dry." He took Scarnato's arm and led him through the terminal. "We watched Rafferty's office and home. Late this afternoon Rafferty turned up at his office with Ryder's wife. They stayed an hour or so, then took off in his Caddy. We followed them to Marina del Rey. I almost lost my lunch when they hopped on board a boat and took off. I never expected that."

They exited the terminal and walked toward the parking lot. "But we got the name of his boat, *The Melinda*. And I noticed a pennant flying from his rigging, a Trade Winds Yacht Club pennant. I know the logos for most of the good yacht clubs around here, I've got friends with boats. It was too late in the day for him to be heading out to sea, so I figured he was going down the coast to another marina to shake us. I called ahead and sure enough, Rafferty phoned the Trade Winds to have his power and water connections turned on before he got there. I tromped it down here and sure enough *The Melinda* had just pulled in.

"We moved close and watched. About nine o'clock a gray Mercedes pulled up and Ryder got out. I recognized him right away from the telecopy photo Sal sent me. He took something out of the Mercedes trunk. It was wrapped in a blanket and the light was going, but I put a pair of binoculars on him. Tony, he had at least two rifles wrapped up in that blanket. He's on the boat now."

They had come up to Parisi's Lincoln Continental. Before entering the car Scarnato leaned on the doortop, his eyes drilling Parisi. "They can take off in that damned boat any time, can't they? They might be casting off right now. What have you done about that, Ray?"

"Taken care of, Tony. My men will rush the boat if anyone tries to cast off the lines. They're six of my best. Don't worry, that boat isn't going anywhere."

"He'd better not," Scarnato said, and ducked inside the Lincoln.

"Who's this Rafferty?" Genovese asked.

"A builder. One of the high rollers in this part of the country."

"Connections?"

"Heavy. You don't get the big construction jobs in L.A. unless you're wired into the power structure."

Vincent Malle, no longer able to conceal his contempt for a *mafioso* who knew the pennants of yacht clubs and used phrases like "power structure," just like a damn politician, joined Scarnato in the limousine.

"Why the hell is Rafferty sticking out his neck for Ben Ryder?" Genovese asked.

"No idea," Parisi told him. "We haven't had time to dig into the guy."

"Let's *go,*" Scarnato growled from the depths of the back seat.

Parisi got into the front seat and told his driver to take them to the Trade Winds marina. The only space available to Genovese was between Scarnato and Malle. He gritted his teeth and wedged himself between the two thick bodies. Scarnato gave off an aroma of alcohol and Malle of cheap cigars. The combination almost made him gag. He didn't know which he despised more, the *capo* or his toad. They were both peasants. Well, he wouldn't have to put up with either of them for long—not if things kept moving according to plan back in New Jersey.

THE MELINDA resembled Sean Rafferty himself: sturdy, with unexceptional lines but plenty of power and speed. The superstructure had a traditional look . . . the craft originally, some thirty years earlier, had been a fishing trawler. Rafferty, looking for a boat, had spotted the neglected old trawler in a messy corner of a boatyard where it had been hauled out of the water for repairs its owner couldn't afford.

"I bought it and scraped the hull myself. Tore out the rotting timbers and replaced them with seasoned oak. Melinda and I had a lifelong dream. We wanted to fix up an old boat and take her up the

313

coast all the way to Alaska, the inland waterway. But Melinda died before we had a chance to make that particular dream come true. Afterwards I just didn't care to make the trip without her."

"You did a marvelous job," Donna said. "She's beautiful."

The main cabin, located just behind the bridge, had been converted to a lounge. The original mahogany woodwork had been refinished to a soft amber glow. A brass barometer and lamp fixtures had also been retained and polished. A dark-pine captain's table in the cener of the cabin was bolted to the deck through heavy carpeting for safety in a rolling sea. Under the starboard windows, a banquette covered with mildew-proof upholstery provided additional seating. A counter at the rear of the cabin served as a breakfast bar; on the other side was the galley.

Donna particularly admired the compact efficiency of the galley. It contained a propane-gas range and a refrigerator that could run on either gas or electricity. While they'd waited for Ben she'd used the stove to make a pot of coffee. When he'd arrived she had carved up a small roast from the refrigerator for sandwiches.

Now it was past one A.M. and they were sitting at the captain's table finishing the sandwiches and coffee and making their plans.

"Harry could be here any time now," Ben said.

"If he's coming." Rafferty squinted through the window at the moonlit silhouettes of masts. "He'd be a fool to walk into a set-up like this."

"I threatened to disappear with the money if he doesn't show up by dawn. He believed me . . . he wants that money. More important, he wants *me.*"

He had recapped his phone conversation with Harry and told them about the house and the girl Harry called Tina.

"Let's get in place," Rafferty said. "Harry is bound to try something special . . . come at us from the water, for instance. There are plenty of dinghys around here. He might steal one and come over the stern. So Ben, you cover the dock from the bridge with your shotgun. I'll be on the fantail watching the water. Give a low whistle if you see anything move, I'll do the same."

They picked up their weapons and checked the loads.

Donna's mouth felt dry. She hated guns. The Walther automatic Ben had pressed on her rested in the pocket of her slacks with

314

an unpleasant heaviness, a dead weight, she thought, not caring for the unintended pun. However, she'd dutifully practiced operating it before letting Ben load the weapon for her. There wasn't much to learn . . . Ben had inserted the clip and levered a round into the chamber; she'd only need to push the safety catch forward with her thumb until the red dot appeared, then pull the trigger. She devoutly hoped there would be no need to put her newfound expertise to work. "What are you going to do? Just start shooting when you see him?"

Ben and Rafferty exchanged uncomfortable looks.

"Good question," Ben conceded. "I suppose even now I'm not ready to do that—"

"Nor I." Rafferty slipped extra rounds of ammunition into his shirt pocket. "And we won't have to. I mean, Harry isn't coming calling with a box of candy and a bouquet of flowers. We won't see him until he's almost on us, and he'll have a knife or a club or a gun ready. There'll be no cold-blooded action on our part. It will be self-defense."

Rafferty was right, Ben thought. He slipped his arm around Donna's waist. "Turn off the lights and stay at the back of the cabin. Don't do anything, just keep that pistol close. Listen for strange sounds and if you need me, yell."

"You can count on that," Donna promised. She didn't smile when she said it.

They kissed as if they were about to be separated for a very long time. Ben went up on deck. Donna cleared the table, cleaned up the galley, turned off the lights and huddled in one corner of the banquette, her back against the woodwork, her fingers around the hand grip of the Walther in her pocket. She felt, for God's sake, like the last defender of the Alamo. Harry wasn't one man. He was an *army*. Suddenly she was afraid that this so-called trap was a terrible mistake, an invitation to disaster . . . But there was nothing she could do now except sit quietly in the darkness and shiver.

HARRY TOOK THE San Diego Freeway to the Newport Beach turnoff and found the Trade Winds marina with no trouble. His rented car was a brown Chevy that attracted no attention, but because it was two A.M., he took pains to look as if he were a resident on his way home. He didn't slow down in front of the marina's entrance and parking lot, just cruised by at a steady speed while casually directing glances at the mass of anchored boats.

He saw only two boats with lights on, neither of them berthed near slip A-12. There appeared to be a party under way on one of them. He also glimpsed his own Mercedes in the lot . . . Brother Ben had certainly latched onto it fast enough.

Several blocks up the avenue Harry found what he was looking for, a sporting goods store. He circled the block, parked the car on a side street and went up the alley to the rear of the building.

He located a circuit box on the wall. The alarm system undoubtedly fed into it. Cutting the wires would set it off as quickly as prying open the door, so he went up the fire escape to the roof. He had seen the outline of a raised skylight, which might be less secure.

Sensor wires were built into the perimeter panes of the skylight. Harry took a rolled-up newspaper from his hip pocket, placed it carefully over an unsensored pane and pushed down with the palm of his hand. The glass shattered and fell to the floor of the sporting goods shop ten or twelve feet below. He repeated the process until he had a square of broken panes large enough to climb through.

He leaned into the hole and grasped a sprinkler pipe near the skylight that looked strong enough to support his weight. Taking great care to avoid breaking one of the sensitized glass panes, he swung through the hole and let his feet drop. The pipe bent slightly as his full weight fell on it, but held. He swung from the pipe while he tried to make out what was below. It looked like a rack of jogging shoes. He dropped onto the wooden shoe rack, which shattered under his weight, and tumbled to the floor.

He rose quickly, sweeping a jumble of shoes out of his way, and listened for an alarm. He heard nothing, but the store might be equipped with a silent alarm. Harry went to the rear window and looked out into the alley.

When a few minutes had passed with no sign of the police, Harry left his watchpost and prowled the shop for the equipment he needed. He selected a pair of swimming trunks and black wetsuit, the best scuba gear he could find, a lead-weighted belt, a seven-inch knife with a cork grip and leg sheath, fins and mask. The last item he took was a speargun made for underwater fishing that fired a yard-long shaft with a falanged steel tip.

He thought: Now I'm ready to catch a really big one.

THE LINCOLN CONTINENTAL turned into the parking lot fronting the Trade Winds marina and slid into an unobtrusive corner space. Parisi tapped his driver on the shoulder. "Go tell Artie to switch on his receiver."

When the driver had left, Parisi swiveled around so that he could talk to Scarnato over the back seat. "Slip A-12 is over there, Tony. You can see the outline of Rafferty's boat." He frowned. "The lights were on when I left to pick you up. We'll know what's going on when Artie checks in." He picked up a walkie-talkie from the floorboard and cradled it on his lap.

Scarnato felt relaxed, almost exhilarated, now that he was on the scene. Catherine would be able to rest soon; he'd promised to avenge her, and now he would . . . With a start he realized he'd been talking to himself and that Parisi was watching him too closely. "Nice lines on that boat," he said, embarrassed and angry at the same time.

"You know cabin cruisers, Tony?"

"Yeah, I keep a twenty-eight-footer down at the Jersey shore. Me and Vincent go for a cruise now and then."

Malle was the only person who knew that the cruiser was the only place where Scarnato could relax and still feel safe. Sometimes they would take off in a boat at seven A.M., just him and the boss, and cruise a few miles offshore all day long. Scarnato would begin drinking as soon as they left the dock. By ten o'clock he would be bombed. Usually he remained that way until midafternoon, when Malle would pour coffee into him until he sobered up.

"That must be a forty-eight-footer," Scarnato said, looking at *The Melinda.* His interest in the boat quickened. "Yeah, looks sea-worthy, doesn't she, Vincent? We could handle her for a short cruise, just the two of us."

Malle muttered agreement, following well his *capo*'s train of thought.

317

"We'll use the boat," Scarnato said. "Take that creep out to sea where he can scream his goddamn head off with no one to hear. His wife and this Rafferty too. We can get rid of all of them out there. Sharks' bait, all of them, right, Vincent?"

"They say Ryder's wife is a looker," Malle said, "Maybe, before we give her the deep six I can—"

"She's yours," Scarnato said expansively.

The plan alarmed Genovese. He had no desire to go out on the water. The sea scared the hell out of him. He could hardly swim a stroke. Fifty feet of dog paddling was all he could handle, then he'd sink like a load of bricks. "Tony, I don't think that's such a good idea. That's a big boat. It needs a big crew, doesn't it?"

Scarnato showed his teeth. "Hey, that's right . . . you can't swim. I almost forgot."

The hell you did, Genovese thought.

"Don't worry, Sal. You fall overboard, I'll throw you a life preserver." Scarnato winked at Parisi. "Ray, tell him what it takes to sink a forty-eight-footer."

"A tidal wave," Parisi said. "Or sea monsters. Don't worry, Sal. I'll come along too, and bring a couple of the boys."

"No," Scarnato said quickly. "You've done enough, Ray. Once we've got the boat and those people, you can take off."

The walkie-talkie on Parisi's lap crackled into service: "Ray . . . this is Artie . . . do you read? . . . are you there?"

Parisi put the instrument to his ear. "This is Ray . . . I read . . . what's happening on the boat?"

"Fifteen minutes ago Ryder and Rafferty came on deck . . . they're covering the dock with guns, Ray . . . stern and bridge . . . I can see them . . . moonlight . . . any instructions?"

"Sit tight . . . out." He switched off the walkie-talkie and put it on his lap. "They're expecting us, Tony."

"Us, or the cops," Genovese said.

"The point is, we'll make a lot of noise if we try to grab them now." He banged the walkie-talkie against his thigh. "I should have moved on him before. I'm sorry, Tony."

Scarnato put a hand on Parisi's arm. Now that Ryder was almost in his net, he was himself again. The effect of the whiskey he'd had on the plane was fading. His mind was clear and clicking. "You were told to find Ryder and watch him. Okay, that's what you did. How long can we stay here before some cops cruise by?"

"All night," Parisi said. "This is private property. Very exclusive. The cops don't poke their noses where the rich folks play without an invitation."

"Let's sit and wait, then. Sooner or later one of them will go to the head." He smiled at Genovese. "The head. That means the can to landlubbers like you, Sal. So they take a leak, or go below for a cup of coffee. Then we move. How close are your men?"

"Artie and the others are on that sloop near *The Melinda.*"

"Tell them to stay awake. When Ryder gets careless, we take him."

Genovese looked at his watch. Two thirty A.M. Five thirty in New Jersey. "I gotta make a phone call, Tony. Be right back." He quickly left the car before Scarnato could object and walked to a phone booth at the far end of the marina. He dropped in a dime and told the operator he was making a collect call to Newark, New Jersey. Mr. Genovese to Mr. Pavo. Within moments he had Geno Pavo on the line. "This is Sal. Has the job been done?"

"We got back an hour ago, Sal."

"Did the customer have the merchandise I was looking for?"

"He did. You can have it C.O.D."

"You'll get your money. See you tomorrow night." Genovese hung up the phone and walked back to Parisi's car with a lighter step.

Scarnato gave him a look when he climbed back into the car. "What was that all about?"

"A horse. I had big money on a nag at Belmont yesterday afternoon. Things have been moving so fast, I didn't have a chance until now to see how she ran."

"How'd she do?" asked Malle, always hungry for racing news.

"I won a bundle." Genovese grinned.

BEN CHECKED THE hammer on his shotgun for the ninth or tenth time and cradled the weapon in the crook of his arm. The Great White Hunter in repose, for God's sake. He felt foolish and scared. What am I doing here? I should be running for my life. I've no business tangling with Harry. He's killed people. The toughest thing

I've ever done was punch out Larry the mechanic at Al's Exxon, that time he tried to switch my good snow tires for a pair of bald old junkers. Even then I spent the next six months worrying about being sued.

Rafferty's presence on the fantail did give him some sense of security. He was a tough old bird who'd as soon shoot Harry as say his name. Ben broke off his observation of the quay and looked through the bridge's rear window toward the stern. He could see Rafferty's silhouette against the moonlit water. The older man was alert yet relaxed. Apparently in control of himself and the situation. Ben envied his confidence, and his familiarity with guns. He still worried he might accidentally shoot off his own foot with the big shotgun, which was growing heavier by the minute.

He laid the shotgun on top of the control panel and resumed his scrutiny of the dock. A few minutes before, he had seen someone come up the fingerdock. But whoever it was had boarded one of the other boats. Even from a distance he'd known it wasn't Harry. The man had been too short and thin, no breadth through the shoulders.

Suddenly he sensed a difference in the boat. It seemed to dip gently to starboard. But most of his boating experience was on smaller craft, and he was unsure of his instincts on a cabin cruiser as big as this one. He looked in Rafferty's direction. Apparently Rafferty had felt it too because he was standing with his rifle at the ready.

Something silvery streaked through the darkness from the direction of the midship rub rail. Rafferty's large bulk quivered and Ben heard his rifle clatter to the deck. Rafferty swayed and toppled backward over the stern, his legs striking the flagstaff. There was a splash, and silence.

Ben snatched up the shotgun and ran out the starboard companionway of the bridge in time to see a black form slither across the deck and into the deeper darkness next to the superstructure. The form disappeared, but didn't remain still. Ben could hear it scurrying like a rat.

He hurried up the ladder to the flying bridge and swung the shotgun toward the stern. From there he had a 360-degree field of fire, which seemed to do him no good at all.

Harry had found a hiding place.

He wants me to come to him, Ben realized. But I won't. I'll outwait him. He gripped the shotgun tighter and rested the barrel on a grab rail.

Minutes passed while Ben waited for some movement or sound. Sweat drenched him. Donna was still in the main cabin, he hoped, probably still unaware that Rafferty had been killed. Rafferty *dead.* What the hell had Harry used on him? Something silent. Something metal. Something long and sharp. A spear? An arrow?

It occurred to him that he still held a slight advantage: Rafferty's money. If Harry killed him straight off, he'd forfeit the money. Which probably meant Harry would try to cripple, not kill him—for the moment.

Above all Ben wanted to find Donna and insure her safety. But he couldn't risk going to her until he had some idea of Harry's location. Damn him, why didn't he move?

Something changed nearby. The aroma of rubber and salt water filled his nostrils. Bare feet slapped against the teak decking. He swung the shotgun in a slow 360-degree arc, still saw nothing—

Harry came scrambling over the windscreen. Ben brought the barrel around, too slowly. It smashed across Harry's shoulder, but he kept coming. They hit each other like opposing linemen, with a crunch of bone and gristle. Ben drove his knee into Harry's groin and chopped at his head with the shotgun stock. Both blows connected. This time Harry swore and grabbed the shotgun with both hands. They wrestled for it, using elbows and knees on each other.

Ben was losing the shotgun. He pushed Harry backward, quickly picking up momentum. Harry's bare feet couldn't match his sneakers for traction on the smooth deck. They hit the rear grab rail and went over, landing with a crash on the top of the cabin house.

Donna screamed out Ben's name, which seemed to give Ben additional strength. He'd lost hold of the shotgun during the fall, but he had hold of Harry's throat. He banged Harry's head against the cabin house, lifted it, banged it down again. The edge of a knife flashed past his face. He sank his teeth into Harry's wrist and bit down hard. Harry yelled and tried to pull free.

"Ben? Where are you?"

Donna climbed up onto the cabin house. There was no way Ben could warn her away without letting go of Harry's wrist. He shook his head like a dog chewing a bone and the knife disappeared from Harry's hand. Letting go the wrist, Ben gasped out, "Donna, run, get off the boat—"

"*No.*"

Donna appeared above them, her right hand held high. At first Ben thought she was aiming the Walther and hoped to hell she would shoot the right twin. But her hand came down and a heavy metal cleat thudded off Harry's skull. He gagged and rolled away. Donna hit him again. He became still.

"Ben?" Her hands groped for his face. "Ben, darling, are you all right?"

"Yes . . . except . . . I can't catch my breath . . ."

"Rest a minute."

They huddled on top of the cabin house like survivors of a storm until Ben recovered his breath. "All right now. How did you know which one of us to hit? Oh, God, of course, the wetsuit . . ."

"Where's Sean?"

Ben waved his hand miserably at the fantail. "Harry shot him with something, a speargun I think, he fell over the stern. If he wasn't dead when he went into the water, I'm afraid he must be by now—"

"Oh no, *no* . . ." She fought back an urge to scream, to carry on like a banshee. "I didn't hear anything until the two of you crashed down right over my head."

"Where'd you find the cleat?"

"There were a couple of them near the engine hatch. Strange. I completely forgot about the gun." She shoved a hand into her pocket. "It's still here."

Ben forced himself to his feet. "I'm sorry, honey, guess you'll have to help me drag Harry into the cabin."

They each took a leg and pulled Harry's inert form across the cabin house, rolling him off without exactly worrying about the four-foot drop to the deck. After climbing down they dragged him into the main cabin and turned on the lights.

Ben now understood how Harry had gotten so close without being seen. The black wetsuit had camouflaged him very well. He shuddered at the sight of Harry's face, his first glimpse of that profile in eighteen years. Harry had changed very little. Their resemblance was still extraordinary.

"Seeing the two of you together is eerie," Donna said.

"Give me the pistol."

"What?"

"The Walther. *Give* it to me."

"Ben, you can't just shoot him while he's unconscious. That would be murder."

He reached into the pocket of her slacks and yanked the pistol free. Donna moved back against the banquette, hating what was about to be done. She put both hands to her mouth as Ben placed the muzzle of the gun at Harry's temple and flicked off the safety catch. Ben's hand was shaking, but he cocked the hammer with a show of determination . . .

Moments later, the hand holding the gun fell to his side. "Damn it, damn *him,* I can't do it. God knows I want to . . . he deserves it . . . but I can't." He shook his head.

Donna went to his side and pressed against him. "It's okay, I guess I'm even relieved. Ben, let's call the police. That's the only way we're going to get out of this now."

"Yes." He took a deep breath and tossed the pistol onto the banquette cushions. "First we'd better find some rope and tie him up—"

A voice boomed out from behind: "Jesus, there really are two of them."

Startled, they turned to see men with guns entering the cabin. Ben stepped forward and was clubbed with the barrel of a heavy automatic. He staggered and fell, forming a cry that never left his lips.

CHAPTER 22

FROM TEN miles out to sea, the dawn over the California coastline was breathtaking. Burnt orange shadows crawled from the dark canyons of the Santa Monica mountains and spread across the glistening ocean.

"Sal," Scarnato called. "Come look. You never see this kind of sunrise off New Jersey."

Genovese ignored Scarnato's invitation. He was in the main cabin fighting a queasy feeling at the pit of his stomach. The up-down motion didn't bother him nearly as much as the side-to-side roll of *The Melinda.*

"I'll pass," he finally said, which made Scarnato laugh.

Tony the pig, Genovese thought. You won't laugh for long.

The ocean was soon bathed in brilliant sunlight.

"Turn off the running lights, Vincent." Scarnato climbed to the flying bridge and scanned the ocean with binoculars. He saw only a couple of sloops heading west and a freighter grinding its way toward San Pedro. The Coast Guard worried him, but according to the charts they would soon be out of the area regularly patroled by their boats.

Scarnato eased forward the throttle handles regulating the twin diesel engines and felt the craft pick up speed. Plenty of power there.

325

He smiled over the stomach problems the additional speed would cause for Genovese. It would do the prick good to sweat some of that English cologne out of his system. He was smelling more like a Forty-second Street whore every day.

He went back down to the bridge, where Malle in his shirt-sleeves had taken the helm, an enormous pistol in his belt, and whispered in his ear, "Keep the bow into the waves, Vincent. Let's see if we can make Sal toss his cookies overboard."

Malle smiled and checked the oil pressure and RPM gauges. "I give him another ten minutes." He looked over his shoulder to make sure Genovese was still in the cabin. "What's the plan, Tony? Do we take off Ryder first . . . or Sal?"

"Sal."

"Which of those guys do you think killed Catherine?"

"I dunno. I never expected twins, for Chrissake."

"Then which one do we slam?"

"We do them both."

"The woman, too, right?"

"Her too." Scarnato thought of his daughter, momentarily saw her sweet face float in front of him. "Let the whole damn Ryder family pay for what was done to Catherine. That's justice, yes?"

Scarnato left Malle at the cruiser's helm and went back to the main cabin. He found Genovese groaning and holding his head. The Fixer's face was gray and pinched.

"Tony, we're going too damned fast . . . this thing's coming apart . . ."

"Naw, we're making less than seventeen knots."

"Jesus, I'm gonna throw up." Genovese bolted to his feet and walked unsteadily out to the starboard rail, where he bent over the side and retched violently.

Scarnato watched with amusement. "Careful of your trousers, Sal. You don't want to ruin that fine custom tailoring." He strolled to the captain's table, where Genovese had left his suit coat, and slipped his hand inside its folds. One of the custom features of Genovese's suits, which surely must have astounded his London tailor, was a special pocket built to the exact size and shape of a .765 Beretta automatic. He found the weapon and removed it. While Genovese was still throwing up he went to the port rail and tossed the Beretta overboard. Then he walked around to the galley, where Donna Ryder was handcuffed to a guardrail that ran around the stove burners to keep hot pans in place at sea.

"I only admire one thing about cops—their handcuffs. Handcuffs are a great invention, Mrs. Ryder. I use them a lot."

"Is my husband all right?"

"The Bobsey Twins are locked up in the stateroom. And handcuffed. Which is yours?"

"*Please.* Ben's the one in the slacks and sports shirt. It's Harry who killed your daughter . . . he's insane. Please don't harm Ben—"

"Sure, you'd say that. And how would I know if you fingered the wrong brother? Maybe the guy in the bathing suit is your husband, and the other one is Harry. And how do I know which one killed my little girl anyway, never mind who he is. You can see my problem."

"My God . . . you're going to kill all of us."

Scarnato's heavy face became sad. "Let's not talk about such things." He took hold of her wrist and examined the handcuffs. The steel was tight against her skin. She couldn't possibly wriggle loose. "I will not make you suffer in pain, Mrs. Ryder. That wouldn't be proper." He remembered his promise to give her to Vincent and felt a twinge of guilt at having lied. But it wasn't a deliberate lie, and she wouldn't be in pain for long.

"You're too kind," she said bitterly.

Scarnato overlooked the rebuke . . . "Sal, are you feeling better?"

Genovese nodded dully and went back to his chair at the captain's table. "I'll be all right, I think."

"Can I get you a drink?"

"*No.* I can't take anything on my stomach. Hey, aren't we out far enough, Tony? Can't we take care of them and turn back to shore?"

"A few more miles, Sal. I want to get well clear of the Catalina channel first. You get too many Coast Guard patrols and other traffic in a busy sea lane."

"Busy? It's like a graveyard out here."

Scarnato considered his plans for Genovese, and nodded. "Another five miles, Sal. Then you won't have to worry about getting seasick any more."

BEN'S VISION WENT in and out of focus to the rhythm of a pounding headache. Moving only made it worse. He massaged his forehead until things became a little less blurred and rolled over on his shoulder.

Someone laughed nearby . . . "Just like the morning after a beer bust. Remember those days? We could hardly stand up. Had to help each other to the bathroom."

Ben saw himself in a mirror. Strangely, he seemed to be smiling. His clothes were gone, he was wearing only a blue bathing suit. He blinked and realized there was no mirror. That was . . . Harry.

He lunged at Harry's throat, only to be held painfully in check by a manacle around his wrist. Now he realized that he was in the pilot berth of *The Melinda*'s stateroom, his wrist handcuffed to the guard rail. Harry was in the quarter berth on the opposite side of the cabin, his wrist similarly manacled. There was no way they could get at each other.

Harry laughed again. "You can break your arm that way, dear brother."

"*Donna*. Where is she?"

"In the galley with one of these on her." He jiggled his handcuffs. "God, I hate these things. My first year in Camarillo, I spent most of it in restraint, as they liked to call it. Handcuffs or straitjackets. It took me a long time to realize I couldn't bust out of there, had to learn their game . . ."

Ben was reluctantly drawn into Harry's reminiscence. "What game?"

"The psychiatrists have this game they play. It's called The Sanity Sweepstakes. They want you to talk in a quiet, controlled voice. Examine your emotions. Agree with their conclusions. Think of them as *friends*. Pass their silly damned tests. And when you can do that for enough years in a row, you win The Sanity Sweepstakes —they set you free."

"Did it ever occur to you that maybe they just wanted to help you?"

Harry winced. "Psychiatrists are damn fools. While they were trying to manipulate me I was playing my own little game with them. There was one asshole—Dr. Trice—who was really pathetic. During our sessions I'd be very alert and attentive whenever he leaned forward in his chair. If he leaned back, I'd yawn or pick my nose or just stare at the floor. After a few months of that Trice always leaned forward during our sessions. I'd damn near pinned him in that position by rewarding him with my wonderful attentiveness, and he never even realized it. Believe me, I knew more about behavioral psychology than any of those jerks."

"You were always brilliant, Harry."

"*Brilliant but unstable.* Do you know how tired I got of seeing that on my school records?" Harry rapped the bulkhead with his fist. "All my life people have been trying to turn me into a sniveling conformist. Well, Harry goes his own way."

"Who are those men, the ones with guns?"

"Mafia. Couldn't you smell the garlic? The only one I know is a guinea named Genovese. He's the one who grabbed me at your house. Another face I recognized from the newspapers, Anthony Scarnato—Tony Scar, they call him. There's only one other guy out there, some kind of damned dwarf. The others stayed on shore."

"Harry, did you kill Scarnato's daughter?"

"A mistake. I didn't mean to hurt the silly little bitch."

"You left enough evidence pointing to me. Scarnato found out the police suspected me of killing his daughter and sent his people after me. They got you instead . . . isn't that what happened?"

"Yeah, that's it . . . took me half the night to shake loose of them."

Ben looked over the stateroom. "Scarnato will have to kill both of us to be absolutely certain he's gotten rid of his daughter's killer. Then he'll kill Donna too—"

"Burial at sea." Harry sighed. "Not my idea of the best way to go."

"Then let's do something about it."

Harry's head came up. "You've got an idea?"

"We can't do much if they decide to kill us here, in this cabin. But we've got a chance if they take us up on deck first. And if we work together."

329

"*You* and *me?* I don't believe it. You wouldn't help me if I was drowning in my own shit."

"I'm thinking of Donna, Harry. I'd work with the devil to get her off this boat alive."

"Then you're in luck." Harry sat up and swung his legs over the side of the bunk. "I'm his duly appointed deputy. What's your plan?"

Ben gingerly moved around so that he could better talk to Harry. "Do you remember the time we were collecting subscription money from customers on our paper routes and those older kids jumped us?"

"Sure," Harry said with almost a smile. "We were in . . . what . . . eighth grade? There were three of them and each one had five inches and thirty pounds on us."

"And we left them lying on Oak Knoll Boulevard with their heads on backwards."

"They didn't have guns."

"It's a longshot, but we might be able to use the same gag."

Harry shrugged. "Who's going to act chickenshit, you or me?"

"Me," Ben decided.

Harry was staring at him now with what seemed a genuinely pained expression. He stroked the welt Donna had given him when she struck his head with the cleat. "Ben . . . there's something I've wanted to ask you for the last eighteen years. Why did you desert me?"

"What?" And then realizing what he meant . . . "That's bull, Harry. Because I wouldn't confess to a murder you committed—"

"Never mind that part. I'm asking why you never came to the courtroom once during the trial. Not until the jury was coming back with a verdict did you show your face. That got to me, brother Ben. The way you just wrote me off."

"I didn't write you off and you know it. The judge barred me from the courtroom until the jury returned with a verdict. He said the fact that we were twins would be prejudicial if the jury saw me."

"Is that straight? No one ever told me that."

"The judge made the ruling in his chambers before they started selecting the jury. Your lawyer was supposed to tell you. I would have told you myself but you were so sore over my refusing to make that phony confession that you wouldn't even come to the visiting room."

"My lawyer had a brain like a dead lightbulb. He could hardly make out a bill to the court for my so-called defense." Harry gave the manacle on his wrist an exploratory tug. "That's really true, what you just said?"

"You can look it up in the court records—"

"Sure, I'll do it right now," Harry gave the handcuffs a more violent pull. "Asshole judge, he was against me from the start."

"Anyone who doesn't see things your way usually is."

"I had some bad breaks."

"Harry, for God's sake, you've committed *rape* and *murder*. You knifed my son, your own nephew. Bad breaks excusing all that . . . ?"

"Get off my back, you don't know anything about it—"

"Don't I? I've seen some of your victims. I'm married to a woman you raped."

Harry's front deflated. "You know, maybe you're lucky, Ben. Maybe you got a good one. But most women are sluts, or worse. Believe me. I never in my life found a woman. Not once. I could tell you a story . . ." He shifted around. "Ah, what's the use? Ancient history."

They both flinched at the sound of a gunshot that seemed to come from the main cabin, forward of the stateroom.

"*Donna* . . ."

Ben pulled savagely at the rail he was handcuffed to, trying to yank loose its bolts.

"Save your strength, Ben. Remember the plan."

"To hell with the plan. Donna, *Donna* . . ."

He was rewarded with an answer, muffled but definitely Donna's voice. He slumped back onto the bunk. "She's alive. Thank God, she's alive . . ."

"The plan," Harry repeated. "It's her only chance too."

"What the hell do you care? You were going to kill her yourself, weren't you? And me. And our children."

"That's *right,* brother Ben. Nothing's changed, except that we need each other. We need each other just this once."

There were two more gunshots in quick succession.

SCARNATO HAD WAITED until they reached the outer Santa Barbara Channel before ordering Vincent Malle to throttle back the engines and tie down the helm on a south by southwest course. "Use your thirty-eight," he whispered. "Save the hook for the ones in the stateroom."

"You've got it, Tony."

Genovese was still at the captain's table in the main cabin, his face in his hands. He looked up and turned a new shade of gray as he read their faces. "So that's it . . . the Ryders *and* me. I guess I felt it coming but didn't want to believe it—"

Scarnato actually looked dejected. "Sorry, Sal, but you've taken to acting like a *capo.* It might have come one day, but you wanted it too soon . . ."

"Wait." Genovese held up his hand. "Would it make a difference if I had your stash, Tony?"

"What stash?"

"The stuff in your basement vault. All that evidence you've been putting away on me and your other good pals."

"That's a pretty stupid bluff, Sal."

"No bluff. I sent men to your house last night. Remember the phone call I made from the marina? My horse paid off, all right. His name was Geno Pavo."

"Geno." Scarnato suddenly knew Genovese was telling the truth. Geno Pavo was an enemy who'd been waiting years to strike a blow at him. Losing the cache of documents on his business associates was a big setback. It would probably cause him trouble for years to come. "I believe you now, Sal. But it doesn't make any difference. In fact, it settles it. Do it, Vincent."

Malle fired.

Scarnato's left leg was blown out from under him. He fell to the deck in stages, like a collapsing bridge. He reached for his knee, but it was no longer there. The joint had been smashed. Astonished, Scarnato rolled over on his back and saw Vincent Malle's face smiling down on him. "Vincent . . . why? I was good to you. You were *family."*

"Family? I drove your car, walked your dog, took your suits to the cleaner, killed your enemies. You call that *family?* I was your servant. I stayed with you all these years only because of Catherine."

"Catherine?"

"I was more of a father to Catherine than you ever were. You had your business to run. Who sat up with her when she had the measles? Took her to the dentist? Picked out her Christmas presents? Me, Tony."

"Vincent, she was my daughter. I loved her—"

"You don't love anyone. I let you live for her sake. The day she died, you were finished."

The morning had become very cold for Tony Scarnato. His body temperature was dropping as if he'd been thrust into a deep freeze. Even his teeth were cold. The gun in Malle's hand was now leveled at him. "For the love of God . . ."

Malle fired twice, punching out both of Scarnato's canny brown eyes with .38-caliber slugs. In an instant the don's huge head was turned into a skeleton's skull.

From his chair, Genovese put a curse on the dead man's soul in guttural Italian.

Stunned, disbelieving, Donna watched the ceremonial execution in silence. She had screamed when Malle shot Scarnato's leg out from under him, but now she was deliberately quiet, terrified she'd draw attention to herself.

Genovese got up and walked over to Scarnato's body. He kicked it once, then said to Malle, "Help me give our late friend what he was going to give me." Together they lifted Scarnato, carried him to the rail and pushed him over. The sound of his body hitting the choppy sea was barely discernable. "Tough Tony Scar." Genovese shook his head. "He begged for his life, didn't he?"

"They all do," Malle said.

"You did the smart thing, Vincent. You're going to be an important man, just like I promised. Let's take care of the others and turn this thing around. I get nervous on the water." Genovese searched through his coat pockets. "My gun is gone . . . Tony must have taken it."

"Use this." Malle handed him the Walther he had taken from Ben and Donna. "I'll bring up those twins from the stateroom. You cover them."

"Kill them down there. Less risk."

333

"I need room to work on them. The one who killed Catherine is gonna die slow."

"Be careful."

"Just cover them, Sal."

Malle disappeared into the stateroom and Genovese took up a position on the banquette, the Walther covering the companionway leading below. He said now to Donna, "I hope your husband didn't kill Catherine, lady. Vincent was nuts about that kid."

Donna hardly heard him, her attention on the tiny galley, hoping to spot something like a weapon. There wasn't much of use—one butcher knife and a small fire-extinguisher.

Ben and Harry emerged blinking into the extraordinarily bright morning. They exchanged a look that Donna couldn't decipher. Ben was relieved to see her alive and safe, even if temporarily. Both brothers seemed to have recovered from the blows they'd taken.

Malle pushed them down onto the banquette seats. "You can make this easy on yourselves, or hard. Which of you killed Catherine?"

Harry looked directly at Ben. *"He* did."

"Liar."

Harry ignored Donna's outburst, shook his head sorrowfully. "Ben's crazy. He's been seeing doctors for years. Look, I don't care what you do with him. I've got money, plenty of it. You can have it. Just let me go and don't make the mistake of—"

"I didn't kill her," Ben whined, and then, to Donna's astonishment, he began to crawl, to plead. God, she was ashamed for him. It wasn't like him, and after everything he'd stood up to over the last week . . . She saw the look of amused contempt that passed between Malle and the other one, Genovese—

Ben, who had dropped to his knees, suddenly moved forward and hit Malle at waist level. In the same instant Harry leaped for Genovese, but he was quicker on his feet than Malle. He jumped backward, trying to aim the Walther at Harry as he moved.

Donna, coming awake, leaned as far over the galley counter as the steel chain on her wrist would allow and sprayed the fire-extinguisher in Genovese's direction. A thick stream of monamonium phosphate hit him in the face. He swore and fired high. Harry kicked out and sent him flying.

334

What happened next surprised Harry as much as it did Donna. Instead of following up his attack on Genovese, who was frantically trying to clear his eyes of the corrosive chemical, Harry veered toward Malle, shouting, "Ben . . . *drop.*"

Ben jerked his head as Malle fired and the cabin window exploded behind him. Harry rammed into Malle, whose midsection was like stone.

For a split second Donna was able to catch Ben's eye. He was half down, wrestling away from the muzzle of Malle's .38. She tossed the knife toward him. It bounced along the carpeted deck and came to rest a few feet from his hand. In a single movement he scooped it up and drove the blade into Malle's chest.

At first the thrust seemed to have no effect. Malle's thick body continued to bear down on Ben, the gun swinging relentlessly about. The only sign that he'd been wounded was a damp red spot on his shirt and a puzzled look in his eyes. Then, abruptly, his breath became labored, his strength ebbed, and with a muted grunt he toppled over on his back. A rattling sound came from some deep recess of his throat, and Vincent Malle died.

It happened so quickly that both Harry and Ben continued struggling with Malle for several moments after he'd become dead weight. Only when the .38 slipped from Malle's hand did they realize he was gone. They stepped back guardedly, as if Malle were a wild animal that might still have life in him.

Genovese had been momentarily forgotten. The Fixer stumbled into the starboard companionway as he rubbed at his eyes. When his vision cleared, he saw the twin brothers standing over Malle. He still didn't know which one had killed Scarnato's daughter, nor did he care. He raised the Walther, aiming first at the twin in the sports shirt and slacks . . . And then the one in the bathing suit noticed the movement and, damn him, shoved his brother out of the line of fire. Now he was coming on toward him. Running. Grinning, eager for contact. Legs pumping. No hesitation, just the opposite. Jesus . . .

Genovese fired point-blank, spacing his shots. Red holes appeared in the muscular chest, but Harry Ryder kept coming. Genovese, disbelieving what he was seeing, backed through the companionway until he banged against the rail. He fired the remaining rounds in the Walther, both slugs tearing through flesh and bone as

335

Harry Ryder slammed into him and launched them both into open space. They hit the water with a smack.

Arms and legs flailing, Genovese fought for the surface, but Harry refused to break his death grip. They went deeper and still deeper. The sea became a mammoth weighted hand, pushing down, driving breath from their lungs. And then, as the last bubbles of air floated by, there was no pain. There was nothing at all.

California:
six months
later

CHAPTER 23

"THE SCHOOL bus is coming," Ben called out.

"Be right there," Sharon called back.

Jeff echoed a "Me too."

The patio of their new home in Santa Barbara overlooked a mile-long slope down to the highway fronting the ocean. Several other houses built on terraced lots similar to theirs dotted the intervening landscape. The view of the golden-brown hillside and the shimmering Pacific was pleasant. It had become Ben's habit to breakfast with his family on the patio, then while the kids collected their books he would finish his coffee and watch for their school bus.

The kids came pounding downstairs and burst onto the patio. Jeff clapped his father on the back. "See ya, dad!"

Ben's glance went automatically to Jeff's right arm. The deep knife wound Harry had given his son had healed nicely, though an ugly scar would be a permanent reminder. "Basketball after school?"

"Yeah. I'm a 'maybe.' "

"A maybe?"

"Maybe I'll make the team, maybe I won't."

"Well, I've got my money on you."

"Thanks . . . you know, it's strange, dad, playing basketball when it's so hot . . . Do you think we'll *ever* go back to Connecticut?"

339

"No," Ben said softly, shaking his head with emphasis. "We can't, Jeff. Does that still bother you?"

"Aw, I miss Tony once in a while. And the woods and ponds by our house. And . . ." He saw that he was upsetting his father and changed the subject. "If I make the team, can I have a new pair of gym shoes?"

"What kind?"

"Converse All-Stars."

"I guess we can hack it."

Jeff gave his father a quick hug and ran through the patio gate toward the street.

Sharon had hung back, looking for an opportunity to speak to her father alone. She had come out of their ordeal more slowly than Jeff. For weeks she had said almost nothing to her parents. Even when they were coaching her on the details of the new family identity she would only ask or answer questions. But when school began in September and she was faced with the prospect of close association with new people, Sharon had rallied and made an effort to be more outgoing. Gradually she had begun to regain her old zest for life. But there was still a shadow, a remnant of the horror she had gone through. She understood the need for the name change, they'd done their best to explain it to her. But it was still a reminder . . .

"Bus is coming," Ben said.

"It won't leave without me. Freddie, the driver, thinks I'm neat." She smiled.

"Just so long as he keeps his hands on the wheel." A strange thing to say, he thought with annoyance at himself. "What's up?"

"I wanted you to know that I have sort of a date tonight."

"Oh? Who's the lucky boy?"

"His name's Rob. Nice guy. He rebuilt a Datsun from scratch last year, but he collects opera records too. Rob's an all-around . . . I like that."

"Sure. Well, I'm glad you're starting to see people again. I'd like to meet Rob."

"You will, tonight . . ." And then she came out with it . . . "Oh, daddy, I feel so *guilty.*"

"On account of Oop?"

"Yes."

340

"Time has a way of softening even the worst hurt, Sharon. Terrible things happen to us and people we love, but we go on. We have to." He was talking, of course, about Oop, except, to his surprise, he was also talking about a dead brother. "Oop was the kind of person who'd understand that."

"I suppose so." She bit her lip and was about to say something else, when the school-bus driver honked his horn. "I gotta go. Can we talk more about this later, daddy?"

"You bet."

Ben watched as his daughter ran for the bus, a girl of true beauty and fierce loyalties who was still coming to grips with the first tragedy of her life. The last thing he wanted or expected was for her to forget Oop, although he did hope she could learn to put Oop's memory in a special place where it could be treasured without dominating her life. In time, he hoped. In time. For both of them . . .

"More coffee?" Donna came onto the patio carrying the coffee pot. "There's a smidge left."

"A smidge is just what I want."

"I'm a genius. I finally figured out what that switch in the hallway is for, the one that doesn't seem to make anything go on or off. It's an outlet for an attic fan. We could install one next summer if you'd like."

"Good idea. They say it can be like an oven here in the summer, in spite of the ocean breeze. You like the house, don't you?"

"Of course I do."

"Then what's wrong?"

"I don't *know* exactly. So much has happened in the last six months, I can't put my finger on it . . . I just know that I'm worried . . ."

Part of it, she realized but didn't say, was that the terrible morning on Rafferty's boat had been only the beginning of their odyssey, not the conclusion to it as she'd hoped. Her thoughts, as they had done a hundred times before, went back . . .

Ben had found a hacksaw in the chain locker and cut loose the manacle on her wrist, and they'd debated their next move. She had wanted to find the nearest Coast Guard station and tell them everything. Ben had opposed the idea. He'd argued that with Harry dead, and Genovese and Scarnato too, there was no way in the world to prove what had happened. Sean Rafferty could have backed up their story, but Rafferty was dead. Ben was still wanted for murder in Connecticut, and now he had even less chance of clearing himself. None, really.

She was forced to agree. As far as the police were concerned, Harry Ryder had still died more than a year ago in an auto accident. Without his body Ben would never be able to convince the police that Harry had committed those crimes in Connecticut.

In the end they had lifted Vincent Malle's body to the rail and consigned him to a watery grave too, and with the act forever cutting themselves off from their previous lives . . . The final irony was that Ben's only choice had been to become Harry—Harry Bond, of course . . .

They'd flown to Boston to pick up Jeff and Sharon and bring them back to California. While Donna looked for a house Ben had cautiously searched out people who could provide him with documents for the rest of the family: birth certificates, Social Security cards, a driver's license for Donna—all in the name of Bond.

Jeff and Sharon had been tutored to think of themselves as Jeff and Sharon Bond, newly arrived in California from the East Coast. The man Ben had found to provide documents had even produced school transcripts for Jeff and Sharon.

None of that could have been accomplished without Sean Rafferty's money. They would have felt obligated to return the money if Rafferty had had a family, but with his wife and daughter already gone, he had left no one, and Donna believed Rafferty would have wanted them to use the money as they had, though it occurred to her more than once that that might be only a rationalization.

At any rate, they had kept the money and bought this home outside Santa Barbara. Ben had opened an art gallery in downtown Santa Barbara, with a large section set aside for selling do-it-yourself picture-framing equipment. The place was beginning to catch on. In a year or so it would be making a good living for them.

In spite of all that, Donna had not been able to exorcize her nagging depression.

"Is it the house in Connecticut?" Ben prodded. "You still miss Westport that much?" Of course he knew that wasn't it.

Donna shook her head. "I don't even think about Westport

342

anymore. That house seems like a place I once visited for a weekend. How strange, after all the work and planning that went into it."

"I understand, you still remember what happened, it upsets you. But damn it, Donna, you can carry it too far. Sometimes you seem to look at me as if you didn't know me, like I was a stranger or something. Almost as if you didn't feel at ease with me . . ."

He was right. "Things do seem . . . well, different between us."

"How?"

"You're . . . I don't know . . . aloof, you act like you're above it all, including me. I don't get much warmth from you, Ben . . . not like before . . ."

"I'm *sorry*. These past months haven't exactly been easy for me either. All right, I've been moody. I'm not sure why, some kind of itch I can't seem to scratch." He hesitated, finally blurting out, "I guess it has something to do with Harry."

That surprised her. Harry's name hadn't been mentioned in months.

"I keep wondering why he did what he did back there on the boat. He saved my bacon, hell . . . he did it *twice.*"

"You'll never know, and you'll only make yourself sick thinking about it. I thought we had agreed to forget Harry."

"I'm *trying.*" He lowered his voice. "I'm trying. But I'm having a hard time shaking him. It's like having your own personal ghost."

"Ben, don't let Harry get inside you."

"Inside me? That's a strange thing to say."

"You know what I mean. Don't credit him too much just because he did one decent thing in his life. He had a lot to make up for. And whatever you do . . ." She hesitated, afraid to anger him, but she felt she had to take the chance, too much depended on it . . . "Please, Ben, don't try to be like Harry, I mean, the way you did as a boy . . ."

"But I am Harry," he said, and for a moment she couldn't tell whether he was annoyed or amused, or both . . . "That's the joke. And it looks like I'll be Harry for the rest of my life."

He turned from her then and went upstairs to shave and change. When he came back down, Donna was hanging pictures in the living room. "I'm going to the gallery," he said. She could only nod, not wanting to look at him. That last crack about being Harry had chilled her.

Their new home was north of Santa Barbara just off Route 101. Ben backed the Mercedes out of the driveway and began the short trip into town. He enjoyed the morning drive along the coast, especially in the smooth-running Mercedes. Donna had been after him to sell the car because it had been Harry's, but he'd felt reluctant to do so. The car seemed to fit him.

Usually he was a careful driver, even conservative. But today he found his foot inching down on the accelerator. The speedometer needle jumped to seventy. Then eighty. And finally ninety. Ninety miles an hour! He'd never driven so fast in his life, passing cars going seventy as if they were horse-and-buggies.

Donna may have had something there about Harry getting inside him . . . speeding, spending, the Mercedes . . . they were all, face it, manifestations of Harry . . .

Well, so what? Ben Ryder had been too damn inhibited. Straight-arrow. Always playing it safe, doing the so-called proper thing even when it made no sense.

As the city limits approached he eased up on the accelerator and let his speed fall to just over fifty.

A young hitchhiker appeared at the side of the road. A girl of twenty or so. Long dark hair and nice tits. Without thinking he pulled off onto the shoulder and waved to her through the rear window.

She ran up and jumped into the front seat. "Thanks, mister. I'm on my way to Ventura."

"I can take you into Santa Barbara."

"Terrific, that'll help." She settled back as Ben pulled out onto the highway. "Say, this is a great car."

Ben glanced more than once at his passenger. Lovely almond face. Ponytail. Carrying a canvas beach bag stenciled with the logo of the University of California at Santa Barbara, which, like his home, was located north of the city. Probably a student on her way home for the Christmas vacation. And her tits were not just nice, they were terrific . . .

"My girlfriend has a Jag," the girl was saying. "She's thinking of trading it in on a Mercedes, if she can talk her dad into coming through with the extra money. You ever drive a Firebird? That's not in your car's class, of course, but I'd like one. Yellow. A yellow Firebird. It's a shame they don't make convertibles any more, I'd— hey! What are you doing? Look out!"

Ben had swerved the car violently out of its lane onto the shoulder of the road, narrowly missing a telephone pole and destroying half a row of hydrangea bushes along the side of the highway. He put his head down on the steering wheel, barely able to breathe.

"My God! You could have killed us, you jerk. What's the *matter* with you?"

"Get out."

"Huh?"

"Get out of this car!" Ben raised his head. "And take a little advice, miss. Catch a bus or a train or a llama, but keep off these roads. There are too many creeps around."

"Yeah, right, I can see that." She threw open the door, swiveled her legs and jumped out.

Ben watched her run up the road, and finally was able to draw a deep breath. God, the things that had been going through his mind about that girl . . . sick, creepy. No question, there was more of Harry in him than he'd wanted to admit. Much more. And it would always be there. For years he'd tried to shut out Harry, pretend he didn't exist. A costly mistake. He fondly touched the faded old scar on his neck, and resolved to stay in touch with that Harry, the boy who had cared.

When he felt calm enough to drive, he pulled onto the highway and continued on at a more decent speed, fighting the itch to tromp the accelerator to the floorboard.